★ CENTURY STUDIOS ★

"You are what you are and sometimes a little more."
—Billy Sunshine

The Life and Times of Homer Sincere

BOOKS BY THE AUTHOR

Cricket, A Novel

Mindstyles-Life Styles:
A Comprehensive Overview of Today's Life Changing Philosophies

Stages: Understanding Ethical and Moral Decisions

Self-Health: The Life Long Fitness Book

Blueprinting: Rebuilding Your Career and Relationships

The Emotional Maintenance Manuel

The Moral Responsibility of the Press

The Cigar Connoisseur:
An Illustrated Guide to the Worlds Best Cigars

Dispatches From the Front:
The History of the American War Correspondent

The 10 Best of Everything:
An Ultimate Travel Guide for Travelers

The Life and Times of Homer Sincere

WHOSE AMAZING ADVENTURES ARE DOCUMENTED

BY HIS TRUE AND TRUSTED FRIEND RIGBY CANFIELD

An American Novel

NATHANIEL LANDE

THE OVERLOOK PRESS

NEW YORK

This edition first published in hardcover in the United States in 2010 by
The Overlook Press, Peter Mayer Publishers, Inc.
141 Wooster Street
New York, NY 10012

Cataloging-in-Publication Data is available from the Library of Congress

Billy Sunshine poster © J. Hitch

Book design and typeformatting by Bernard Schleifer
Manufactured in the United States of America
FIRST EDITION
ISBN 978-1-59020-328-6
10 9 8 7 6 5 4 3 2 1

ACKNOWLEDGMENTS

This story could never have been written without the contributions of extraordinary people who helped shape this work, making me better than I am. They are the heroes, the friends, and life enhancers. To Aaron Schlechter, Erin Brown, Marie Cantlon, David Groff, Mickey Freiberg, Jane Lahr, Paul Fedorko, Milton Glaser, and most essentially, Natalya Lande, I salute you.

For literary legend Peter Mayer, my deepest thanks and admiration, along with my many colleagues I worked with at TIME. Their words and contributions leave fond recollections. I'm thankful for the words and selections from articles, books, and archives. They are greatly appreciated.

From the editorial bandstand the cheers from Gary Springer, Hugo MacPherson, Vincent Kamin, Mary Posses, Alanna Ramirez, Sheena Berwick, Ralph Thomas, Norman Twain, and Andrew Lande, brought Homer home.

From the beginning of my career, I must thank William Styron, a mentor who carries the appreciation I can never fully acknowledge. No one can style a story like Styron. Often, I read a phrase he had crafted and when I mentioned how perfect it was, he encouraged me to make his words my own. I was amazed when he assured me, "Natty, I've been stealing from William Faulkner all of my life."

In the making of a novel, a lot of things happen, magical and amazing, things unexplained. I remember a few years ago, after writing around the clock for months, I was rushing from a copy center in Santa Barbara with my manuscript. I blacked out on an empty street near the old mission here. I had fainted. During those precious minutes, a stranger looked after me and called an ambulance. On a stretcher, I asked for his calling card; he smiled curiously, presenting one to me. A few days later, when I was discharged from the hospital with a pacemaker, I wanted to thank him. Dialing his number I found it had been disconnected. On further investigation, I never found the man who in measure had guarded over and protected me. He did not seem to exist. I write this because I have documented proof that there are personal signposts appearing when we least expect them. Are they angels? Who are they? This much I know: they write the songs of it all. They know who they are and why, and to them, I dedicate this book.

Over many years, I've grown to love the characters on these pages. Through many revisions, the story may have changed, but their spirit has not. In this book you will be introduced to Homer, Rigby, Daisy, Waldo, and Father Rivage, and I hope you will remember them.

—NATHANIEL LANDE
Montecito, California

INTRODUCTION

Nathaniel Lande admired his colleagues at TIME and I should know. I was both Publisher of TIME and Chairman during his salad days when this lean and lanky six foot six inch "cowboy" blazed through the corporation. I remember a versatile talent. When he was not writing first hand narratives about shipwrecks at sea, or marching for civil rights in Alabama, he was in Viet Nam making documentaries at a time we essentially focused on print. He loved the film medium. When one of his first documentary films, Montage, won all the awards, we took notice. Twenty years ago, before Kindle, he was awarded two design patents for his prototype for the first electronic book and New York publishers took notice. He created TIME World News Service broadcasting the pages of TIME to 70 countries around the world. When he was missing from company action, Nathaniel was consulting with the President at the White House on the moral responsibility of the press. We celebrated TIME's 40th Anniversary together with an amazing notable evening. Much to my amusement, as creative director, he was the only man at TIME to have a piano in his office. But all in all, he was indeed a *Soldier of the Word*, and no one respected and appreciated his colleagues at TIME /Life more than he. With his new novel, he includes tribute to a heroic editorial landscape singing the song of it all. It was a more innocent time then, but a wonderful time; and within these pages, spanning three decades in America, there is a spirit I recall with affection. Nathaniel Lande has crafted unforgettable characters and a beautifully written cinematic story that will not easily be forgotten.

—RALPH DAVIDSON
Washington, D.C.
January 2010

PROLOGUE

COMING ATTRACTIONS

On a steamy summer afternoon in New Orleans, a cool breeze stirred in the Delta before lifting and crossing the Mississippi into the French Quarter and up to the Garden District, where I sat sipping mint and lemon iced tea, rocking back and forth in an old ladder-back pine chair on the front porch of my past. This is the place where I grew up, my family's plantation house with its tall wooden columns and floor-to-ceiling windows covered with slatted shutters to keep out the summer's heat.

The rocking and the thick, humid air lulled me into a dreamlike state. My mind wandered, as it often did in those days, back to when I was a boy playing cowboys and Indians, or getting into mischief with my best friend, doing what boys do on long, hot, lazy afternoons.

A distant rumbling noise shook me out of my reflections. I looked far down the road and saw a truck that left blooms of yellow dust in its wake until it came to a stop at my door. Two men jumped from the truck and unloaded a crate. "For you, Mr. Canfield. Sign here," one said to me.

The shipping paper revealed that the crate had come all the way from California with an attached note from Daisy.

Dear Rigby:

I've wanted to give you something that was essential to Homer because, without each other, neither of you could have been the men you became. He mentioned once that you always admired his desk and I would like you to have it now. I'm always thinking about him and feel his presence in many ways. I'm fine. After all these years, the ranch has grown so much that you would not recognize it, but a lot has also stayed the same. I send my love.

Daisy

As I opened the crate, brown cardboard wrappings fell from an old pine desk. I swept a layer of dust off the top and, for an instant, remembered when I had first seen it. That day and the present day seemed to meet and melt together, becoming one. For a long moment, I rubbed my hand over the smooth surface with a mixture of memory and emotion.

This rolltop desk had accompanied Homer all his life. When I rolled back the top, I found that the cowboy cards we had traded as kids were still in the secret compartment, and a few pictures of my first encounter with attractive Sweet Lorraine. And there was something else: A journal written in inky solitude.

After moving the desk into my ground floor study, I read Homer's journals. They had recorded our marvelous adventures and amazing times. Homer and I had grown up in a time of heroes, in the quiet landscape that was shattered by the events of the Second World War. For boys, it was a time when radio and movie personalities filled airwaves, when carnivals cruised into town and cowboys gave popcorn memories every Saturday afternoon at the Rialto before the last ticket was sold.

The more I read, the better I understood how his life was shaped by the most extraordinary circumstances. With each entry, I realized that his was a story that needed telling, a tale about not only friends and heroes but also about a golden age in America, a time that will not likely come again. Homer was proof that once upon a time there was more to movies than special effects, more to photojournalism than paparazzi shots of the latest tabloid sensation, more to New Orleans than Mardi Gras, more to New York than a parade of passing artists and writers. And that there was a side of California perfect for dreamers to fly into a world of make-believe.

I began making notes. Words became paragraphs and pages.

There is a sentence in Homer's journal that haunts me to this day: *Sometimes a single voice has a quiet message and, sometimes, a single voice carries a message from the spheres.*

In the recesses of my mind, I continue to hear Homer's voice, reminding me of a relationship between two boys that began in New Orleans, a friendship that spanned decades and that I realize never ended.

—RIGBY CANFIELD, *New Orleans, 2008*

Part One

NEW ORLEANS
1946

Chapter 1

THE EARTH TURNED

One late winter day in 1946, the earth turned. Its revolution was a bit clumsy, slightly lopsided as if the weight of some force of nature had shifted after a sluggish, post-alarm roll. Like a quilt tugged away, a patch of Louisiana was pulled along from the brightly lit morning into the lazy blue afternoon.

In the eventful 1940s, our soldiers returned from the war, the lights went on again all over the world, round-the-clock radios caught the Andrews Sisters sitting under an apple tree, and Kate Smith took to the airwaves singing "God Bless America."

New Orleans, where I grew up, was a city that has always had a firm grip on unreality. Apart from the delirium at the end of the war and the annual insanity of Mardi Gras, the land itself had a giving quality that thwarted any sense of solidity. New Orleans was like the deck of a boat moored on a thick crust of earth that heaved gently, imperceptibly, over layers and layers of Mississippi-soaked soil, sluiced down through the centuries by the river's falling rush to the sea.

Like the water-laden land on which it rested, New Orleans was a place of yielding, a depository of differing soils, the city settling into a garden of nationalities: French, Spanish, Creole, Indian, Haitian.

Within this humid metropolis was a thirty-square block dubbed the French Quarter. Here, the tropical climate that bathed the city condensed into a dampness that pervaded everything, as if from a primal swamp. The senses were saturated. Sounds squealed, slid, and vibrated into a mix of aromas folding over one another until their edges set the nostrils singing. The notes were a little too sharp, a little overripe. Color cloyed the eye as two-story buildings—candy pink and sunrise peach—glowed in a collage of facades fading into each other. The drenching, steamy climate and the narrow, clinging streets gave the Quarter a close atmosphere, felt by some as the clutch of wet clothing on the skin, by others as security.

For kids, the womb-like atmosphere of the Quarter was a cushion of sensations within a wrapping of fantasy. Its very architecture encouraged illusion: courtyards forced inhabitants to look inward, to forget the existence of the world outside. The balconies everywhere were high enough to blur the grit on the street below.

Under the right circumstances this overwhelming of the senses produced an exquisite imagination that brought the depth of the world into focus. Under any other circumstances, the same atmosphere might have been too rich, overloading the imagination until it became unhinged from reality.

MARBLES

Just as my father knew the Latin names for every disease known to medicine, I was, at eight years old, a virtual walking encyclopedia on marbles. I knew the dizzying array of colors offered by the Christenson Agate Company. I could tell the difference between Indian Bands, Transparent Swirl Ribbons, China Balls, and Cat's Eyes; Orange Peels, Flames, and Cobalt Blue Submariners.

Every kid said, in either awe or irritation, that I had "the eye." Regardless of the competition—Poison Ring, Ringer, or whatever the game of the moment was, I knuckled down, took aim with my shooter nestled like an opalescent cannonball in the short gun barrel of my curled forefinger, and fired.

I intended to shoot for Willy Crompton's Orange Peel. Right in the middle of adjusting my thumb pressure to apply the proper hunch and backspin to the shot, I noticed out of the corner of my eye that a newcomer had tentatively joined the game. He was standing outside the circle. I glanced up at the kid who wore an oversized cowboy hat. He opened the pockets on his patchy jeans to reveal a motley collection of ordinary marbles.

On the ground, his Peppermint was in my way. It sat between my shooter and the Orange Peel, nothing more than an irritant, so undistinguished that I probably wouldn't even bother adding it to my collection. The other boys urged me to shoot.

It was an easy shot. With a clear angle on Crompton's Orange Peel, all I had to do to send the Peppermint flying was to shift slightly to the right, reset the cock of my thumb, and launch my shooter to glance off his marble, knocking the Orange Peel closer to the perimeter. My miss was met with hoots of derision from the other knucklers.

The new boy looked confused and then knelt with difficulty, but without complaint. He took the Orange Peel and one of my favorite Red Devils, leaving just his humble Peppermint in the circle. He had won.

I caught up with him as he walked away. He told me his name was Homer. He was my age and a scrap of a boy, a long, thin, raggedy scrap. Stringy, lithe, butter-brown from days spent in the streets and on the levee. His dark brown hair straggled too far down his neck, flopping hopelessly into his wide brown eyes that were the color of strong tea. Occasionally, his big eyes blinked because they were vulnerable to fatigue and stress. Homer's eyes wandered and blinked almost imperceptibly because, as Waldo Emerson Jackson—a man who would play an important role in our lives—knew, Homer was "a kindly gives hearted boy," who felt a lot of pain in what he saw. His eyes, Waldo said, "were just making sure he took some time off by blinking a little extra once in a while."

Most of the time his eyes shifted smoothly, until he saw what he wanted: beauty and sometimes a hint of magic. His mouth, not used much for talking, was wide and smiled easily, with an upper lip falling straight from under his nose onto a lower and fuller lip that waited without pouting. My attention was caught by his brace. It was fitted to his leg, armed with two steel rods reaching from a round leather band on his knee to his shoe.

As we walked, we didn't talk about the shot or anything important that I remember, but I gained something that would stay with me for the rest of my life, and that was my friend, Homer Sincere. I had never felt as good about winning as I did about losing that Red Devil to Homer.

SUNRISE

"Shadows followed me every day and only disappeared after the sun had set. Then Billy Sunshine smiled. In my room, my heart lifted a bit. My troubled thoughts often wandered to the squares of glossy paper posters on the wall and, like the tap dancer in the Quarter on the pavement squares, my thoughts skipped recklessly, naively to an anticipated but unknown destination. And I was fearless, able to go anywhere and do anything. There was someone to inspire me. I had seen every movie he ever made and, except for Waldo and Rigby, he was the most important person in my life."
    —Homer Sincere's journal, looking back to 1946

Homer Sincere was caught, in childhood, somewhere between an empty place and a wish. New Orleans was up and ready each morning before he opened his eyes. He wrinkled his nose, sniffing out the day, smelling time to the hour by the scents that drifted up to his second-story bedroom. There was rich chicory coffee, chewy and black (Waldo said it was possible to smell colors), and the sweet sachet of deep-fried beignets dusted with sugar—a companion to the fragrance of white grits whose ubiquitous presence complemented the piquant magical flavor of the Quarter.

As Homer turned over onto his stomach and pulled a crumpled

down pillow over his head, the growling in his belly nearly drowned the vendors' cries from the street market. He had not had a real meal in two days. Homer accepted that the inviting aromas seeping through the wrought iron balcony outside his window were not intended for him. He forced himself to think about something else. Once on his feet, he headed for the two other rooms in the converted carriage house, the only home he could remember. He considered walking into his parents' bedroom, but didn't hold much hope of finding anyone there. His father, an angry man when he went on a bender (or a "tear" as Waldo called it), wouldn't be back. He had been gone for a week. His absence was more worrisome because Homer's mother wasn't at home either.

She had been spending less time with him. In her place was a rocking chair, a favorite pleasure when rocking brought him a secure, relaxed feeling, serving as a surrogate momma. When he needed her, he just conjured up the precious times she had held him in that old chair, perhaps as much to soothe herself as Homer, reading to him from *The Velveteen Rabbit.* He didn't understand many of the words, but her voice transported him as they rocked, sliding melodiously over her long sentences. For the moment at least, Homer had been comforted and the veil of his loneliness lifted.

On the landing, he checked the stairwell where he sometimes found his father asleep. Having drunk too much in the hours before, he would not have been able to make it all the way to the second floor. The stairs were empty. Avoiding one particularly arthritic stair that would resonate his presence, Homer left the hall quickly to avoid the landlady, a mountain of a woman whose bosom spilled out of her apron with hesitation. Every time she heard the creaky stair, she popped her head out of her door like a cuckoo clock.

Back in his room, Homer picked up the khaki pants where he had dropped them the night before. Scooping up his one laceless tennis shoe, he flopped on top of his cot, stuck his spindly leg up in the air, and struggled to pull up his trousers while lying on his back. He halted the gyrations long enough to fling his pillow at a fly bumping against the closed pane of the window. Affronted by such crude tactics, the fly turned from the window and headed down, dive-bomber fashion, over his bed. Then haughtily, the insect flew in a straight line back out of the open half of the window as though it had known all the time where the opening was. As the tiny buzz disappeared into the general music of the Quarter, Homer's sorrow faded with it a few days before Mardi Gras.

And with the sunrise, he saw his hero. He let his eyes feast on his new wall of posters, movie souvenirs that had been hidden under his cot. The night before, in an effort to fend off a scary feeling, he had decided to tack them up. And sure enough, he felt better once the slick photos were in place.

On every piece of paper, from the nine trading cards I had given him to the four tattered, but beautiful posters gathered by Waldo, thirteen vivid yellow letters glowed:

"BILLY SUNSHINE!"

Billy wore a magnificent, swooping white Stetson banded with circles of Indian silver matching those that studded his white vest and the side seams of his white boot-grazing pants. In various poses, the cowboy hero sat astride his palomino, Apollo. Whether twirling a lasso, pointing his six-shooter, or saluting the American flag, the cowboy hero held Homer's attention. In each picture was the same wide, comfortable smile that pushed his bronze skin up around his handsome face. At the outside of each sparkling blue eye, a fan of crinkled skin indicated that the smile was real. Billy Sunshine was smiling right at Homer.

HIDDEN CARDS

I climbed heavy-footed up the stairs to Homer's apartment, hitting the creaky stair that would bring out the cuckoo lady. Other than his often-missing parents and Billy Sunshine, Homer's real family consisted of Waldo Jackson, friend and philosopher, and me. His pain and fear evaporated on those quiet warm days when I visited, bringing a set of new Billy Sunshine cards to trade. After our detailed study and admiration of each card, we hid them in the secret compartment in his momma's desk.

I yelled as I ran. "Hey, Home! Guess who's coming to New Orleans? I heard it on the radio yesterday."

Before Homer had a chance to do any guessing, I burst through the apartment doorway with a smile of delight.

Out of breath, I offered a hint.

"At the State Fair on the twenty-sixth."

No clue. Homer offered a blank stare.

When he couldn't stand the suspense any longer, and I could no longer hold the secret, I announced the big news. "BILLY SUNSHINE!"

Homer's voice almost hit high C.

"How much are the tickets?"

"Only a buck—two for the price of one."

He wavered between joy at the good news and the flinty realization that he didn't have the money. He shrugged, and then mumbled, "Great."

Grinning, I said, "Look, I have it all planned out. We'll sneak into the tent between shows and hide until he appears."

Homer could never understand why a kid from a rich family had to be so inventive, but I always felt that I could not enjoy an event if I had to pay rather than sneak in. And I couldn't understand what a threat such lawlessness was to a kid who didn't know where his parents were most of the time.

I took a picture of Homer. Long before my father gave me my first camera, I had developed a habit of rearranging and composing nature into snapshots, always trying to balance the swirl of life around me. I saw landscapes of people and stunning events one frame at a time. After I heard the shutter click, I advanced the film in my new Kodak Brownie, pausing long enough to notice for the first time the black and blue bruises on Homer's arms. I reasoned that maybe he had dreamed in the middle of the night that he was riding with Billy and the boys and that he had fallen out of bed when his horse bucked him out of the saddle.

"You OK?"

Homer didn't say anything and I was pretty good about not pressing for answers he did not want to give. As if on cue, the cuckoo lady's footsteps sounded outside the door, saving Homer from having to answer. To avoid her, we dove out the window onto the balcony. He had learned how to shimmy down a pole despite his brace and we were soon in the Quarter.

THE BILLY SUNSHINE SHOW

Jumping on a rickety, rattling streetcar on St. Charles Avenue, we were at the fairgrounds in minutes. It could have been longer but anticipation made time fly.

"This is it!" a man in a red jacket announced as we entered. "The Official Billy Sunshine Program." We took seats up front, close to the arena floor.

The stage lights were dim compared to Homer's shining face. Billy Sunshine at last! His anticipation was only matched by his affection for the cowboy who occupied a comfortable corner in America's legend.

When the great theater was filled, the lights dimmed as a furious drum roll vibrated through the crowd. Billy's theme song, "Paper Moon," floated over a round of applause, the first of many that night. A pool of warm light poured across the stage as Billy Sunshine entered the yellow oval. He was atop Apollo, his powerful horse rearing and pawing the air. Billy waved his hat in a theatrical grand sweep, just like the picture on Homer's poster.

The yellow light spread like hot sunshine across the arena until it covered thirty golden cowgirls, all on white horses, dressed in silver-sequined western spangles, each carrying an American flag. They circled Billy in a glistening, glittered embrace. The audience held its breath a little at the dazzling spectacle. Then Billy sang:

It's only a paper moon
Sailing over a cardboard sea,
But it wouldn't be make believe
If you believed in me.

Billy got off his horse and sauntered to a microphone with a plac-
ard that read NBC Radio. In a low, confidential baritone, he murmured, "Good to see ya! Good to be here," encouraging the audience
to continue cheering and stomping. Then with more enthusiasm,
"Right here—the governor of Louisiana—Earl Long—glad you're
here, governor."

A spotlight hit the governor's face and he beamed from the
applause shared with Billy.

"And a special treat, ladies and gentlemen, Louisiana's own great
golfer, Slamming Sammy Snow."

After the show, we went around back for an autograph, planting
ourselves at the stage entrance of the amphitheater where Homer
wanted to see Billy, if only to say hello.

There was a string of work lights hanging overhead when a door
opened to reveal an entourage with Billy at its center. They hustled out
and I noticed near him a man dressed in black—as black as his ebony
skin: Johnny Diamond, who had the reputation of being the best poker
player in the world. I recognized him from his small parts in Billy's
films, recalling a particular role in *Under the Western Sky*, when they
played poker because the ranch was at stake. Having been rooted to
the spot, Homer broke the tension, "Hi, Mr. Sunshine, I'm Ho-Homer
Sincere."

"Hiya, son, good to see ya. Yeah, good to see ya."

"Thank you for your letter and your picture, Billy."

"Glad to do it, son." Billy tipped his hat and sauntered away.

With my arm around Homer's shoulder, the two of us walked in
step, brace and all, Indian fashion, careful to avoid any cracks in the
pavement.

"Billy was just great," Homer said excitedly. "And he was with Johnny Diamond."

"Johnny is his pal," I said. "They play cards and stuff."

"For fun or for keeps?"

"I don't know. I wonder if he plays marbles. I betcha I could beat him."

"I think you could too, Rigby."

We relived and laughed at every joke, savoring every nuance and every gesture of Billy's show, rubbing our palms that ached from clapping so hard. When we were some distance from the fair, still with happy memories, we walked on in silence.

"Billy said it was good to see me, Rigby," Homer said, breaking the quiet. "Can you believe it?" Homer was lost in endless applause.

We ran out of laughter when we found the eviction note.

THE UNEXPECTED NOTICE

"Mr. Sincere,

I sympathize with your wife being unwell and all, but your rent is several months overdue and eviction proceedings will begin unless we can come to some arrangement. Your son is running wild in the streets. Changes need to be made. Mrs. Partridge."

"Your mother's sick? Maybe you should come and stay at my house."

Homer nodded, unwilling to admit he didn't know where she was.

"I gotta be here when she comes home."

"You okay—being alone tonight?"

It was a silly question. "I'll be all right," Homer said.

Under the door, he found another note and more concerning news in an envelope marked "The Office of Welfare and Adoptions." Nausea washed inside Homer at the thought of losing his familiar surroundings. His mother was away for just a few days and his father would be back soon. When his father wasn't home, he was in the Quarter. Had Mrs. P. noticed? As Homer stepped on the creaky stair, she opened her door. As he looked at her, her eyes skated away from his.

"It's really best for you, Homer, for your own good." Mrs. P.'s voice trailed off as she shut the door. He knew there was nothing good inside the envelope.

Where was his mother? She could be in a hospital; there were several in the Quarter. When he had tried to visit the nearest one, a nurse told him she wasn't there. Only old people around the neighborhood went away and never returned. Homer quickly dismissed the thought and wished for something better.

THE BACK OF TOMORROW

"No one who ever heard my father play the trumpet could forget the way he performed. With his familiar golden horn, he was a general dispatching rising and falling notes under his command. He loved playing his trumpet and I wanted him to care for me as much as he did his music. If he wouldn't come to me, I would go to him. But when I was just near his club, I was unable to go forward and stood at the edge of the Quarter."

—Homer Sincere's journal, 1946

Wishing. Homer had wished on the balcony for as long as he could remember. Protected by the curling wrought iron that encircled the balustrade and hanging his arms over the railing, he wished for the usual things that the gods of ten-year-olds brought.

He wished for things he didn't have, existing somewhere in the place Waldo called the "back of tomorrow." At the top of his all-time wish list was to have a family. His father played trumpet in a smoky room on Bourbon Street, in sets that took him to another time and place. He played musical riffs in uncertain combinations and familiar melodies requested by sleep-worn spectators. Lost in addiction to both drink and music, his father lived in a place Homer could never visit.

Sometimes at home, when Homer found his father's hidden bottles, he tried to reason with him about his drinking. His father would then take his anger out on Homer. Didn't fathers love their sons? His father never hugged him and was rarely around. If it were his fault, he would change. People could change. At least that's what Waldo said. The war had changed a lot of people. In '46, everyone was talking about how the war had changed men. Not just the injured, like the war veteran in *The Best Years of Our Lives*, but everyone, in more silent ways. Just how or why, Homer couldn't figure out, and that's when he wondered if something might be wrong with him.

With Mrs. Partridge's note crammed in his pocket, he headed for the club where his father played. He stopped two blocks from the building, frozen with the realization that he would never find the man he was looking for.

Returning home to his room with only a wish, Homer fell into a deep sleep. He was awakened by noise and then laughter. The laughter became louder, his father's voice, answered by a giggle, soft at first, with muffled words, a woman's voice. She's home, momma's home!

He ran into his parents' room. Momma! Before the laughter stopped, he smelled a perfume that carried an unfamiliar scent. His father turned from rustling sheets. In the dim light, Homer saw a trail of clothes across the floor leading to an occupied bed. Beside the bed, the night table supported a half-empty bottle of bourbon. There was someone scantily dressed, almost naked, and not his mother. His expectation became a bewildered blur that was immediately extinguished when his father leaped up, chased him back to his room, and caught him mid-stride with a hard smack across his back. Homer managed to lock his door and heard a furious drunken slur, "You better stay in there, and don't you be coming back out and disturbing me." His father's voice trailed off. "Pain in the ass." A door down the hall shut, reinforcing Homer's hurt and confusion. A few minutes later, the laughter began again. He went out to the balcony and quietly dropped down the pole into the Quarter and went to work.

FAUCHAIRE & CO.

Mr. Fauchaire owed him fifty cents for his new job. Two hours' work in the morning earned Homer a dime a day, making doubloons, souvenir trinkets to be thrown to the street crowds from the King's Float on Mardi Gras. No one was to know about it. That was a secret between him and Mr. Fauchaire, who told him he could just forget working for anybody on the block if he found out that Homer had gone around bragging. The other kids who worked for him kept it quiet.

"You do the same and you'll do fine."

Mr. Fauchaire's shop was crammed with old house furniture upholstered with big red, orange, and yellow flowers. Frazzled ruffles hung limply from the bottom of every chair. When Homer arrived that morning, he was surprised to see someone at work in his place. He approached the stranger, who had cracked lips, silvery whiskers where he needed a shave, and a stern look on a long face.

The man glared at him, then continued to thread orange plastic pearls on a waxed string. He was doing Homer's job.

Mr. Fauchaire was nowhere in sight, so Homer asked in a voice that quavered despite his best efforts, "Are you working here now?"

There was no reply.

He looked toward the door, not knowing what to do. He couldn't imagine what he would do without the job, especially now. Maybe this was a mistake and the man was working temporarily. He shrank into the shadows and waited for Mr. Fauchaire to appear from his home over the shop. Leaning against a wall, he slid down slowly and knelt where he could see the entrance.

Squashed in the corner, waiting for his boss, Homer was confused.

He tried to understand what was happening when Mr. Fauchaire's silhouette filled the doorway. Homer released his breath.

"Ah, so you have met Louis. I wanted to be here to explain. Louis is my wife's brother from France; he lost his home in the war. He is working here now to earn the boat fare for his wife and two children." Mr. Fauchaire shrugged and spread his palms in a gesture of helplessness. "You understand that, Homer? I'm sure you can. You are a good worker, boy, but he needs the job more, so he can make a new home for his children."

Listening with a sinking heart, Homer looked over at the man with respect, asking a question that took Mr. Fauchaire off-guard. "His children . . . do they know that he's trying to get them back together?"

Maybe his own father was trying to fix up his family and he didn't even know it.

Mr. Fauchaire said, "You came to work today, and I will pay you for the day I owe you; but I cannot afford to have you both. I'm sorry. You wait right here. I'll get some change to pay you."

Pulling his shirt, Homer smoothed his palms over his chest in a futile gesture to tidy himself up.

He had tried to save some money to have in reserve in case his father forgot to stock the pantry. But more importantly, for a present to buy for his mom when she returned. Those dimes added up. At least this job was just seasonal. His job at Western Union was more secure.

With no place to camp for the night, it occurred to him that the loss of his job was a sign, what Waldo called an "omen." In that case, he should return home with a rush of good feeling. "Maybe my mother will be back tonight." If she came, she would need his care. "Maybe losing my job is a good thing."

Standing there in the relative security of Mr. Fauchaire's shop, with his five shiny dimes, Homer stopped worrying about the adoption people finding and taking him away. Then he took off.

* * *

Halfway down the block, he heard Mr. Fauchaire call his name. "Homer . . . Homer!" The shop owner stood out on the banquette, feet spread, and hands on hips. All Homer could hear were the morning sounds originating from the Quarter.

"Homer, come back here."

His hazy understanding warned him not to return. "He is probably going to turn me in," Homer thought. When Mr. Fauchaire saw him hesitate, he started down the street after Homer, who panicked and took off running as best he could.

His heart pumped loudly and hard. Homer saw ahead of him the sidewalk, the shops and the stands selling beignets and café au lait, and the man called Waldo!

THE MAN WHO PLAYED THE DOZENS

"There was no one like Waldo. A man easier to feel than describe. Unique, original. Not a carbon copy to be found."

—Homer Sincere's journal, 1946

"Homer? Is that you, boy?"

More powerful than the Lone Ranger's cry, more beautiful than the rainbow over Oz was the sound of Waldo's voice at that moment. "You gone deaf, child? What you doing out so early?"

Homer turned at the sound of Ophelia Lou's slow hoofbeats traipsing along the cobblestones, following a rutted path in her brain. His world quickly fell into another perspective, emptying all the sadness out of the moment. Waldo was on top of his stagecoach!

Waldo Emerson Jackson, the best vegetable vendor in the Quarter, had made his way up Governor Nichols Street with the dignity and wisdom of the patriarchs of Genesis. His crooning invitations to buy chickpeas and okra had their own melody. And Waldo carried on a tradition of playing the "dozens," matching words of advice in rhyme, speaking to aspirations. New Orleans' unofficial patron saint had been dispensing wisdom and vegetables from his cart for as long as anyone could remember. He was an observer who knew everybody and everything in the Quarter.

It was Waldo who first told me about being real friends and why Homer needed one, although I couldn't think of not being Homer's friend under any condition. What Waldo told me touched me with affectionate understanding.

Homer had polio when he was five, when little was known about germs and infectious diseases. Having been isolated in a sanitarium in the Garden District, he spent a lot of time alone. The masked nurses and doctors offered little company and when his momma came to visit, she could only view her son from a distance through a pane of glass. I'm sure she wanted to hold Homer when he reached out his arms to her. It must have been as hard on her as it was for him.

When he recovered, the disease left a calling card on his leg, leaving it limited in movement and appearance. I couldn't imagine how hard it must have been for Homer to survive, begin the road to recovery, and overcome his handicap. I was too young to understand emotional repercussions and wondered what it might be like to wear a brace. Homer was usually cheerful and stoic. He had slowly walked a path on the grounds of the hospital. It had been a long time before he could run a little.

Being with Waldo was an amazing experience; he gave more of himself to us than we gave to him.

Driving his wagon around the Quarter for most of his fifty-eight years, Waldo could negotiate every turn and pothole in his sleep, trusting Ophelia Lou. Lou was short for Louisiana.

The horse always made her morning debut wearing a bonnet garnished with vegetables—carrots, celery, and green peppers left over from the previous day's wares, topped by a huge, hot-pink plastic crab. Waldo never failed to put the crab on every one of his millinery creations, holding the firm opinion that real class was established by being ridiculous and secure at the same time.

But Waldo wasn't ridiculous. For a man of color, living in the American South in the forties, he had educated himself pretty well and was smarter than anyone I knew. His patrician presence was a mainstay of the glorious Preservation Society Marching Band. They played for weddings, and when a member died, they marched to New Orleans Number One cemetery, escorting the departed soul to heaven.

"What you doin' boy?" Waldo asked Homer, pulling back on Ophelia's reins.

"I'm looking for my mother."

Reaching for the letter from the welfare agency in his shirt pocket, Homer showed it to Waldo who read it and let out a slow sigh, a half whistle, then patted the seat next to him.

Waldo pulled Homer closer to him in the wagon. Ophelia started forward as Homer pleaded, "What am I gonna do, Waldo?"

"When there's a lock on the gate, you wait. Don't start mopin' till it's open."

Homer leaned against him, just to touch someone. He wasn't sure what Waldo meant, but the words felt better than the crazy thoughts careening around in his head.

Their kinship came from the heart. The years separating them didn't matter; Waldo understood that Homer needed someone to take him from a place he called the "Land of Loss."

"I have got to find my momma."

If anyone knew where she was and when she was coming back, Waldo would know.

"You ever get scared, Waldo?"

"Sure."

"What do you do about it?"

"Nothing to do, 'cept maybe pretend you ain't."

"And that works?"

Waldo smiled. That was always his best answer.

THE GLORIOUS MAGIC OF MOVIES

"Life was at the Rialto. There was no better place to be. Surrounded by the cavalcade of stars, swimming with Esther Williams, we were part of every scene. I danced with Gene Kelly in Paris and flew in glorious Technicolor from rooftop to rooftop. We laughed with Abbott and Costello and rode into sunsets with Roy Rogers and Hopalong Cassidy."

—Homer Sincere's journal, 1946

From the beginning, the bond that held Homer and me together was the movies. Making films was the most important pastime in our lives and when we weren't shooting scripts Homer dreamed up, we lived in the Rialto, a magical palace of make-believe.

On Saturday afternoons, sitting deeply in the comfortable seats of the Rialto Theater, sharing popcorn and Baby Ruth candy bars, we enjoyed ourselves immensely. We postured like Edward G. Robinson and crooned along to "The Bells of St. Mary's" with Bing Crosby. We eavesdropped on romances between Gable and Lombard, Hepburn and Tracy, but the movies we liked best starred Billy Sunshine, especially after his stand for the Indians in *Trail of Sorrows*.

Spending hours alone before a mirror, Homer practiced Billy's look, walk, and posture. "You are what you are and sometimes a little more." I knew that Billy Sunshine had more influence on Homer than anyone in his life.

One day after a movie, Waldo picked us up and took the long way home through the Quarter. Homer sat close to him, as if he were in the bosom of Abraham. When the landscape changed, grabbing our attention, we saw generous sugarloaf ladies in light ruffled aprons drinking iced tea, making pralines with pecans and burnt brown sugar, children dancing through a sprinkler, men in straw hats lolling in conversation at the corner, a sleeping dog, deep green lawns interrupted by garden hoses, wash on the line; all snapshots and a prelude to another photograph. People's lives rolled by in narrow frames, one moment at a time. We stood up in Waldo's wagon with our fingers looking through an imaginary range finder and invisible camera. How great it would be to actually make movies, I thought, to capture what I saw as moving images. Nothing could be more effective or important.

We wanted to know more about Waldo since he was the main feature in our cinematic life. More than a performer or an actor, he had it all. But where did he live? We knew the carriage house where he kept Ophelia Lou, but nothing else. Did Waldo have a family? Where did he sleep? Homer and I tried to find out but couldn't. We wondered if maybe he just lived with Ophelia, like a cowboy who never left his horse and bedded down by the campfire or slept in the back of his wagon. We accepted the fact that Waldo was magical, like a god appearing from nowhere when we least expected it.

On summer afternoons, we ran through empty fields, fooling around until evening, pretending to play musical instruments in almost perfect cadence. Sometimes, straddling a broom, we rode horses over the western Wyoming plains, riding under a moon blazing like a giant pendant, still and calm, just the two of us trailing through the crisp night air.

But it was always the movies that got our attention.

The day after we saw Billy's *Montana Sky*, we asked Waldo a question that had been bothering us, "How are movies really made?"

"You know how, boys, With cameras and actors and such."

"No, how are they made so that they seem so real?"

Waldo thought about it for a few seconds. "To me," Waldo said, "imagination has more feel than what most folks consider real."

"What's imagination?" I asked, turning the word over in my thoughts.

"A place by itself, a separate country and a good place to be. You've heard of China now, and the French nation? It's like that. You can make snowballs in the summertime, fly in the air on a great balloon, ride with the cowboys in the afternoon. Imagination is a good place to be."

"China is real. Is imagination real?"

"As real as the movies."

"But Waldo, how do they make the things on the screens really happen?" Homer continued.

"Just pretend, boys. Think about it, you can make it happen in your mind."

Homer closed his eyes for a while. "Nothing's happening."

"Sometimes," Waldo said, "What we can't see is the most real thing of all."

"So what is real is what you can't see?" For once, we thought we had him. "Ophelia's real, and I can see her. You're real. This cart is real. What's more real than that?"

"Lots of things. Trust, friendship, honor. Tell me, what does honor look like?" Waldo opened his palms. "Look at me, ain't got much, do I? Don't dress nice 'cept on Sundays. Don't drive no fancy motor car, but I know what I got in here." He tapped Homer's chest where his heart beat inside.

We looked at Waldo in awe. He was the greatest man we knew, but there was no visible sign of that greatness—no money, no fame.

"So, the heart is the most real thing?"

He shook his head. "Only one thing greater."

"What's that?"

"Love, boy. Plain, old-fashioned love. It's what we all need and when we get it, we should give some away, even things up a bit."

The thing Homer wanted most in the world was for Waldo to love him. I remember looking at Waldo's eyes at that moment and knew that Waldo could melt the stars.

Chapter 2

INTRODUCING DADDY GRACE

"Hallelujah! Be anybody, and anywhere I wanted to be? Wow! I closed my eyes, and I was riding with Billy Sunshine, and Rigby was the world's greatest photographer. It was all a matter of VISUALIZING."

—Homer Sincere's journal, 1946

We learned more about make-believe and expanding our imagination in an old wooden church surrounded by a large, sweeping porch at the edge of the Quarter. The black people in the community prayed here.

Waldo asked us if we were ready to face the man himself, Daddy Grace! Before we knew it, we were in the House of Prayer for All People, loading our magic cameras.

Long, slender, freshly painted white pews topped the wide, scored oak floors. Open windows allowed warm breezes inside where the members of the congregation fanned themselves with round straw fans. The preacher imparted hope and talked about the "Main Street of Heaven." Every week, the message to his congregation was the same, "Let the Bells Ring for Freedom."

"Let the bells ring, close your eyes an' visualize."

"Yes, Daddy!"

Sitting between Homer and me, Waldo closed his eyes.

"Are you visualizing?" Homer whispered to Waldo.

"I am."

"Can I?"

"Sure can," Waldo whispered back.

"Anything I want to be?"

"Anything."

"Can do," Waldo said.

Homer closed his eyes tightly and saw Billy Sunshine. Then his expression changed, lost in worry as he thought of his momma.

We were interrupted with a chorus of "Hallelujah!"

"How do you say that word—hallo-you-yah?" Homer asked.

"Hallelujah."

"Hallelujah!" we cried, but there was no visualizing for me. I was a real photographer, and I took a picture of Daddy Grace, a black and white photograph of the man standing before his congregation. When it was developed, I would give my snapshot to him.

In salutation, Daddy pronounced, "We are all flowers in the field."

After services, Homer took Waldo aside. "Did you hear anything about my mom?"

Waldo turned his hands, fixing the reins.

"We're going to ask your daddy 'bout that real soon. And I best look around. Don't pay to worry 'cause we going to find her and she's coming back. I know you are missing her and all, and that's natural, and that's okay. You love her and she loves you. Now listen up, Mardi Gras is coming. People are flyin' and don't be sighin'."

As a skilled player of the "dozens," Waldo had a distinct advantage in this manner of speaking. Homer and I first heard Waldo talk in rhyme when a man walked up and hurled nasty insults at him. I can't remember exactly how they went, but Waldo, without a pause, patiently tested his mettle. "With all that sass, let it pass."

Waldo could reply honestly and with some experience that no, it didn't pay to worry. I was a bit of a skeptic, but in the end, we went along with his advice because his optimism was boundless; it always had been. His wagon was magical and his band paraded celebration like no other.

Waldo's broad, grape-black face topped a steady posture. Under the fringes of the red canopy protecting the vegetables, his hat didn't budge; it stayed at the same rakish tilt. He had proven to us that he was a true friend when he confided how he used the sap of a pecan tree on the band inside his hat. And no one, not anybody, had ever seen Waldo without a hat except inside of the church. Every Sunday he wore it when he lifted his arms to strut a fancy shuffle in the lead of the Preservation Society Marching Band. Waldo led the way, pretending in a most real way, down St. James Street, with sixty black men dressed in dark gray formal suits with bow ties and silk top hats, a brass band formation with trumpets, coronets, tubas, trombones, and a big brass drum. He waved his long silver baton. Women dressed in flowing white gowns, carrying umbrellas in pastel colors—blue, pink, white, peach, and lavender—followed the band, sashaying from side to side. We were devoted to the man at home in the Quarter, Waldo, the eminent collector and distributor of all wisdom.

As we rode away from the church, Waldo's face brightened with a smile that dazzled me, one that I often caught with my imaginary lens. When he smiled, Waldo's one gold tooth sparkled in the slanting sun.

When he dropped us off, he tossed several apples from his "engine's" bonnet. "Now be sure to eat right," he said as the cart lumbered away.

I followed Waldo and the carriage with my eyes down the street as the rays of the February sun were beginning to soft-shoe their way along the tall French windows of the old square, the Vieux Carré.

THE NATION OF KNOWLEDGE

"We made a wide sweeping shot, stretching from Waldo's wagon to Cadillac Mama's restaurant across the way, then to the Western Union Office where the telegraph keys had an attractive rhythm, like the man who tap danced on the corner sidewalk."   —Homer Sincere's journal, 1946

Touching the tips of our thumbs to our forefingers, we both made square viewfinders of sorts, putting our hands up to our eyes to see through our homemade frames, moving smoothly in a slow, 180-degree pan like we imagined a Hollywood director would do.

Our titles were simple, appropriate, practicing for our major feature film, *Mardi Gras*. Today we were filming *Food Capital of the World*.

Opening shot: a wide angle stretching from the square, with a sweeping shot of the neighborhood—careful to avoid the Voodoo House as usual, because the locals said that anyone taking a picture of the Voodoo Lady, Madame LeVeau, would make her angry. I didn't believe the part about the camera stealing the soul, but I did respect Madame LeVeau's power; our camera eye was carefully averted whenever anyone came out of the house.

The camera panned and paused on the Western Union office where Homer had secured his other part-time job delivering telegrams and cleaning. He didn't have a bicycle; it would have been hard for him to ride one. His deliveries were concentrated within the Quarter but when a delivery was far away, he hopped a ride on Waldo's stagecoach, insuring a prompt arrival. When we finished framing our opening shots, Homer headed to work.

The first words Homer discovered had come by way of a telegraph. Mr. Harvey Adams, the manager, wore a green visor and a yellow vest and proudly sported an "Elgin Accurate" gold railroad watch.

"You can send a message to anybody, anytime, anywhere."

"To my friends?"

"Yup."

"To my mother?"

"Sure."

"To New York and California?"

"Anywhere, just send the words over the keys."

That afternoon, Homer heard a clacking as he typed with one finger, learning the keyboard and advancing his secret ambition to make words to send messages. His first telegram was dispatched Tuesday afternoon at 4 o'clock, on January 8, 1946, from a Western Union office on Royal Street, in New Orleans, Louisiana:

MOMMA I'M WAITING FOR YOU STOP PLEASE LET ME KNOW WHERE YOU ARE STOP I LOVE YOU STOP HOMER SINCERE STOP

The keys clacked rapidly and then paused.

He didn't have an address, and Mr. Adams looked down saying, "That's okay, son. We'll just send it out."

"Will she get the message?"

"I expect so."

Homer thought it would go to the "Land of Loss," where Waldo said a lot of things were left: skate keys, gloves, toys, loose change.

Mr. Adams assured him that no word was ever lost.

"It enters the great ether; it is recorded in the 'Nation of Knowledge.'"

"The Nation of Knowledge!" Feeling comfortable with that information, Homer sent a dispatch to Billy Sunshine in California thanking him for coming to New Orleans and asking him to please stay in touch.

The keys were hard to find at first, but the words soon came and he addressed his wishes to the Nation of Knowledge, even though he wasn't sure where it was.

THE FIRST FLOAT OF MARDI GRAS

"Wide angles and cutaways, each day we tried something different in order to see sections of the Quarter in different ways, from different points of view. Rigby was the cameraman and I wrote the script."
—From Homer Sincere's journal, 1946

My father, due to my persistent prayers spoken out loud for weeks, gave me an amazing 8 mm Bell and Howell movie camera with a three-lens turret. It shot twenty-four frames per second. This was the most exciting and formative moment in my life and, in a film metaphor, a preview of coming events. That camera shaped our lives. It was the same light, portable camera that news teams had used to make war movies. "What you see is what you get," made for Movietone newsreels. It had a comfortable feel, a natural extension of me, like a glove in hand. For Homer too, it was the opportunity to explore the beginning of a dream. Each day, we viewed different sections of the Quarter through the turret housing the three lenses. This time it was real!

As Mardi Gras approached, the face of the French Quarter was erupting in a profusion of garish color. Costumes, masks, and accessories, sewed and painted in backrooms all winter, were displayed in brief, tantalizing glimpses near doorways and windows, until the last spot in the Quarter on Royal Street was being draped in the traditional green, gold, and purple of the Lenten festival.

Waldo's colorful horse-drawn cart would rattle into camera range. We would train our lens on him and title the film something like *The First Float of Mardi Gras*. The old horse sometimes shuffled to a stop under Homer's balcony, sending all of Waldo's jiggling wares threateningly backwards. Waldo wasn't the least bit disturbed. He'd wave to us, spin a smile, and then go on his way. Usually he rode on past, but now he never failed to linger for a minute, fascinated, watching us film.

Though we made homemade films, we strove to make each feature, even a short subject, have the snap and pizzazz of the movies at the Rialto. Homer shared my enthusiasm. But I never knew what he was really thinking. Sometimes he would bubble over with excitement and comments, at other times he stayed silent, as if he was working a knot out of his frayed shoelace. I was more outspoken, with a knack for causing trouble by infrequent insensitivity and sometimes making an error in judgment.

UN, DEUX, TROIS

Behind a brick-walled garden and boxwood hedges, deep in the shade of hollyhocks, trumpet vines, and bumblebees, was the land-marked Beauregard-Keyes House, recently appointed as a Garden Club. On Tuesday and Thursday afternoons, it was home to Madame du Bois' dancing class. Like most expensive homes built in New Orleans by the cotton brokers before 1850, the home had a wide veranda and held a large ballroom for formal occasions.

I took Homer with me to dancing school one day, especially to meet some of the decorative magnolias that fluttered effortlessly in our presence. These pretty girls with their sweet virginal drawls and moist painted lips, white gloves and little freckled bosoms that rose and fell as they breathed, gathered together waiting to take their prim and proper places before the lesson began.

Even those who were less physically favored were just as attractive due to their manners and charm. Southern ladies, probably more than those anywhere on earth, have for generations been valued for their beauty. It was a plantation tradition to be reckoned with. Generally speaking, this heritage of the South produced generations of beautiful women, but with a diminished emphasis on their higher education. Yet, they always excelled in the finishing schools during the 1940s. Behind the facade of beauty and innocence, they were very astute and smart. Among the most remarkable was Margaret Mitchell—whose physical stature and lack of prettiness created a compensating drive—who gave benison to the greatest romance of the Civil War, with flawless understanding, ability, and an unshakable intensity.

Homer had been reluctant to go with me and he was right. Madame du Bois did not warm up to a boy in a brace. Homer did not measure up to her standard when she dismissed him from participation in the class, asking him to sit by the piano, banging out three quarter time, and watch.

Madame du Bois wore a well-fitted red wig and heavily caked makeup that highlighted well-rouged red cheeks, reminiscent of a

Toulouse-Lautrec poster. In her practiced and disciplined hands, she held a tall, slender, wooden brass-crowned pole, topped with multi-colored ribbons. It served as a musical metronome that she tapped with the music. Standing in the center of the large ballroom, she called out in a slight French accent, "slide, two, three, turn, deux, trois," as the class circled around her over the well-worn, polished parquet floor, past the large floor-to-ceiling windows where Homer sat casting his eyes outside to hide his hurt feelings.

Afterward, in the Quarter, Homer relieved my embarrassed excuses. "Aw, that's all right, Rig. I'm just not up for dancing right now."

I felt bad for my friend and almost quit dancing school then and there. My feelings were confused and blurred, tinged with empathy, colored by my own privileged circumstances, wobbling between my attraction for ladies and friendship. My selfish need for the companionship of girls took precedence, I am ashamed to say. But I aimed to compensate in other ways.

THE POKER GAME CAPER

"All his life, Rigby noticed details. It was his way of seeing the drama of life around him. And he always had a plan."
                                            —Homer Sincere's journal

Waldo had a lot on his mind. He collected his small savings in a sock, kept under the seat of the wagon. But not enough to pay Homer's rent. The boy must have his own bed, he thought. When I noticed that Waldo was a little nervous and not his easy self, I pumped him several times for information. At the same time, I looked for a way to keep Homer from being evicted or adopted. I always believed that if there was a crack in the door, or even a window, I could get it open all the way for some fresh air.

A lucky and unusual opportunity presented itself to get us out of the Quarter, when Waldo confided that there was to be a big game with Johnny Diamond, the best poker player in the world. I learned that Johnny Diamond had family and friends here, and had stayed behind for a few days after the Billy Sunshine Show moved up river. Johnny was still in the Quarter!

Being a gaming sportsman myself, and although marbles wasn't played for the same high stakes as cards, I wanted to know more about the coming game.

"Are you a good poker player, Waldo?"

"Black man plays blackjack, poker's for the joker. I used to be pretty good but I gave it up."

"You afraid of getting rusty, Waldo? You're not fidgeting about playing Johnny Diamond?"

Waldo told me that he had appointed himself as a delegate on behalf of Daddy Grace and the church. But I suspected the real reason was to help Homer, not only with the rent, but just some basic expenses, matters that had weighed on Waldo's mind ever since Homer had showed him Mrs. P's note. He was going to add money from his own savings to the church's contribution, play, and bet.

"I have it in my mind that I can give Johnny a run for his money. I can beat him, as such."

"I know you can! Where you gonna play, on the river?"

"Johnny's not a river man. He plays on land."

"Waldo, take us with you!"

"Now I can't be doing that. Everyone would think I'd lost my good sense."

"It's for my education," I pleaded. "I have a new camera, Waldo, and it's a way to learn. You've seen us shooting film, and to shoot a real live poker game would be dramatic, just stunning. A way to keep us out of trouble."

"You'd be in a lot of trouble if I take you to the game. The genuine poker folks wouldn't like it a bit."

"We'll hide. They would never know we were there."

"You're not goin' to be learning any bad habits," he said with a note of finality in his voice. It was like when I requested something from my mother and she replied, "I'll speak to your father." Especially if my father wasn't in town. I pressed Waldo so he wouldn't side step me.

"I can learn the protocol of poker and can make a stupendous and colossal film."

"Don't be using those big words on me."

"Please, Waldo, you've been teaching us about imagination. This is a real break to test our skill and, as you say, test our imagination."

Waldo relented.

I discussed the new production plan with Homer. We were a team, and this would be our first professional joint venture and collaboration. Waldo was our star. We had a cast of supporting players, including the great Johnny Diamond.

Waldo let us watch that night above the hall with our promise that we would be quiet, stay out of sight and, as Waldo said, "You're not to be saying anything, to anyone, now or anytime later." We couldn't wait.

At a little before nine o'clock, we hid in the rafters above a bunch of men in a warehouse on Rampart Street. It was in the old Government Building that had been gutted. The large crowded room with wooden plank floors was wreathed in smoke. A green-shaded lamp cast light over a large, round table covered by a ceremonial green felt cloth. Homer and I had taken our position in the building early, scouting out the best angle to shoot from, staking the best point of view among the beams. We found a niche that offered an added advantage. Two swirling overhead ceiling fans made just enough noise to suppress the clicking sound of the movie camera. To insulate any sound, I had also taken the precaution of improvising a shoebox by making a hole at one end for the lenses and lining it with pure cotton taken from some fresh bales.

We recognized some of the notorious card-playing sharks in New Orleans. Louie the Bank took bets around town, Happy Jack Carver, the richest man in the Quarter who made his money from sugarcane, and other familiar faces of men whose names we didn't know. Waldo was dressed in a crumpled cream linen jacket and bow tie, clean and ready. Through my range finder, the scene played perfectly for our movie.

The animated poker companions sat around a table. Even though we were in the segregated South, it didn't matter if you were black or white, as long as you brought chips. We were about twenty feet directly above Johnny Diamond. The dapper, commanding J.D. was magnificently costumed for the occasion. He wore a black suit with a red handkerchief and sported initials on his sleeve. He was smooth, impeccable, and unflappable. No question, he was our new star. Homer steadied me when I leaned over the large beams, just far enough for an unobstructed view without being discovered.

The men settled into a relaxed routine with underlying conflict and tension. Johnny Diamond had a large stack of chips the size of quarters and threw some to the center of the table, forming a red and green mosaic.

Raise! Fold! Raise!

Waldo was winning big. Every card was dealt to his advantage, and then something happened to reverse his fate. The stakes doubled. Johnny Diamond was playing intensely. After several more hands, as I watched carefully, I noticed a barely discernible movement—his tell.

One of the reasons I was so successful at marbles was that I had learned to observe everything around me carefully, knowing when I had my opponents by a look in their eye or by the way they knuckled under pressure. It was in the detail. A shift. A nod. A slide.

"I saw it! Homer, I saw it!" I said under my breath. "Johnny Diamond doesn't have the cards when his left foot slides back." Homer was on the lookout for the slide as well and when I was shooting a long shot, he nudged me, anticipating the motion. I changed the turret to a longer lens and filmed up close, cutting to Johnny's cool expression, and then back to his doubling the bet with such casual confidence that everyone folded, including Waldo. The drama repeated several times, and there was a lot of money on the table. I got a clip of that, too.

Johnny Diamond, the greatest gambler in the world, was tipping his hand. Right there and then, we had peak moment. I figured that after careful editing, we would send the film to Billy

Sunshine who had always lost to Johnny. With this news, he could win all his money back, having the advantage, the upper hand—not by cheating, but with valuable information. He could win a million dollars! Waldo could win too! I tried to signal him with convoluted body language, hoping more than anything he would look up. I couldn't risk being discovered. Waldo never noticed, concentrating on the game.

When we got the rushes back from the lab, we could hardly contain our excitement. As we cut the pieces together, the film worked out beautifully, revealing how the fans cast shadows, making the game mysterious, full of suspense. It was quite an achievement, a hit, for Canfield and Sincere!

"You realize we have box-office gold, Homer? We have a way out of here and our ticket to Hollywood."

"Hollywood!"

"How would you like to be out there with Billy Sunshine?" I asked, playing into his fervent wish.

"You kidding, Rig? I've got other matters, more important things."

"We got the film, we've made a winner."

In reality, he was still trying to reestablish his family. I imagined his feelings were all jumbled up, but I could help.

A few days later, along the old courthouse square, I tried to explain our secret discovery to Waldo, but he kept interrupting.

"Now it just doesn't pay to gamble. I lost a hundred dollars."

"Waldo, I can win it all back."

"You just forget that right now, Boy. No one can beat Johnny. He's just too good."

"But we can, and we have the evidence on film to prove it." Then Waldo said, "Have you completely lost your mind?"

"I know I could beat him, Waldo, for sure."

"Oh, you film an evening of poker and now you know everything about it? Johnny Diamond's been playing the game since long before you were born. He's a professional, and you're not to be gambling with anybody."

"But Waldo . . ."

"I'm tellin' you, boy, the gambling way don't pay. Now you take the oath, no gambling, and don't be following Waldo's ways."

Waldo made me take a solemn pledge that I would never play poker.

"What are you going to do now?"

He wasn't sure.

I discussed the matter with Homer. We had proof of Johnny's poker playing habit. We decided we would keep it for Billy.

We mailed the film to Billy Sunshine at his ranch in Hollywood.

In the days that followed, a selection of household items and silver objects mysteriously appeared in the back of Waldo's wagon. I made a contribution from my family's household: a serving spoon, a tray, and a large sterling silver bowl. Waldo knew a pawn shop and deposited the money we got from the "collection" under Mrs. Partridge's door.

Relieved by appearance of gifts from the Almighty, Waldo accepted it all as compensation from that great Poker Player in the sky. I waited for word from Billy Sunshine.

A NEW BEST FRIEND

Waldo was the son of slaves and my Grandmother Rachael was the daughter of slave owners. We had something in common but hardly a shared past.

I remember hearing stories from Grandmother, whose name was Rachael Morrison, Rachael from the Old Testament, and Morrison, a family name holding pride; they had produced generals that fought for the Confederacy. She was a storyteller in the best southern tradition, handing down recipes and reflections from her illustrious past, about the slow and easy times before the war. One thing she shared with me, that I remember to this day, was how she was raised by her nanny Mamie whose devotion to her was deeper than all the psalms in scripture. Sara-Belle was Mamie's daughter—a sweet black and giving girl who helped with the washing, and Rachael's best friend. My grandmother spoke with unshakable affection about her. They loved each other dearly, played together as "sisters," growing up holding a deep and abiding love for each other. After the war, Sara went north on the "underground railroad" for a better life, an adventure that fascinated me. Rachael stayed behind and they missed each other terribly, being inextricably linked to each other in friendship. I still have a sepia tintype photograph of them as children, arm and arm, smiling, both dressed in lace and innocence, and smelling of lavender I'm sure.

I mention this as a prelude, because of an indelible incident stained with color and whose memory I hold with shame.

It happened one day, when Waldo introduced us to his nephew, young sporty Lincoln Jones, whose smiling brown eyes and broad smile were only matched by his outgoing personality and friendship. He had come to visit his Uncle Waldo for a few days, and after making rounds on his wagon with him, we accepted his company readily. He was a good guy, became our new best friend, and we never saw or knew any difference except he lived in another parish far away. We played and filmed, little rascals right out of a Hal Roach *Our Gang* serial.

Lincoln taught us to sing harmony, and although we three pals had not reached an adolescent bass, we tried in *Ink Spots* imitation. Lincoln introduced us to the best of soul food—corn bread hush puppies with honey—and how to fish the streams near Lake Pontchartrain where we learned as much about catfish one summer afternoon as anyone could learn in a lifetime. Lincoln Jones had the touch, and we netted over a dozen or more.

When we invited him to share our pastime enthusiasm for movies, he couldn't come, since the Rialto accommodated only white patrons, with no segregated balcony, where we would have gladly sat. It made no difference to us, as long as we were together. This injustice should have diminished our movie-going forays, but it didn't, and we let the matter pass. I had come from a family who wore their sentiments and tolerance with quiet gentility. Waldo never said anything about it, but it stayed with Homer and me.

THE UNEXPECTED VISITOR

"I leaned forward with the camera rolling on this live event. It was the color or lack of color that was out of place with the pastels of the Quarter. The car had writing on the side that was hard to read, but a long lens brought the words into clear focus."

—Homer Sincere's journal, 1946

In my camera, I caught a view of Waldo's carriage as it turned down Iberville Street then panned back toward Cadillac Mama's. So many of our films began and ended at the same place. We had no literal understanding of why that was a good thing to do but it gave us a feeling of comfort when we watched our movies end.

We were becoming better filmmakers. I had suggested to my father that he upgrade me on my next birthday to a Filmo 16 mm movie camera for Kodak film with a strip of magnetic tape that could be applied for single sound. There was a lot of activity in the Quarter and sound would give our films a more realistic dimension. A background score would add a vital touch, amplifying the action. A film without a score was like a house without furniture.

For *The First Float of Mardi Gras*, Homer and I, still unsure of a plot, had spent all day on the roof of Homer's home shooting cutaways. We had not graduated beyond a few establishing shots. As we were about to call a wrap, we saw something that didn't belong in the Quarter. We had stumbled into a short-subject event that suggested that we continue shooting and that we were at the beginning of a new episode.

A strange car had stopped in front of the carriage house. Homer knew every car that was parked regularly within a three-block radius, including the cars of visitors and vendors. I knew the frumpy cars that tourists used on occasion and the elegant, gleaming cars that were parked near Antoine's restaurant on Friday and Saturday nights. With post-wartime shortages, there were a lot of old models around. My favorite was the Studebaker that everyone laughed at because they never knew by its sleek design whether it was coming or going.

But this car was ugly. Homer narrowed the focus of his fingers, and I zoomed in tight on the vehicle that was parked right under his window. It looked odd in black-and-white and out of place. Everything on it was the same non-color with no gleam or even rusty chrome to break the grim monotony. The car was clean but didn't shine. The door opened to let out a lady who looked a lot like her car.

For a closer view, we switched to a telephoto lens as if for a news-reel. Homer liked newsreels almost as much as he liked Billy's movies. *The March of Time* had grand stirring music with as much pomp and pageantry as a film like *Gone with the Wind*.

The lady was talking to someone under the balcony below us. Homer didn't want to be seen. While he viewed the strange woman through a wider virtual lens, another character entered our new film, a woman in gray who was talking to the landlady, Mrs. Partridge. I wished we had sound. The new visitor was tall and bony with her black hair swept back in a round knot. A narrow-brimmed, black straw hat topped a face with a prim, pursed expression. It was exaggerated by her gray complexion, thin lips, and small hazel eyes. Her white gloves held a thick manila envelope.

The stranger's voice filtering out of the growing racket in the Quarter was easier to hear because it was different from the background sounds. It was dry and papery, speaking in a monotone, like when we read aloud at school.

We moved in carefully to listen, to know what was being said so that we could get the title and the mood right for our film, a preview of things to come. When Mrs. P.'s arm extended up to point directly at Homer's apartment, Homer ducked fast, still peeking through his personal range finder with a focus on the balustrade. We heard her familiar voice continue, "A damned shame . . . good boy . . . bruises . . . alone three days now . . . ." Homer's father had not appeared again since Homer caught him cheating with that loose woman.

Homer's face flushed. Mrs. P. was talking about him, telling all that to some stranger, and breaking confidence. It was a betrayal.

Crouching lower, he could make out the words on the side of the automobile: Department of Child Welfare and Adoptions.

Homer's hands dropped from his eyes as he stared at the car door. I continued shooting.

"It just won't do, Mrs. Partridge." There was a slight rustling of papers before the stranger continued in an arid voice, reporting that the department had tried to locate Homer at school on Friday, but she had gotten there too late, and she would go again today.

"As soon as I hear him come in, I'll call you," Mrs. Partridge said. "I'll know when he's home because a certain stair always creaks."

"Rigby," Homer whispered urgently, "This is no movie. This is real, and she wants to take me away!"

Turning to Homer, I again noticed the same purplish-blue marks on his upper arm and body. He had recently taken to wearing long-sleeve shirts, explaining that it was for protection from mosquitoes, but not today. Even Waldo had noticed the discolorations. He had lightly rubbed Homer's arm while he hugged him, hoping they would disappear, but it was not enough.

I didn't say anything, pretending not to notice, but wondered how Homer could be so cheerful. I figured that his father might be beating him up pretty bad. How could someone hit a kid with the same hand that made music?

Homer longed for a family more than he let on. In the meantime, I was sure all he had to do was tell the adoption people that he wanted to stay with his parents, whether they were around or not. He'd say he had been in a fight after someone called his father a name. That should discourage anyone from wanting to take him away.

Sure, that's what he would say, but he needed protection. Later that night, when I mentioned the situation to my father, he looked me in the eye for a moment, but all he said was, "Oh, I see." Since he never mentioned it again, he must not have believed me.

I was on the case. Until we heard from Billy, Homer could come home with me. He had to escape from captivity. Surely, sending our film to Billy would bring an invitation to his ranch. That was my plan.

TAKING COVER

"Waldo loved me. I knew that. But I also knew there was something unspoken. It was somewhere else, somewhere beneath the surface, and I could not understand."

—Homer Sincere's journal

Homer quietly snuck away and found Waldo in the shade along the Square.

"What you want, boy?"

"I—I—" It was harder to ask than he had imagined.

"Just tell me, boy."

"Will you adopt me?"

Waldo leaned way back in his carriage seat and eyed Homer for several short eternities.

"Oh my, wish I could. You don't want to be adopted by anybody. You be your own man, not someone else's."

"That's easy for you to say, you're already a man."

He peered at Homer from beneath the brim of his hat. "You think it's easy bein' a black man? Black people been having trouble worse'n yours since this country began."

Homer didn't argue, but he wouldn't give up just yet.

"What am I going to do?"

Waldo's sigh was louder than one of Ophelia's snorts, shaking his head and patting Homer's hand.

"Gonna find a place, and we are on the case," and added, "It's gonna be okay, you listen to Waldo, now. You stay with your own people."

"But my people are hurting me."

"Give it time, son. Just a little more healin' time."

It was anybody's guess whether Waldo said that to prevent Homer from having any ideas about running away. As a willing caretaker, but not being Homer's real father, it was perhaps a good thing. In sum total, letting anyone else replace his parents wouldn't make Homer's life better. It occurred to Homer that maybe Waldo didn't have a house.

He returned home. Being alone was not easy for him. Mrs. Partridge was at best a chilly compromise, and not very trustworthy. Homer's parents owed her money.

Homer rattled around a bit upstairs in the apartment, pretending to have conversations with his father. For sound effect, like in films, he clomped across the floor with his hands in his shoes. He stayed out of sight.

But the next morning, over different clumping sounds, he recognized Mrs. P's voice, stern and strict, coming up the stairs. Clump, clump. A knock on the door interrupted a temporary silence in the hallway. Homer stood on the other side of the door in the center of the living room foyer, careful not to move, scared and quiet. The knocks came harder and deeper.

"Homer, I know you're there. It's Mrs. Partridge."

The knocks were fast and furious with a full echo.

"I want to talk to you, young man."

Outside, the noise made by mid-morning workers, decorating lampposts with streams of wide silver and black ribbon for carnival, distracted him.

"Homer Sincere, there is a court order here, and I have to speak with you."

An order, what kind of order? Homer thought, as he considered sliding off the upstairs porch and dropping himself onto a window ledge until he reached the ground. He had done it a thousand times before, a safe and economical route to his daytime world. Right now, there was too much going on outside. The thumping continued.

"Open up, Mr. Sincere, open up," the voice snapped with exasperation.

Homer splashed some water from the kitchen sink on his face and wet his hair down. With a towel around his arm, he opened the door.

"Good morning Mrs. P. . . . I was just washing up."

Mrs. P. entered quickly.

"Where are your parents?" she demanded.

"Just out, just now." Homer felt her uneasy stare.

What did this woman looming in front of him want? Mrs. P. distanced herself in the background, fidgeting with her apron strings.

"Have you been going to school?"

"Yes, ma'am." Homer was nervous at this interrogation. He had missed school on and off a few days over the past several weeks because of his job at Western Union.

"Answer me, boy. You're not going to school. Where is your father? Have you seen your mother? Who's looking after you? Are you eating properly?" The questions came in torrents. Homer felt he was a fugitive, a menace to society, yet he had done nothing wrong.

"Just look at you, running around the Quarter. Look how you are dressed," she said. Homer thought he was dressed all right. Maybe there was a tear in his khaki pants, a button missing from his shirt.

"Like the hat?"

Mrs. P. disapproved. "That floppy dirty hat."

Homer crammed his hat tightly down on his head. No one was going to take his hat. No, siree. Changing the subject, Homer offered the lady some hot coffee.

"It's very good," he said brightly.

"You shouldn't be drinking coffee." Mrs. P.'s eyes were intense, her eyebrows raised. "I have some papers for your father to sign. You must be taken care of, and we know how to do it."

"My mother will be here today. My father will be back soon. He takes care of me and he's a good man. Honest."

There was nothing good about this situation. Not for him. Mrs. P.'s eyes squinted as she pointed a warning finger at him, leaving a message.

"I know all about you. I'll be back."

Just the thought dimmed Homer's hopes that life would get better.

We spent more time at the Rialto, and Homer saw his mother in every film smiling like Rita Hayworth, her hair rippling across her exquisite face, glowing like Veronica Lake's. Sometimes her expression was as fragile and ladylike as that of Mrs. Miniver or sad and filled with longing like Merle Oberon in *Wuthering Heights*. Other times she would have the immense grace of Ingrid Bergman. Homer became less sure about what was real and what was a dream. His feelings slipped into pretending.

THE GREAT CHASE

"I remember the green leafy lanes between the carriage houses in the Quarter. My mother pointed out things I missed seeing in our walks. The dark paneled doorways, the tall second-floor balconies, the flower boxes on windows. She would recite and ask me to repeat the name of every flower. Her favorite were peonies; she loved pink and red ones."

—Homer Sincere's journal, 1946

The social worker returned, telling Mrs. Partridge, "These abused children are forever protecting their parents. He needs a home." Her words echoed up to the balcony.

This was really getting serious.

The creaky stair! It dawned on him why Mrs. P. had missed the cue to open her door when he returned home. She had been on the telephone talking with the Department of Adoptions.

Her words were chilling. "After all, I don't think his mother is coming back, and there's no reason for him to stay with that man another day. The boy's upstairs now."

Scarcely breathing, his mind fastened on Mrs. Partridge's pronouncement, he had to get away.

Homer slipped out through a window. Cutting through courtyards,
his limited ability to move quickly was compensated by his determination.
He crossed Governor Nichols and St. James, heading toward the Square
to look for a safe place for the time being . . . until he could think of something. His attempt to run gave his stride an awkward, uneven rhythm.

The courtyards had been replanted with flowers. The last remnants
of the victory gardens were gone; even the war was being forgotten.
Homer passed a street corner, where Mr. Music, a one-man band played
an old banjo, drum, and harmonica, strumming musically away wearing a black top hat, red-engine socks, and black-and-white wing-tipped
spectator shoes. In close competition, Dirttooth Seneca played tunes,
shaking his spoons at Homer in a noisy greeting, a *clicky-clack-clack-
clack, clicky-clack-clack-clack, a clicky-clack*! A railroad train was taking
him far away.

Like in the movies, life was one chase after another.

A couple of blocks inside the Quarter, he headed toward the
House of Prayer, reaching the door near the open windows. He
stopped to listen before knocking. Utter silence until a shout rang out.
"Yes, Daddy. We hear you!"

Turning the doorknob, he saw the preacher dressed in a purple
flowing robe, his arms reaching up to the ceiling. "You can be anybody, you can be anywhere, you can be anything you want to be," he
wailed. The congregation echoed back, "Hallelujah!" The bells rang,
"Freedom!"

A dozen or so people in the congregation bowed their heads as
they responded to each phrase of hope, "Yes, Sweet Daddy."

Sweet Daddy Grace dropped his arms to his sides and lowered his
massive head. From under his dark eyebrows, he glared threateningly out into the congregation as he exhorted them, "Close your eyes,
children, close your eyes. Let the church bells of freedom ring."

Daddy's bass voice lowered further, rumbling from the depths of
his spirit in a booming summation.

"VISUALIZE!"

This word brought Homer back to his mother. He visualized when they had walked together through the Quarter to the café they went to for cold limeade and a hot apple tarte tatin.

These were better days and better times.

Visualize! Leaving the church, he found a temporary refuge as the images dissolved one into another. Making his way down the narrow street, he ran past rich pecan-paneled doorways past shops where Mardi Gras costumes were being sewn; the Carnival was coming fast and preparations had speeded to a furious tempo. Sequins and lace, velvet and feathers flew from one room to the next, ball gowns and chain mail, harlequin suits and mad court clothes, all to be worn before Lent.

Inside a kitchen near the plant-lined patios, a Creole lady made a bowl of orange cream from fresh orange juice, sugar, sweet milk, and eggs, encouraging his taste buds to explode.

Homer hopped on a streetcar whose familiar rattling comfort took him along tree-lined avenues that shaded passengers from the hot sun. Not unusual in February when the flat earth seemed to swim in vapors. He could almost sniff things growing. A few blocks from the lake, he got off, and the singing trolley receded into the noon stillness with a jangling metallic whir. He walked to a small counter run by an old woman with black braids and gold earrings, and produced a nickel and, she a sandwich. He feasted on a long loaf of crisp French bread hollowed out and filled with meatballs flecked with red peppers and a rich sauce topped with layers of herbs, fresh sliced tomatoes, and mayonnaise with a sharp bite. On this day before Carnival, Homer Sincere was safe, but it was to be not for long. There was a black telephone on the linoleum countertop, and he made a call.

NO ALARM, NO HARM

Waldo told me he had searched for Homer's mother, asking for her at all the hospitals in the Quarter because it wasn't like a momma not to return home, and he supposed that the lady was in trouble. There was something going on at St. Exupery's Infirmary, and it wasn't easy for Waldo just to walk into a white hospital, but he did, with the excuse that he was just delivering some fresh fruit to Mrs. Sincere. He found who he was looking for in his most polite way. "Ma'am, I'm looking from Mrs. Sincere. Her son needs her." A very compassionate Sister told him that a young boy called Homer had come looking for his mother, but she had not yet been transferred from the clinic. His mother had finally been admitted just a few days ago. Weak and injured, she had fallen into a coma. Her body had been battered. The nurse sadly informed Waldo of something else. A blood test revealed that Mrs. Sincere had leukemia, a very rare kind, and she was very sick. The news shocked Waldo, putting hope on hold.

"Oh, Lord. No. Oh no, please Lord." I knew his eyes watered, because he was that kind of person, and the nurse, feeling bad for the man who had come with fresh fruit and vegetables, offered a warm towel to collect his sadness. Waldo discussed the matter with the nurse. Where was Mr. Sincere? He had not been around and didn't know the situation. He was probably ashamed of beating his wife, or just too drunk to care. And the boy? Waldo would find Homer. What could he tell him? Maybe it was best not to say anything. Look after him, take his mind off things until his momma was up and around. He was sure that was what she would want. Best to pray. "Take a rest and think the best." She would be well in a few days, and he would bring the boy to her. But not now, not while she was unconscious. The nurse agreed. Waldo left behind a large basket of his best "selected" fruit for Homer's mom to enjoy when she got better.

With a respectful nod, he said, "Just tell her that Waldo came by, no bother, no worry. Thank you, yes, I'd better be going on along now."

Waldo didn't want to upset young Homer. "No alarm, no harm." He knew with all his heart the woman would pull through, and he was going to make sure Homer and his momma would be happily back together. It was too hurtful to be apart.

"The lady's been away, but she'll be okay!" he rhymed to himself.

INTO THE BAYOU

"The water's polished surface was marbled by swirls of deep, shiny green with azalea bushes blooming, purple and red and white, their colors mingling with the passing landscape. Scents of magnolias and gardenias folded into each other. As we moved through the bayou, it felt like being wrapped in clean, wet smoke."

—Homer Sincere's journal, 1946

At water's edge, I found Homer in the same place we often spent summer afternoons on the lake, dangling our legs from a cement ledge in the warm water, looking at our rippling reflections. Then, at other times, without warning, rain would begin to pour down and we would run for cover under a moss-laden tree waiting for the squall to pass. Today was no different, with water lashing and soaking us as Homer hunched over his po' boy sandwich, protecting a Billy Sunshine postcard, his special good luck charm. Suddenly, an exhilarating subtropical squall had whipped up a swirling wind, and a dark cloud dumped buckets of fresh rain over us. Afterward, we sat by the lake until the sun dried our clothes bakery-warm.

Leaving Homer on a jetty hidden by tall shrubs, I went to my special spot to retrieve transportation to get us home. Before I got his phone call, I was figuring it was a good day to skip school without anyone noticing. The mailman had just arrived, depositing a large envelope postmarked "Hollywood." As soon as we were further upstream, I would tell him the amazing news, but I had to ensure secrecy.

Homer was waiting patiently when I returned in a cypress pirogue that slid through the glassy surface of the bayou stream. I picked up my old straw hat, stored with my equipment in the bow, and directed the boat's light, graceful movement. My camera eye put nature in balance and kept the tipsy craft upright.

I couldn't tell whether Homer marveled at my skill or was petrified by my daring; he held his breath while he sat in the pirogue, a boat used by Cajun people in the bayou. The bayou, too, held its breath. A heavy, wet silence hung over the sluggish waters that ran through swamps and marshlands, past low-lying farms and plantations with lawns unraveling to the sea.

The bayou was a place of lurking, we both felt that. Attakapa Indians, said to be cannibalistic, had once traded nearby. More danger waited in our imaginations. We could quickly find safe harbor from the frequent sudden storms by hiding in the high tangled grasses. Tossing Homer my Filmo, loaded with a 100-foot roll of film, I thought it was an opportunity to add some scenic footage to our movie and at the same time calm Homer's anxiety. If he started filming, he might have the same calmness and exhilaration that I felt, losing myself as I concentrated hard on everything around me. And now I had a letter and a photo from Billy Sunshine, with an answer, encouragement, and a solution to Homer's dilemma.

While we were swiftly moving into the production, it was a good time to pause and let Homer have a go at the camera, even though it was difficult to keep the boat steady and to keep the news to myself until we had hit dry land. I instructed Homer on ways to lock his elbows tight to his chest to compensate for the boat's movement as he used the hand-held camera. Then with a swift current, the craft sliced and glided through the bayou where we observed incredible nature, flowers, and beauty from every angle.

Homer crouched along the side of the craft, the button pressed, the lens sharp.

Putting the camera to his eye, he muffled, "Looking good, Rigby, real nice."

The land was queasy with water, lined with streams and raked by stretched-out shadows of ancient live oak trees hanging with moss that looked strange and alien. Paths bordering the mainland marshes led through the grasses to old houses, wide porches, and beds covered by mosquito nets. Knotty cypress trees bent over the water from the banks, genuflected over clumps of motionless cane and palmetto fans; the stream was choked with water hyacinths. Pine trees and magnolias sweetened the syrupy air; the pirogue made only a temporary knife's crease in the water.

"How's it looking?"

"Getting some nice stuff," Homer said, following focus.

"This is going to make a great series for *National Geographic* or something," I suggested.

"Keep moving, Rig, I almost got it," he answered with the camera close to his cheek.

He was very involved, and I was almost a little jealous. I was supposed to be the director and the cameraman in this crew. "Nice job. Ready for a break?"

He didn't respond. As we passed beneath the trees, Homer continued to film patrician oaks, reaching out in an arch to darken the waterway.

He was filming all of this mystery and beauty, and I felt a little competitive until I noticed the dark bruise marks on Homer's arms, wondering if they were the same or new ones, and I couldn't restrain my concern.

"Homer, your father on a bender again?" Then I looked away, waiting for Homer's usual excuse.

He put the camera down and looked at me.

"You fell, eh?"

"Yeah."

The scenery wasn't enough to heal his hurt. "Rig, they're going to get me," he blurted out.

A hiding place would help, but Homer faced bigger demons. "Maybe she went on a trip."

"I don't think so, Rig. I think she had to go away to get well. But I shouldn't worry. Isn't that what Waldo says, not to worry?"

Dipping the paddle to dislodge us from the marshy bank, I confirmed his thought. "Hey, we'll work somethin' out." I needed to hear those words as much as Homer.

In a moment, the boat was free, floating again.

I brought my dripping hand in from the water and momentarily pointed to Homer as inspiration struck.

"You can stay in the room over our garage."

"Sure good to be out here . . . have a friend like you, Rig."

Guiding the boat into a weedy area, we found some walk-worthy land and came ashore for an hour to crawfish. I needed to rest for a while before talking about the letter. We needed clear and unencumbered thinking. I would ask for the guest room, but my mother had an appointment book full of invited friends. No, that wouldn't work—she probably would not want to hide a boy who was on the run. Then I calculated that I could put Homer into the garage apartment, a makeshift room used as a temporary office, until our plan developed. I'd get permission from my father who used the space when people broke a hand or got sick so he could be close by to look after them.

Conversation naturally turned to our fathers.

"I'm not at all impressed with mine," I confided and turned to Homer as I prepared a fishing line. "He's the perfect person to con because he always wants to be in control of everything. I can get my dad to do anything I want by persuading him that it's his own idea.

"For instance—and you gotta keep this a secret—why do you think my kid brother is at home and I'm here gliding around in the swamp, enjoying myself?" I checked the line before I dropped it in the water, jerking on the chunk of bait to be sure it was secure. "Because I convinced the kid that he wanted to become a doctor. He had to. It was the best way to meet girls and make a lot of money. What was his piggy bank for? Just to save pennies? No, he needed respect, the big bucks and security and a good life. And didn't he like blood and stuff? He agreed and that took the pressure off me. Now, my father likes to say my little brother will carry on the tradition. I will just carry on somewhere else, and he has no idea that I had anything to do with it."

There was my mother, too. My relationship with her had always been distant. She was rich and privileged, and she expected the same of me. Yet, when I looked to her for advice and for emotional support, she was incapable, perhaps having compromised for convenience in her own life—too busy with her garden, her friends, her charities, her parties. Not that she was uninvolved, but just oblivious to the deeper feelings and needs of a young man growing up. Since my life was pre-ordained with expectation, I could never depend upon her, and as a result, I turned to my father, who in his own way framed me in his own likeness, seeking recognition and accomplishment that held meaning for him and not for me. I didn't know then that I would be left searching, someday and always, for both a career and a relationship that would win his approval.

I waved my fishing line back and forth to divert Homer's attention. "You know how else I keep my father in line? See my hat? I wear these crazy hats because my father always wears a hat. I keep my hands jammed into my pockets because my father does and when he sees me acting like him, even a little bit, it makes him happy. So, I keep him happy, and he doesn't pay too much attention to the fact that we don't think alike about anything. Friends, for instance, or school, and sports." I unhooked a gasping crawfish and set it in a basket, then laid back, covering my eyes with my hat. I still needed to confirm to myself, "You okay, Home?" Before I got an answer, I blurted out, "I kinda like this closing your eyes and visualizing stuff."

I was used to seeing light and color and perspective. That was real to me. I saw things while Homer felt them—part of the bond we had, cementing our differences.

"Pretending, it's okay Rig, I guess it makes things a little better." Homer was earnest.

Of course, what else could he say?

I guess I was really sort of visualizing, too. "I want to see the whole world and be a great photographer one day. And I want to have my own boat and sail around the world. I can imagine all the great places to go to and make films on location, like the French Riviera."

"I know that you will, Rigby. I'm sure of it."

"And how about you, Home? What do you want to do?"

"I think I'd like to be a writer like my mom. But for now I'd like be a cowboy, ride a horse like Billy Sunshine."

Homer would love riding a horse; it would be a lot easier on his leg. But you can't be a cowboy forever. And the way he thought about things and suffering a lot, he could be a good writer. That would be something great.

Putting feelings on paper and telling an action story could be part of my developing plan. He'd stay at our garage apartment; we'd look for his mom, and in the meantime, I would keep sliding through life like a pirogue on the edge until we got to California. I figured now would be a good time to produce the letter from Billy Sunshine.

"It's all possible, Home. This is the moment we've been waiting for. I got a letter and picture back from Billy but wanted to be sure how you felt before we had an important meeting."

"A letter from Billy!" Homer couldn't contain his happiness. "What does it say?"

The news caused Homer to lunge toward me, taking the letter and photograph out of my hand. We almost tipped over our bayou galleon.

To Homer and Rigby,
"You are what you are and something a little more."
    Billy Sunshine

"Wow, Rigby, what a great photograph." Billy was standing in the doorway of his ranch, in a folksy welcoming sort of way.

"Yeah," and I began to read the letter.

Dear Homer and Rigby,
I really like your film, great quality, like your natural style, and you giving me the advantage over my pal Johnny Diamond, the best poker player in the world. Thank you! Now I can beat him fair and square! If you get out to Hollywood, look me up. I look forward to seeing ya.
    Your partner,
    Billy Sunshine

"Partners! You read that! Billy sent us an invitation. Home, I'm on the case!"

"But how are we going to get there? We need money, tickets, and I've got to find my mom. Then we can go for sure, Rigby. I'm with you."

We were somewhere in a Louisiana swamp, gliding over slender streams in the bayou, in a dream called Hollywood. Maybe not yet, but sooner than someday we would get there. "Wow," Homer said over and over. "Billy wrote us a letter. He liked the film and *The Poker Game Caper*!"

When we arrived home, my dog was waiting for us. He was a pleasing young mutt, soft auburn hair, with adoring brown eyes, curious, with a waving tail like an antenna, retrieving the latest news and events. "Like your dog, Rigby. What do you call her?" Homer asked a little awkwardly as the boat slowed and rippled into shore.

"It's a him, I think."

"His name?"

"Doesn't have one yet. What about Walter? I have a cousin who looks like him."

The dog circled around Homer.

"Where did you get him?"

"He found me in the Quarter."

"I didn't know you had a dog."

I saw Homer's affection and then looked at the dog. "He's yours. Take care of him!"

"Really?"

"Yep."

"Wow, Rigby! Thanks! He'll make a great movie dog, like Lassie or Rin Tin Tin!"

Walter the mutt and Homer the boy took to each other immediately as if each had been looking for the other for a long time.

Homer asked with hesitation, "If anything happens to me, will you look after him?"

"Sure I will. But nothin' bad is going to happen. What are you talking about? Things are looking good. We're on our way to Hollywood!"

A MATTER OF LIFE AND DEATH

"Rigby's house was a stately home, one that became alive with people and parties. Inside Rigby edged closer to his father to ask him about the room in the garage. For the few minutes I watched through the window, it seemed like I was looking at a silent movie. The players performed with hands flailing like signal flags, sending a message I didn't understand."
—Homer Sincere's journal, 1946

Our house was a wooden plantation just beyond the Garden District, taking full advantage of the Delta's late afternoon breezes. Mother's garden was a showplace carefully cultivated with rows and rows of dogwoods and camellias, framed by formal boxwood hedges and bordered by pansies. Old brick lanes wound through weeping willows and magnolias. To say my mother actually gardened or had any semblance of a "green thumb" would be an overstatement. But she did maintain the landscape, giving directions in a voice as smooth as southern molasses. The garden was considered by experts to be as beautiful as any that Capability Jones, the great English landscaper, had designed. She had a "green finger." Her gardening secret was "pointing." Dressed in a white cotton gown with light lace to reflect the sun's rays and a large sweeping hat brimming the unusual winter warmth, my mother addressed Ham—for Hamilton—our yardman, appointed chauffeur, butler, handyman, and personal gardener who followed her impeccable instructions: "Ham, replant the pink camellias over here." Pointing. "Ham, the pink dogwoods here." Pointing. "Ham, the lawn needs attending." Pointing. "Ham, have you pruned the roses?" Pointing. "Ham, I've told you a dozen times not to overwater the azaleas." "Ham, the guests will be arriving shortly."

Guests, dressed to the nines, were already coming through the tall, imposing gate, pulling up to a circular drive and entering through a massive oak door where a party was in progress. A perfect diversion.

I smuggled some blankets and a pillow into the garage, then went to the kitchen to lift some food from the cook. It was the first night of Mardi Gras and, to use one of my father's favorite expressions, "All hell was breaking loose in the Quarter."

With the sound of crickets in the distance, a yellow light poured from the windows of the big house. Under a broad, carved wooden archway, my father greeted his visitors while my mother stood nearby in a graceful white satin gown. Ham, in a black jacket and white tie, holding a silver tray, would do any butler proud. With gentle aplomb, he followed Mother's quiet instructions. There was no pointing in the house. He moved easily, serving drinks. Two gleaming mahogany balustrades wound symmetrically in opposing directions up to the second floor, and high overhead a sparkling circle of hanging candles from wedding-cake ceilings sprinkled light over the dark woods and heavy satin fabric. Everything glowed, making the house itself a source of light. A green velvet carpet ran past a black marble fireplace with shining brass implements. It was a home clinging to the past as almost to imitate it, holding to familiar customs, playing old tunes, fashioning out historic scenes with elongating shadows extending from the past and still hesitant of the future.

Years ago, Creole balls and banquets were held in such great rooms, full of movement, where French girls in long skirts whirled away from their chaperones to their young men formally dressed in uniforms with brass buttons, swords tapering down from their hips to fancy boots. Outside, men had quarreled beyond the wide verandas, dueling under oaks that twisted high in the air in front of the great white columns and terraced black iron grillwork.

My father was not a tall man but he carried himself so correctly that everything about him was obviously cared for and under control, from the thick head of prematurely white hair to the mustache that overhung his upper lip just enough to mask the movement of his mouth. He was tall, and carried his confidence and success comfortably. His well-fitted vest covered an elegant gold watch tucked away in a side pocket, with a matching chain hiding a gift from my grandfather. Standing next to him, while my mother attended her guests, we spoke until my mannerisms became exaggerated.

He stood with his hands in his pockets, and I tried to affect that same stance. I had my father's closely set eyes that just didn't see well. There was one interesting difference: my father's eyes were deep gray while mine were blue and transparent, evidently using up all the blue in the family.

Lace-shouldered women and dinner-jacketed men were seated at the long, gleaming dining table. Only candles lit the room, their deep yellow light flickering over polished crystal and silver. Languishing ladies nodded to their gentlemen companions to acknowledge their compliments.

They were the wives of important men in New Orleans. A word from any one of them could get someone on or off a Mardi Gras float. The women were carefully scattered among their men, turning their attention in such a way that their faces were meant only to provide a reflection of their male companions. Governor Long invited the approving looks of the ladies. So did the president of the city's biggest bank.

Two lines faced each other over platters of crabmeat sprinkled with breadcrumbs and baked to a high golden color, not to be outdone by the oyster soup served in a silver tureen.

A frozen punch contained oranges, kirsch, pineapple syrup, lemon juice, strawberries, and champagne. Mounds of spiced beef followed, flanked by grilled tomatoes, carrots, and onions seasoned with cloves. An eggplant soufflé was accompanied by Ham's tossed salad. A platter showing off a variety of cheeses was offered to the guests for a sharp aftertaste before dessert.

And for dessert, the guests were considering a frosted bowl of delectable caramelized bananas drowned in fresh cream, when a platter of paper-thin orange-sauce-soaked pancakes appeared, illuminating the room with blue flame and small yellow flares.

Homer stood outside the window, watching and hungry. I brought him a napkin full of glorious food; we ate swiftly, satisfying our appetites.

When we were far enough away from the house, I could no longer contain myself. I exploded: "I have some news," and I grabbed Homer by the shoulders, shouting, "Your mom's at St. Exupery's!"

FADING COLORS

There was a kaleidoscope of sequins and painted bodies, a parade of headpieces with towering plumes, freewheeling shouts and answers, bands and horses, more and more floats, colorful and loud. At every turn, there was joy and jubilation. Huge papier-mâché heads moved ponderously from side to side, masked riders tossed trinkets from their prancing horses. We had been in pre-production for weeks, getting ready to film the big event. Waldo was expecting us on his float to film the mystical Krewes carrying torches along their own path of golden light, down Esplanade to Jackson Square toward the French market, moving in march-time rhythm. We found Waldo and the Society Marching Band alongside a long moving platform. With his help, we hopped aboard the float.

"You boys got your camera?" he shouted over the compelling parade. I explained that we were going to St. Exupery's hospital because my father had told us that Homer's mother was finally at St. Exupery's. "You've found her!" Waldo nodded in happy agreement, although I did not know why at the time I saw concern in his eyes. Jumping off at the corner of Royal Street, we headed into the infirmary, into the white corridors, peering hopefully into one room after another, even calling for her. Down the wide white halls, in the long wards, we scanned, followed, searched, and patrolled, finally landing at the admissions desk.

"Which room is Mrs. Sincere in?"

The nurses huddled together like a giant white umbrella unfolding to protect Homer from the cold rain that would soon fall over him.

A nurse looked up from the roster.

"You're Homer?"

"Yes, I am. Is my mother here, please?"

"And I'm Rigby Canfield, Dr. Canfield's son," I added with some proud authority. "My Dad told us we could find Mrs. Sincere here."

"My name is Ms. Alice. If you'll wait just a moment, Homer, Doctor Lansing wants to speak with you."

She pointed down the hall to a man in white who looked defeated, his arms folded, leaning against the wall that supported his exhaustion and frustration.

"May I see my mother?" Homer asked quietly. "I'm Homer Sincere."

The doctor turned and came closer, speaking gently with inflections that revealed his concern.

"I'm sorry, son, we tried everything we could but we couldn't do enough. She was very sick, and she didn't want you to know."

"What do you mean?"

"We finally had to operate. Your father was here earlier. I'm deeply sorry, son."

"Sorry?"

"We wanted so much for her to make it, but she didn't."

His words turned to ice.

Turning away before the doctor could finish, Homer ran as fast as he could, out into the crowded streets with me close behind. I tried to say something to him. But what could I say? Running, we passed stately buildings and voodoo houses where secret rooms once kept slaves in chains. Spectators were reaching, calling out for throws. Homer was reaching too, but what did it matter. Floats passed and bands played in toneless dissonant sounds and, finally, in this blurry haze, Homer saw the glass frontage announcing Mr. Lereaux's Funeral Home on a plate glass window in gold letters: "At Rest and at Peace, Serving New Orleans since 1873." We came to a sudden stop.

Through the window, we saw Homer's father standing inside, taking a few bills from his wallet and handing them to Mr. Lereaux, a large, imposing man in a crumpled suit. After hesitating for a moment, Homer entered the parlor. A small bell announced him. His father turned in surprise, steadying himself against the counter.

"She's gone, son, your momma's gone."

Homer's tears muddled over his face as he heard his father's words. Mr. Lereaux showered shopworn words of sympathy. When he could stand no more, Homer fell into a crimson Victorian chair. Walter, whom I hadn't even noticed, had followed us. In some spirit of loyalty, he licked Homer's unmoving legs.

His father, faltering, sat and put his head in his hands. I could smell the liquor on him.

"Gone," was all he said over and over, with no expression of comfort for Homer. The repetition of this one word crowded out the sounds of the Mardi Gras outside and faded like life itself, floating away, just passing by.

"We better be getting on," his father said, turning out the door and heading for home, with Homer following. I was left watching two figures fading into the distance, leaving me with just the sounds of unsteady footsteps. It wasn't supposed to end this way; there was no happy ending.

Approaching the stairs of their home, Homer's father lost his balance and slipped, crashing down on Homer. Walter was caught underfoot and let out a frightened yelp.

"Get up, Dad. Please, Dad, you're hurting me." Homer felt a cracking and a sharp aching pain in his ribs. His father was still. Homer wanted to cry out but couldn't move, and it hurt to breathe. "Please, Daddy."

His father had passed out. Where was Mrs. P.? She would call the Adoption Lady for sure. But she was somewhere else, watching the carnival.

Homer managed to slip from under the weight of his father and relieve the pain that had caused his brace to cut into his leg. Frightened, he made his way upstairs, leaving his father where he had lain so many times before, a felled boulder. Taking the quilt from his momma's room, he tried to fall asleep. With Walter next to him, he was grateful for the warmth and closeness of his furry companion.

A BEDTIME STORY

"The tree was too pretty to be a lord, even prettier than a lady. I recalled a noble princess in a movie and how she had offered her hand to the knight who had come to save her—that was it, each branch was her outstretched hand, but offered to whom and to what? To the world, I decided at first, then, more judiciously, it pointed to some place, some place I didn't know anything about."

—Homer Sincere's journal, looking back to 1945

With threatening visions of his father looming over him—a fearless, tall, strapping marine—Homer felt ugly and helpless. Shadows were fragmented and diluted and curled up tight. With the quilt securely enfolded around him and a snoring dog nearby, he stopped thinking of his father long enough to remember his mother, reading to him. He daydreamed about her soft voice. Her foreign-sounding words were appealing, and he liked it as much as when she was just thinking, her pencil eraser gripped by even white teeth, and when the right words came, she put them in her diary, mouthing them or even murmuring aloud as she did. From time to time, she looked up and gazed out the window, then at her magical desk, where the words flowed. Homer was close enough that her perfume seemed to waft over him.

"Momma," he said, looking up at her and climbing into her lap after studying her for a long time. "You know what it's like being close to you? It's like being in a garden next to a lovely tree." He paused, more in contemplation than in hope of any response, knowing that even though she occasionally pushed his hair out of his eyes, she often forgot he was there. That didn't matter to him; he imagined lying in deep grass, feeling sunshine coming through the leaves, warming him, soothing him. And the leaves seemed to be lifting in swirling currents from a breeze.

"Tell me something, Homer," his momma asked gracefully. She was writing, but a bit more slowly, "Can you see the tree clearly? I mean, can you see the leaves? Is it a summer or a winter tree?"

He closed his eyes tightly to get the right answer. "Summer!" he pronounced. "It must be summer—lots of leaves dark green, except for the ones being heated by the sun like hot coals in a greenish-yellow glow like that silky dress Daddy bought you."

His mother was calm and mumbled something about that being "a long time ago."

He remembered that he had started to say something else but stopped. His mother returned to her reverie. The breeze must have been going through the tree, making the sound of many small voices, as if they were planning something. Perhaps they knew a storm was coming, or had the sun lost its way through the branches?

"Homer, is it a big tree?" His mother, her pencil at rest this time, seemed to be concentrating on something out the window. "Does it look like it will go on being there forever?"

"It's big," he said, "and it's been there for a while."

He had seen many such trees throughout the Garden District and even in the bayou, especially after the last big Gulf storm, trees yanked by the wind right up out of the swampy earth, with roots stuck out every which way, claws tearing at the now quiet air.

Homer felt his momma's eyes on him. Her pencil had not moved, she was waiting for one more answer. Thinking deeply about the question, he replied slowly, "Maybe not forever."

He drowsed somewhere between sleep and waking, and the next morning, feeling the soreness in his ribs, he made his way to the landing. Standing for an instant, he heard the sound of a tap filling the basin coming from his father's bathroom. He was shaving.

"Get dressed, boy," his father called. And then, a bit softer, "It's a sad day."

Looking up, his father seemed to be sober, and Homer was too fearful to ask the questions he wanted to ask. He took a breath. The adoption people! Was his father getting him dressed for the adoption lady?

"I told you, boy, get dressed. We have to go and bury her."

He stood stock still hearing the words, studying his father's face looking into the mirror.

As he reached out for his father's hand, his father turned away from the sink to get a towel, and Homer was left with a hand full of nothing.

A FAR AWAY MELODY

"We heard the shuffling feet of a slow, beautiful march just below the muted music. Waldo led the slow, somber band, in a New Orleans tradition that had come to celebrate my mother."

—Homer Sincere's journal, 1946

A bright orange sun scaled a clump of trees at Number One Cemetery and cast a forgiving light over the irregular stone structures as we followed Mr. Lereaux. The graves were made of elaborate squared blocks of granite and marble that sat high on the swampy earth, like little houses, with some of the elaborate ones looking like temples with marble carvings and columns. Others were brick, stuccoed, and whitewashed.

All morning Homer had worried about the fitting of his new dark suit. He stood beside his father, and I inched up to be closer to Homer, and a look between us said this was a setting we had seen in so many films, the light so sad and perfect, but I did not dare to think about even one frame. It was a beautiful setting, and I'll leave it at that.

I was dressed in my Sunday suit, and I had sent an arrangement full of peonies, mixed red, pink, and white, in a tan basket.

"That's really nice of you, Rig. Her favorite flower."

Mr. Lereaux, sweating but calm, bowed his head and said a prayer over the wooden casket. "Ashes to ashes, dust to dust, may she rest in peace."

Only when his father opened an old leather case, lifted his silver and gold trumpet to his lips and played softly, did Homer start to cry.

It was a faraway melody, transcending time to a happier place, but the man with the horn stopped playing and stood, still jiggling the three keys of the trumpet up and down until his fingers stopped moving. Once he had been young and had owned a uniform with shiny brass bars. He had presented himself proudly and handsomely to Homer's pretty mother. Now older and worn, he had drunk away his dignity. He drank away his dreams.

After the ceremony, Homer tried to match the stride of his father as we moved past the miniature, house-like structures through the cemetery and down some steps. Then, from the distance, coming closer, we heard the shuffling feet of a slow beautiful march just below the muted music. Tears streamed down Homer's face, dropping into a wet handkerchief as he looked at the congregation of black men who came to honor his mother. I couldn't help noticing how gray Waldo's hair was when he lifted his top hat. Out of step, Mr. Sincere pulled Homer along then stopped in a bar, leaving Homer and me to watch the procession.

Toward evening in Homer's room, we heard the uneven sound of his father's stumbling footsteps. Homer ran to the top of the landing, his face still swollen by tears.

"Daddy, Momma's left forever."

"Be a man!" His father swayed like weeds in the bayou.

Homer looked up, and for an instant, his father loomed like a thundercloud, his face darkening and his big frame tensing.

"It's your fault!" Homer cried. "It's your fault, Daddy. You're a drunk and a cheater! You didn't love her. She was sick and couldn't take it anymore!"

His father slammed his fist into Homer's back, telling him to shut up. "Call me a cheater? Toughen up, goddammit!"

Holding on to his father's pant leg, Homer shielded his head. "Don't hit me, don't."

As I ran out to get help, the man slapped me hard across my back, and I shouted back, "You son of a bitch!"

Homer's father tried to gain some control over himself, tried to shake his son off in exasperation. In his unpredictable movements, he hit a banister.

"Why didn't you let me say goodbye?"

Stopping in mid-stride and like a dark cloudburst, his father's anger exploded with a furious gust of emotion. Perhaps a deeper instinct not to hurt his son caused him to strike low and hit the dog Homer held him close to his chest.

"Stop it," Homer screamed. "You're crazy!"

His father looked down at him with rolling and unfocused eyes. Homer had been knocked backward, holding the puppy. Walter moved only slightly then went limp, his head bent back horribly.

Homer, terrified, struggled to sit up and checked the animal. Whispering and crying, he pleaded to the broken dog.

"Oh God, Daddy, oh God, not my puppy."

His father yelled, "Can't you take it?"

Staggering through Homer's room, his father gave vent to all the fury left in him, ripping the posters off the wall. "You little bastard! My fault? You call me crazy?"

He whirled around and landed a crashing blow that rendered Homer unconscious.

A VISIT FROM BILLY SUNSHINE

"I saw Billy in his white Stetson with silver trim . . . Billy Sunshine was looking right down at me. He was usually in the movies, but now he was in my room."

—Homer Sincere's journal, 1946

Later, Homer opened his eyes and reached for Walter before he remembered. His body shuddered with the added grief. He looked around his room, and the posters on his wall appeared more alive than usual.

Suddenly Billy was neither a poster nor a photograph. Homer saw the man in the white, swooping Stetson with silver trim at the foot of his bed. He didn't even have to leave town. Billy Sunshine had come to him. Without moving a muscle, he whispered, "Billy? Am I dreaming?"

"I'm here, son."

"You're supposed to be in Hollywood."

"You need me now, son. I'm here."

"Got your letter and your picture. Really, thanks!"

"That's what partners are for."

His eyes narrowed, blinking again, not believing that Billy Sunshine was at his bedside.

"It's a bad feeling to lose someone you love so much."

"Why didn't she tell me she was sick?"

"Maybe she didn't want you to know."

"If she loved me, why did she go and die?"

"A person doesn't have any control over dying, but they have control over who they love."

"She did love me, Billy?"

"More than anything, Homer."

A great gush of air that he had been holding in flooded out.

"She used to tell me that."

His hurt gave way to tears, and he felt himself being rocked in Billy's arms.

"I feel badly, Billy. They are going to take me away. Why did Momma leave?"

"Sometimes you have to wait for the answer."

"Is there an answer?"

"You must wait. The answer will come."

"Promise?"

"Promise."

"I know everything hurts right now."

"It's kinda tough."

"It's part of the deal."

"Bad deal, Billy."

"Never give up son, never."

"I'm trying."

"And there is something you should know."

"What's that, Billy?"

"You're a cowboy, right?"

"Yes."

"You are going to ride with us."

"But I can't ride."

And then Billy disappeared.

"You're going to be okay," I said to Homer, over the *cloppity-clop* of Waldo's horse. We were resting in the back of Waldo's wagon as Homer looked around, dazed, trying to focus where he was.

"It really hurts," he said. "I really hurt."

Waldo couldn't find any words as Homer tried to sit up. "Where's Walter?" Then he lay back and closed his eyes. "Don't leave me, okay, Rigby?"

"Aw jeez, Homer."

"They're going to take me away now."

"You'll be safe," I answered. "And no matter what happens, we'll be together. You and me and Waldo."

The wagon stopped. Waldo turned back from the front seat and said, "We're here, boy."

I looked up at our destination as the hospital orderlies came to collect my friend, and we watched as they carried him inside. Waldo motioned for me to follow, as he climbed down from the wagon and talked to the lady from the adoption department in front of the hospital. He shook his head "no" to every unexpected word.

Climbing back onto the wagon, Waldo flicked the reins. Ophelia Lou tossed her head, then took her first steps kicking up some dust. Waldo pulled out his handkerchief and rubbed his eyes, realizing that the abuse by Homer's father and the loss of his mother would leave a unwelcomed early sorrow always tapping at his door.

I went into the hospital to find Homer and ran into my father who asked if I would have a soda with him. I followed him down the hall to the cafeteria.

PARTING WORDS

Dear Homer,

For a long time I pretended I would get better, that after a cruel invasion had insulted my body, I would get well.

After the hurt, after the pain, after the tide of sorrows subside, after it all passes into yesterday, you, dear son, are left with the emptiness of it all.

I wish I could hold you and soften your loss. I don't want to die. But I have no choice. It doesn't make sense.

You are a special miracle, a delight, and I love you. Please know that the short time we had together was a lifetime for me.

Your father was a loving man. Something happened to him in the war. Something happens when he drinks, something that takes away his goodness.

What happened to him I don't know. He used to play the softest music I ever heard. Sometimes love between people is lost and broken. We pick up the shattered pieces and try to put them all back together, but the images are fragmented. They don't always fit, the reflection is not always true . . . I can't tell you why things happen.

I have asked my doctors to help me find a place for you to live. I have a little money to leave you from the stories I managed to write, some that I saved to help with your education. I want you to have my pine desk, Homer. That's all I can give you, and I hope this desk will be with you always. I hope that someday you will keep a notebook and return to it for your thoughts. Keep them for me; words help me express the love I feel for you like a bridge crossing and connecting us.

I want you always to feel the cool winds of change, always see the stars casting their lights ahead, long after they have gone out. Yet words are like stars.

All of us have each other for only a little while, and then like a summer cloud, we move on.

These next few years will shape the rest of your life. Learn well. Be gentle. I know you will grow into a stunning man. You will always find something of value, and know most of all how very much I love you.

Your Momma

Chapter 3
LA VIEILLE MAISON
CONVENT, LOUISIANA

INTRODUCING FATHER RIVAGE

The earth turned a time or two more, and the world was a series of images losing their shadows into one another, fading into a big, blurry, blowsy Louisiana evening.

There was no squeaky stair to warn him, no balcony over which he could escape, and a bruised, red-eyed Homer was on his way to a new home—a foster home, the social worker called it.

She frowned, but acceded, when I insisted that I be allowed to accompany Homer to his new residence. Homer was unsettled, and in his tenth year on earth, he made a wish—that I would always be his best friend.

The lady struggled with the wheel as we bumped along a road heading out of New Orleans. Experienced enough to be disillusioned, but still new enough to do everything the hard way, she was probably wondering how to handle Homer. My camera was shaky, and I wished she would drive a little smoother, a little more carefully. But she would have ignored my wishes if I had asked. Still, I filmed as steady as I could in true cinema-verité fashion. Homer was seriously occupied, deep in his own thoughts, almost forgetting I was in the back seat.

In Homer's lap, under his helpless-looking hands, lay two mangled glossies and a poster from his room. "Who is that?" the social worker asked. "Billy Sundance? Or Sundown? Billy Something, anyway."

She didn't notice beneath the photos the marble-colored composition book that would later hold his words, a Chanel perfume bottle—his mother's—and a letter, concealed in his coat pocket close to his heart, that he hoped would become part of him by osmosis.

"It's only a temporary placement, Homer." Her voice betrayed her cool manner and official words. She was taking him to an institutional limbo, beyond the reach of an angry father and of bigger blows that society might deal him.

The lady need not have worried about his reaction; he wasn't listening. As we left the outskirts of New Orleans, Homer had kept his face against the cool window, watching his whole world fade away. I'm sure in his own way he saw everything through a gauzy film, a leftover image from a slow scene in a movie, one picture lingering over another. By contrast, my lens was clear and sharp, not insensitive to Homer's feelings, but the drive was a transition, the beginning of a new episode to include in our film library.

My camera turned to the winding road that climbed ahead. I was only too aware that this was different from the Quarter—flat and empty, the surrounding countryside was even more featureless as the light shadowed over it. From an indefinable distance came a long, ragged moan, a sound as gray as dusk. The social worker swayed the car, glancing at Homer, but he just stared.

"Don't worry, Homer. Father will take good care of you."

"I have a father."

"No, a priest, Homer, a Jesuit. Father is just his title."

She didn't comfort him, or tell him some little personal detail about this foster parent—this father who wasn't his father—as we began the isolated, winding climb on a rough road. She concentrated on driving.

Finally, when the car came to a noisy stop on gravel, Homer and I stepped out and looked up at a forest of dusk-piercing towers. My eyes narrowed trying to comprehend what I was seeing.

"Criminy, Homer. It's a palace! A mansion!"

Next to the house was a millpond with skating water bugs. A silver-colored haze of winter sunlight over the water silhouetted waving sycamores. The calm image awarded me a glimpse of Homer looking at me with his innate cheerfulness, lasting a moment to rekindle warmth and hope.

As we viewed the green shuttered windows and Palladian doors in walls of stone, questions began poking through our protective web of numbness. Had we traveled through time and space? Were we in a movie? Was this Oz? We had gone on automatic and lost all sense of reality.

As Homer was briefly taken with the scene, I began filming, panning the landscape, another opportunity to set up shop to produce our features.

I managed to take my eyes away from the camera and the old house long enough to look down at the gravel beneath my feet: shouldn't it be yellow brick? A person speaking calmly and authoritatively stood beside Homer. The stranger's hand was on his shoulder, and I was startled, realizing that I had missed the social worker's introduction.

Peering up almost as high as the tops of the tall, leaded glass windows, I had my first look at the man everyone called Father.

Standing up close, I thought he was bald, but he wasn't. He had a thick shock of white, fluffed hair coming out all around the top of his head. From a distance, it had the appearance of a silver halo.

Even though he was old, gray, and heavy, Father Rivage conveyed an aura of strength, maybe partly from wearing heavy-looking robes, and I remembered that Robin Hood's Friar Tuck wore robes like Father Rivage's, except Father's robes were black—which were made to appear even blacker by his black shoes, worn over white socks.

As we entered the open doors into a large room of the main building, I saw a painting of a castle in France with archers on an expansive lawn. Archers! Looking down at Homer's brace attached to his shoe, Father realized he would not be a candidate for sports and announced

Homer could learn archery if he wanted to and "learn the secret of the target." I wondered what kind of secret he was talking about.

We crossed a large open area dotted with several small undistinguished buildings used to store rusting garden equipment, tools, and fertilizer sacks. Standing in the center of the courtyard, I saw a little house near the keep where Homer's room was to be located. We would continue to make films. The location was just an interlude before we would take off to the great studios out west, but I had a hunch that I would find out more about this place and this Father.

ONE HUNDRED GREAT BOOKS

"I turned to find Rigby, but he was gone. The distant jiggling noise of an automobile, not so surely driven, jumped back at me, but then came a more reassuring sound saying in a very considerate voice, 'Let me show you around.'"

—Homer Sincere's journal, 1946

I had left Homer, having given in to the rude impatience of the social worker. She had little time and I did not have the chance to say goodbye.

Father Rivage and Homer made their way up the spiraling stone steps. Lumbering shadows followed, fearsome figures silhouetted by lights stationed in niches with candles. To ward off his fear, Homer asked questions.

"Who built this house?"

"It was built by a man called Maximillian who was France's Superintendent of Buildings. He called it *La Vieille Maison*, which means the old house."

"When was it built?"

"I think the year was about 1700. It was intended as a home for a ruling viscount, a position like a governor."

"Who lived here in the old days?"

"Hardly anyone. The viscount ended up staying only fourteen days a year. His successor even fewer, and the project was abandoned as suddenly as it had been created."

"Who lives here now?"

"It's a school for about twenty boys, all of them good. I am in charge, and I very much hope you will like it here."

A sixteen-foot-high fireplace in the refectory held prominence over several idle others located throughout the house. It stood under the thirty-five-foot-high ceiling, rising from a floor of glazed, cracked ceramic tiles.

"Helloooo," Father shouted.

His voice, which had started as a quiet whisper, shot up, smashing against the high ceiling, then burst like Mardi Gras sparklers. Homer tried it. "Hello." The sound bounced from one place and then "hellooooo" echoed from everywhere. At first, this made him feel big, then small, very small, because the voice seemed so much bigger than he.

Blind at first to great jagged cracks in the walls, not feeling the constant drizzle of plaster and paint, and unaware that everything of value that could be sold had been removed, leaving grandeur and mystery, Homer thought that this great house could have been a home for the head of a country. It was as fantastic, wonderful, and gloomy as anything in the movies.

His mind returning to his personal pain, Homer whimpered.

"My mother died."

"I know," replied the Father.

"I didn't have a chance to say goodbye."

"Sometimes that can be a beginning of sorts."

"She was a writer, but she had to go away."

"I know that too."

"Why did she leave me?"

"The answer will come. It takes a while." Father leaned back, measuring the boy.

"That's what Billy says."

"Billy?"

"Billy Sunshine."

"I see. And your father?"

"He hurt me a lot."

"And you want to hurt him back?" Father asked, knowing the answer.

Homer nodded.

"Just as he did to you. You want me to help you do that?"

"Yes, Father."

"I can't, it wouldn't be right," Father started to explain with an expectation that Homer would come to understand.

Father Rivage had Homer squarely in his sights. "I'm here to help you find your way in life. Even the bad things that happen to us can be useful and important if we handle them the right way. You're going to find a lot of amazing things to help you write your own stories."

"What kind of stories?" This was strange to Homer. "I don't know how."

"That's why I'm here. I'm here to help you."

"Are you the viscount now?"

Father thought for a moment and shook his head, "No, I'm a Jesuit."

What was a Jesuit? Homer wondered.

SOLDIERS OF THE WORD

"I remember Father's words well: 'We Jesuits have what we call the four Nobilities: Spirit, Discovery, Truth, Reason. We fight for right. We use words for weapons.'"

—Homer Sincere's journal, 1946

"Jesuit soldiers are organized into 'Nobilities.'" Strolling into a library, they continued walking among stacks of dusty books. Father's robes left a track of dust. "I'll show you," Father continued. "We Jesuits have been around quite a while, you know. Four hundred years! Not bad, eh? And we started small, with only seven men getting together in a group, a club you might say, to serve people in a new way, offering ourselves to the pope as soldiers."

"Soldiers?" The idea sparked Homer's curiosity.

"Well, soldiers in the sense that they had to be strong and disciplined and fight for good." Father Rivage stopped to search for a book and found what he was looking for in a stack. "Here is a book about Jesuits who took the church into distant lands, hostile places. Soldiers on foreign battlefields, you might say. The spirit of fighting men, the excitement of traveling to distant lands, surviving in difficult places without hurting anyone."

"What did they use for weapons, Father?"

"Others had swords and cannons, we Jesuits used words."

Did Billy have words and nobilities? Homer didn't want to compare a four-hundred-year-old tradition to a movie cowboy. Father tapped his head. "Words! Books! Cowboys are soldiers of the word too, in different ways. Homer was surprised by the comparison of cowboys and soldiers. Was this more than a coincidence?

"Our mission is the same. Our weapons give more protection than an arrow or a bullet."

Homer had never seen so many "weapons." They were everywhere in the room—thousands of books stacked on tables and along walls, piled on chairs and along the floor.

"One of your responsibilities will be to arrange them, in preparation for the great battle."

"What battle?"

"To prepare and to get ready, they must be lined up in perfect order, with serial numbers, a regiment in rank and file, available to march."

Homer was astonished by the number of books scattered around, needing to be organized alphabetically—a seemingly awesome task.

"These books are ammunition," Father added mischievously. "Anyone who wants to be a Jesuit has to study! The first two years, we call it being a novice, are spent in classical studies." At that he pulled out various books with mysterious names. Reading the titles, he pronounced each one carefully, *The Iliad, The Odyssey, The Aeneid*. He referred to them as "the Greats."

Homer's eyes bugged, having never seen such titles, even on his mother's bookshelf.

"Look at who wrote these first two." Father's finger pointed to the spines, to the gold lettering: "HOMER," arousing Homer's attention.

"Can I read that someday?"

Father Rivage nodded. "You'll read a lot while you're here."

They passed masses of tables with stacks of books on philosophy, mathematics, and the physical sciences. "After he has studied these, a soldier spends time learning about theology," Father Rivage said.

Theology? Jesuits? Soldiers? What did it all mean?

"It's about God. The commander of knights, the profession of faith, the guardian of the Grail, learning about God, how to think of God, the part of you that is His spirit." Father Rivage searched for the right word, then gave up and just repeated, "About God."

"Is God the answer to my questions?"

"That depends on you."

"If God is the answer, why did he take my mother away? Why do I feel so bad? Why am I here?"

Father explained as much as he could to Homer on that first day, responding to his questions to help him feel at ease. Thoughts of the Quarter were soon jettisoned, and Homer decided then that he would learn how to fight with his words to find some answers.

Homer leaned down to adjust his uncomfortable brace. Teacher and student studied each other, not missing anything. "Oh, your brace," Father said. "Helps you to walk, does it? I think that makes you rather distinguished.

"Each of us has a job the heart can recognize." Father Rivage continued his explanation. "Each of us is a soldier, and each of us has a job to do in the great realm. In fact, I want to present you with a gift."

Father crossed the room to a brass container with black umbrellas.

At its center, a slender object stood out, a black lacquered cane with a polished sterling silver handle.

"One of my prized possessions, for a Soldier of the Word. In fact, I wish I had an excuse to use it. In spite of a few extra pounds, I seem to get around okay, so if I walked with this magnificent walking stick, my peers would think me odd." He presented the cane to Homer. It was as beautiful as it was thoughtful.

Homer was in awe of the Jesuits. Why had he never seen a movie about them?

Looking at Homer intensely, Father Rivage asked, "Do you know that your family name comes from the French Saint Cyr?"

That was new to Homer.

"Yes, the *Academie St. Cyr* in France is a military school like Annapolis and West Point, a school in France to train soldiers to fight. Its name is pronounced in French just like yours. I think you'll fit in nicely, Homer. There's a reason you're here."

Maybe he would become a soldier and learn archery, like the men in the painting.

Looking out the window, he saw a long, grassy knoll behind the gardens, a range for archers with a target in the distance, and Father, catching his gaze, commented, "Someday at that range, you'll learn the secret of the target. In the meantime Private St. Cyr, I'm recruiting you into an army of words." Private St. Cyr, Homer thought, was never going to read all those books. Impossible! He had other interests, too.

When Father saw the cowboy poster in his room, he confided to his new young novice that he has seen most of Billy's films, but he seemed more interested in someone else and asked, "Can you tell me more about your friend Rigby Canfield, the boy with the camera?"

"He's my very best friend, Father."

"And as your friend, I suppose you trust him very much?"

It seemed to be a statement that did not need defense. "Of course, Father, without question. He's not only my friend, but we are partners, and I'm going to miss him here."

"Partners? What sort of partnership?" Father was inquisitive, and Homer responded freely.

"We make films, it's what we do. I should say, what we plan to do. Make great films, go to Hollywood, be with Billy."

"Rigby is always welcome here, Homer, always."

"Thanks, Father, I appreciate your saying that. I'm sure Rigby would like to spend time at this place. It's a fine setting, and we could even make a film. You look like a film star, Father, you do. I'll become a soldier, you become our star, a featured player. How does that sound Father?"

Father considered the thought. "Hmmm, a star, thank you, I accept your compliment."

THE SECRETS OF LA VIEILLE MAISON

When I got back to the Quarter, I wanted to make sure Homer was alright. In asking around, I learned that during the war, La Vieille Maison had been requisitioned by the government to use as a special center for shell-shocked soldiers, a place to help them overcome the trauma sustained in battle. The setting of the building was beautiful. The villa once had a handsome library with red leather chairs and limestone walls. Its dining room was equipped with long refectory tables for the veterans who came there for R & R, the Army's Rest and Recreation program. When the war was over, the entire property was deeded as a school for children who had been abused and abandoned due to wartime circumstances, and that was how the *Maison* had become a sanctuary for such children.

I had met the man in charge, Father Rivage, who had taken to wearing a black robe that—I discovered later—he had found in one of the large boxes stored in the cellar. With his black robes, and distinguished look, everyone called him "Father," and he liked his new title. While he had no formal training in literature, Father served as a willing caretaker, reading to his students from his yellow and black

CliffsNotes. But the school needed funds to survive.

He had found something else, too: in one of the green army storage trunks filled with supplies and equipment, there was an Auricon Cine-Voice camera in perfect condition. It was the very useful type used by the Army Signal Corps during the war and had been left behind, still packed in its own case. Father would later give it to me.

"I understand you boys make films, and I have something that may be of interest to you. After all, I consider you a professional!"

When I opened the box, I couldn't believe Father's generosity! The Auricon was a camera that used film with a magnetic strip for single sound, an advantage that would add a new dimension to our films through synchronized sound with better quality. Homer would become more involved, using a clapboard to help me identify scenes when we edited our rushes. It was a remarkable gift from Father. I had wanted a camera like this, and I planned to take full advantage of it, thinking ahead to sound, special effects, and color.

On a return visit to see Homer, I quickly pulled out the camera from a closet that Father had requisitioned for me and took some establishing shots. By this time, Homer was familiar not only with the many books in the library, but he had made new friends with the other boys as well. They were some of the twenty students on the premises, all required to wear a uniform like French schoolboys: gray-flannelled suits, short pants, high socks, white shirts, blue and red regimental-striped ties, and brown oxford shoes. I wondered if the dress code was flexible enough to allow Homer to wear the cowboy hat he had tucked away in his things. I was fascinated by "Father," though I sensed, and hoped, that I might discover some mysterious plot with twists and turns.

Father enlightened the boys about the distinguished order of Jesuits whose teaching was traditional and demanding, but whose tenets encouraged those who wished to explore and examine new ideas and concepts. This was an agenda beyond the playground code some of the boys had in mind; Father had his work cut out for him.

"All the words, all the books, all the questions and answers are found in this room," Father told them in the library. "It's up to you to find the right door to open. The books are the keys." The "keys" might be wasted on the others, but not on Homer. He took the matter seriously, and I thought that he was better off here than having a key to the room over our garage. This could be his great opportunity, and I wouldn't have minded it at all if I could have been with him every day. What great pictures, what a cast for a movie! I'd title it *The Secrets of La Vieille Maison*.

We kept in close touch. Homer explained that he was trying to understand what Father was talking about, viewing him as a friar, master of a medieval castle, and I hoped that Father would help Homer build a foundation for the rest of his life. I also believed the company of the older boys would offer him some companionship, though I knew that no one would take the place of Waldo and me.

A SUPPORTING CAST

"I was surprised by the language directed at me. They were curious boys in an even more curious setting. 'Hallelujah,' Bobbo said, throwing up his hands. 'Nick's father was gone in a tornado . . .'"

—Homer Sincere's journal, 1946

On the bench before a fire, as Homer folded his laundry, came a startling question.

"So, why the fuck are *you* here?"

It had come from a boy dressed in the neat gray flannel suit the boys at La Vieille Maison were required to wear. Robert Frame was a pudgy-faced, neatly disorganized sixteen-year-old. Using two pencils on his belt loops, he introduced himself with a drum roll: "Bobbo! Impressionist-drummer-whistler-of-the-blues."

Bobbo urged Homer on. "Okay, cowboy, what was it? You can tell us." He tossed a murky-looking T-shirt up in the air and on its downward descent speared it with his hand. "What? Rob a bank? No? Steal a horse? No? Run out of town?"

Homer sputtered, "My dad, it was my dad, he just got, uh..."

"Got what? Sick? Well? Up? Down?" Bobbo examined his own shirt for wounds. "Mad?" His scrutinizing narrow blue eyes looked for a cotton casualty then back to Homer. "Drunk?"

Before he could reply, Bobbo's voice changed to a W.C. Fields mode. "Ah, yessss, my little chickadee. That's it! Well, well, well..."

"Hey, don't worry, kid," interrupted another boy. His accent was right out of a George Raft movie, the voice of an emaciated teenager whose entrance had obliterated the laundry pile. His name was Nick, except to Father Rivage who always called him by his full name, Nicholas Xavier.

"Hey! Listen up. So he's gone. So what? Fathers don't mean nothin'. Everybody's got one somewhere." A wad of gum shifted from one side of his cheek to another to underscore his point. "Hey! You heard Bobbo, didn't ya? His father's a goddamn preachah!"

Bobbo bowed deeply. "Praise-the-Lawd-hallelujah-and-how-right-the-little-man-is!" He plopped down on the laundry he'd been folding.

Staggered by the stream of language directed at him, Homer felt that he was expected to say something, probably swear. In desperation, he brought up Waldo. "Waldo, he's a philosopher."

No one said anything.

"And then there's Daddy Grace."

"Daddy Grace?" Bobbo asked.

"And he's a preacher, like Bobbo's father. Close your eyes and visualize, and you can be anywhere you want to be."

Bobbo walked slowly around, imitating the sonorous tone of a deacon. "You hear that, boys? All you have to do is visualize. That's all there is to it, praise the Lord."

"Hallelujah," Nick muttered.

Nick seemed like a good guy, but not one to mess around with, a little over the top.

"Fathers are okay, kid, but Nick's . . . ," Bobbo said, "Gone in a tornado."

"Gone where?"

"Oh, well, uh." Bobbo tried to be casual and careful at the same time, though it was not his style. "It's like, well . . . for example . . . I mean . . . like his dad, that is . . . his family, they—"

"I'll tell it," Nick said, rescuing Bobbo. "It's my story." Though he hadn't seemed to be moving, he was now facing the fire, hunched forward at the edge of his chair with his elbows on his knees. "I'm from Shreveport," he began. "My folks, Mom and Dad, are okay types. Kid sister: nag. Baby brother: pain. Two years ago, we're all sitting around the living room radio. The news is on: tornado. Soon as we hear that, we start arguing, of course. About everything, you know what I mean? Yelling, showing off. Dad said that arguing was the real Italian language." Nick's voice became softer. "Anyway, we got on tornadoes." In the tone of someone who had been mightily tricked, and once more, with emphasis: "Tornadoes!" His head jerked a little toward us. "You know, like what a tornado is. Mom, she's the reader in the family, goes on and on about air pressure in a tornado, how much damage one could do. Dad had been in a big one. He said it was big. And what are the signs that one is coming? Yellow sky, animals acting funny, calm air."

Like a fighter's, Nick's handsome head began to bob and weave. "So, I'm gonna do this right, right? One tornado demonstration coming right up. My mom hasn't read everything, my dad hasn't lived through everything." A pause made the next bit of information seem very important. "I make 'em all sit together on the couch, like an audience and I'm blabbing about whether you stay inside or out, that you should go to the basement, when my sister pops up." Nick's voice became high and prissy. "'But what if there is no basement, Nicky? Jimmy doesn't have one.' I say, 'Easy, toots. Watch.' Pointing to our heavy, Formica-topped dining table, I say, you see the table over there? Well, when the old tornado comes, that's where No-Basement Jimmy goes. Under. Like this." Nick's firm shoulders hunched up around his ears. Elbows bent at his sides, hands in fists, his arms pumped comically like Charlie Chaplin. "I make for the table myself."

Nick's voice escaped inside him, and at the same time, his gaze extended beyond the fire, stretching the distance between the memory he saw in his mind and the feelings he was trying to put into words.

"And then, whoosh! Front door flew open. Whooshed away—and a hard wind, a roar, and then it's over. I see. I hear." Nick's tone was baffled, the rest of his words came out elongated, pushed by a dying, volcanic anguish: "— but, but I—I can't move...! No one else is there in the room. Four people! My whole family! Gone!"

Nick was unreachable. The look from Bobbo was unclear as Homer picked up a towel from the laundry, his mind adrift with Nick's story, unlike anything he had ever seen in a film. He thought about Nick's family, their disappearance. Why? What did it mean? Nick returned to his chores, Bobbo whistled. The laundry piles grew neater by a few inches.

Nick and Bobbo were featured players, and Homer was both overwhelmed and frustrated. He longed to tell me what he had heard. He was right, it was an improvised performance never to be seen again, and we did not have it on film. A thought came to Homer at that moment. Am I seeing life from the inside looking out or from the outside looking in?

Father Rivage came in, cutting the unsteady silence. "Boys, how's the laundry coming?"

Bobbo flung his head back dramatically, waggled his sticks at the heavens, and in a rumbling, sonorous voice shouted, "Glory, I say! Glo-ory, hallelujah, my brothers!"

As Father Rivage walked out shaking his head, Bobbo intoned a gospel hymn with Nick clapping, swaying, and chanting "Amen."

In this strange ecclesiastical setting, Homer established daily routines: laundry, cataloging books, studies, chores, gardening, housekeeping. As the smallest and youngest student, but soon to be the best reader, he was given library duties. It was his job to dust and sort the hundreds of volumes piled up in the large drafty room that Bobbo claimed had once been a prison.

He summoned thoughts of his mother, but the feeling was elusive and he couldn't get a confirmation of her warmth. She was only in his mind, and that was all he would ever have.

THE MAKING OF A STAR

"Father said, 'It's the words, always the words—timely, beautiful, and illuminating.'"

—Homer Sincere's journal, 1946

Father Rivage asked the boys into his study to discuss the procedure and process for their studies. Prominently displayed on the walls were paintings, as well as framed black-and-white engravings. Homer noticed eighteenth-century prints, fine etchings, portraits, and landscapes, and Father was pleased that Homer admired some of the collection.

Homer's first assignment was to read *The Adventures of Huckleberry Finn.* The novel's story would be one that would eventually influence Homer with immeasurable understanding.

"I want you to discover Jim's essential humanity." Homer went with Huck and his friend Jim, a runaway slave, down the Mississippi River to freedom on their raft. Although he did not know it then, Father, with the help of Mark Twain, planted a literary seed that would someday identify Homer's values.

Nick and Bobbo were in charge of the agricultural program at the school. Since that required a lot of physical energy, Father thought Homer was better suited to continue on with library duties, reasoning that in the company of literature around the classic books, he would somehow accept their influence and importance.

"There are great books, many of them," Father lectured. "They will be your teachers, and you will learn to think about the great questions, as I have done. What is reason? What is passion? What is beauty? Freedom and equality?

"Take the beauty of words. With a rhythm for the right words in the right order, your soul will run along with them. They are timeless and timely, illuminating and questioning, speaking to us in more than one way—a poem, a play, an essay—linking together and advancing knowledge, so we can express ourselves freely." Father sighed, pleased with his thought, quickly adding, as fast as Homer could write, "You become what you behold." Bobbo and Nick rolled their eyes.

On my next visit with Homer, much was accomplished toward our goal when I had a chance to set up the Auricon Father had presented to me. I was astonished by its technology, its ability, its beauty from lens to case. While it was just a little heavier than my Filmo, and would on some occasions require a tripod, it was light and sleek. I suggested to Father that he allow Homer and I to film some of his lectures. It would help refresh and review his essential lessons, and nobody had the authority, the style, and the deep resonant voice he did. "You'll be like Spencer Tracy starring in *Boys Town!*"

Father took to the idea. "Rigby, that's exactly what I had in mind!" I don't know whether I had appealed to his ego or his mission, or if he truly considered the notion as a learning experience. In any case, we were back in business.

Father had advised Bobbo, Nick, and the other students that Homer and I would be filming classes, to try not to notice, but pay attention to the day's lecture. After placing a microphone at Father's podium, we set up in the rear of the room. The natural light was appealing. Homer flashed the clapboard, the camera speeded to twenty-four frames per second, and I gave Father a wink and a nod. Action.

Father told the boys a bit about himself, not at all self-conscious, lowering his voice just a little, playing to the camera in such a relaxed way that you would never think a star was being born. "Along the way to becoming a Jesuit," he said, in an engaging, friendly voice, "I found my love for books, taking me anywhere I wanted to go. Or to a place I didn't want to be. By correspondence, I studied the Great Books at a university in Chicago with Professor Clifford. I then joined the Jesuits in Joliet to acquire the spirituality that provided a comfortable home for me, realizing that one person can make a difference in life by good words and thoughtful action. I know that if you make a difference, you can wear a medal, like soldiers do. If we are lucky, we can earn one."

This explanation took Bobbo and Nick farther away from the lecture at hand. They were more interested in Homer and me than Father at the moment.

THE WEST!

The film series continued with great enthusiasm. I beckoned, "Father, how about a lecture that will interest us and will help advance our education? I mean, that's what you are supposed to do, to help us find our future, right?"

"Until then, I want you to build upon the classics to house a foundation!"

"Understood, Father, but how about some practical rooms in the house?" I replied with Homer's full encouragement.

Father, taken back, agreed, "I'm open to any subject and suggestion."

"The West! We want to know all of it," Homer and I chimed in.

"And a bit about cowboys?" Father added.

"Yes, that too."

Father Rivage willingly agreed that we set up the camera for his next presentation.

He began his lecture with Lewis and Clark, and their exploration of the way leading west, their vision bearing witness to the "westerning" of America, recalling frontier values, the beauty of our land and natural resources, our lakes and forests and trees, ending with the writers Hamlin and Garland, summing up the lore and legends of the West and, borrowing a phase from Willa Cather about "our precious and incommunicable past."

To keep our interest and attention, Father spoke of cowboys and

Indians, good guys and bad, fistfights and gunfights, covered wagons, and action-filled film chases from Tom Mix to Billy Sunshine. We were excited about the image of our self-sustaining West. The latest episode would get us out to Hollywood faster than we hoped.

As soon as I could edit the film, another installment would be dispatched.

"Homer," I said, "Father really came through for us on this one! We'll wrap it up and send it to Billy. This is a pilot for a series!"

After completing his narrative, Father wrapped the lecture, for a quick preview of future attractions. "In our next film, I'll tell you about the deeds and journeys described by the poet Homer in his *Iliad* and *The Odyssey*. They are wonderful tales." My friend Homer had not forgotten seeing the book written by his namesake that first day.

"Father, Nick and I want to be in the films, too," said Bobbo.

"That can be arranged, boys. I want you to study hard and think of some intelligent questions and answers. We'll rehearse, just to be sure you have your lines down." Their attention returned, reawakened.

I marveled at Father's scheme.

Putting the camera away, I congratulated him.

"More than a screen test, Father, you were real, and we are going to learn a lot."

Pleased with his accomplishment and keen to reinforce Homer's learning skills, to keep him from becoming overly preoccupied by extracurricular shooting, Father took him aside. "Let's make a deal: if you apply yourself as much to reading each book carefully as you do to making films, you can have special permission to go to the movies in town once in a while, looking at them from a different perspective, learning more about your craft, how they are made and cut together." Father seemed to appreciate films more than I had realized. Did he have something in mind, or was he just being a good guy?

Homer was happy with this promise. It was also an incentive for Nick and Bobbo, who viewed the movies as entertainment more than a learning experience.

TURNING PAGES

"I was surrounded by books and words, and new experiences that were leading to discovered places."

—Homer Sincere's journal, 1948

Homer could never read all the books, but he was diligent in keeping his end of the bargain. His vocabulary expanded rapidly into his literary world. In his room were some of my photos, a poster of Billy Sunshine, a letter, and his collection of secret dispatches. Occasionally, he confided, there was a dispatch to Billy from the typewriter that Mr. Adams, the manager at Western Union, had given him.

Father Rivage encouraged Homer to write to his father. He did, but never mailed the letters, nor did he mention his mother. The envelope to his momma was empty, but that did not keep her out of his mind.

Into his imagined reality, Billy checked in from time to time.

"How's it going, kid?"

"Fine. A lot of reading."

"Treatin' you okay?"

"Yes, I'm pretty good. Just thinking. How are you doing? Father tells me you are a Soldier of the Word, too."

"Cowboys and soldiers, one and the same, son. Same purpose, same mission. Looking after the studio and stuff. Getting ready for you to come out."

"We're planning on it. But it looks like we're stuck here for a while."

"Well, that's not a bad thing."

"Rigby and I, we're getting a few more films made, and we're getting better."

"And that's a good thing. Got a new film coming out, try to catch it. It's called The Alamo! *Some great special effects and if I had some tickets with me, I would give you a pair."*

"That okay, Billy, we'll try to catch it, and I've meaning to ask you, could you do me a favor?"

"Sure thing."

"Look in on Waldo, make sure he's okay and tell him I'm missing him."

"Will do. See ya, partner."

"Good to talk to you, Billy."

"I'm around if you need me."

"You hear that?"

"Yep. Sounds pretty folksy. Coming from upstairs?"

"Father's room, I think. Why don't you check it out?"

THE ART THAT IMITATED LIFE

The music came from just overhead. Then a thumping two-step began, and the sound of someone dancing. Was it coming from Father Rivage's room? Homer decided to investigate just as the music stopped.

Slipping upstairs and peeking through a narrow and slender arched window, he saw that Father wore a green eyeshade. He was sitting over a painting and spread around him were artist's tools, brushes, paints, and canvases—islands of artist materials. Father was wearing a paint-smudged apron and painted in a distinctly monastic rhythm, imitating brushstrokes from an impressionistic painting before him. He fashioned a swab of pigment into the canvas then applied a deep yellow varnish..

Just as he was finishing a piece of artwork with the detail and patience of a watchmaker, suddenly, in the distance, there was the sound of car sliding over gravel then stopping. Soon, visible from above, two men wearing black suits entered. They looked like hoods. Father hastily left his room, with his robes whipping around him, skipping down the wide stone stairs in twos to greet them. One of the men called Father "Ralph." Odd!

As they climbed the stairs, Father reported, "Just adding the finishing touches, Anthony. It aged quite nicely and has the patina of a hundred-year-old painting. I used some specially formulated pigments and old canvas from France. You will be quite impressed with the faux craquelure. The fine webbing is magnificent."

Hiding behind a stone column, Homer tiptoed back to the window. As they passed, the elongated dark shadows folded into each other.

What was going on? Who was Ralph? Where was France on the map?

Father spoke of the impressionist painting, then, handing it over, spoke about a Blue Period.

"Exquisite," Anthony replied, looking the work. "The colors and detail, perfect."

Receiving an envelope in return, Father advised, "You realize this is my last commission."

Anthony was surprised. "But don't you need funds for the school?"

"I'll work it out. I'll work it out with God."

"You better work it out with us first."

"I can't," Father replied.

"Are you really sure about that, Ralph? You are doing your best work, and we wouldn't want to see anything happen to that fine hand of yours."

"I've paid off the loan on the mortgage to the bank, I've taken a vow, and I can't do it anymore. The only reason I've done these was to help the school, and I've found redemption."

"You think again about your redemption, Ralph. We'll be back." He pushed Father in a threatening and unbecoming way.

The figure with a hat carefully wrapped the rolled up canvas in plain newspaper and placed it under his arm. The two men hurried downstairs and into the waiting black Packard, which was soon lost into darkness with its receding taillights leaving a trail of red clay dust.

Before Homer crept back across the hallway, Father wound up a RCA Victrola and carefully rolled up a few canvases. The music started up again.

Then he started to dance.

There was more going on in the room than just music! Not only was Father a dancer, he was an artist. Homer didn't mention to anyone what he had seen, felt guilty spying, and thought what he saw was none of his business. But something unusual was going on, and Homer eventually told me about it.

FROM REAL TO REEL

I loved La Vieille Maison and looked forward to seeing Father Rivage again. I now had a new hand-held Filmo D-180, using fast film, with a wide-angle Angenieux lens that quickly sprang to my eye when I wanted to film a scene. While it was a silent camera, it would come in very handy. I wanted to capture everything, the showering paint and plaster, the cracked walls, the barrenness inside the Maison, all the textures and shades of deterioration that were perfect for black and white.

Homer brought me to Father Rivage's office. I wanted to shoot some footage—his features highlighted by shadows. "Now Rigby, remember," Father said with unassuming modesty, "we are only servants, not movie stars."

"I understand, Father," I said, and that's when I saw the shot I wanted to take, of Father's face, but with lens-like magnification. I saw his white-stocking feet. The contrast between the socks and black robe was perfect.

The camera's lens was a part of me, and I ran a rift of footage. Before I could wind the camera and roll another few frames, Homer hustled me out. "Rigby, we have work to do, and let's not blow it. He's like a soldier. It's like he has a duty and he does it."

"What do you mean he's a soldier? He's a movie star. I like that guy, and I want to know more about him—he reminds me of George Raft." Then I thought maybe Father didn't want me to take his picture, thinking I'm a G-Man or something.

"We should stick to filming the lectures. He's a private man. Think about our future!"

"Father's got that special something, star quality. Wait until you see the rushes. Came out fantastic. I showed them to my father, and he was so impressed that we are making educational films that he gave me this new camera. He thinks the lectures should be shown in every school in town, but still Homer, I think Father understands that you don't always have to live by the rules, you know what I mean, Home? Rules are not always so good."

In the end, I understood Homer's respect for Father Rivage.

"He's a good man, Rigby."

Everybody needs privacy. In my house, I was surrounded by a whole phalanx of people nailed down by rules and expectations. Father Rivage was okay in my book, and Homer was right. Father was a good man, and he was our ticket to Hollywood.

REMEMBER THE ALAMO!

Lured by the latest Billy Sunshine movie and with Father's permission, we hitched a ride to the nearest movie theater, not far away, in a small town called Le Place. Like all of Billy's films, the picture opened with the powerful crescendo of galloping hooves, Billy's horse Apollo was coming straight at us. Hunkered down in our seats with boxes of warm popcorn in our laps, we were captivated as Billy telegraphed an urgent message. "Tap . . . tap . . . tap," his finger punched the key. "Fellow cowboys. Alamo is under attack . . . *tap . . . tap . . .* We need your help . . . *tap . . . tap . . . tap . . .*" Then came the thundering horses, and standing on the top of the Alamo was General Morrison wrapped in the Texas flag. "Remember the Lone Star!" he shouted. "Remember the Alamo!"

When the feature ended and the lights went up, Homer took a deep breath and turned his popcorn-smeared face to me. "Billy was great, the film was great, just like he told me."

"Told you?"

Homer confided about Billy's sudden appearance at his bedside, and his later visits from time to time, checking in, making sure he was okay and even personally recommending *The Alamo!* "If he had had some tickets with him, he would have given us a pair, that's the kinda guy he is!" By the time Homer finished, I cocked my head to one side, asking, "You're not, uh, kidding—right?"

Homer's look gave me the answer.

Billy Sunshine in the Quarter? Not likely, of course, but possible. Then showing up at the foot of Homer's bed and at La Vieille Maison? Was Homer going nuts?

I was too bewildered to press him for details about these far-fetched episodes, but if Homer wanted to think Billy was around, I guess it was all right. After all, Jimmy Stewart had an imaginary bunny in *Harvey*.

My uneasiness made me jump to another subject—one that concerned Homer even more, I figured. I had wanted to tell him before but didn't want to ruin the movie.

"Waldo had a heart attack last week."

All the color drained from Homer's face.

"Is he okay?"

"Like a big, mean charley-horse right in the middle of his chest. He was standing beside Ophelia, huddled over, holding onto her mane, like he was about to leap on her and ride away bareback. When I saw Ophelia's hat on the ground, I knew he couldn't ride away. Waldo couldn't even move, and my dad says he'll have to rest for a long time."

Homer was too jolted to say anything. Before I left I reminded him, like Waldo said, "It don't pay to worry, and next time, we can, well, talk some more about Waldo and Billy's visits."

Homer never talked about Billy's visits again, but he did ask me to make sure to get word to Waldo wishing him to get better fast.

A VERY PRIVATE ENTERPRISE

I made regular visits to La Vieille Maison, which I preferred over my own. Father Rivage gave an impressive lecture about John Steinbeck and Thomas Wolfe and the promise of the land, reading from his abridged summaries. I knew the CliffsNotes well, having used them myself to get through school. We set up the Auricon at a different angle. As Father lectured, I noticed that he was affecting a formal literary accent, slightly British like David Niven's. Homer noticed it too. Did Father Rivage know he was overacting? I thought the next thing he might do was to start wearing makeup. Wanting to offer a few discreet directorial comments, I wrote in the margin of his notes, "Keep cool, and keep natural!"

I supposed that the church had funded some of the school's expenses, and to help keep things solvent, I wondered if there could there be a real market for the films. Everyone had essential duties, and Father had a pretty sweet deal, wearing all the robes and stuff.

Homer admired him, but my suspicions still ran wild. I didn't want to diminish Homer's respect but still felt something was not quite right.

Although he wouldn't admit it, Homer looked so tired that I asked Father about his health. Father knew that the boys had teased Homer so mercilessly that Father gave him the whole library for his own room. He felt that it was character building, and in the long run it would help Homer to stand up to life's inequities, although I disagreed. Nick had found a letter from Homer's mother and passed it around, poking fun, but that was not all. Bobbo told Homer that in addition to his own chores, he had to acquire the essential quality of leadership, a duty of a soldier. With that admonition, Homer was awarded the duties of five or six older boys—not only taking care of the library, but also making beds, doing laundry, and standing watch several nights a week, guarding what Bobbo called the Secret Tower. Worst of all, I overheard them calling him gimp. I asked Homer about this, and he pretended not to mind, but he was hurt and I aimed to do something about it. I knew from Humphrey Bogart the best way to deal with a bully was to act fast, stand up to him, and never back down.

"Evidently, they like you a lot, Home."

"Why would you say that?"

"They wouldn't take so much trouble if they didn't."

Still, I found Nick and Bobbo and spoke to them in a language they understood.

"What the fuck are you doing to Homer?"

"What do you mean?" they responded innocently.

"Call that boy gimp one more time and you'll have something to gimp about."

"Rigby, we're sorry, didn't mean any harm; Homer's an okay guy and we was just playing around."

"Get another game," I snarled in my best Bogart style and added, "What's with the Tower?"

Bobbo surprised me, producing a bottle of hard apple cider with an intriguing proposition. Taking me aside, he asked if I would like to get in on their prospering business empire. They were looking for a distributor for a special product stored in the Tower, unknown to Homer.

Pointing to the bottle, he said "Moonshine. Only two bucks a bottle." As head of the agricultural committee, Bobbo's enterprise consisted of "selecting" bottles of cider from the dining hall, adding yeast, and letting the juice ferment over the winter months. They had found a letterpress in the basement, and with the "official" school letterhead, designed a label—I bet with Father's help. "La Vieille Maison Vintage." The illegal and private label was in demand. It was doing a brisk business supplying the local townspeople with hard cider. Now they wanted to expand to New Orleans and offered me a percentage. I was their man.

"It's excellent," Nick said. "We had a tasting from September's production, and the apples were perfect then." Bobbo continued, "We can produce about fifty cases."

From this chance chain of circumstance came a plan, not only to fund our films but to help the school as well. I took action independently, not wanting to involve Homer in any dubious activity I might engage in. If I got caught, I didn't mind any consequences thrown at Bobbo and Nick, but not at Homer. He had been through enough. So I kept the secret of La Vieille Maison to myself. If Homer was going to be the scriptwriter, and I a director, he'd better concentrate on his education, polish his verbal skills, and write a shooting script or at least a treatment. I needed an outline. Isn't that how they did it in Hollywood—the writer doing the first half of the work and the director the second? It could only help us at the major studios when the time came: a long-range plan with short-term action.

Nick and Bobbo had fortuitously presented an opportunity to make things better for everyone.

That is how I, Rigby Canfield, became the patron and exclusive distributor for a private label.

Returning to New Orleans, I explored my contacts. There was Mr. du Pree who had a store in the Quarter and a pipeline to the underworld community. I knew about him from Waldo who had taken me to see him. After he tasted the cider, he exclaimed it reminded him of France.

Looking at the label—"La Vieille Maison Vintage"—Mr. du Pree asked, "Isn't that Ralph's place?"

"Ralph's place? You mean Father Rivage's." To be sure, I produced a shot of Father in his black robes that I had printed from a footage frame.

Mr. du Pree laughed. "Yes, that's Ralph all right. I don't mind telling you that moonshine, beer, or wine made in Louisiana is legal. We got a law saying that individuals can produce a certain amount of alcohol for home consumption."

"Is this home consumption?"

"Well, we can expand the law a little bit, home consumption, home cooking, all the same. I shouldn't be telling you this, but if it helps finance the school . . ."

"I appreciate it, Mr. du Pree, but is there anything I should know? I mean I'll keep it quiet. And we want to help Ralph."

"Word on the street is that Ralph is not painting anymore. You know what I mean?"

Had Homer been on to something?

"He's the best in the world but has gone through some sort of religious conversion—either that or the Feds got to him, or his parole officer."

"Did he do anything wrong?"

"Depends how you look at the paintings. They are perfect copies, and he doesn't sell them, but I have friends who are art dealing kind of folks." Mr. du Pree continued. Father had reinvented himself. While serving time for art forgery, he was in charge of the prison library, where he read everything he could find. That led him to find God. And when he was paroled, he was recruited for a few years of community service at La Vieille Maison, where he took to wearing a black robe that he had found in one of the large boxes stored in the cellar.

I couldn't find out any more details, but I did learn from my Dad that Mr. du Pree had been shot by a disagreeable associate and had been part of some gang, maybe the mafia. But in New Orleans you didn't disassociate yourself from that organization on a whim. He had been in pretty bad condition, and my father had saved his life. Mr. du Pree's helping me out was probably his way to show appreciation.

"How can we get cases to the Quarter?"

"I can handle it."

Mr. du Pree was part owner of a trucking firm that picked up garbage in the city. The pick ups were scheduled for every other day; on off days, he leased the trucks to a firm that delivered building materials to construction sites. Magnetic signs were attached as needed to the doors of the dark green trucks that read "New Orleans City Disposal Control." For other contracts, he would replace the signage for the business that needed his services. A new truck sported "La Vieille Maison Vintage." After all, I didn't want our special product picked up or delivered in garbage trucks. The cider found its place on shelves in specialty shops outside the city and inside the Quarter.

After his recovery, Waldo didn't mind quietly making a few deliveries to some of the best restaurants, supplementing his usual inventory. He also sold bottles from his wagon for three dollars each, which became immensely popular. Apples were just a distant relation to the cider. The profits were equally distributed and I received my ten percent commission for services.

As the enterprise became successful, and Mr. du Pree and I became trusted associates, I asked for more information about Father Rivage, especially details about his paintings, with the promise I would not mention them to anyone.

Mr. du Pree and "Ralph" had met in Leavenworth. Ralph had been convicted of art forgery, and there was no one better at it. To pay expenses, he had produced Picassos and Chagalls, art that quickly became popular. One painting sold to the Nelson, an art museum in Kansas. Then Father found God in the prison library and was giving up on imitating masterpieces.

I had assumed that the school was funded by the Church and by a few donations from good-willed people. I was only partly correct. The most affluent families in the Garden District had supported the school inadvertently. "Original" paintings hung proudly on walls in their homes, mine included. New Orleans was becoming the fine arts capital of the world.

Ralph, or Father, I should say, was artfully forging a new life. A major decision faced me. His story could be the subject of a major film. But in the end, I would have to wait for the promise of "someday," and continue on for the greater good.

The cider inventory had been reduced considerably by the time I took my next trip to see Homer. I learned that Nick had forgotten to unscrew the caps of each jug during fermentation, and about fifty bottles deposited in the tower had exploded, jeopardizing our business. We needed quality control, and I spoke to Bobbo about the matter in no uncertain terms. Even though the cider contained a considerable amount of alcohol, the operation was legal, and I recommended stepping up production with quality control.

RIGBY CANBY, M.D.

In time, I was sent to boarding school, due to unintended consequences originating from a personal matter. The cider enterprise sustained itself, but film production was suspended for a while.

But before I left the Quarter, I felt that I was contributing to a good
cause and would also make a difference.

Dear Homer,

*It's going to be harder to come and see you and, in movie terms, we got con-
flict. I'm sitting at a neat desk in a neat little room trying not to notice my
roommate who is studying as usual on a neat bed across from my rumpled
one. I have the Filmo with me, hidden on a high shelf. If you look at the postmark, it will document that I'm being held prisoner in Iberville Parish, an
exclusive preppy place called St. Mark's. First it was going to be a school in
Boston, but I'm here. The only good thing is that I'm not too far away.*

*It's an institution of higher learning, as my father calls it. To me it's more like
an institution of lower dumbness, but who am I to say dumb? I got caught!
Among other things, like skipping classes, I got caught playing doctor in the
apartment above the garage, because I needed privacy!*

*After you went away, I met Jennifer Carpenter, and we became friends.
Not that I was trying to film her or anything. Well, I suppose I could have*

. . . I thought it would please my father if I temporarily demonstrated I had a bent toward medicine. So I borrowed his stethoscope, went out to the garage, Jennifer undressed, and I performed a detailed examination! It was one of the best things I have accomplished so far in life. But in doing so, I walked right out of my father's confidence. I think he thought I was making a porno movie. I tried to explain that I was just interested in learning anatomy. Didn't impress him. He said the things I could learn at Madame du Bois' where I go to dancing school would either come naturally or give me a disease.

I can't talk to my dad about girls. Don't think it would have mattered anyway. He seemed almost glad to have an excuse to send me away. I guess at almost thirteen, I'm old enough to be shipped off.

I thought the Maison would be a great and essential place to continue our work, but instead he sent me here. For a while I went to Assembly. Now I don't go, because I have better things to take care of, like editing the miles of film we've shot. That I really look forward to. I'll keep you in the loop!

Now for the really good news. We got a note from Billy, and he loved The West. *I knew he would. He really wants to stay in touch.*

We both have our troubles, but they're only temporary. You get old fast, and they have to let us out. That's how I figure it, and while you're at La Vieille Maison, you can do that archery stuff. Maybe you'll star in a Robin Hood movie. Ha ha. You can read there too, with some peace and quiet.

But some day, Homer, with Billy's help, we're going to make real movies. And I know they will be good ones. We're going to Hollywood. My father secretly still wants me to become a doctor, but I only want to be a photographer, shoot stills, make documentaries—anything as long as it has to do with film. It's still magic to me. Sometimes I get scared, but I know what I gotta do.

Enclosed find a picture of our Father Rivage. Pretty good and dramatic, don't you think? We should place him under contract like they do at MGM. I promise to write regularly and to send you some more pictures soon. I have my old Brownie stashed away.

Your friend forever,

Rigby

THE BEGINNING OF FATHER RIVAGE'S EXTRAORDINARY PLAN

"Father said, 'I have a great plan for you, Homer St. Cyr! A very impor-
tant engagement.'"

—Homer Sincere's journal, 1950

A gentle ocean breeze rose from the river, filled with the faint cool snap and odor of autumn. Leaves fluttered to the lawn and trooped up a slope and over the hill. Father had been observing Homer at the archery range from his study's window. He had been doing this for some time. "I've been watching you, lad, and I know who you are: a knight from King Arthur's court in Camelot, a man of few words, yet a man who can be trusted with a mission."

A mission! Father always surprised Homer with something new.

Standing in front of a target, Homer took aim, missed, and retreated into silence.

"That's all right, Homer," Father assured him. "It takes time. I have a plan for a knight, a Soldier of the Word." Father was convinced that if Homer Sincere could overcome a handicap, he could accept the challenge of becoming an archer, and Father had another target in mind for Homer to hit.

Dear Rigby,

Thanks for the photo of Father Rivage. I've tacked it up on my wall between the two posters of Billy. Most of my time is spent in the library reading and sometimes on the archery range.

Nick and Bobbo ask how you're doing and hope you'll be back soon. I do too!

Father has a mission for me, a secret mission. I think it has something to do with his plan for me to become a Soldier of the Word! I'll keep you informed. Stay tuned.

Your best friend,

Homer

DINNER AT BRENNEN'S

As soon as I was back in the Quarter for summer break, I checked in with Mr. du Pree. I was relieved to find that production was still in operation, moving toward capacity, although demand was always greater than the supply.

Right away, I invited Homer for a weekend. My father liked him because he had read Melville and Molière and he was sure that Homer was a good influence on me even if I preferred to take photographs and visit my "Louisiana Ladies"—the girls I loved at dancing school—instead of hitting the books. I wanted to introduce Homer around town. Surely, under my tutelage, he could become as accomplished as I, and I modestly mention I could talk my way in and out of just about anything except my father's confidence. In the long run, Homer was better off without added complications. I could see he was beginning to overcome his self-consciousness about his brace, but with girls he was still unsure of himself. Franklin D. Roosevelt wore one, even though he did not want anyone to know it. I guess Homer felt the same. Reinforcing his self-esteem would be my next big plan.

"Dad, the cook's off, and we're going out into the Quarter," I said, anticipating a really fine meal after the Spartan kitchens of St. Mark's and La Vieille Maison.

Of course, my father thought it was a good idea, expecting Homer and I would talk about literature as we pursued gentlemanly pleasures and pastimes.

I particularly liked Brennen's for the banana flambé, Antoine's for the salads, Commander's Palace for the Oysters Rockefeller, and K'Pauls for desserts. Brennen's won the evening where I took a particular satisfaction in paying my way on behalf of my newest enterprise, even though I liked signing my father's name to the bill and leaving a big tip. To top off the evening, I ordered a bottle of La Vieille Maison Vintage.

"Rigby, where did this come from?" Homer stuttered in amazement at the label. With his promise of secrecy, I casually mentioned the business. Not surprisingly, Homer was speechless, more in a state of suspended disbelief. Father Rivage was pretty inventive and, while I never sought out any real evidence, I believe he was in full support of the project. I didn't want to assume too much, making sure not to reveal more than I should. In other words, the cider trade "was on the quiet," and Homer, who had other matters on his mind, had been oblivious to the small enterprise. Sometimes I felt guilty not telling him everything. But not implicating him in any way was a decision I had made. Less known was better gain, and remembering my word to Mr. du Pree, I let the matter pass. We were enjoying the good life as I lit up a Havana when my father made a surprise appearance with his out-of-town guests. The good life was abruptly cut short as we made a discrete departure out the back entrance.

THE TECHNICOLOR LAUNDRY

"Nick and Bobbo took Henry Thoreau to his word. 'When the machine is manufacturing injustice it is the duty of conscientious citizens to resist.'"
—Homer Sincere's journal, 1950

When Homer returned to school, Bobbo and Nick were up to something. Trouble and tricks were endemic. Whispering and planning stopped when Father Rivage came into the room. But when Father talked about Plato's *Republic*, the rights and duties of citizenship, they started another whisper fest that ended when Father Rivage asked them to explain their behavior.

Nick produced his pencil and pretended to be writing on his pad of paper, then winked at Homer who couldn't figure out what they had up their sleeves, but he soon learned.

What Bobbo and Nick didn't seem to understand was that La Vieille Maison was not just a distillery but also a place of classical learning with books taking them to the "Nation of Knowledge" beyond booze-making and fun-making profits.

The day's lecture on individuality left Bobbo and Nick euphoric in a Technicolor way.

"Never be afraid to use your imagination," Father Rivage told his boys. "Your thoughts create the future."

Bobbo and Nick shook hands at the back of the room, and it was difficult to tell from their expressions whether the devil or an angel sitting on their respective shoulders carried the day. Homer was trying to understand their actions and almost missed Father Rivage's assignment to read *Civil Disobedience* by Thoreau, the first book that Bobbo and Nick took with serious intention, and one that would add color to their imagination.

Naturally deliberating with a scholarly pause, Father placed his notes and pens in a well-worn black travel briefcase, concluding the day's lecture.

On Saturday, Homer pulled laundry duty. Normally, Bobbo and Nick complained, but this time they whistled happily, and Father Rivage had obviously struck a chord in them that had released the demon that seduced them.

"I've got an idea that will make our day fly by," Bobbo announced.

"That'd be a relief," Nick replied, wiping the sweat from his brow.

"Here, I'll load the washers. Nick, you set the controls, and Homer, you put in this special soap and close the lids."

They quickly established a working rhythm, and Homer was ashamed that he had doubted them. Nick meticulously checked each load making sure that the white loads had hot water, the dark loads cooler. Caught in laundry engineering, Homer measured out the soap with the same exactness as his comrades.

"Don't forget to use that other soap for the sheets," Bobbo instructed.

Reaching for the second box of soap, Homer continued his part in the assembly line.

Halfway through the rinse cycle, after they transferred the clothes to the dryers, Nick excused himself to work on his lessons. Bobbo bent over with pain just as the first washer finished.

"I'll be right back, think I got sick from lunch," he said, running out of the laundry room clenching his stomach.

Still in the grasp of efficiency fever, Homer opened all the lids, went back to the first washer to transfer the clothes, and popped the first load into the nearest dryer. Returning for the next batch, he noticed a pink residue on his hands and wiped his pants before reaching for the whites in the next washer.

But the white shirts they wore with their gray blazers were decidedly different. A uniform red replaced the pristine holy white. With a sinking heart, Homer looked in at the sheets—all baby blue. He was further bewildered when he discovered Father's socks and underwear were half-blue, half-red.

Then came laughter from the hall. Bobbo and Nick returned, admiring their work and, without saying a word, loaded the dryers while Homer sat on the folding table feeling miserable.

As he folded the socks, he wondered about just what Nick and Bobbo had put into the machines—some sort of dye, he suspected— and what Father Rivage would think when the laundry was delivered.

The expected call to meet Father in the library came the next afternoon. Bobbo and Nick were already sitting at the table when Father Rivage arrived and took a chair across from them.

"Gentlemen, I thought I'd call this somewhat informal meeting to discuss next semester's reading list."

They all wore the same bright pink shirts and confused expression as Father Rivage pushed onward.

"We will continue, of course, our drive through the Great Books, but there are modern classics that might help bring us into contact with contemporary issues," he said, looking at them for confirmation.

Homer nodded. Bobbo and Nick shrugged.

"Any suggestions?" Father asked, sitting back and crossing his right leg over his knee—displaying a bright red sock. There was silence, then he shifted position, reversing legs. The other sock was bright blue. A Kodak moment!

"Before I forget, Homer," Father Rivage said and caught Nick looking at his sock while giving no sign of noticing, "there's a double feature playing this Saturday. I thought you'd enjoy it."

"R-r-really, Father?"

"Apparently they're both quite good films."

"Which ones?" chirped Bobbo. "Maybe we'd like to go too."

"Oh, I'm sure you would," Father Rivage said, with a trenchant cast to his smile. "I'm sure you would."

"Well, what's playing?" Nick asked.

Father was off-handed, more casual than usual. "On second thought, I don't think you boys would like these movies, they both have classical themes. Homer you like westerns, right? Nicholas—action and adventure, and Bobbo, there just aren't enough mystery movies being made, are there?"

"We want to go!" they chorused, hanging on his hook.

"But you don't even know what's playing," Father questioned.

"We don't care. If you say it's good, it's got to be good. We trust you."

"You do?" Father's eyebrows went skyward.

"Yes, yes," chimed Bobbo and Nick. "What's playing at the movies?"

Father Rivage calmly folded his arms on the table and looked them right in the eyes.

"It's really the perfect double bill for this situation." Bobbo started to speak, Father waved him silent. "You trust me enough to put an entire Saturday afternoon's entertainment in my hands without even asking what's playing? That's quite a compliment—it means I've done my job as your guardian." His eyes wavered. "You trust me. Hmmm."

He was silent, looking at them for a day's worth of moments, then a sparkle emerged, gleaming in his eye.

"Gentlemen, the double feature playing this Saturday is *The Blue Angel* and *The Red Shoes*. How does that sound?"

Homer was delighted with the prospect.

Father pinned the boys like a butterfly on a specimen board with his stare. Bobbo chattered something or other about Norma Shearer when Nick shushed him.

"That double feature isn't at the movie house, is it Father?"

"No, it isn't, Nicholas."

"Then where is it?" Bobbo wanted to know.

"In the laundry room, you dope." Nick said and punched Bobbo's arm. "Right, Father?"

Rivage agreed.

Bobbo glanced at Father, then at his socks, the gears in his head finally finding the cinematic connection. He laughed. "That's cool." Then a moment later, "Aren't you mad at us, Father?"

He shook his head. "Every time I teach *Civil Disobedience*, something like this happens." He chuckled. "Maybe I should drop it." He leaned forward from his desk. "You boys only made one mistake. Know what it was?"

"We got caught?" Bobbo just didn't get it.

Another thought from Father Rivage, "God—"

"Catches everything," Nick said, finishing the sentence. "Right, Father?"

"I know you boys said you trusted me. I make a lot of decisions regarding your education and the kind of life you lead here. It would make my life easier to make you all wear black robes and shoes—and follow my daily schedule." He leaned back again. "But that wouldn't be appropriate to your lives. You aren't me and you have to make your own choices."

"What was our one mistake?" Nick inquired, looking for more.

"You made a decision about other people's lives—not a big one, mind you—but your trick means that some people here won't trust you as much as they did before. And just remember for the future," he continued with a grin, "When you do things that affect other people's lives, be sure everything can be washed back to its original color."

Homer appreciated the analogy that fit with his worldview.

They were dismissed.

Father took Homer aside. "Things don't always happen as we expect them to, especially with friends. When you really care for somebody, you invest a bit of yourself and that's called trust. Sometimes that trust is broken, and when that happens, forgive others. And forgive yourself, because in forgiveness there is freedom."

Homer thought about that a long time. These were words to hold with him, a thought to keep. Trust, forgiveness—essential words that Homer had not included in his emotional vocabulary. Maybe that's what Father Rivage meant about considering other people's lives. It suddenly dawned on Homer that this was the kind of thing that happened between brothers in a family, even though this family was different from any he had read about in books.

THE UNEXPECTED LAST GOODBYE

"He had come a long way, and I was amazed by both Waldo's goodness and generosity. My admiration and happiness should have been shouted to the world."

—Homer Sincere's journal, 1950

"You have a visitor," Bobbo announced. "But he won't come in, and he won't leave his horse." The visitor had appeared silently and unexpectedly as if he had been lowered by a celestial apparatus.

It was Waldo! Homer raced down the spiraling stairs.

Remembering Rigby's description of Waldo's heart attack, he was reassured when he saw him standing by his horse, his spine straight as ever, feeding Ophelia, thanking her for making the three-hour trip in only three and a half hours, with a voice that was steady with implacable, sweet warmth.

"Whoo! Long . . . long . . . long kinda trip," said Waldo, responding to the big bear hug Homer gave him.

"You're okay, Waldo. You're okay!" Waldo's reassuring touch on his hand felt good.

Homer asked if he would like to meet the other boys but Waldo was more interested in being alone with Homer. "Knowin' you have friends makes me feel a little better about not comin' to see you before. Of course, when I'm missing you, I remind myself that you are bein' cared for by a man of God."

Climbing on top the wagon, Homer glanced in the back. "What's that?" he asked, discovering a large object covered by a tarp.

"Something important," Waldo advised matter-of-factly.

Asking Waldo for news, he learned that his father had been taken for rehabilitation for the second time since Homer had been at La Vieille Maison.

"Dunkin' torture, that's what he's goin' through. They be dunkin' him in and out of those smokin' hot baths and then into icy water. Oowee, Homer, that's pretty tough treatment."

Waldo was fully aware of the hurt Homer had endured after the funeral. His gaze aimed straight out over Ophelia Lou's hat, talking and listening and, with a long strong arm, he pulled Homer close to his side.

"Real good to see you, son."

Homer loved him. Waldo by any measure filled the hollow in his heart.

"And let me tell you about Rigby. He got his smart self caught right up on the sharp lens of his daddy's eye." Waldo shook his head. "See . . . if you went home right now, he wouldn't be there either, and you wouldn't be learnin' and makin' films as such. Maybe it was time for you all to be outta the Quarter. Got a photo and letter from the boy, of his smart self sitting on the bent right knee of his fancy school's founding father, so we can tell Rigby is the same, can't we? The trip out here was fun for me and pretty short, and for Ophelia Lou—nothin' personal, you understand—it was mostly long, long, long. She's makin' some funny noises nowadays, like an old jalopy. Her teeth even chattered once and it's not even cold, got to treat her right."

Waldo turned from his seat. "Ophelia has class, boy, she didn't even let me know she was sick, yes siree, this little lady done pretty good out here today."

His voice paused. "Homer, this Father Rivage—you like him a lot, don't you?"

"I'm discovering books, a hundred of them. I read them all, learning about new things, but Waldo, please tell me any news about Rigby. We stay in touch, as much as we can."

Waldo was silent for a moment, then he pressed on thinking that he needed to talk about something.

"He's worried about you. So am I. Rigby told me about these visits you have from Billy Sunshine. I know we have to believe in imagination and dreams, boy—and we do—but only to a point." Waldo fidgeted in his seat a bit.

"You mean like Daddy Grace says, to visualize?"

"I'm talking about your visits from Billy Sunshine."

"What about them?"

Homer heard the words in chunks: "Dreams . . . like pretty flies on your hooks . . . pretty and lively, and doin' what they s'pose to do—hidin' the ugly stuff, when life gets unpleasant—like we can get in the habit of usin' the dreams and then—sometimes—and it happens to all kindsa folks—if life gets better, well, there you are, stuck on a hook you don't need. We're worried about you, boy. There comes a time you got to come back to the real world to stay."

"But Billy just comes once in a while and like he sings in *Paper Moon*, it wouldn't be make believe if you believed in me!"

"Maybe he shouldn't be singin' or coming at all." Waldo tried to be gentle. "Got to give it up. I know he is important and all, but you talkin' to him when he's not there, well that's not making good sense."

Silently he carried the weight of Waldo's words and advice. "Come back to the real world." The words were lacerations raising old hurts, bringing them to the surface. His thoughts worked their way out of him, and so did all the humiliation he had been carrying around.

Wrenching himself away from the side of the wagon, Homer started for the door. He whirled around. Real or imagined, Billy was part of Homer. Waldo was sitting there staring down at him, the reins slack in his big hands, his mouth slightly open in a crooked little way.

For the first time, Homer saw that Waldo was getting old—a thousand years old, maybe, all his blackness turning gray; it made things worse and, in a last great effort, he gathered up his hurt and hurled it at him. Waldo could take it; he was a soldier. Hadn't he been doing that for years? Hadn't he? Homer's arms waved wildly, empty.

"You didn't want me," he said. "Remember? Only Billy came when I was alone. You . . . you and your horse and rhymes."

He walked away, going inside, as he heard the wagon rattling slowly away and the dinner bell ring. Homer excused himself from supper, mumbling that he had already eaten, not very hungry, and then, alone in his room, looked at the pictures and posters, his whole body feeling limp and ugly.

There was a knock at his door.

"Go away, please."

"Special delivery for Homer San-Cyre." It was Bobbo's voice.

"Don't want it, come back tomorrow."

"Can't. It's blocking the hallway."

He trudged to the door and opened it. Bobbo, Nick, and two other boys lifted a tarpaulin-covered crate—the one from the back of Waldo's cart—and carried it into his makeshift room in the library.

"Where you want it?" Bobbo asked, affecting a New York deliveryman's accent.

"Don't know."

"Right, lads, then we'll leave it here."

Staring at the large object, he was numb, and then someone cleared his throat at the door. Father Rivage.

"Aren't you curious to see what it is? Let's remove the cover together."

They dragged the covering off only a few inches before Homer realized what was underneath, and he swept the tarp the rest of the way.

His mother's desk! Rubbing his hand gently over the wood, he pulled at the drawers, opening and closing them. But in the midst of his excitement, he stopped, feeling ashamed, remembering the way he had treated Waldo. What had gotten into him? He hadn't even said goodbye. Waldo was a man with a heart condition, a sick horse, and he knew it took him three and a half hours to bring the desk to him.

Turning away from the desk, shame burned over Homer like phosphorus.

"What's the matter?" Father Rivage asked, his eyes appreciating Homer's desk.

"I was pretty terrible to Waldo, said stupid things. I acted badly, didn't thank him . . . didn't even say goodbye . . . I . . ."

"Why don't you write him in the morning? I think it would be a nice way to launch your career, at your desk."

Launch his career! It was at this time, this moment, when Homer's perspective began to change. Writing in long hand replaced his dispatches. By morning's light, he had written eight pages in his notebook and drafted several different apologies to Waldo. In the midst of making his bed, he heard Waldo's name mentioned. Father Rivage stood in the doorway saying that Homer would not have to write an apology. Waldo's body had been found huddled over on the wagon seat, the reins in a death grip so that the horse, trained to return home, had not moved all night, but had stayed in the countryside.

"Massive coronary. Quick and not welcomed," Father Rivage said. "We knew it was coming, didn't we? After all, he was old and had a weak heart."

Homer didn't think it was coming—he didn't know Waldo had been sick for so long a time.

"But why didn't he get help?"

"He tried. Hospitals have some strange notions and wouldn't admit him for the treatment he needed. You know it's hard for a black man in the South. It's not the same as for you and me."

Some things were hard to comprehend at a young age and in the old South. Sitting on his freshly made bed, blinking outside his window, he had forgotten that he was too old to cry.

His mind traveled to a green countryside, becoming pale blue as the night lifted and dark green as the morning came. In vivid color, in all its magical quality, he watched a bright red wagon fade into a shadow with Waldo silhouetted under a dark sky.

"Waldo was an old soul, an inspired man," Father said, folding his hands in prayer.

"What does that mean, Father? Inspired."

"It means touched by God."

Homer asked what words would have been said if the poets Addison, Blake, Browning, Byron, Donne, Montague, and Pope were seated around a great library table, with John Keats reciting a requiem for one of their fallen. In a second, Father paused, and then raised himself taller than Homer had ever seen him.

"When I have fears that I may cease to be,
Before my pen's words and high-piled books
When we behold, the night's air-starr'd face,
We feel that we may someday live to trace shadows
With the magic of chance,
That we shall look upon them again
And spirit the fairy power of unreflecting dream
There on the shore of the wide world we stand alone."

The next day, Homer tried to retrace his footsteps, looking for shadows but came up empty. A wave of anger cheated his memory, and on the archery green, he pulled the string of his bow, firing arrow after arrow. Inspiration? Was that the secret? Was there any nobility in death? He shot hundreds of arrows, all missing the target, and with his supply and energy exhausted, returned to his room.

A thumping started in his ears like minefields being strafed and bombed. His eyelids filled with explosions of light, and just when he thought his head would burst, he realized the sound was pounding hooves. Billy Sunshine's horse, Apollo, was coming straight at him.

The voice was familiar, and his heart lifted as Billy, wearing his big silver-banded hat, stretched out both arms toward him.

"I heard about Waldo."

"I knew it was you, I heard you coming. It's my fault, Billy, and I hurt him badly. He came to see me and I ran away."

Billy sat on the edge of his bed.

"I'm beginning to see the plot of this story. What we have here is somethin' besides shadows. You were a part of Waldo and now he is a part of you. Someday you should do something to honor him. That's important, and you are feeling the loss of a good friend, but that's not all you're feeling. Waldo himself would see that right away and he'd say that what's got hold of you is somethin' we all go through—the fear of growing up. And something else, and there's a big idea here."

Billy stretched out a long leg, running a finger over the creased white fabric.

"Forgiveness, son, forgiveness. Father says your feelings are getting older, maybe they are. And after you get some more learnin', I'll see you in Hollywood."

With that promise, Billy made one of his theatrical exits. It was one of the last times he would come to visit. Homer was moving from his past into his future with a compass still pointing toward California.

TARGET PRACTICE

Homer's journal began recording every thought and sentiment, filling the day's small history. "Keep writing!" Father urged. "What happened, how do you feel, and what can you learn by it? Words will help you define your life, how you regard the world on the great journey. We all have a story to tell, Homer. Write it down!"

Homer began seeing the world differently and made more detailed entries in his journal. He expressed some intimate views of his observations, moments when the blank pages shared his feelings. Crossing boundaries, he knew where they began but was not sure where they ended. Then Father introduced the hard stuff. Einstein and Darwin escaped his grasp. With literary excavation into "the Greats," Father introduced *The Iliad*, the epic legend of the Trojan War, a story of mortals struggling against odds and obstacles. Who was responsible, man or gods? From his desk, Homer charged into battle under extraordinary circumstances, losing some of the sorrow that had formed the pattern of his life. Was this a proving ground? Like *The Odyssey*, a personal rite of passage? Was this a way to the target? Then with Dante, life became curious. In *The Divine Comedy*, Virgil led him from the underworld to the stars crossing the River of Forgetfulness, to the music of the Spheres, to the love that moved the moon. He was happy to have Father's CliffsNotes because his readings had reached an overwhelming scale. But, here and there, a passage got through and made sense. He had been thrown into the language of scholars, though still too young to fully understand and appreciate it.

Father patiently explained his theory of creation. "Like ribbons falling from the sky, ribbons called elements, ninety-two of different colors and sizes, hanging alone until they wrapped themselves around a big package. And something mysterious happened with a big bang, something we can't explain, something like blowing the lid off the box.

"Guess who was inside? You and me. Of course, this is only one explanation for creation. There is another in the Garden of Eden that enjoys a great popularity, easier to accept, but anyway you consider it we're made of stardust, and we're created by God."

Homer's studies became more personal as he traveled in April with the twenty-nine pilgrims Chaucer had assembled in the *Canterbury Tales*. Could he travel alone without Rigby or Waldo or Billy Sunshine, with Father as his only guide?

Father introduced Homer to Cervantes' Don Quixote, a soldier who mixed reality with illusion, and to his love, Dulcinea del Toboso. It was a high-spirited story with the power to leave a sense of revelation and stunning enchantment. Were he and Rigby also chasing windmills? As Homer traveled on, meeting Gulliver and Moby Dick, his education took wing.

He was visiting the Nation of Knowledge, learning about the world that would make him a fuller man. And when Homer was assigned Machiavelli, St. Augustine, and Descartes, his workload doubled.

"Do they live in the Nation of Knowledge?"

"*Yes.*" Father was emphatic.

As Father's literary map guided Homer into an inventory of books, would they help him understand the connection to the target? Could the words help him find the target? In an odd way, Father cared about books and writing with an almost holy crusade. I don't think he ever realized what an extraordinarily fine teacher he was, with or without CliffsNotes. He must have known that he had an ineffable appealing quality in which Homer could respond to the wondrous world he was trying to open to him. It was a matter of caring, and he did deeply, and ultimately with the ability to move his boys into action and feeling, by coercion and conviction. From whatever mysterious wellspring his talent came, he could be regarded as a companionate man floundering on the edge of a controversial past. He told Homer to write, that he could become a writer, and he was bestowed with notions and truths, books and ideas, befitting of a Soldier of the Word. Father had an unshakable conviction and abiding confidence that Homer's armor would not only deflect the inequities of life, but it would someday shine.

A STATELY PLEASURE DOME–DECREE

"Father combined verse with the Constitution. I imagine these principles are part of poetry too."

—Homer Sincere's journal, 1950

"Poetry time, gentlemen. Bobbo, your assignment is Emerson's 'Concord Hymn,' Nicholas, Milton's *Paradise Lost*—that is, I hope, not lost on you. Then, Homer," Father opened a book of English verse, pointed to a page and assigned Homer Samuel Coleridge's "Kubla Khan" adding, "I want you and the lads to memorize it."

"But why?" Homer questioned.

"There are certain things I want you to hold on to," Father replied.

"Memorize after so much reading? I don't get it."

"Trust me, Homer. Let the rhythm of the words overtake you. It doesn't matter if you don't understand them all. Let the words flow over you like a river."

Father's eyes became squinty.

"Because poetry shapes the heart and sharpens your memory. Without memory we are nothing. It is absolutely essential, and it is your right, a precious right built on our Constitution."

"The Constitution, the American Constitution? Part of the Great Books program?"

"Exactly," Father replied. "Reciting principles and phases by heart is one of our basic freedoms. But first Coleridge!"

That night Homer practiced:

"In Xanadu did Kubla Khan
A stately pleasure-dome decree.
Where Alph, the sacred river, ran
Through caverns measureless to man
Down to a sunless sea.
Da, de da, da da de da . . ."

Father was driving hard, but Homer didn't know why, nor what he had in mind. He was beginning to appreciate the classics but was overwhelmed and often became resentful of Father Rivage's all work, no play, scorched earth policy. Homer believed that schools in the Quarter were more relaxed. But he accepted the challenge, and each evening tried to go over Coleridge's verses, only to be interrupted by thumping overhead—zydeco music and Father's shuffling two-step.

Chapter 5
CONVENT, LOUISIANA 1950

<hr>

IN HIS OWN WORDS

"I really hoped my arrows could make it to the target. But if they did, would the arrows carry my words?"
—Homer Sincere's journal, 1950

It was a stifling day with no breeze. The afternoon stood still. Father Rivage announced that Homer's father had written; his own father wanted him back. His father! Where had he been all these years? What did he look like, what did he want?

It stirred up old feelings, and at such times, he took refuge at the ring, shooting arrows at the target.

Homer told Father he really wasn't expecting to see his father again. And according to Homer's journal, when his father appeared, it wasn't a dream but a very real experience.

"Sometimes we have to expect the unexpected," Father said, and Homer was ready.

Homer expressed the day in his journal:

"The library was just an Iliad's throw from the archery ring. Would all the books help me make a connection to the target? I wondered if my arrows could go the distance.

My beaten up quiver held two new spruce arrows, a gift from Nick and Bobbo. I set one in the tightly strung bow. The range at La Vieille Maison was set up in the English manner with targets at both ends. To aid concentration, I've developed a habit of shooting from the east end, keeping the sun and the house at my back, facing the horizon with only the target ahead. Practicing at the same time and at the same station, I have accepted the changing wind conditions and adapted my vision.

With my right hand, I pick up a circlet of black leather and pull it over my left wrist, twisting my forearm until the band is comfortable, almost nonexistent, and with that done, I take a black leather shooting glove and place my right hand into it, wriggling, letting my fingers find their accustomed grooves.

I was intensely focused, unaware that there is more at my back than the sun. Even the wind was cooperating, conditions were right, accuracy is not important yet. I am striving for control.

I feel that I am part of the spruce arrow, the osage-orange bow, the rope-filled target. They are all connected and everything is part of something. If this is true, then no one is ever lost. Not my mother, not Waldo, not my dad, not even I.

This must be the secret of the target. Maybe the target is me and yet the target is in front of me. I sense its thick, circled roundness—vivid, variegated, elusive, and vulnerable.

Targets have great wounds and do not die. The secret is to become one with the target.

My right arm is bent back to the quiver, and with the arrow in hand, my bow arm rises straight, slowing when the weapon is almost waist high and angled into a position more horizontal to the ground so I am able to set the arrow across the bowstring, nestling it next to my grip hand. The fingers of my right hand curl around the string, trying not to squeeze the arrow. Then the bow comes all the way up, a vertical line before my face. A line to divide the visible world. My right arm pulls, bending, folding back in search of the energy needed to separate bow and string, enough to launch the missile properly.

As the string stretches to my cheekbone there is an instant when, in the corner of my eye, a man's shape is visible. While targets stare unblinkingly, they do not see.

I have achieved some measure of oneness with the target. But do I see?

Holding the bow steady, a drawn string began to slice mercilessly at my fingers, 'like the bursting of ripe fruit.' That is the way my fingers should open—like a ripe fruit. I held on. Very soon, the agonizingly tight knot in the middle of my back adds to the pain in my fingers. Thirty-six pounds is the weight of the world.

My world, like that of the target, all quiet and waiting. Close to my ear is a sharp crack and then the thrumming of the string, the rhythm slowing, fast but uneven—like a frantic heart. Ahead of me the whistle-whisper, the vibrato in it betrays the unsteadiness of the arrow's flight. After the recoil, the target stands absolutely still.

Then someone quietly says, 'Jesus!'

My string hand remains frozen, splayed at my cheek, frontal and very accessible. After all, isn't that one challenge of a target—a place you count on hitting sooner or later? My eyes are closed to avoid any temptation of checking where the arrow has landed. The score is not important, I remind myself, control is important. Suddenly my eyes open, and again, a man's voice breaks my silence.

'Good job.' The encouragement is sincere.

Backlit by the morning sun stands a medium-size, dark-haired man in a frayed but freshly ironed shirt and khaki pants. He stands watching. Slightly haggard, but rangy and handsome all the same, with a strong, reminiscent jaw line. The man's hair is combed back.

In a delicate hand, he grips something. His other hand is thrust deep in his pocket to hide a noticeable tremor.

I see the silhouette. Annoyed by the intruder, I intend to ask him to leave. Turning and stepping off the mound, I get a better look at his features. He is not a drifter; there is something familiar about him, and as I approach, I notice he holds a trumpet. This man is here to see me. I look at the trumpet, but my mind is examining the face of the stranger. It could not be. My dad is bigger, much bigger. His eyes down, it is my father.

With only a few feet of ground separating us, I see his hand tremble just a little and I know it is, after all, the hand that had hurt me.

The long walk from the target to me must have been difficult for my father. He sucks in his gut with a deep breath and steps forward to meet me.

It has been four years.

Inside my head are words that hold a sad understanding that comes with the loss of innocence. A few years too late.

Looking at my father, I am strangely calm. My emotions retreat to a safer place, maybe to one of the empty places around the bull's-eye.

'I'm here to take you back, son,' my father says.

I wait silently, staring at him and for a moment gazing directly into my father's eyes. Then his own eyes shift to a place over my head, looking past me. I hear Father Rivage's car pull up to the gate.

'That's the man who takes care of us—Father Rivage. Do you want to meet him?'

My father does not respond, walking around me and away, seeming to hear nothing, yet the sound is clear. I don't know how all this is happening. Then I remember how I had let go of the arrow too soon due to the pain.

Before I can stop myself, the words sputter out. After years of rehearsal, all I can manage is: 'Dad, what about the hurt? Do you, I mean, do you know?' A choking feeling rises in my throat. I stop abruptly, take a brief, feverish pause. And when there is no answer, I turn away, walk back to my starting point and begin twisting my feet into the ground. Again the breathing routine: slowly and gently in, pressing the air down, I take out a second arrow, arming the bow, and with the large weapon positioned horizontally at waist height and the shaft notched, I pull the bow. My concentration is surprisingly good. 'It's up to me, Dad,' I insist in a quiet voice that barely reflects my strain.

Down the shaft of my tightly drawn arrow, the broad chest of my father leaves my view. Though distant, he looks smaller and more like the father I remembered and feared. Around his head, like a sullen rainbow of haloes, is the usual target. There is the white of my father's white-hot rage, the black of his own grief.

The string could have surely cut my fingers off. But still I hang on. 'Like ripe fruit,' I say to myself. 'Like ripe fruit.'

I loose the arrow.

My father is far away, turning, but I see just enough before he finally slides his hand into his pocket.

He does something that I do not want to see. Pulling out a bottle disguised in a brown paper bag, he takes a long drink of bourbon. 'Here's to you, Homer.'

His inelegant conviction is only matched by his inadequate countenance.

Had he stopped drinking? No. Had his guilt, monstrous and unutterable, caught him in an instant of sober surprise, temporarily transcending his actions toward some redemptive hope? Like a mountain climber, fearful of completely losing his way in a blinding snowstorm, getting up one morning, emerging safely from his tent breathing victoriously the clean alpine air—but in a momentary triumph of sunlit goodwill, had relapsed into an avalanche. He was as he is.

He snatches the bottle again in an awkward, greedy motion and drinks, draining it in a gulp, and replaces the bottle in his side coat pocket. Then he walks away. It wasn't the toast or the sentiment. It was the action, not the arrow, that held the answer.

I also walk away. The crescent of osage-orange wiggled as though under water. I swallow hard but say nothing. Then in a moment, 'I'm sorry too.'

Today. Tomorrow. Like the target, I have empty spaces in the circle that holds my sorrow. I won't die when I'm hit in one of those places. Sometimes I hurt. Does the target hurt too?"

—Homer Sincere, 1950

THE GREAT PLAN!

Father summoned me for the weekend, asking me to meet him at the entrance of the Great Hall. Now Father had a plan!

"How you doing, Father?" I began the conversation brightly. "Everything all right?"

He requested I come with him to Chapel. "I'm glad you are here. It's a very serious matter."

He had a roll of canvas in his hand, and when we arrived, he deposited it under one of the angels at the altar. The act was so mysterious that I wished I had brought my camera with me.

"What are you doing, Father?"

"It's a penance," he replied. "I have to put my sins away."

Father dropped to his knees.

"Father, I am but your humble Servant. Father, please direct me. I ask for your grace and guidance for the school. Give Homer strength in the mission I am about to ask of him and of his friend Rigby. They will soar on wings like eagles. They will walk and not grow tired."

He closed his eyes, kneeling for the longest moment, then rose with a refreshed posture, saying, "Ah, I feel better."

What was Father praying about? What was the mission? Father turned to me. "I need your help."

I couldn't figure it all out, and I thought I was pretty good.

"Come along," he said. "I have news." When we arrived at his study, Homer, Bobbo, and Nick were waiting.

"I have something important to say," Father confided.

I knew it! Father was going to come clean. He had guilt all over his face.

"What's to say?" Nick and Bobbo asked.

"Good news for all of us gathered here," Father intoned, assuming a posture I'd not seen before, like a religious conversion or something.

"News?" everyone chimed.

"Homer Sincere will be representing us at Louisiana's annual great competition at the Academy of Word and Elocution."

Homer was startled. He couldn't imagine what Father was talking about. Nick had been in Father's vision for it in previous years.

"What do you think, Bobbo?" Father asked.

"Perfect choice," Bobbo replied easily. "Congratulations, Homer. We don't feel slighted. We know you'll do a great job."

"Sure," Nick agreed, "and if you need any help, we're here for you! As a matter of fact, I'm sorry I failed you, Father," Nick commented, "but I've improved over the years. Right, Father?"

"Nick, I have great admiration for you, and I know you understand. We must begin preparations."

"Can we go now?" Bobbo asked.

"Yes, we must work out logistics."

"Good luck, Homer." Nick said, happy to escape the mission.

Father gave Homer "Self-Reliance," an essay by Ralph Waldo Emerson about trust and honest convictions.

"In a few weeks, a competition will be held at the Academy of Word and Elocution, and students will compete in public speaking. The winner will earn statewide recognition for their school, not an easy task. It's going to take considerable work to get ready. Funds have arrived, and I have paid the entrance fee."

Realizing what was to come, Homer jumped in, "Nick can really tell a good story. I think he would be the best candidate," he urged. "Give him another chance, Father, he's dramatic. I've seen him act, he is a natural!"

"I've made my decision, we need a fresh voice," Father said, remarkably pleased but firm in his decisions. "Homer Sincere will be representing La Vieille Maison."

"Father, you are kidding me!" I was amused. Homer was going to represent the school!

"Me! Mmmm-me?" Homer stuttered.

"I know you feel you know nothing about public speaking."

Leaning closer, I said to Homer, "I think you are up for the task. You can do it, and I'm going to film you." Homer's face was beet red.

"Father, you are nuts! Where did this crazy idea come from? Why me?" Homer asserted himself in a way he had never done before. I loved his confidence, every word, every minute. This could be a great adventure, a great film episode, and now I knew why Father had invited me for the weekend. I was to be his cinematic acolyte.

I studied Father Rivage, and Father Rivage studied Homer. "I have had this in mind since the very first day I met you," he said.

Turning to me, "You'll be doing me a personal favor, son. Will you help us? Getting the word out on film?"

"Father, I must agree. This is truly important. And when I think of the contribution to the film library, for posterity, I cannot think of a better assignment, a better proposition, a better contribution. Of course I will help."

"You're nuts too, Rigby," Homer said, sensing he was being rounded up for the slaughterhouse.

"We have to pick a perfect and impressive subject, and I'm thinking Louisiana. I'm thinking civil rights. Here are a few essays on the subject. You can handle it."

I would have to admit it was an assignment we had not been expecting, but I believed if Homer practiced, and I coached him, he could get the job done. I concluded this would be part of the confidence-building program I had thought about, and now Father was laying it out before us.

With a kind of exultant momentum, I joined the team. "He can do it, Father!"

Turning to me full of skepticism, Homer calmly asked, "Do you know anything about speaking in front of people, Rig?"

"Well, you just do it. I'll be your coach."

"What am I supposed to do?"

"Just get out there and talk."

"And you are my coach?"

"Well, I'm your supporter! When I film you, I'm going to make you famous!"

"I don't want to be famous!"

Father thanked me for my generosity and said he would get permission from my father for me to take some time off. A few days off from school, even better! "We'll need you along, my boy."

Homer sighed, thinking the whole matter was a conspiracy, not knowing the first thing to do and, except for instinct, neither did I. Father Rivage assigned the most difficult challenge yet. Homer had to memorize stuff about civil rights and the Constitution, but first, to get into shape, he had to continue reciting poetry about that stately dome in front of a mirror. To tell you the truth, I was happy to have been selected to be part of the task force, with an opportunity to film a short subject starting from the beginning, with a middle and an end.

"You've got to do it for yourself, Home. It's a learning curve, and it will make a great film. Father has done his part, now you've got to do yours. And besides, it's a chance to get up to Baton Rouge. You will really be helping more than you know."

"How so?"

I confided to Homer a little that I knew about Father from my asking around. I told him just enough so I didn't break my agreement with Mr. du Pree—a little but not everything. Homer had to give his best for the school. His success could help secure state funds so the place wouldn't have to close.

"Close? Why didn't you tell me this before, Rig?"

"I didn't want to say anything bad about Father. I didn't think you would understand. He has a past but he's trying his best to change for the future, Home. And it costs a lot to keep this place open."

RUNNING WITH THE WORDS

"Father Rivage told me how Father George made a difference in his life, adding that he very much hoped he had made a contribution to mine. One thing he said made a lasting impression. 'It's up to you to make a mark as well. It's not so much what you do that matters, it's what you don't do.'"

—Homer Sincere's journal, 1950

A few weeks later, after working on his memorization skills, Homer asked Father for a meeting.

"Let's talk about your essay. I'm counting on you."

"I'm not going to do it, Father."

"I don't understand. Why?"

Pausing, Homer blurted, "I need to know the truth, and I don't trust you."

"Maybe you don't trust yourself." Father looked away.

"You have to be honest with me, Father."

"The school needs you, son. At the Academy competition, there will be many officials who have great influence on the budget before the legislature. We are low on the list for funding, and if you do well, it could make a huge difference. We need to get word out about what we are doing down here. You know all of us are doing the best we can, and it is God's work. From the very beginning, I knew you were a Soldier of the Word!"

"If I'm a Soldier of the Word, then who are you?"

"What I want to say is that it's not about me. It's about the school."

"Are you who you pretend to be, Ralph?"

Father paused, taken back.

"Okay, you know something about me. I don't know how, but you do, and I won't lie to you, Homer. I'm an artist, and you know that."

"I do?"

"You looked in on me shortly after you arrived and saw me painting in my room, when Anthony came the last time."

Homer was surprised, thinking he had been undetected all these years.

Father didn't dwell on the matter. He had an artist's eye for unseen detail. He continued, "You'll find some of my best art work in the chapel hidden under the altar, safe and secure. Ask Rigby. I know someday Anthony will come around looking for them, and for a while the paintings helped achieve some measure of financial independence. Yes. I was an art forger, and I can copy the best artists in the world perfectly, without a flaw, a gift bestowed upon me. But I got caught a few years ago."

"By God?"

"By the Feds."

"You're not a priest then, a real priest?"

"Father George was a Jesuit priest I met in prison."

"A soldier?"

"Yes, he started this station as a home for people like you and me. He arranged for my parole here, giving me a chance to change. You might even say I reinvented myself. It changed my life. Father George introduced me to books. I read everything, made friends I never knew I could have. No forging, no cheating. I realized I could do better."

"Father George made a difference."

"He made a difference, and you can too."

"How, Father?"

"For the school! We all try to help in a significant way, and that's the truth."

"You really believe I can do it?" Homer needed confirmation.

"I do, son. And so does Rigby. We all do. I've spent considerable time measuring you."

"What will I talk about? The Constitution?"

"You and Rigby are like Huck Finn and Tom, and I aim to send you rafting on the Mississippi."

"What!"

Father had something on his mind, and it wasn't the adventures of Huck or Tom, but an underlying theme. "In that case, I think freedom is really the subject."

"And you really think I can do it?" Homer asked again.

"You've been serving in my army for a long time."

Homer took the challenge. "Let's go to work, Father."

Father was at ease. "You're going to have to think like Huck, be self-reliant, confident. It's not only the words, but also how you say them, one word at a time, run along with them, Homer. God is on our side. I've a few thoughts here to help you on your way to a miracle. It matters most to a soldier of the word." With that, Father turned his notes over to Homer.

"It will take a miracle for sure," Homer thought.

He tried to summon Billy for help, but Billy was away, riding somewhere out West.

TWISTS AND TURNS

"'Life is a gift, son, and we should all be writing thank you notes from time to time,' Father mused in a Jesuit sort of way."

—Homer Sincere's journal, 1950

"It's a good thing, Homer, the Lord's work," Father offered encouragingly. For the trip, Homer's brown hair was wetly combed after a long cold shower. His face spanking clean, Nick and Bobbo had even pressed his gray flannel suit and school tie.

"Before your journey, I have something special for you: a well-deserved dinner for a well-dressed man, not any kind of dinner, but one I think you'll like." Father walked quickly ahead in his long black robes with his disciple following.

Looking forward to a good meal, Homer had almost forgotten what real southern food tasted like, maybe a po' boy, one of his favorites. "Try to keep up son. Don't want to be late."

Arriving at Convent, a small town in Jefferson Parish, Homer saw the boat station at the water's edge. A foghorn signaled early evening, breaking the sound of swishing water along the levee, and Homer wondered whether he'd be traveling on a garlanded steamboat—a boat with a calliope like Mark Twain's and a gambling salon where he could play poker with fashionable men and women on deck. He looked forward to the pleasure of the river slipping away easily, the great rolling red wheel washing ahead, leaving clouds of puffed white steam over a river so wide that at some points one could hardly see across. A mist settled over the Mississippi, like the basin of the Atchafalaya River. The trip would take overnight. Father introduced Homer to Stationmaster Duval of the Louisiana Water Conservatory who was dressed like a train conductor, wearing a blue suit with brass buttons and an oval badge. He announced that the *Louisiana* would be arriving in about an hour, plenty of time to catch dinner.

"Just a slight delay, taking in a little water down at Le Place. Got to fix the bilge pumps."

Homer saw photographs of the great steamboat on the station's walls, then his eyes followed to a separate waiting room. Over the door at its entrance was a sign, "Colored." A few black people waited politely inside.

"You'll be waiting outside here, boy," Mr. Duval admonished. "It's much cleaner, with fresh air, and it's more comfortable out front."

"Better get that boat up here," Father interrupted. "This boy is representing Jefferson Parish in the great competition at the Academy up in Baton Rouge."

"He speakin' at the competition?"

"Statewide!"

"Ooowee, there's a whole lot of speakin' going on these days up at the capitol."

"What else is going on up there?"

"Just sent a group up to the legislature. Governor Earl Long's going to be there."

"Legislature is in session?"

"Whole lotta talk about deee-segregation and votin', mixing whites and coloreds. Whole lotta trouble. You think that's a good thing, sir?"

Father let the question pass him by.

"Mr. Duval, let me know when the boat arrives. We'll be up with Louise at the Snack and Chat. I'm going to get this boy something to eat. We'll be expecting Mr. Rigby Canfield to arrive any moment," Father advised.

"I'll keep a look out! Enjoy yourselves!"

LOUISE'S SNACK AND CHAT

"Come, Homer, I'm going to introduce you to some Cajun culture that I regard favorably," Father said as they left the station.

Up a dusty dirt road was a cabane, an old weather beaten wooden shack with faded green shutters, falling at every angle, framing the yellow light and the shadows inside.

Along the road, Homer asked, "Why didn't you say something to him about segregation, about the blacks and whites, Father? I'm speaking about freedom, and you say nothing?"

Father again didn't reply.

In protest, Homer kicked up some red dust from the clay road.

"Now don't be breaking your brace. Save your anger, son, for the right time and the right place."

Father changed the subject. "They have some really good food at Louise's snack shack ahead. Sautéed fresh shrimp and sweet mustard sauce, southern fried chicken and gravy, New Orleans dirty rice and beans, sweet potatoes spiced with cinnamon sugar topped with melted marshmallows, biscuits and honey, lemon meringue pie, and cold sweet iced tea with fresh mint." Father's rambling recipe and the thought of a real dinner distracted Homer's mind from the issue.

It was more than a shack inside. The seductive aroma of home cooking took precedence over his sensibility, and Homer's stomach growled for one delicious taste.

Louise was just as generous as she was fat. "Come on in. Been expectin' y'all. Is this Homer?"

"Sure is." Father made the introduction.

"Well, bless your sweet heart. Sit down, darlin'."

They dined at a long pine table set on wide plank floors with the river wind whispering through the open windows. "Louise, my dear," Father said and waved, "Bring forth, with bountiful plenty, your magnificent treats!"

Each dish was better than the last. At their table some of the men and women spoke patois, a broken French, and Father talked with them fluently, "Ça va bien." Everybody was Cajun or Creole, black or white, all different shades, and all very friendly. Homer wondered why Father was so comfortable is this setting. Was it the food, the culture, or the companionship?

JUST IN TIME

I was on my way early, taking precautions not to be late by taking a bus to Convent to meet Homer. When I arrived at the boat station, the Dock Master told me that the *Louisiana* had not yet arrived and Homer and Father had gone just a short piece up the road to Louise's

Snack and Chat to get something to eat. Heading over that way after checking my bag, holding on to my Filmo, I soon heard music coming from the wooden cabin. Looking through a side shuttered window to make sure that I had found the right place, I saw Father and Homer at a long table and a band in the back of the room.

After warming up, the small group called Rockin' Dopsie Rubin played. Father took a break, patting his lips on a white linen napkin, listening as a drummer, a washboard, an accordion, a violin, and the piano transported him to another world. Homer looked for a trumpet, but there was none to be seen.

The music wasn't Dixieland; it was more like ragtime, carrying a sweet French memory with an African beat, the same music Homer had become so familiar with late at night, the same tunes that had come from Father's quarters at La Vieille Maison, when the sounds of a-clunk-a-clunk brought home the two-stepping rhythm of the zyde-co. Father was born to dance and utterly unable to resist the tempo.

I moved around to the side of the cabin shooting through another shuttered window to get another angle.

HOMER SINCERE MEETS DAISY PHILIPS

"Father could not resist the music. He lifted his black robes and danced!"
—Homer Sincere's journal, 1950

Father loved it, taking two steps out, then two steps in, shuffling in a circle around and across the floor as people clapped and hollered. Homer was amazed by Father's dancing ability and enthusiasm. Then Father pulled him out to the floor. "Father, I don't know how! I'm embarrassed!"

"Just follow along beside me. It's easy, two steps in and two steps out, and one and two and turn and turn. Feel the music, son."

Two steps in and two steps out. Homer felt clumsy, and it was not easy, but he managed and although he was not perfect, the music was infectious. He stepped through his embarrassment. No one seemed to mind—one step, then two. A pretty blonde girl standing nearby joined him. Others joined in and some of the more practiced gave a little hop, a tap, and click to the step. Round in a circle, back and forth, in and out, with easy show-off steps. Homer admitted it was fun, though he was not as accomplished as Father.

When the girl took his hand, he filled with fear, but in a few minutes, he was more relaxed. It was hard for Homer to accept the notion that someone wanted to dance with him.

It was too good to be missed, but there were too many scenes in a whirl of activity of what I called *The First Dance*. I wasted no time winding the motor to focus on Homer and the girl, capturing the mood of the developing emotion, resulting in a montage of expressions.

All the tension that had been building in Homer's life lifted at that moment. He forgot he wore a brace, or how self-conscious he had been, even how nervous he was about speaking at the Academy. The girl smiled not at him, but to him, and he was enchanted as she turned gracefully, following the music. He pretended not to look directly at her, and he could find no shuffling excuse to step away from her. Most of all, more than anything else, he liked the lovely smile below her clear ocean blue eyes. When the band paused for a break, Father reminded them that he and Homer had to get back to the station: it was past the hour and the boat was due. Father needed to drop Homer off and return to La Vieille Maison. Nick and Bobbo could be out of control.

Thanking Louise, waving goodbye, Homer and Father departed for the docks, with the pretty girl skipping behind.

"You sure are a good dancer. What's your name?"

"Why, thank you," Father replied.

"I mean the young man with you."

"Oh." Father introduced them. "This is Homer Sincere."

"I'm Daisy," she responded openly, extending her hand to Homer. "I love the zydeco."

Daisy! She gazed at him. Homer thought that if he could dance on a floor in a brace, surely he would be fine at the competition.

Following along, Daisy asked, "Are you going on the steamboat?"

Homer announced with some pride, "I've been accepted to take part in a speaking contest."

"Wow, that's really great. I hope you win. No one from here has ever won."

Father frowned, assuming she referred to his former contestant, Nick.

"Are you going too?" she asked Father.

"No, Homer is a good man, an independent man." He nodded. "He can handle this responsibility by himself."

Homer raised his eyebrows in astonishment.

"I wish I could go. I live a few stops down the river in Le Place."

Is there really such a place as Le Place? Homer wondered. Yes, hadn't he gone to the movies there?

"It's right next to Convent. And a nice place to live."

Homer was comforted to know that she lived nearby.

"I hope you don't mind me walking with you for a while?"

"Sure. This is Father Rivage."

The boy is very polite, well mannered. I've taught him well, Father thought to himself, pleased to have been introduced.

"You can really dance, Father. Where did you learn those steps?"

Father gathered himself to his full height to express his dignity. "Just a pastime."

When they reached the station house, Mr. Duval called to Daisy, "Hi, Sugar."

Daisy! A perfect name, Homer thought. And "Sugar."

"Hi, Mr. Duval," Daisy said sprightly.

"The *Louisiana* hasn't arrived yet," Mr. Duval shouted to Father. "Won't be long. You have my word, Father. They'll be heading up to Baton Rouge in no time, and I'll make sure they have first class accommodations. Don't worry, I'll look after them."

Father left Homer with a hug. "I'll be praying for you, son. Do your best."

It was anybody's guess if Father stopped to dance a final round at Louise's. I don't think he could have resisted one last dance.

Daisy lingered on for a few minutes.

"I'll be thinking about you." Then she kissed Homer.

He looked down, not knowing what to say.

"Hope to see you again. I've got to be getting home." She was gone.

Daisy! Homer had never been kissed by a girl and was swept away. He needed a word. But what word? What exquisite word could he assign to the girl he did not really know. Nice? Pretty? Pleasing? Magical, yes, magical, that was it. Wow, he couldn't believe that he had met someone as nice. Maybe he could have a girlfriend some day, he thought. One thing was sure: he had no intention of introducing Daisy to me, under any circumstance.

THE UNUSUAL VOYAGE OF THE DAVE-CAN-DO.

After catching the amazing footage of the dance and the emotions between Homer and Daisy, and having successfully remained out of sight, I rounded the corner out of breath.

"Rig, you made it!"

"Nothing would have stopped me. Where is the *Louisiana*? Has it come yet?"

Before he could explain, a telephone rang in Mr. Duval's office.

"Yes, okay. I have two boys here waiting to get up to Rouge."

We heard singing, a choir of voices floating over the water that seemed nearby. It was an opportunity to create a visual treasure.

"Come on, Home, we gotta get this!" We set up for the shot.

"You hear those voices, Mr. Duval?" I called over my shoulder. The stationmaster was on the dock, wondering where the singing was coming from.

"Sounds nice."

Into the camera's view, a boat turned into the bend on the river, and a choir broke into:

*"We're marching to Glory
With Freedom on our side,
Marching to gloooorrrrreee
With Jesus to abide."*

"Must be the *Louisiana*?" Homer said, slating the shot.

"I don't think so," Mr. Duval replied. A tugboat, sounding a deep-throated horn, was pulling a long flat platform, a barge, and on it was the entire congregation from Daddy Grace's House of Prayer for All People.

"Holy criminy," Homer exclaimed. "It's Daddy Grace!"

A fire flickered from an oilcan, centering a shining light on Daddy Grace who sat like a sultan on a golden throne. Two black ladies in white gowns fanned him with large green palms, creating mysterious shadows that reflected off the water.

I panned a banner on the side of the barge that read, "Floating to Freedom!"

The wall phone rang again, and Mr. Duval hurried inside to receive an update. Nine o'clock chimed on the round black clock over the arched door of the station.

Several black people who had been waiting in the colored waiting room rushed out into the commotion, shouting and smiling widely.

"Where ya'll goin'?" they yelled.

"We're floatin' to freedom," sounded a hundred voices. "We're on our way up to the legislature. Daddy is going to speak for all of us."

"What about?"

"Brothers and sisters are protesting the votin' test so we can vote!"

"Hallelujah! Can we go too?"

Caught by the enthusiasm, Homer yelled, "We'd like to go, too."

"Come on board!"

The barge took on another few passengers for freedom.

"Sweet Daddy, praise be! Good to see you, Daddy." We folded into a big family reunion.

Mr. Duval shouted to us from the station's office.

"The *Louisiana* will be steaming in here in a couple of hours."

A voice replied from the barge, "That boat is not coming—we traveled past it a few hours ago down at Le Place!"

The whole scene had more visual contrast than I could ever imagine, and Homer was equally thrilled as the drama played out until I broke the sequence with "Cut!"

"We'd never make it on time, Mr. Duval. We've got to go," I shouted.

Mr. Duval considered for a moment, then stepped into the small tugboat to speak to Captain Dave, a man we would come to know and film. The name on the back of his boat, written in a fancy script, was *Dave-Can-Do*.

"Dave, can you take on these passengers?"

"What the hell, I'm pulling a ton of niggers in the back of this boat, a few more don't count," he smirked, as he navigated the tug as it reversed in the thrashing water off the stern into a docking position.

We winced, hating the word "nigger."

"I'm talking about white boys, Dave. Can they ride inside with you?"

"I'd rather be with my friends, Mr. Duval," Homer suggested. "I'll be very comfortable."

Suddenly, the crowd became silent and parted the way for Daddy Grace to come dockside.

"We'll look after the boys, Mr. Duval," the voice spoke in a quiet reverential tone directed at Homer. "I remember—that's Waldo's boy."

"Waldo's boy," resonated through the crowd. "Waldo, he passed on, you know," the group whispered to each other.

"Hi, Reverend Grace," Homer exclaimed, pleased to be remembered. "It is nice to see you—close your eyes and visualize!" The congregation whooped and cheered as Homer led the way to board the barge, and I followed unnoticed, letting the camera run, making sure Mr. Duval or Captain Dave didn't see me filming.

"Come on board, son, we've chartered this boat. We're paying our way, and I do believe we can take on anybody we please, that is, if it is all right with Mr. Duval."

"That true, Dave?" Mr. Duval questioned.

"Oh, yes, *they* paid, yes, they sure did, and when the money is right, Dave can do and is good to go."

"What time will you make Rouge?"

"In twelve hours or so, the river's high, water's calm."

"Here are the tickets you can cash in later," Mr. Duval gave Dave two passage accommodations endorsed from the *Louisiana* to the *Dave-Can-Do.*

Checking my watch, I knew twelve hours would be nine o'clock in the morning. We could make it to Front Street with just enough time.

"Come aboard," Daddy said, extending his hand, and in a second we were standing on the barge. *Dave-Can-Do* chugged from the pier, moving into the lapping, rushing water, pulling the freedom barge. The congregation sang again "Marching to Glory . . ."

"Homer," I confided, "We'll get there all right. I think you might call it another divine intervention, and we have a stunning prelude to our film on civil rights. Can you believe it?" I was more interested in film at this moment, but Homer was more concerned with his speech and getting up to the Academy on time, true to his objective.

We weren't traveling on the stately *Louisiana*, but we were on our way to Baton Rouge, feeling protected in familiar territory with Waldo's congregation. We weren't on a grand steamboat or rafting *down* the Mississippi with Huck Finn and Jim. No, we were steaming *up* the Mississippi with Daddy Grace, a speech, and a Filmo.

"Why you boys going to Baton Rouge?"

Homer explained to Daddy Grace that he had been selected to compete in the elocution contest.

He sized Homer up. "You scared? I mean, are you kind of nervous?" The Reverend was curious.

"I'm nervous, but I have my good friend Rigby for support and . . ."

"So you going to be competing," Daddy Grace said, intervening into Homer's thoughts. "No one has ever made it from Jefferson Parish, certainly no one of my color."

"Why is that, Reverend Grace?"

"You can call me Daddy."

"Thank you, Daddy."

"Most folks don't have the education. Poorly paid, poorly educated, all we have is a lot of family."

Homer had a family—maybe he didn't have a Dad, but he had Father Rivage and me as a pair of familial bookends.

"Are you going to speak to the legislature?" Homer asked.

"Gonna try. I got a permit. Black folks need permission, you see. We're going to be joining with lots of people who need to be heard. And I'm speaking for them. I suspect there's going to be a whole lot of polarized pushing and shoving. Some for, some against, and I hope to be very persuasive."

"What are you talking about?"

"The votin' test . . . our right to vote."

"What's the voting test?"

"Oh, it's a trick to keep us from voting. Every time there is an election for a senator or president, or even a mayor, if you are black, well, you don't stand a chance to be counted. Ever since the poll tax was repealed, all sorts of local segregationists have required a test about the Constitution, with questions even white folk can't answer. They grade, pick, and choose, and you can be sure that none of us gets an A plus. Makes it impossible to register—costs a whole lot to even take the test. And if you can't take the test, you can't register, and if you can't register, you can't vote, and if you can't vote, you can't have an equal voice. Equal, like the Constitution says."

"We've got something in common," Homer said. "I'll be talking about civil rights. You speaking at the legislature and me speaking at the competition." They looked at each other and shook hands; they were constitutionally alike.

"So, this boy is really saying somethin' in the competition!" Daddy let the thought settle in.

Homer sat next to Daddy Grace by the dim fire, keeping warm. I was going to try to get some sleep while the night air over the water had turned chilly. Some of the passengers spoke quietly in small groups. Daddy Grace began talking about the slave trade and slave ships and it aroused my curiosity. It was likely that if this brief account had been given at school, I had not paid any serious attention. Daddy told of the *Queensland*, the *Blackbird*, the *Benito Cereno*, schooners and brigantines sailing from Africa to the West Indies and Cuba, carrying a cargo weighed with misfortune. I was trying to get some sleep but instead listened to his tale of slave merchants who for three hundred years had sat in the fine counting houses of London and Lisbon.

Not much currency for the human spirit when I heard about human hardship—hard to endure and a generation lost somewhere without hope. I heard about fathers taken from sons, mothers taken from daughters, beatings and lynchings, about Nat Turner and Jim Crow, about sharecroppers and poor people. Homer absorbed every word, learning a lesson Father had never taught. Daddy Grace continued, speaking about legislatures who proclaimed laws that were separate and hardly equal on the great scale of history. He was on this ship, floating to freedom. I had never realized what it was to be spit on, denied, called *boy* or *nigger*, work from morning to dusk, and even refused at the Rialto to see a movie. I didn't know that in the whole state of Louisiana, less than six hundred blacks were eligible to vote, but they were fixing to do something about it. It all ran through my mind like an epic film. It was a remarkable coincidence that Homer had chosen civil rights as his subject for the Academy.

Some members of the congregation slept alongside each other in blankets, some dozed on benches, and others on the side of the long boat watched the dark water slide by. In the tugboat up front, Captain Dave listened to a muted Hank Williams song on a country radio station.

"Is it all true, Reverend Grace?" Homer needed confirmation.

"It's all true. You tired?"

"Not very much."

"How you think you'll do?" Daddy asked.

"I don't know, but I've spent a lot of time rehearsing and hope to get through without shaking and my knees knocking. I wish I could talk like you, address a lot of people like you do in your congregation, Daddy."

Then Homer asked the inevitable, "Do you think you could help me a little?"

I was astonished. I hadn't helped much, because I didn't have the experience, except for visualizing. Now, Homer asked for a real coach, the kind of godly intervention we needed. Out came the Filmo to record the background for Homer's starring role.

"Well, I do know a little something about talking," the Reverend Daddy Grace confirmed.

"Where did you learn so much?"

"At Bible college in Savannah where they gave a lot of attention to scripture, and even more when it came to preaching."

"Did you read a lot? Ever read *Don Quixote*?"

"I see somebody has been teaching you pretty good. Yes, I took my major in literature, before I went to study the Bible. I was one of the only students at Grambling who wasn't an athlete. We had a great football team, long on yardage but short on the smart stuff. Yep, I've always liked to read."

The Freedom Barge passed another marker as it traveled, leaving waves of undulating ripples of water behind. Here and there, the river opened and narrowed around long, winding river bends, and occasionally, a puff of smoke was discharged from a throaty motor.

"I'm reading the great books. You ever read them?"

"I have," Daddy replied.

"But they don't teach you how to talk to a lot of people," Homer said. "I don't know why I'm telling you all of this. It is usually hard for me to talk to *one* person, and I've never faced a hundred."

"Well my boy, you've come to the right place—that is if you want to win the day."

"I want to win."

Daddy offered, "It's not always so much what you say, but it's how you say it."

I was about to observe secrets from the master himself. This was authentic. I asked Daddy whether he would mind if I filmed quietly in the background. I told him that I didn't want to intrude, but I thought what he had to say would be helpful and important and that I had been assigned by Father Rivage to record a visual history. Reloading the camera with high-speed sensitive film to compensate for the late evening, I asked Daddy if he would move a little closer to the fire so I could capture better light. Daddy was gracious. "Okay, young man." Homer was preoccupied with his speech and, aware that film was just a natural extension of me, accepted it easily. I stayed far enough away so as not to intrude, shooting just a long shot, then sneaking up for close-ups when I could.

"What I have to say, I think it's pretty important," Homer confided. "And I've got to find a way to say it very well."

"I understand. I've been practicing myself. And I know a little something about talkin'. You've got to inspire, like Waldo would say, 'Inspire and light the fire!'"

I laughed under my breath.

"I do believe that." Daddy was serious. "If you light the fire, folks can feel what you mean to say."

"Tell me more."

"Mind if I look at your speech?"

Homer carefully took the white pages from his bag and gave them to Daddy.

"Write it yourself?"

"With some help from Father Rivage."

"Oh, yes. Uh huh." The man from the pulpit took his time reading. "Now let me hear it."

Homer collected himself and, after a minute, began.

"The Mississippi . . ."

"I think you might change that a little and start by saying, 'The *great* Mississippi . . .'" The Reverend looked down again, making notes, then interrupted, "You might add, 'bends and turns.'"

"I didn't write that, Daddy. I've got to be honest."

"Just a little improvement won't hurt. I call them points of illumination. You want to get their attention right away. Start again."

"OK. The great Mississippi bends and turns . . ."

"Softly at first," the Reverend suggested. "I'll tell you a secret: let
the audience bend in a little to hear you, then talk up a bit louder,
build a cadence."

"A cadence?" Homer asked.

"Rhythm!"

"That's what Father Rivage says. Feel the words."

"Father Rivage is right, he is on top tonight!"

Homer continued, the Reverend Grace interrupting, suggesting a
word, and offering a point, *the illuminating points of light.*

"Feel it, Homer, stand steady, look eye-to-eye, don't be looking
down or to the back of the house, look at everybody in front of you,
talk to each and every one of them."

Homer was finding his stride.

"We . . . areathousandseparatefeelings," Homer rushed.

"Easy, listen, what do you hear right now?" asked the good
Reverend.

"What do you mean?" replied Homer.

"You hear the river?"

"Yes."

"Then feel the river, let the words flow with you . . . Let the words
flow and take your time. That's important." Homer looked to the
river, and occasionally saw large spreads of grass leaving their plantations to meet the river's edge.

"Yes, sir." Homer paused, accepting words of encouragement
from his new mentor.

"Folks talk a hundred miles an hour when they get nervous. You
should talk in a slow kind of way. Like with a fishing pole, cast out a
line, wait a bit, hook 'em and reel them in."

"We are . . ." Homer continued, ". . . a thousand separate feelings
that fill in time."

"Better. Now try, 'the day's small history,'" urged Daddy Grace.

"That fills the day's small history," replied Homer with more confidence.

"A store of things."

"A store of things what words were said."

Daddy admired his courage. "That's it, stand steady."

"We grow older," Homer continued.

"We wake to see ourselves a season older."

"We wake to see ourselves a season older, wanting to," Homer faltered.

"Say 'sifting through the hue and cry'."

"I not sure what that means, Daddy."

"Means understanding."

"Sifting through the hue and cry, trying to understand . . . and balancing the best we can, what matters most."

Daddy's eyes lit up. "I like that. You can talk, boy."

"Do you think I can do it?"

"I believe you can!"

Homer was fired up. Inspire and light the fire!

"And Homer, don't forget to visualize, just for a few moments, before you go out on that stage." The preacher finished with a few words. "By honoring humanity, we honor ourselves."

Daddy continued polishing here and there while Homer looked up new words in his pocket dictionary. Some of them were bigger than he had ever seen, but if he understood them, he would be authentic. He read his speech over and over, occasionally asking the reverend to explain a thought.

"May I use some of your words, Reverend?"

"Make them your own. I do it all the time."

Homer's focus was on the words, committing as many as he could to memory, then afterward he fell asleep with his arms folded across his chest. Daddy Grace found some blankets among bags and bales stacked in the front of the barge and covered him. The newly minted orator looked comfortable lying on a bed of clean, fresh-picked cotton.

The Reverend worked on the speech alone in the night air, mumbling a few phrases under his breath, testing a thought. I watched him add a few more sentences and return the draft to Homer's small bag. Off the riverbanks, moss fell from trees overhead like passing curtains.

Having heard a little of Louisiana's history from Daddy, Homer had had a terrific lesson, a one-to-one tutorial. Father Rivage taught knowledge; Daddy Grace put knowledge into action; Father was a teacher and artist; Daddy was a poet and preacher. I couldn't wait to develop my hot footage, a knock-'em-out scene, from Daddy's lips to Homer's ears. For the next few hours, there would be just the hum of the engines and the sound of the river flowing around the boat. I put the camera away. I loved being on water and drifted to sleep rocked by the gentle motion of the river.

At five o'clock, I woke to a heated discussion. The tugboat had come to a stop at the ferry junction in Iberville Parish, the forty-five-mile marker. Reverend Grace was talking with a burly police officer whose boat and crew had pulled alongside the *Dave-Can-Do*. The congregation was compressed into the end of the barge listening to the conversation.

I quickly got the Filmo out again.

"You can't proceed. I have orders to have you stopped. This trip is illegal!" The officer had a white badge nameplate that read: Bull Parker.

"I don't understand," Reverend Grace replied with concern. "I filled out all the papers. I have a permit from the River Authority."

"Sorry, Reverend, I am not authorized to let you travel on. You ain't going no further. Release the ropes, Dave."

"But we paid and hired your barge, and I need to be at the legislature."

Word had traveled up the river fast.

"These neeeegra folks got any lifeboats, Dave?" Bull Parker inquired with a dose of contempt.

"No, sir," Dave answered, trying to hide his satisfaction. "I only have two life jackets, no life rafts on this barge."

"Now you should know better, Dave. You breaking the law."

"I'm sorry. I just better head back to New Orleans. I don't want to be on the river doing anything illegal," Dave uttered sarcastically, winking at Bull.

"What do we need lifeboats for?" an old man from Daddy's congregation asked.

"In case you collide with something."

"The only thing we are colliding with is the law."

"It won't do to have a bunch of *coloreds* drowning in my river, you understand?"

"What do you mean, your river?"

"Shut up, mister." The officer was irritated. "Any more guff and I'll run you in." Bull's crew nodded in agreement.

The frustrated reverend said calmly, "We have to learn from our mistakes. We will prevail."

"Sorry, Reverend," Bull Parker said, his voice coupled with insincerity.

"We'll walk," Daddy said.

A file of people began to disembark, and we were about to join them.

We were forty miles away. Could we arrive at the Academy on time?

Captain Dave finished securing the ropes that connected the barge to the stubby posts beside the dock.

The Reverend knew the incident was bogus, an obstruction to keep him from reaching Baton Rouge. Yes, they would walk the rest of the way. Daddy would march with his people.

"I'll be turning back to New Orleans. Sorry I can't take you folks, no life rafts. Now that's a shame," Captain Dave said over the throaty-sounding engines of the tug.

"Not so fast, Captain," Daddy walked closer. "I believe we chartered your boat to Baton Rouge."

"But you ain't going."

"But the boys are. I think you have tickets for passage from Mr. Duval, head of the River Authority. You got two life jackets, you got gas, you got a river, and I am sure the *Dave-Can-Do* can do!"

Officer Bull Parker reluctantly agreed. "You better take him on up there, Dave."

"The boy has business upriver," the Reverend continued in an easy tone. "We both know, Captain, we know what the right thing is to do. Better get goin', son."

Homer was reluctant to leave the group.

"Son, there's no argument; legislatures come and go. Don't let this opportunity at the Academy pass you by. You be attending to your business and remember the points of illumination. Make each one count."

"But what are you going to do?"

"Don't you be worrying about me. I've got the Lord leading the way. Now you get going."

Emotion washed over us, and reason was clouded in this moment though we knew it was the only thing to do.

"But Daddy!"

"On your way now!"

As Daddy left, there was vast sorrow. Then, spreading his arms to heaven, he lifted his beautiful face toward the dusk and spoke to his congregation, "Be not afraid . . . we are but flowers in the field."

We boarded the small vessel and Captain Dave throttled the boat into full gear, speeding up the Mississippi.

The scenery receded as the boat was propelled forward. It was hard for us to look back passing another marker, but we did, as a slow dissolve with the crowd waving Godspeed and wishing us good luck. Homer and I had grown up, like Mark Twain, on a river that affected so many lives. No American river had carried so much racial history.

Homer was silent and didn't have much to say to Captain Dave for the rest of the trip. I hated the racist son of a bitch as much as I disliked Bull Parker. I filmed the passing landscape, a few skiffs, cabins on the river, fishing boats, and weeping willow trees.

I said to the captain, "What you did wasn't right."

"Those niggers wouldn't make a difference to the legislature."

"You know that for sure?"

"Doesn't matter."

"It does matter, Captain, it matters."

"We better not be talking about this." Captain Dave turned to his country station on the radio; Hank Williams was singing "Your Cheating Heart."

When Dave flicked the radio off, the only sounds we heard past the fifty-five and sixty-five mile markers were the chugging boat and the swoosh of the morning wind. We would reach the battery in Baton Rouge in an hour.

Opening his small bag, Homer politely asked to be excused to wash up in the head just off the galley. Father had prepared a bag with fruit and a baloney sandwich with mayonnaise. He removed the contents and offered half to Captain Dave, a gesture he did not want to make, but he evidently felt better doing so. Why, I don't know. I wouldn't have done it, for sure.

"No thanks, but I wouldn't mind half of that Hershey bar you got."

Homer gave him the bar and went to freshen up and I joined him, not wanting to be left alone in the stinking company of Captain Dave. When we returned, he had chomped down the whole sandwich.

"Changed my mind. Sure is tasty." Dave had devoured everything. "Shouldn't eat before speaking." He grinned with a mouthful of food.

Homer didn't reply but checked for the folded paper with the speech that was in his coat pocket, ensuring it was still there. He kept his hand over it until we got to Baton Rouge.

There was a lot of activity on the docks when the *Dave-Can-Do* arrived. Under the working arms of giant cranes, boxes and cartons were being unloaded from a dozen freighters on the crowded piers. A longshoreman pointed the way to Front Street. It was ten thirty;

we were late. Homer had forgotten his bag in the cabin, and I retrieved it fast.

"You'll see the square next to Jackson Park down on the right of the river," the longshoreman shouted, shading his eyes from the sun. "Two blocks past on 400 Front Street. It's a white building with a big porch out in front."

I knew every turn in the Quarter, every short cut where I could save time. In Baton Rouge, the only route was straight down Front Street for at least two miles. Ten forty-five. The clock was ticking.

I found a bicycle nearby and borrowed it. If I had known who the owner was, I would have bought it right then. I left a note and a few bucks.

"Hop on, Home!"

Negotiating around people and places, street cars and carriages, I skipped around fire hydrants, ran through stop signs, past the fire station and over a bridge, until we came to the massive oak doors of the Academy. Taking a moment to clean up, check his tie, and comb his hair, Homer closed his eyes and took a deep breath.

"Thanks, Rig. Wouldn't have made it without you!"

We opened the door and walked down the long hall where a receptionist waited. We had made it!

The hall was almost empty. Upstairs, a wooden balustrade squared the double-height room. In preparation of the big event, I took my camera out of its case. Already I was scouting exactly where I could shoot. The competition had started. Neatly dressed contestants came and went quietly. In the background, I heard the muffled tones of a speech.

The receptionist spoke in a whisper, "May I help you?"

"I'm Homer, Homer Sincere from Jefferson Parish," he whispered back.

"I'm Rigby Canfield, I'm his friend," I piped up.

"May I have your registration please?"

"Yes ma'am, just here. Father Rivage told me to give this to you." Unbuttoning the bag, Homer unzipped the compartment and discovered that the registration papers were missing. Frantically, he looked everywhere and came up empty, turning his bag inside out as his belongings spilled across the floor, scattering a few pennies. An orange rolled across the room, pencils bounced, and papers slid. I was on my hands and knees when the lady spoke to us with a dose of contempt.

"Mr. Sincere, please, I must have some identification."

"Yes, of course," I said to the erect woman with cold clay lips.

I thought, We're not going to make it. Then I figured that Captain Dave had taken his registration, and probably the money Father Rivage had given to Homer, even the ticket for his return passage home.

"I'm sorry, we can't make an exception," the receptionist said as she arranged files in a stack. "You were scheduled to speak at ten o'clock, Mr. Sincere, and we are always prompt to meet the guideline regulations of the Academy. What if everybody were late? I'm afraid there is nothing I can do. If you read the rules, you will find that they are very clear."

I countered, "Ma'am, this is important, we couldn't help it, the boat was late and we took a barge and then . . . is there anyone . . . ?"

"Mr. Canfield, I am sorry."

"Could we at least listen to the other contestants?" Any plan to get upstairs.

"Your friend has no identification."

"Damn it, lady, he's Homer Sincere!"

"Security!"

A guard came over and escorted us out.

Frustrated, defeated, and dejected, we sat alone on the cold limestone steps in front of the building. Homer felt he had let Father down, his school, and himself. Exhausted, he put his head in his hands, trying to bury his disappointment.

I wondered how Billy Sunshine would handle the situation, and I turned to Homer and said in a drawl, "Son, I don't like prim, I don't like prissy, and at a time like this, we gotta ride on."

THE GREAT STATE OF LOUISIANA

Walking toward LaFollette Square, we heard shouts and chants. The legislature must already be in session, I realized.

The noise from the square got louder. Then a motorcade of twenty state troopers on motorcycles, followed by a speeding black Cadillac, raced down the magnolia-lined street.

Son of a gun, it was Governor Earl Long.

"This could be pretty exciting. Let's go, Homer!"

We moved as fast as we could, Homer stumbling a few times, hurrying to the capitol and to the hundreds of black protesters holding large posters on wooden poles.

"Freedom Now!"

"Pass the Voter's Rights Bill!"

"Equality for All!"

Through the crowd, I saw Governor Long in a white linen suit, wearing a Panama hat. A security line stopped me before we could reach him. Rushing him from his car, a company of bodyguards and secret service agents escorted the governor of the Great State of Louisiana into the legislature. The governor had visited my house on many occasions, but I was blocked from getting near him. Rows of state troopers armed with 12 mm shotguns stood in front of the white marble building.

The crowd chanted, "Freedom. Freedom. Freedom."

A group of hooded Klansmen yelled, "Nigger. Nigger. Nigger."

I could hardly believe what we were hearing or seeing. I started to film. An imposing hulk of a man shouted orders. He had albino skin, a shaved head, and green cat eyes.

The man commanded by megaphone: "You people be on your way. You cannot be coming into the legislature without an official permit. I repeat, you must have a permit. You do not have a permit. You have no right to be here. Go back, go home!

Homer turned to me. "Maybe we should get out of here."

"You are denying us our rights," a few protesters yelled.

"MOVE ON, this is an unlawful gathering."

Men from the Ku Klux Klan yelled, "Rights for the Whites. Rights for the Whites."

"Nigger, Nigger, Nigger!"

"This is bad," Homer yelled to me.

In the confusion, Homer asked several people if they had seen the Reverend.

"We are waiting for him; something must have happened on his way."

Homer recognized one of the passengers who had been in the waiting room at the river and had taken a bus. "Is Daddy coming?"

"I don't think he will make it here on time. I got the last seat on the Greyhound and offered it to Daddy, but he wanted to march with his people."

"BREAK IT UP," the officer with the megaphone yelled. A platoon of mounted policemen with batons charged into the crowd on horses, clobbering everyone in sight. Heavy sticks crashed down on innocent people.

A man next to us fell to the ground, helpless and silenced, his head smashed and blood gushing past his tears. Homer took his handkerchief and helped him to his feet. A woman tore her dress to bandage the man's wound. Screams of outrage shot out from different parts of the crowd like steam from erupting geysers. The protesters were cut with whips, their arms and legs bleeding from blows that slashed shirts and trousers as if through paper. The hard sticks left purple and black bruises—not an unfamiliar sight to Homer. The crowd pushed us toward the shouting Klansmen in white sheets, and one of them lashed out with a rope, just missing us. It was mayhem.

A burly trooper came after Homer. "You little prick!" he snarled. "I'll get you." As some people from the congregation folded in to hide him, another trooper lashed out with a vengeance. "You little bastard!" he snarled, and then smashed my camera with his stick.

The Filmo broke open. The shattered lens and film spilled out.

The son of a bitch! Before he could hit me, I dashed away.

I ran to find Homer. "Follow me," I shouted. "We gotta get out of here." We escaped into the crowd.

The officer spied us. "Get those meddling white boys! They don't belong here."

A fireman shot an explosion of water into the crowd, hosing it with powerful bursts. We ducked and turned into a doorway on the side of the building. A guard admitted us without questions. We were the "right" color.

Outside, the screams continued, but in a few minutes, the crowd had calmed. It was almost quiet.

"They are crazy, Rigby. Jesus, it was bad out there! Where's your camera?"

Homer could not imagine my disappointment at that moment. But I held on, not giving up, feeling better knowing I had preserved a few rolls of film from the *Louisiana* in my pocket, even if I had not gotten footage of the riot. There would be more, I figured.

"I know what we gotta do."

"What's that?" Homer asked, catching his breath, drying off on a bench in the rotunda.

"Daddy didn't make it. He won't be able to speak to the legislature. Every voice has got to be heard. You have your speech. Just go inside and wait your turn, Homer. It's a public hearing."

"I don't have a permit."

"Get one, white boy." It sounded sarcastic, but it carried a message. "We didn't come all this way just to be stopped by lack of a permit."

"Rigby, are you crazy? The legislature? I can't do it."

"Look at me. You've got a speech about civil rights right in your pocket. Do it for Waldo."

Waldo! Homer pulled it out and read it as he had done many times. He had it down pat and noticed that Daddy Grace had even punched it up.

"Didn't Reverend Grace tell you to go with the flow, boy? Do it for your friends. Get going! Every voice has gotta be heard, and you, my man, are a Soldier of the Word!"

"You coming with me?"

"Nope, I'll be in the great hall, and even if I don't have a camera, I'll be waiting to hear what you have to say. I'm rooting for you! You just go down and find the Speaker of the House and get yourself a permit."

Now was the time. Homer was on his own, and I prayed, even though I had never been that religious: "Please God, give him confidence."

Homer walked down the wide hall, along a long arched corridor hung with paintings of the history of Louisiana, too upset to notice the details. Looking for the office of the Speaker of the House, he found a large mahogany door and edged his way in.

"Is the Speaker of the House in?" Homer asked politely of a lady behind a large desk. "My name is Homer Sincere, and I'm from Jefferson Parish."

The lady was nicer than the one on Front Street. She was about fifty and wore a blue and white polka-dot dress. A pink Camellia was pinned to her blouse.

"Well, I do declare," she said.

The warmth written over her face surprised him. "You've come up here all the way from Jefferson?"

"Yes, I have, my friend and me."

"My mother lives down there. Make yourself at home. How old are you, young man?"

"Thirteen, ma'am," Homer said proudly.

"Have a seat and rest a bit, seems like you've had a long trip."

"I have."

"Wanna freshen up? There's some lemonade on the table and some brownies I baked myself. We always have them ready for the Speaker at the first session; he loves my brownies."

The brownies with a long drink of cold, sweet lemonade were perfect. "These brownies sure are good!

"Bless your little heart, have as many as you like. Put a few in your pocket for later, and for your friend. Now you freshen up, you've got plenty of time. You know, I work in a very special place, and the legislature is for the people and by the people, where our state laws are made."

"I know that, ma'am!"

"You are so polite and intelligent, of course you do."

"It's a really a great privilege to be here, talking and all with you. My friend down the hall knows the governor. Fine man."

"I think so too."

"And your name?"

"My name's Miss Helen."

"That's a pretty name, Helen. Helen of Troy had a nice name and a pretty face too!" Homer was progressing nicely. He could not only recall classic images from Father Rivage, but also something from me. I had always been pretty good at talking myself into situations, though I was much better talking my way out of them.

"Helen of Troy! No one has ever told me that before. Why, thank you."

"And thank you, Miss Helen," Homer replied, helping himself to another glass. "But I don't want to miss the legislature. I've heard much about our representatives and the governor and all in school."

The lady leaned over and quietly asked, "You got something to say? Folks come up all the time and talk to the legislature." Then Miss Helen leaned back in her chair, speaking in her normal voice, "If you don't, it's all right if you just want to observe or listen from the gallery. And I'm sure the Speaker would like to talk with you afterwards, but just now he is in session with the governor. He's such a nice man, nice man, a gentleman. You are welcome to go on into the Great Hall."

"Can I do that? I do have something to say."

"Of course you can. It's open to all folks who live in Louisiana, except those folks who are makin' all that ruckus. Happens all the time on opening day of legislature, but I think things have quieted down, don't you?"

"Yes ma'am, but don't I need a permit?"

"I have one for you, and you have my permission to go in."

Ms. Helen carefully inscribed a permit made out to Mr. Homer Sincere of Jefferson Parish and handed it to Homer.

Mustering all his remaining courage, Homer left for the Great Hall to observe the legislature of the Great State of Louisiana that was sitting in a chamber lined with mahogany paneling and richly carved crown moldings. Above the hall was a gallery and on the floor all 103 state representatives had green leather chairs and their own polished desks, housing Yea and Nay buttons, and silver inkwells.

I was already inside, looking around, but could not spot Homer.

A row of fans whirled from the white paneled ceiling. The crowd outside had dispersed, and the room inside was all order and business.

The Speaker of the House sat on an elevated platform. Hanging over him was the Great Seal of Louisiana. *Union, Justice, Confidence.* On his right, behind a low wooden enclosure, sat Governor Earl Long. I wanted to greet him as soon as I could.

A small column of people, noticeably in white, stood in a slender line behind a microphone waiting their turn to speak about issues and bills to be considered or passed before they were sent to the Senate. They had five minutes to make their case.

My enthusiasm peaked when I saw Homer take his place in line. He was lookin' good!

Like the governor, most of the legislators were dressed in traditional white linen suits and panama hats, the official uniform for Louisiana politicians. Handshaking, backslapping, congenial cronies surrounded the governor, talking closely, with an occasional secret whispered in each other's ear. An attractive, redheaded lady sat with the governor. She was Blaze Starr, the governor's friend from New Orleans and a contrast to the cheery, cherub-faced man with a small potbelly, presumably from too much barbeque. The summer was over, and there was work to do.

When Homer's turn came, he took his time. The moment was before him.

He had come a long way and had something to say, if not at the Academy, then to this gathering. He was speaking to the Great State of Louisiana!

"Mr. Speaker, governor, honored representatives."

A few members were surprised by Homer and called the Speaker's attention to him. Looking down from the podium, the Speaker slammed down his gavel.

The House became quiet.

"Mr. Speaker, governor . . ."

"State your name and parish," the Speaker called.

"Homer Sincere. I'm from Jefferson Parish. Good to see you folks."

Sympathetic laughter came from both sides of the aisle. My enthusiasm exploded. Way to go, Homer! The Speaker slammed his gavel again.

"What did he say, who did he say he was?" The governor asked the Speaker.

"Homer Sincere."

"Speak up, Mr. Sincere," said the governor.

"I'm here to speak about the Constitution."

Comments swept through the House.

"And what matters most."

"Let the boy address the legislature in proper fashion," the governor said to his friends. "I wanna hear what he has to say. He's talking Constitution and what matters." He patted his knee with a chuckle, then turned to Blaze Starr who was fanning herself with quick passes of an oval straw fan.

Holy criminy, I thought, he is going to do it! I tried to catch Homer's eye, but he didn't see me right in front of the chamber.

Homer introduced himself again, very softly.

"I'm Homer Sincere from Jefferson Parish."

The legislative body leaned forward to hear him better.

"Mr. Governor . . ."

"Yes, sir, that's me," the governor acknowledged, with an expansive wave to the legislators.

A photographer took Homer's picture as he launched into his speech. It bugged me that I didn't even have a still camera.

"There is a river that bends and washes over names like St. James and St. Charles. Evangeline and Solitude Point."

Homer paused and looked around the hushed assembly.

"Small parishes represented by big people."

Represented? One of Daddy's words. Sounded good, that . . . represented by big people.

"A gumbo of folks, Creole and Cajun, English and German, Spanish and French."

A gumbo of folks! Homer pressed ahead. The Academy was going to miss a great speech. He was doubling his efforts now, challenging the legislature to think.

"It wasn't long ago in the fields when a treaty guaranteed cotton and sugarcane to a future called Louisiana. Between dawn and twilight, there flows a river through history, people, and plantations—Point Coupee, Belle Grove, and Allendale—whose memory was built on hard times and dreams."

A stir rippled across the audience, some turning to each other. What was the boy saying? But they were listening! Homer had his speech almost memorized word for word. He was natural and comfortable, looking each representative straight in the eye, just like Daddy told him. "Let the words flow like the river."

"The Mississippi is God's river, mighty and yielding, reaching to the Rocky Mountains before reaching the music of New Orleans. We are many people, but we are one soul. We are the currents of words and promises running in America's river."

Then Homer let go!

"Mark Twain wrote about this great river, the Mississippi, and the extravagant voyage of Jim and Huck and Tom. You all know the story. They were kids, like me, with no notice of color, no care for prejudice. What happened to you when you grew up and stepped out of the playground? Have you forgotten the kids you once were? Have you forgotten that Huck and Tom are a part of you too?

There was profound silence in the Great Hall. Homer has struck a chord.

"Louisiana touches us profoundly, and nothing has more meaning than equality. In far too many ways, black people have been treated as another nation: deprived of freedom, crippled by hatred, and doors of opportunity closed to hope. Men and women of all races are born, tall or short, rewarded or cheated by the neighborhood they live in, by the school they go to, by the poverty or the richness of their surroundings. Let all know we can extend no special privilege and impose no limitations in parishes we call our own."

Daddy Grace's points of illumination were delivered with the impact of a voice well beyond Homer's young years.

"And yet, in the words of an African proverb, 'No fist is big enough to hide the sky.'"

Homer was in full stride.

"A voting rights bill is a voice to fulfill the fair expectations of every person. Beyond this community of law, I'm told the Fourteenth Amendment governs the poetry of our land, a rich land, glowing with abundant promise. Here, unlike any place yet known, this legislature has the glorious opportunity to end one huge wrong of our nation and, in so doing, lead Louisiana into the same immense discovery that gripped those who first looked toward freedom. It is a time, our time, to define who we are.

"And on this journey, can we not go to a place called courage, somewhere beyond colored waiting rooms, to a far better place called change and reconciliation, to create a long legacy? And by that I mean a legacy of Governor Earl Long!"

Homer had their attention and sent his words home.

"We are a thousand separate feelings, now a new generation, sifting through the hue and cry, trying to understand and balance our intentions and concerns as we follow our river to what matters most."

The entire legislature, dumbfounded, sat silent in the Great Hall. The governor turned to his lady beside him. "You hear that, Blaze? You hear those words? Where did that boy learn to talk like that?" The governor began clapping, then another in the assembly, then two, three representatives, until the entire hall resonated with applause.

I liked the part about a "Long legacy." The governor beckoned to the state trooper beside him. "Bring the boy over, I want to meet him."

Then Governor Long spied me in the gallery and waved to me. I went to greet him before congratulating Homer.

As the governor pointed toward Homer, a platoon of state troopers rapidly approached him. Ahead of them was the menacing trooper from outside, coming straight for Homer.

"You! Come with . . ."

In a panic, Homer moved through the standing crowd and was small enough to wriggle through a side door on the side of the chamber, looking for an escape route. I tried to follow.

He turned down Front Street, across to the riverbank, looking over his shoulder for the trooper until he saw no one following and he felt safe. He looked for me, but I had lost him in the huge political crowd mingling on the floor of the legislature.

ON A WING AND A PRAYER

"Unpredictable weather often came fast and furious over the Delta from the Gulf of Mexico. A white windsock filled with a western wind. Rolling gray clouds lost their formation in the increasing darkness. One cloud moved quickly at the leading front and would slice into rain any minute. The remaining leaves on surrounding trees rustled to each other, warning of the approaching storm."

—Homer Sincere's journal, 1950

With no money or identification, an orange and a brownie in his small blue bag, Homer ran with great difficulty past the outskirts of Baton Rouge. He limped past sharecroppers and cash crops, over railroad tracks, muddy marshes, battlefields, and graveyards. He was miles away from home but he walked on just the same, feeling like a fugitive, imagining the trooper not far behind. Following the river for hours, he reached Iberville Parish. Even with the sun boring down like fire, he kept going. He wondered what he would say to Father Rivage about missing the Academy. All of Father's trouble and time, all his hope and pride in him—gone. His life was a mess, he thought.

At the ten-mile marker heading southeast, he found a sign posted at the workers' entrance of a cotton plantation: "A dollar a day is the pay." Behind a hedge of thick green trees, he spied a cotton gin and barn, with men, women, and children unloading bales of cotton. With a dollar a day, he could earn enough money to buy some food and a ticket home.

Entering the warehouse, he saw long lines of black women grading unprocessed clusters of cotton.

He asked the foreman about the job, referring to the notice. "Sorry son, pickin' and sortin' cotton is for experts, not for tender hands."

Evening was coming on fast. Following the fields of sugarcane along the wide river, he stumbled toward a small airplane hangar, bouncing orange rays off a tin roof. A narrow clay runway, stretching a few hundred feet and bordered by cornfields, led to a rusty corrugated structure.

A sign, written in large letters on the side of the building, read:
"Flying Hap Harrison
Crop Dusting"
A white windsock, filled by a western wind, forecast a squall.

Taking shelter inside the hangar, Homer called, "Anyone here?"

Hearing no reply, he scanned the structure, pausing at lettering on a glass office door—Hap Harrigan, President. There was a toolbox between a torn sofa and an old GE refrigerator, and a banner from Key West: "Last Flight Out." His eyes came to rest on a spectacular red bi-wing de Havilland, a radial single-engine airplane with an open cockpit. The plane was as dusty as Homer at that moment. Admiring it up close, he marveled at its beauty.

There was a sponge and a bucket near the wing and, after weighing the possibilities, he had an idea. He was safe from the trooper but needed a place to sleep for the night, so he decided to wash the plane in return for his stay. The proposition seemed fair. Filling a bucket with hot soapy water from an open sink in the bathroom, he washed the plane carefully, polishing as much as he could after it was dry. When he had finished,

Hap Harrigan's plane sparkled underneath the green-shaded hangar lights. It had taken much longer than Homer had anticipated and was much harder than washing a car. Pleased with his work, his image reflected off a portion of the plane, signaling satisfaction and a job well done.

Dimming the lights, he wrapped himself into a green blanket with a 34th Airborne Division emblem and dropped onto the sofa. His orange and Miss Helen's brownie were enjoyed in glorious combination, with the sound of rain pinging against the tin roof, until he fell into a long, comfortable sleep.

"Son of a gun," Hap Harrigan exclaimed in the morning, after rolling back the large, perforated hangar door. "Wow. That's the cleanest and best lookin' plane I've ever seen!" Hap was standing by the cockpit. He was tall and fair, with blond hair highlighting easy blue eyes, dressed in jeans and a brown leather flight jacket. He carried a newspaper under his arm while sipping coffee from a Dixie Cup.

Homer woke and quickly got up.

"Excuse me, sir," he said, peering around the plane.

Hap was startled. "Who are you?"

"I'm Homer Sincere, and I washed your plane last night because I needed a place to sleep and it was raining."

"Aw, you didn't have to do that, but it was really a real nice thing to do. I love this plane."

Homer was relieved. He had made a new friend.

The pilot smiled and shook his head. "I don't know what to say, except you better clean up, too, and we'll go have some breakfast."

Duke's Diner was just a few hundred yards off a dirt road. They entered the chrome-paneled building, equipped with a long white counter and linoleum floor with a menu at the head of each plastic-covered booth. A rainbow of jukebox sounds enveloped the restaurant, a lovely wide spectrum endlessly shifting, a man singing "Take me back darlin'," a hillbilly song with gentle and genuine sorrow.

The first thing Homer saw through the moving colors, glaring at him, was a newspaper rack with his picture on the front page.

Oh God, I'm a fugitive from justice, he thought to himself. I've been found out!

Hap had the same edition under his arm. Homer concluded Hap probably always read the news while having breakfast, part of his morning ritual.

He pretended not to notice and said nothing.

Hap looked at the newspaper on the stand, then at Homer, then at the newspaper again, not believing what he was seeing and reading at the same time.

"You're Homer Sincere!"

"Yes, I am," Homer replied, unsure what to say next.

"You're famous!" Hap shouted.

The headline read: "Equal Voting Rights Bill. Homer Sincere Speaks to Legislature!"

"Read this, Duke," Hap said excitedly, showing the article to the man behind the counter and pointing to Homer. "This is Homer Sincere."

Duke, a tall black man about sixty, with uncharacteristically hazel eyes, scanned the article. "Well, somebody finally got to those bozos in the capitol. Says that the governor is going to introduce a new civil rights bill. Breakfast is on me!"

Not knowing know how to react, Homer knew one thing for sure: he was starving. Over scrambled eggs and Wonder Bread toast, Sunkist orange juice, and heaps of melted butter over hominy grits, he told Hap how Captain Dave had taken his money, identification, and even the return ticket home.

He confided about Father Rivage and La Vieille Maison, how he had missed the Academy and visited the capitol.

"Well, no worries. I've got to admire you, Homer, I really do, and I've got some dusting to do this afternoon. Convent is just fifty miles by way the crow flies, and you'll be back home in no time. I'm flying down to New Orleans anyway to pick up dusting supplies for some fields I've got to spray."

Back in the hangar and studying a flight chart, he remarked, "Don't see an airport in Convent. Gotta find a place to land . . . I can put my baby down most anywhere . . . Any roads around school?"

"There's a long road leading to where I live, and a lawn in back, where I practice archery. At least a hundred yards."

"As long as that runway?" Hap pointed to the clay strip outside. "Check it out."

"Oh, yes, much longer."

"Well, let's fly. You'll be my navigator! I'll call the school. You said the name was Father Rivage? I'll let him know we're on our way."

Homer had never flown in an airplane, much less one with an open cockpit. The thought of flying under blue skies, over white clouds, was thrilling, almost taking his breath away.

Tossing Homer a leather helmet and goggles, Hap pushed the plane onto the strip.

"Check." The engine revved up until the instruments marked 1800 rpm.

"You ready?" After thumbs up, the plane rolled down the runway and was in the air in seconds. Hap eased his left rudder to compensate for the torque generated by the rotary engine, then banked to the right as they gained altitude. Homer looked down at a checkerboard of green and brown patches and miniature houses. And the great Mississippi River, the flowing signature of the land. He asked Hap to point out Le Place where Daisy lived.

The plane soared in lazy circles; the engine sputtered as they flew over La Vieille Maison several times before landing. Down below, a string of motorcycles and state troopers were standing beside a long black Cadillac parked at the entrance. Had they followed him home?

On the runway, Nick and Bobbo were running and waving.

A PERFECT THREE POINT LANDING

Inside La Vieille Maison, Father Rivage entered the library deep in conversation with the governor and his companion Blaze Starr.

"I knew your brother Huey," Father said, "when he started out as a salesman, selling Bibles."

"You both had the good word on your side. When Huey was governor, he did a lot for the state, building roads and schools and all."

"He surely did, Governor."

"Y'all call me Uncle Earl, Father. That's what everybody calls me these days, and after all, you knew Huey."

"Thank you, Uncle Earl, a pleasure. And I think you know my young friend here, Mr. Rigby Canfield of New Orleans."

"I do, I surely do. We drove down from Rouge together. I know the family well, fine folks!

The governor made me feel more important than I was. I wished I could have taken a shot of the governor and Father Rivage right then and there. I had told the governor about the incident outside the capitol, and he said, "Hell, Rigby, that's no way for the troopers to act, and I aim to do something about it. Y'all get yourself a fine new camera, anything you want, and send the bill to Uncle Earl!"

I was grateful for this kindness. A new Filmo D-90 was coming on the market, a 16 mm by Bolex, and another made by Kodak, and I intended to consider them all.

Turning to Father, the governor said, "Things got out of hand, but all in all, a damn good session."

"How did Homer Sincere do at the Academy competition?" Father was in the spirit of things, as was the governor.

"Competition, hell. What competition? He won the whole damn legislature! You should have been there to hear some fine, mighty fine words. We got it all on a tape-recording. We tape everything, all my speeches, everything, and we got that boy a-speakin'. Rigby tells me you are doing some fine teachin' and preachin' down here. Even got some of your lectures on film! Now that's what I call a fine idea. I wanna see 'em. And your boy Homer is a fine example, sir, and a mighty fine boy. I didn't know what was goin' on down this way, 'til young Canfield told me how you are doing some great educatin'. And educatin' is something I'm for and have always been. I want particular folks to take notice."

The governor liked the word "fine" and was strongly enunciating par-ti-cu-lar. "I want to do all I can for the Great State of Louisiana. Can you design a program for the board?"

"The board?"

"Louisiana School Board. And funding, you need some funding down here I know."

Father beamed.

"That boy made a great speech, and you know the Long boys can whip up a crowd, but this was extraordinary. Really helped me get the legislature fired up."

"Wonderful, Governor, a miracle."

"Where is the boy now?"

Father pointed upwards, to the sound of the plane overhead. "I think that's him, coming in on a wing and a prayer."

"I declare, Blaze, this is an amazing place!"

The governor looked to the ceiling, then back at Father. "One thing I want to say to you. Not everybody in Louisiana has a red neck, we have good people in this state. Sure we have some troublemakers, and change is hard. Some folk don't know how it is. Hard to walk to a place you have never walked to before, takes time. But we're tryin', and we're startin', and we're doin'. I'm running for re-election, if they don't haul me off to the loony bin first. Right, Honey?" The governor turned to Blaze, sitting at his side. "I need a little help with my speeches, and I would like a little companionship. Yes, we would, and if you folks can help me with the words, I mean your boy Homer, I'd be mighty grateful for the contribution, and I know that you know what that means."

"Governor Long, we support you in every way. Homer is a Soldier of the Word!"

Landing on the long driveway, Hap Harrigan taxied to a stop, but not before the engines revved up with a burst of smoke shooting out of the exhaust. Then the noise subsided.

Nick and Bobbo danced around the plane, and the state troopers scratched their heads—they had never seen a plane land so perfectly on a driveway before. Father had come outside and was standing on the long driveway strip to meet him.

"Here's your boy," Hap said to a waiting Father Rivage. Homer gave me a big hug and then embraced Father.

"Thanks for flying him down."

"Afternoon, Governor, Miss Blaze."

Father introduced Homer to the governor, and Homer extended his hand.

"Son, I've been waiting for you. Very honored to meet you. You do me proud, and all of Louisiana. I've been talkin' to Father, and when I run for re-election, I want you with me. You got the right southern style. Yes, sir! We'll be seein' ya. Vote for Earl!"

With that pronouncement, they got into their long black limousine. The motorcycles roared their motors in unison leading down the dusty road. Then Hap Harrigan took off. Before flying south in his red plane, he circled La Vieille Maison, tipping his wings side to side, and disappeared into the sky.

"Did I do all right?" Homer asked. "I mean, I never made it to the Academy."

Father put his arm around Homer and mused, "The joy of the soul lies in the doing!"

Father mentioned that the Dr. Reverend Daddy Grace had called him, saying, "Father, the good Lord works in strange ways, and your man is an expert!"

"Do you know him?" Homer asked.

"I know many men of the cloth, but I was surprised by one little thing, Homer."

"What was that, Father?"

"I didn't know you were going to address the governor and the entire legislature of the Great State of Louisiana!"

Homer received a lot of letters. One from Daisy made him especially happy. Another, a thank-you from Daddy Grace's congregation, was signed by every member.

SOMETHING REMEMBERED

"'You will go from here as a Soldier of the Word.' Father said. 'Learn to accept that which you are not. Stay strong for what you are.'"
—Homer Sincere's journal, 1954

Homer wanted to stay forever at La Vieille Maison, the place he had grown to love, but Father decided the time had come for his next station, as he called it. Homer wondered if he was ready. But Father felt he had learned well and grown older, the perfect age to embark on his next great journey.

"You have a story to tell," Father confirmed.

Uncle Earl, who had taken a hiatus and was ready to run for re-election, invited Homer to another home, another experience, another journey. Father viewed Homer's honorable discharge as a divine lesson. Was he ready? Would he find a home of his own?

Father expressed his deepest thoughts to the boy he had grown to love. "You will go from here to live a life in which you will find yourself keeping appointments that you never made. You have important work to do, and when you have finished, you will have made a difference. It is not always the big things, Homer, but small ones, too. Some people might not even notice. What is often most important are the things that we can never see."

"The things we can't see . . ." Just what Waldo had said a long time ago. Was that the secret of the target? Or did the arrows carry the secret to the target?

On his last evening, he lay in bed searching the ceiling, and then wrote in his journal.

"It wasn't a word I was thinking about, but a sound, neither wind, nor river—it was the sound of my father's horn, off in the distance calling to me. I didn't know the name of the tune, but I could hear it clearly. It was somehow sad. My father was lost on the edge of nowhere, and it had been that way for as long as I could remember."

Homer had not only found a home, he found himself.

Early the next morning he left for New Orleans, taking the same road that led him to La Vieille Maison. It seemed like yesterday.

Father's last words to him were ones Homer kept close, ones he would always remember.

"You will go from here as a Soldier of the Word. Learn to accept that which you are not. Stay strong for what you are."

THE GREAT LOUISIANA HAYRIDE

"He was an unforgettable character. Everyone called him Uncle Earl and beneath his public persona of a plainspoken rural Louisianan with little education was an astute political mind, a master campaigner."

—Homer Sincere's journal, 1954

Homer's amazing adventures were on high alert as Governor Earl Long's campaign caravan crisscrossed the great state of Louisiana in the 1950s, a time when Strom Thurman continued marching the Dixiecrats in a segregationist parade. And a governor in Louisiana fought back, bringing a colorful new drama to American politics.

It appeared that so many white people in Louisiana were irredeemably racist. Earl Long, behind the clouds of his cigar, chomping White Owls, struggled over the moral terrain of inequality and injustice. In his own way, on his own time, he sought equal rights. Behind the façade of his old boy, hell-raising, non-conventional persona, he was a decent man. Nor was Uncle Earl a Soldier of the Word fitting Father Rivage's characterization.

"Are you a Soldier of the Word?" Homer asked, as they sped over the winding back roads of Louisiana, exhaling trails of dust from the governor's once-black limousine.

"Well, a soldier somewhat."

"Who gives you your orders?" Homer asked inquisitively, wanting to know more about the governor.

The governor looked toward the heavens. "They come from up there."

"From God? Do you have meetings?"

"Well, it's complicated. I'm not always sure, but I reckon so, if you want to call it meetings or appointments. I try to follow his command, not always exactly, but I got a map of sorts—my work is laid out, not to many dee-tours!"

The governor in Louisiana was a soldier "of sorts" who fought, bringing a vivid new drama to American politics.

They traveled past sleepy river estuaries, groves of loblolly pines, sawmills, cotton gins, all parts of the unexceptional features giving color and tone to Louisiana geography. Down dusty roads, past neat white churches built on yellow acres of newly cut grass, reaching skyward with an air of grace and tranquility, and nearby, a mule team in some sun-splashed field. The wail of country music in a backwoods roadhouse was always heard when they stopped for an ice-cold Royal Crown Cola for Homer—the governor himself was partial to Dr. Pepper. Back in the car, Homer noticed the sad, wet faces of maids and gardeners and cooks standing in the pouring rain, waiting in the late afternoon for a city bus to take them home.

In this southern landscape, a battery of household help, Secret Service, and a platoon of journalists took Homer under its wing and looked after him. As a Soldier of the Word, he was on the go and on the road, a welcome companion in the governor's motorcade. Approaching adolescence, he made friends easily with reporters, met new people, discovered new places, and got a down-home education from Uncle Earl, who had a battlefield of advice.

"Homer," Uncle Earl said, "It's my duty and responsibility to tell you: never write anything you can phone, don't phone anything you can talk, don't talk anything you can whisper, don't whisper anything you can think, don't think anything you can nod, don't nod anything you can wink—and I say this because in my business, there's a whole lot of winking going on."

In his office, Earl Long got on the phone. "You tell Mayor Chep Morrison down there that I need some dee-ducts, or he is going to feel my displeasure."

"What are dee-ducks?" Homer asked.

"Contributions from my political backers. They got a lot of money in Orleans, and I need it for the rest of the state. We gotta have equal distribution. I'm not against anybody, poor or rich, reasons of race, creed, or any ism except nuttism, skingameism, or communism."

"What's skingameism?"

"A word I made up. Sound good to you?"

VOTE FOR EARL!

Wearing a jacket and a white shirt, the governor adopted a statesmanlike conventionality. On nights when everybody below the platform was coatless, his pearl white tie exhibited a quiet pattern of Rorschach inkblots set against his white shirt and black suit, perhaps a portent of what was to come.

He was an unforgettable character. Everyone called him Uncle Earl and beneath his public persona of a plainspoken rural Louisianan with little education was an astute political mind, a master campaigner.

He ran his speeches by Homer, who in turn consulted Father Rivage, who sought advice from Daddy Grace. This triumphal trio, riding the Long merry-go-round, contributed considerably. Homer never had a better time. Whenever I could, Homer and I met up. With my new FilmoSound, I took the opportunity to film the colorful cavalcade.

Long, savvy, and a natural in the political arena, Uncle Earl adored Homer, maybe because he and Blanche Revere Long, his wife and partner in power, had no children. They offered a life that was generous and kind. Homer asked for only one promise: that Uncle Earl would get the voting rights bill passed.

His travels with Uncle Earl gave him hands-on experience in local politics and a departure from the grind at La Vieille Maison. He was part of the election show. When the governor took Homer's hand, leading him on stage, Uncle Earl graduated to parental status. I showed up in Jefferson Parish, taking the occasion to film some new episodes on the colorful campaign. Homer always made sure the governor sent a car to bring me from school. My father was immensely pleased that Homer was keeping good company, for he liked the governor.

Telling the governor that I was a film journalist he could trust, Homer assured him that I was not like those muckrakers down at the *Times Picayune*. Even though we were the same age, I was much older than my years. The governor thought we were a "hoot" together, and before I could say lickety-split, we were filming—me shooting with the Filmo and Homer slating the scenes. In some ways, Homer was much more political than I was, with a deep concern and passion for the poor and all the black folks in Louisiana. I had more of the southern sentiment, appreciating tradition and heritage. It's what I had always known. I wasn't prejudiced. I should have spoken up with a point of view, but I didn't, keeping it for my camera.

On one occasion, a group of black doctors and nurses came to see the governor, asking why there were only white nurses and doctors working at the black hospital that he had just built. Wasn't there work to be had for black nurses who were immensely qualified? "Why, that's an outrage!" The governor rushed to the facility to reprimand the administrator. "You mean to tell me you got white nurses cleaning out the bedpans of these coloreds? Never heard of such a thing in my life, doing such 'loooowly and suuuumissive' duties. Can't have whites waiting on the 'neeeegras.'" Overnight, the governor secured employment for his black constituents; it was his way of doing things and getting his way. Homer didn't particularly like the method. Still it was an indirect step—an ugly one, to be sure—toward equal opportunity.

Uncle Earl got the voting rights bill passed. Blacks could vote, oiling his political machine. No other politician had been as smart. Blacks were a large voting block and in the long run had a pretty significant say in the Great State of Louisiana.

I joined Homer in the Hotel Roosevelt before we traveled up to another parish. Homer said, "Well, Rig, I guess we are seeing some history in action these days."

We certainly were. In the governor's suite, where we sat with a bunch of his traveling cronies, there was always a good down-home barbecue spread, corn bread, and potato salad made with chopped celery, lemon mayonnaise, and sweet pickle juice. It was the best. And while we ate, every so often we heard a thud of packages hitting the floor after being thrown over the door. One of the men picked them up to deliver them to Uncle Earl. They contained wads of cash that must have been several thousand dollars in rolled up bills. The governor said to us, "Boys, that's 'transom money' from a few of my loyal contributors 'cause I can only accept contributions in an indirect sorta way!"

The "thuds" were in fact kickbacks and bribes for favors. The governor never apologized for them. And since he had done more for education, hospitals, voting rights, and schools, plus a fifty-dollar monthly check for every senior citizen in the Great State of Louisiana, no one seemed to mind. He was even known to walk into the legislature when a bill he needed passing was up for a vote, head up to the podium, and push the "yea" button at the desks of state senators before leaving a bunch of large dollar bills as he passed. "Thanks for your support. Vote for Earl!" That was the mantra. "Vote for Earl" was the Governor's salutation with every handshake. He was so refreshingly dishonest that if he was confronted about a broken campaign promise, he simply said, "Well, I lied."

"Folks, this is Homer Sincere," the governor said, taking Homer and stepping up to the red, white, and blue bunted and bannered country platform. "He's the future of this great state. For Homer, we're gonna make some changes."

Sometimes Homer was called upon to say a few supporting words, an appeal for better teachers' pay or better roads, then before Uncle Earl launched into his agenda, Homer raised his hands and said, "Folks, my

Uncle Earl is not only a good man, he's a good soldier. And if you vote for him, it is a vote for better times. He knows what folks need in our great state, and I think Uncle Earl knows the Louisiana way."

"Hallelujah!"

Homer, polishing his public speaking lessons from Daddy Grace, became an effective speaker, pretty good in front of a crowd, but off-stage he was still shy.

At Jefferson Parish rallies, Daisy was often in the audience. She wore a newly pressed petticoat, tied in the back, and wisps of long blonde hair swept past her freckled face, a freshly welcomed contrast in this crowd. She smelled like lilies in the valley, and was just as soft and pretty. When she came she'd run up to the stage saying, "Homer Sincere, you are not only a pretty good dancer, but a fine speaker. I've never known someone so famous."

Of course, Homer blushed, and they would go off to have a soda, with the governor's blessing. "You treat that boy right," the governor said with a deep drawl, calling after them. "And you get him back heah before midnight." It was only afternoon, and Homer and Daisy would return after fifteen minutes or so. What they talked about I don't know, I stayed mostly out of sight when Daisy was around, but I do know that he adored her. She was his first love, and Daisy returned his feeling.

Whenever Homer and the governor were campaigning nearby, Daisy was sure to show up, applauding from the front row. The governor made sure she voted at least four or five times; the small legality of being underage didn't seem to matter.

Homer didn't talk to me about Daisy, except for confiding that he had a girlfriend. He wasn't sure if she felt the same, but I knew she did.

With no background in psychology, Uncle Earl was an expert practitioner everywhere he went. He had never enrolled in a Bible college, yet he knew both Testaments inside and out. And when he didn't know, he would hold "The Book" in the air and make something up.

"Verily I say into you, if you plant the democratic seed, it will bring an abundant harvest to those who are faithful, to those who are righteous, so sayest the Lord."

He had no training in either economics or government administration but changed from a shoe-polish salesman and political camp follower into a sound businessman. Other governors had formal education and diverse business enterprises, but no one surpassed Uncle Earl in the politics of getting elected.

In his long Cadillac, he talked the talk and he liked the company. "Homer, they called my older brother Huey, Kingfisher. He always said, "You gotta leave some jam on the bottom shelf for the little guy." And he was quite a man, even if he didn't fish. We came from Winnfield Parish and started the great Louisiana hayride.

Our roads, our bridges, our schools, our friends and enemies are everywhere that your old Uncle Earl goes, no matter if I'm here with you or up at the mansion or down at Pea Patch."

Pea Patch was Uncle Earl's old county cabin that Homer loved. Especially the governor's cook, Miss Sadie, who looked after Homer like he was one of her own. And sometimes, the governor made sure that Miss Sadie invited Daisy over for lunch. Miss Sadie had a special talent for producing grilled cheese sandwiches. Her secret was placing two slices of American cheese on Wonder Bread, spread with fresh churned country butter, then grilling them in an iron skillet well-seasoned by years. This dish was accompanied by Campbell's tomato soup, with carefully crunched up Ritz crackers, and remained one of Homer's all-time culinary favorites.

Daisy was fast becoming an accomplished musician and took to a rinky-dink upright piano next to the porch. Homer loved to listen to her play, and sitting next to him, she taught him the "Heart and Soul" doo-wop chords—C major, A major, D minor, and G major—improvising a melody on the upper part of the keyboard, which would stay with him for the rest of his life.

The governor's mansion was the big spread that his brother Huey had built to look like the White House, so he would feel at home if he ever became president. It was where Earl's wife Blanche resided most of the time.

Down at the barbershop in the King Hotel having a shave, the

governor had the "Long Look." Earl understood redneck, tobacco-chewin', Bible-carrying Baptists and easygoing French Cajuns, often saying, "I know about voodoo and vice and sugar babies and sugar-cane. Vote for Earl!"

"Homer, here's some advice," he'd say, launching into his thought of the moment, spinning shrewd observations and sometimes stretching the homilies beyond reason. Homer always remembered them. "Son, you don't rewrite the Old Testament when you run for office. Look at Bob Maestri—the man sold mattresses to the biggest bordello, that's a whorehouse, son, where his constituents convened, and in New Orleans when he got elected mayor, his mattress sales shot up like a rocket, a loyal following, with "a bed for every vote" which says to me he is one shrewd man. I cultivated him after Huey died, because a politician's first job is to make people feel good when they see you—especially people who don't like you."

Politics was his obsession and authority.

"The kind of thing I am good at is knowing every politician in the state and remembering where he itches so I know where to scratch."

Politics may have been wasted on Homer who had no real interest in scratching, but in the custody of his Uncle Earl, his life perspective expanded from book sense to street smarts, fast becoming the youngest supporting Southern Democrat in the history of the Great State of Louisiana.

Every Parish was Uncle Earl's favorite: Evangeline, Jefferson, Assumption, Orleans, St. John's, and St. Mary's.

On their way up to Evangeline, Uncle Earl advised Homer, "Politics, like sweet corn, travels badly. It loses its flavor every hundred yards away from the patch or if you get too far away from it. Corn tastes best where it grows."

Homer collected everything the governor said, especially one speech about how Uncle Earl got out the vote. I filmed it and still have it in my personal archive.

"Evangeline Parish? One of my favorite parishes. All those

Broussard weddings I attend! Evangeline is a fine, beautiful parish.
Ancient oaks, Spanish moss, fertile fields. And you live here! Where?
Behind the courthouse? That's the best place to live and be buried! But
while you are alive, you can get in and out on Election Day, cast your
ballot, four, five, six times. Sign your name right here, son. Let your
Uncle Earl take care of the rest."

He could sell shoe polish, stove polish, car polish, cotton oil, gas
oil, and snake oil.

When a reporter called up from the crowd, "Can you manage
those legislators up in Baton Rouge?" Uncle Earl replied, "You know
the Bible says that before the end of time, billy goats, tigers, rabbits,
and house cats are all going to get together, and let me assure you
that's what makes the legislature manageable."

Homer wondered if the governor's words would ever reach
immortality. But it was the man he cared mostly about, and he wanted
the governor to ease the governmental indignities placed on African-
Americans, calling for their full participation in Louisiana elections.
Sometimes Uncle Earl was politically reluctant, but Homer kept him
to his word. "Don't let me down, Uncle Earl. You can lie all you want
to anyone else, but you got to keep your promise to me," Homer told
him. In some small way, more than talking civil rights, Uncle Earl was
making a real contribution.

Blaze Starr was traveling with the caravan more and more, and the
campaign trail slowed when the governor introduced Blaze as "the
future first lady." She was not only his "on the side" companion, but a
stripper in the Quarter. Like Father Rivage, the governor saw some
good in everybody, and Blaze had that sometime lovin' goodness. His
immoderate behavior didn't sit well with Miss Blanche up at the big
house in Baton Rouge. Not at all.

Blanche Long was aggrieved and said that Earl had a bipolar disor-
der. She managed to have her husband committed, not to Blaze, but to
a mental hospital in Mandeville. During this period, Homer spent more
time with Miss Sadie at Pea Patch. And even from the state hospital,

Uncle Earl kept in touch with Homer, making sure that he was being properly tutored and seein' to his learnin', and that his political machine was looking after him, with the staff paying extra attention to his boy.

The visiting hours were short for Earl Long. Louisiana law required him to relinquish power due to a hospital commitment but the governor, in true fashion, ordered the head of the state hospital system fired and replaced him with a pal who had him released. They were soon back on the road in the Great State of Louisiana.

He appointed "colonels" with a lavish hand and in a simple ceremony made us colonels. I'm not sure what it was good for, except getting out of traffic tickets. Homer, the Soldier of the Word, had officially joined the ranks as a freedom fighter in the governor's army.

"Homer, I love you, boy," he said, handing Homer a certificate and badge.

When his journey came to an end, Uncle Earl was elected by the biggest vote in Louisiana history—422,766 folks cast their ballots for him. He invited everybody to his inauguration in Baton Rouge. Ten thousand came, including Daisy, Homer, and even Father Rivage. Everyone drank free pop, ate hot dogs, and listened to country music; it was Louisiana heaven.

After years of "schoolin'" and after the last rally, having just turned eighteen, Homer entered Tulane. His mother had put aside a small account for his education, and the governor, always mindful of his responsibility and friendship, got a scholarship for him, which helped. It was not by chance that the governor made the university what it is today, with the funds he approved for education. Homer had an amazing journey with Uncle Earl, and learned not only about the movers and shakers in politics, but in a unique and satisfying way discovered more about life, and more about himself. It was one of those appointments he had not made, but one he kept, as fate took him on a path that would bring new and amazing adventures. Homer would miss the governor of the great state of Louisiana.

THE EMERGENCY ROOM EPISODE

"The governor says, 'Never trust anyone in Louisiana who owns a newspaper, 'cause if they own the suit, they surely have got their hand in your back pocket.'" —Homer Sincere's journal, 1955

Uncle Earl had run for the Senate and won. Outspoken and controversial, he carried the day. He was still just as generous when Homer wrote asking for his help in getting a part-time job as he worked his way through college. The now Senator Long introduced him to the editor of the *New Orleans Times Picayune*, a newspaper that was "a pickle" and a lukewarm advocate of the Long Machine, while receiving some benefits from the state. Most of the "respected" papers carrying a southern tradition were slow to meet change. Father Rivage also sent a letter about Homer's good work in the library at La Vieille Maison, reporting that his professional career included research that involved clipping articles from newspapers around the country on a host of subjects.

Uncle Earl told him to be careful. "Can't always trust those folks. Freedom of the press is only guaranteed to those who own one." Uncle Earl never owned one, nor did he ever make it to the Senate—he died three weeks after his election. The news left Homer distraught, but not the editors of the *Picayune* who seemed to rejoice and were better off by Long's passing. Homer stood in line with thousands of Louisianans in the rotunda of the capitol of the Great State of Louisiana to say goodbye to a man who had been very good to him.

Between his studies and two nights a week at the *Picayune*, Homer volunteered several hours a week at St. Exupery's Infirmary; his job was lending books to patients. Wearing a formidable white coat with a badge, he went from room to room on each floor, pushing a cart. On his rounds, he could watch medical students, interns, and residents gaping through clinical rotations. For a very short time, he toyed with the idea of becoming a doctor to find a cure for his mother's disease, but failing biochemistry three times sent a clear message. It confirmed that a career as a writer was what he wanted and was meant to pursue. Although he was interested in medicine, words were Homer's prescription.

One day, when the hospital was quiet, just a few people checking in for operations, he stood outside the operating theater. He eased his way inside and took a place with interns. Fifty students were observing Dr. William Canfield in action. He had perfected remarkable surgical techniques. Other doctors and nurses in operating room greens surrounded him, their sexes indistinguishable except for nametags. Only the glass-enclosed area in the amphitheater separated Homer and the young doctors-to-be from the procedure.

The bouncing light on the monitor receded to a steady line. Stilled by crisis, the patient's breathing had stopped. Without a moment's hesitation, my father applied the paddles to the patient's chest, the life-giving shock ran through his body and the line on the cardiogram jolted back into its rhythmic dance.

My father motioned to his resident.

"He's going to make it. Sew him up." A machine started to hum with healthy rhythms, drawing an undulating graph of hills and valleys, signaling that the crisis was over.

Homer wrote to me about watching my father and I was impressed. He asked if I had a boat yet, knowing that my dream of sailing around the world had never left me. We were still close while far apart. My father and I had grown more distant—I was taking journalism classes at Columbia, still aiming to be a photographer, and even though I could admire his profession, he had trouble accepting mine.

Homer's adventure at St. Exupery's Infirmary peaked one night. As he pushed his cart down a corridor, he passed a black man in the segregated area who was slouched on a bench, with evident chills. Homer asked the nearby admitting nurse to help, but she didn't bother to look up from her paperwork.

"We'll take a closer look later."

"Has anyone written up a history?" Homer pressed politely.

There was no response.

Finding a thermometer, he took the man's temperature, which read 105 degrees.

"Isn't anyone going to help this man?" he petitioned the nurse.

She shrugged, pursed her lips, and glared.

"Has he been examined?"

Still no understandable reply.

"Don't feel too good," the man said weakly.

"How long have you been waiting?"

"About nine hours."

Placing his own coat around the man, Homer asked, "Where does it hurt?"

"My chest, it hurts real bad." He was sweating and shivering uncontrollably. Concerned that he might get worse, Homer leaned closer to listen to his heartbeat.

"We'll get to him when we can." The nurse was indifferent. "We don't have any forms filled out. Besides, he's colored, how will he pay?" She turned away.

Black or white, Uncle Earl would have kicked ass, Homer thought to himself, finding it increasingly difficult to contain his anger.

The man was wet, dripping with perspiration. Homer inspected his tongue. His pulse was faint. He breathed with difficulty, suffering with each breath.

Homer called to the nurse, "We've got to do something."

"You have to clear that with Dr. McGuire," her words echoed down the corridor.

"Then find him!"

Homer remembered passing a room on his book lending rounds whose cabinets were filled with antibiotics and prescription drugs. He went to find them. When he entered the brightly lit office, a few residents were at a white table, reviewing charts.

They thought Homer was one of their own, recalling they had all been in the amphitheater together observing Dr. Canfield. "Can we help you?"

"Thanks." Then he pulled a "Rigby."

"Canfield sent me down for penicillin; my patient's got pneumonia." He filled out a requisition for several bottles of 500-milligram capsules of penicillin, cough syrup, and aspirin, grabbed a blanket and signed his name and time on a clipboard.

A few minutes later, he gave his patient the medicine. From his personal past experience, he knew to prescribe one capsule twice a day.

"This will help," he said, handing over the medicine. "And if you're not feeling better in a couple of days, come back and ask for me, Homer Sincere."

"Thanks, Doc," the man replied gratefully. "My name is Williams."

"Yes, Williams, drink plenty of fruit juice, stay warm, and take this blanket. Do you live in the Quarter?"

"Yes, sir."

"How did you get here?"

"I walked."

Homer gave him a few dollars and called a taxi. "You're going to be OK."

"Thank you, sir . . . and God bless you."

Ding, ding. "Calling Dr. McGuire. Dr. McGuire, call extension 27." Ding. "Dr. McGuire. Stat!"

The attending doctor on duty ran down the hall, demanding an explanation.

"I was just helping the patient," explained Homer.

"Where's his chart? Who admitted him?"

"He has not been admitted. I saw him slumped over outside the admitting office, and he was here for hours. He needed help."

"We have procedures."

"Yes, sir."

"And you just arbitrarily treated him?"

"Was I just supposed to leave him there?"

"You're not a physician."

Regulations. They held a hearing about Homer practicing medicine without a license.

"I can understand the empathy that you had for Mr. Williams," the committee's representative said, "but the patient could have died. It was a lucky diagnosis that saved his life. Going against regulations could have lost us our accreditation. You are not a doctor!"

Homer wrote a piece about intolerable treatment and injustice for the paper and submitted it to the editor, Bill Stone.

Not much had changed. There were still colored waiting rooms for folks considered second-class citizens. Not what Uncle Earl had in mind.

His article was called "The Emergency Room," and even the articles editor at the paper gave it a chilly reception. His words were summarily rejected, a wound for the Soldier of the Word.

"The paper might lose subscribers," Stone said. "We're not trying to win any prizes."

Homer tried to determine if the editor was gratuitous, bigoted, or if the writing was not up to that of a professional newspaperman. He found no support. Not enough had changed in Louisiana, and he figured that somewhere else might be more welcoming.

Sitting in the window seat of his apartment, he thought of the times when we sat on his balcony recording the world with our invisible camera.

It seemed he was now looking at a different world. It was time to march on.

Part Two

NEW YORK
1960

FAST MOVING TIMES

The earth turned several thousand more revolutions. With passing years, friendship stays as expected and constant as a passing day bringing sunrise. There were dusty brown photographs in my scrapbook, snapshots, sepia-toned pictures of Waldo and Homer—one taken the day I had gotten my new Kodak 35 with a time-release shutter, when I had set the camera on top of a brick wall, pushed the button, and ran to get into the picture. Snapshots. There were more to come, more pictures, moving pictures, film clips, more words, and another journey.

After earning my degree, I was young, fancy-free, twenty-one and making rounds of the various national magazines. A foot in any door would have made me happy, but there were no takers. I had a montage of film clips that I had shot following Uncle Earl, some good footage, a prelude to civil rights in changing times that I left off at several news organizations. I thought *Time* would be interested, but when Earl Long sued Editor-in-Chief Henry Luce for eight million dollars charging defamation of character, well, I'd call it a fade out. Still, I persisted. New York was where I wanted to be, and I kept my camera aimed at Time-Life. Making documentaries was my life's dream, but there were limited opportunities then. So I reinforced my skills by becoming a better still photographer, studying light and composition, improving my ability by taking additional courses in photojournalism at Columbia. My father was ever more convinced I was wasting my time.

Then fate, in the guise of a drunken philanthropist, appeared and tapped me on the shoulder. It was Herb Dingle, an AP photographer who had addressed one of my classes.

I was sitting at the bar at the Overseas Press Club on 41st Street, nursing a drink and a wounded ego, when Herb's great ham of a hand pounded me on the back. He grabbed me by the collar, lifting me from my barstool.

"I know you. You're one of those wise-assed Kodak stuffers I saw at Columbia, ain't ya?"

I introduced myself. "Rigby Canfield."

The front of my collar dug into my windpipe, but I managed to squeak out an affirmative.

"Good. You got a camera with you?" His breath would have been visible, unfocused, from across the room.

"Yes."

"Great." He reached into his vest, pulled out a roll of Plus X film, and tossed it at me. "I need you to shoot a roll for me. Kids at this school or something." He burped.

"Great," I caught the film and grinned. "My first AP credit."

Dingle looked at me through blood-red filters and shook his head. "Ever heard of an apprentice?"

I nodded. "Michelangelo, who created the Pietá, had apprentices."

"Yes. Good lad."

"Did Michelangelo pay his apprentices?"

Dingle reared back, and two newspapermen behind him caught him before he could do any real damage—like spill their drinks.

"We'll discuss pay when I'm a little more clear-headed, and I see the shots you take."

"Fair enough," I said, popping the film into my top pocket. "Where do I find this school, or whatever?"

Dingle handed me a crumpled piece of paper. An assignment form already filled out.

As I started out the door, Dingle called to me.

"And no close-ups!"

"But it says here these are kids, and close-ups would be more powerful—"

"They're blind, damn it. Expressions going every which way, and you can't show that. There'll be enough power packed into the captions."

I nodded. There was nothing else to say.

When I walked into the building near Columbia, I was sure I had the wrong address. Kids dancing and pirouetting, some hula-ing off in the corners, others playing instruments. It looked like a rehearsal for the Nutcracker, in a large open ballroom with graceful arched Palladian windows, which allowed streams of light to fall across the floor. And there was the head fairy, drifting like a queen through the bedlam, correcting the kids' movements with easy words. Her blonde hair was tied back with one wisp that kept falling out. She pushed it back distractedly, headed to the next creative emergency, and pushed it back again.

Whimsical and familiar, I decided.

"Someone here to see you, Daisy," cried a dancing urchin just to my left.

"May I help you?" Daisy asked, walking over.

"Is this the Special School for Performing Arts?"

"Yes."

"I was supposed to take pictures of some kids."

She gave me a funny look. "And you are? Have I met you? You look familiar."

We couldn't place each other.

"Rigby Canfield, AP photographer." I offered my hand.

She didn't take it and frowned instead, thinking, curious, and replied, "I forgot that you were coming today."

"Which days do the blind kids come here?"

Her glance was withering. "Every day."

Amazingly, I hadn't noticed their blindness. "Then why can't I shoot today?"

"I want them dressed up." Her gaze sharpened. "I want them to look their best."

I put down my camera bag containing my new Leica and began to unzip it.

"What are you doing?"

"It's hard to get good pictures when the camera's still in the bag."

"But I don't know if we're ready today."

"Excuse me, Daisy, but here's the deal: if I don't shoot this today, you're going to get stuck with a photographer who is either drunk or has a severe hangover. Believe me, I've met the man." I waved my hand toward the students. "He doesn't care about this assignment, and he's going to take shots in such a way that no one's going to know who these kids are or what you're really doing with them."

She started to walk away, and I called after her.

"Don't pretty them up. Let me show you how beautiful these kids really are." She studied me for a moment, amusement crossing her face. "I know that already." She had caught me off guard.

"You have a great smile," I said.

"This is an important assignment for you, isn't it?"

"Every assignment is."

She chewed her lip and nodded.

"I really want to tell your story."

"Are you good enough to do that?"

All my life seemed to have led up to this one question, this one moment, and I looked her squarely in the eye.

"Yes."

True to my operatic arias sung to Louisiana Ladies, I asked her out. She was reluctant at first, a bit nervous, but I think pleased that I had taken an interest in her kids as a photographer. But I was more interested in her. Daisy Philips was attentive at dinner, but beneath her emotional surface, she was cautious of me. She mentioned that she was just getting out of a relationship with an actor who would never make a commitment; deep down she had always known. He was an attractive man she had met at Herbert Bergdorf Studios on Bank Street where they took acting classes. His name was Jeffrey O'Neil. He had been offered a lot of parts but was temperamental, often getting into trouble on the set. She wanted more, a deeper relationship.

Then it came to me. She was very much the same Daisy that Homer had known back home.

Our friendship began like a photograph on a roll of slowly developing film.

WATCHING THE WORLD FROM FRONT ROW SEATS

Close-ups from that assignment were included in the portfolio I submitted to Dick Clurman at Time-Life, which often shared assignments with AP. Apparently Clurman knew Dingle's work and recognized that this definitely wasn't his. My foot-in-the-door charm was better than my film clips or any fortune cookie reading "You have interesting future." I was working soon as a contract photographer, doing what I had always wanted, taking pictures and getting paid for it.

LIFE Magazine had been spectacularly successful for more than twenty years when I went to work there. After a few special assignments, I caught the attention of Peggy Sergeant, the photo editor who was Clurman's assistant and coordinated most assignments. Given a small office on the twenty-eighth floor in the Time-Life building, I found myself in the company of photojournalists whose images are forever imprinted in history's memory: Alfred Eisenstaedt's impressionable moments, Dmitri Kessel's architecture, Philip Halsman's portraits, Gordon Park's landscapes, Larry Burrow's wars and conflicts, Carl Mydan's profiles, George Silk's nature—all masthead masters whose pictures had the capacity to move people in ways that nothing else could.

My job at Time-Life provided me with astonishing opportunities to sit next to a film star on a couch, photograph the first American astronaut, witness a liftoff from Cape Canaveral, and observe a president in the White House's Oval Office. Time-Life was charged with energy; ideas bounced around like balls in a ping-pong tournament. There was a sense of expectancy—long waits interrupted by given assignments that changed suddenly without notice.

An inventive staff shared stories with each other. Once, when Queen Elizabeth attended a tennis tournament at Wimbledon, a senior editor hired an interpreter from a school for the hearing impaired to sit across the court with binoculars to record what Her Majesty was saying. "Good shot," was the silent comment as her head turned back and forth to follow the match. With a passport to virtually anywhere, a seat in *LIFE*'s theater was front row center. The best the magazine had to offer was its people. I felt lucky to be one of them and hoped Homer would someday have the good fortune to join me in these front-row seats.

DINNER WITH DAISY

I asked Daisy out to dinner again. The photographs turned out great and gave me an excuse to see her, but when I called, she pleaded at first that she was too busy. When I pressed her, she sighed and said it was nothing personal.

"You're just not my type, Rigby Canfield."

"You need a type to be friends?"

"I'm not as smooth as you, Rigby."

"Smooth?"

"In relationships."

"I'm not sure what you mean."

"Believe it or not, I'm just an old-fashioned girl, and right now, my time is taken up with teaching kids, learning my craft, pursuing my career as an actress. And besides, I am seeing someone."

"Are you in love?"

"That's rather a personal question, don't you think?"

"No, just direct."

"Are all you guys alike, but with different faces so we can tell you apart?"

"I hope not." She was making a forthright point.

"I'm involved, not in love," she said. Daisy was studying voice and piano at Juilliard and at one time was considering opera. She knew she didn't have the training or discipline to compete at the Met, but she had a nice voice and a passion for theater and musicals. Daisy pursued her goal in that direction, and in another, worked part-time giving children her full-time attention. When she first came to New York, just in her early twenties, she had a crush on one of her professors. They had started as friends then progressed into a more serious relationship until she realized she was just his student of the moment, young and vulnerable. He had taken advantage of her trust. She had been hurt, and old patterns die hard. Daisy had dated a few men, some actors. She had hoped that one of them in particular, Jeffrey O'Neil, would want a relationship based on what she called "simply good stuff." Someone looking with her in the same direction. Right now, her direction was to be an actress. Teaching kids to play the piano helped pay the rent.

"Have you ever had a woman for a friend?" she asked, peering over a menu.

I didn't have an answer.

"Do you know how to be a friend?" she persisted.

The question didn't actually bother me as much as she seemed to want it to. To break her defense, I nodded, adding, "Don't you remember me?"

"I thought we had met. But no, I'm afraid I don't remember."

"I'm a friend of Homer Sincere. We met briefly in Jefferson Parish."

Homer was the magic word. "My God, I do remember," she said

with immediate recollection. "We were kids, it must have been ten years ago!"

"Yes, I think just about that long."

"Well, nice to meet a hometown boy. Why didn't you say so?"

"You didn't give me a chance."

"And Homer, he was adorable. My first crush!"

Then I played my next card.

East Hampton was a people and parties town, where an extraordinarily affluent society summered from Southampton to Montauk and a few hamlets in between. Originally called Maidstone, after a town in England, it still looked as if it had been broken off from New England. Its pleasing Main Street was lined with towering elms that shaded gray-shingled, sloping-roofed houses. Beautiful dunes bordered a white sandy beach overlooking the open sea, with tall slender reeds of grass stranded by high tide.

The place had inspired artists for over a hundred years. A pal of mine who had a beach house was glad to let me look after his summer place when he was on assignment.

Daisy was as alluring as any southern belle. I could easily have met her at dancing school in New Orleans. She was beautiful, and if Homer hadn't met her first, I would have put her first on my dance card of Louisiana ladies. In fact, I would have discarded the card all together. Daisy was that special, and I thought about asking her out for a weekend. We may not have been looking in the same direction, but we were coming from the same place on the map. And if we talked about New Orleans, it was dividend we could share. It seemed there wasn't anyone serious at the moment, and if there were, in an all's fair in love and war sort of way, I asked:

"Daisy, I'm driving out to East Hampton, ever been there?"

"No," she answered, cautiously. "Why?" Was she flirting?

"With your job, working so hard and all, I thought you might like to get away for the weekend. I would surely love some company from home."

There was a reluctant pause. "That might be fun, Rigby."

I hadn't been sure how she would respond to such an abrupt invitation, how she might feel. I was heartened. The pause continued. I waited. Had I made the right decision?

"I really miss home and we'll have fun, I promise. Can you leave around noon on Friday? It's about a four-hour drive, less if there's no traffic."

"I finish work about one o'clock."

"Perfect."

I was dressed in a cashmere charcoal crew neck sweater with a scarlet scarf smartly knotted around my neck when I picked Daisy up in my spiffy green racing MG. Daisy wore a summer dress that looked better on Daisy than a Laura Ashley; they were made for each other. She was prettier than I remembered from the other times we'd met, which regrettably had only been twice. Three times held charm, and she was just down-right-down-home-town beautiful.

After unpacking our things and appreciating the well-designed driftwood house with views to the sea, we took to the white sandy beach and swam. The water was brisk, refreshing. Afterward we built sandcastles, then took a walk as a prelude to the dinner we would prepare together. I got the signal I was hoping for, coming by way of holding hands. It was an informal act, a sensitive gesture I developed during my salad days, and while not always clinically accurate, it worked as a romantic barometer for me most of the time. Just by holding hands, touching tightly, softly, gently, limply, I could sense to what extent my relationship could progress. Appearing casual, I considered this on a measurable scale: if a response was tepid and unyielding, nothing was lost, but a warm response signaled a gain. Daisy was cordial and receptive, holding my hand tightly.

Daisy fashioned a fresh green salad with three kinds of lettuce, drenched in ginger-flavored soy dressing. I roasted corn on the cob and grilled fresh lobsters over mesquite on the wooden patio facing the beach outside.

Afterward, at twilight, Daisy swept away a few strands of rebellious hair and melted into my arms.

We made delicious love as a cooling breeze from the Atlantic wafted over us. Falling into a spacious bed was exciting, new, and wonderful.

I looked at Daisy. "You want to know something?"

Nestled together, with closed eyes, came her pleased response, half purr and half affirmative, "Hmmm."

"This is so perfect, so amazing, I have never felt anything like this before!"

"Tell me . . ."

"I think these cotton percale sheets must have at least a three-hundred thread count!"

Daisy came alive. "What?" She pounded me with her pillow, and then her amusement subsided into a warm embrace.

The afterglow.

If I had my camera at hand, I would have taken a picture of Daisy at that moment; the blush, the confusion, the perfect loveliness of her shining face.

Instead, I filed it away in my memory.

HOMER SINCERE GOES NORTH

My career as a photojournalist took precedence over everything. I photographed landscapes at every opportunity, often the Brooklyn Bridge, taking pictures each hour to capture the changing light. I watched people and places, waiting for the unexpected. Texture and light are the basic ingredients of a fine photograph, and I used them to full advantage. But I still yearned for the immediacy of documentary news photography and traveling on assignments.

I soon received great news: Homer was coming to New York!

Before his arrival, Homer sent me a copy of his story that had been rejected by *New Orleans Times Picayune*—first rate reporting in every sense. He had something important to say. Along with the article came a letter describing his appreciation for Earl Long, the most bizarre story in Louisiana's political history.

More significantly, he added:

"Every day I write and craft a description about an object or a person, like an artist copying a painting in a museum. I try to rewrite Steinbeck, emulating his style until I can find my own voice."

I did the same with photographs, analyzing the landscapes of the great Ansel Adams until I found my own distinctive style with much to photograph in New York. No place on earth had been so rich in diversity of its new arrivals seeking freedom, a better life, or following a path to fame on Tin Pan Alley and the Great White Way. In this immense and brilliant display of energy, scented with sophistication from Upper Eastside world-wide society, braking into brashness of Lower Westside wise-cracking cabbies, was a dynamic tradition made by Irish cops with night sticks, Italian impresarios chomping cigars, a family of Wall Street stockbrokers, and Seventh Avenue tailors cutting fabrics. Slums and penthouses, a creative air in a killing climate of perpetual decay and rebirth. I glimpsed the sky as a series of zigzag shapes crafted by the shape edges of surrounding buildings, dazzling and arrestingly beautiful patterns of light and shadow emerging spontaneously with the city's upward growth. So much happened in and around the city and it happened so fast that New Yorkers sometimes feel they have been observers to all of history. I tried to photograph it all. Time was telescoped—events piling upon events with bewildering speed.

And at its core, Central Park, a great expanse of land, 840 acres in fact, in the shape of a rectangle, a park for all seasons. Autumn gave it a touch of magic. In the sharp air, leaves turned yellow and then gold, cyclists whizzed through the gathering mists, early morning riders fitted on smart English saddles cantered on horseback at a leisurely pace over dirt trails, and joggers trampled the thickening carpet of fallen leaves, until the park became a winter playground, bare and bitter, the city's hurry hampered. Skaters glided on the lakes and pools and children swished down hillocks, providing a quick rush of excitement in deserted expansions of calm. In spring, picnicking parents watched their kids scramble on rocky outcrops surrounded by shrubs and flowers; early rhododendron blooms mingled with yellow forsythia and fields of purple bluebells. Fifth Avenue parades, migratory birds, and spooning lovers made their seasonal appearance on hot summer days. Running baseball players drummed dust from worn grass, while others played tennis, sailed model boats, or simply walked, grabbing a steaming hotdog with deli mustard topped with sauerkraut from a Sabrett pushcart stand, then gathered to hear a concert in the great band shell at dusk.

Homer was looking forward to this city with enthusiasm and hope that his life would come together, like in a good story. He needed a job, a place to stay. A plan took shape in my mind. Apartments were quieter and cheaper in Greenwich Village, home to students and self-styled artists, where the Euclidian geometry of the city broke from its traditional grid. And in the Village, Henry James memorialized Washington Square with its stunning neo-Grecian homes, the epicenter of Village intellectual tremors, chess players, poets, and folk singers with guitars. There were pocket squares interrupted by narrow streets and alleys with coffee houses. The unique geography was as creative as the names that came from its past. Washington Irving and Thomas Paine lived there, as had Henry James and Eugene O'Neill; John Mansfield mopped the floor of a village tavern, and a lost poet, Dylan Thomas, wrote verse in another. I knew of an apartment nearby, a perfect place for my pal.

Our reunion took place in an Indian restaurant in the Village—two Louisiana boys in their twenties taking New York City by storm. Homer had finished Tulane top in his class, and a young man who wore a smart linen suit appeared, true to the South. In contrast, I was in a rumpled tweed jacket, my cavalry twills falling to my brown English shoes, the neatest part of my appearance. On a final interview at *LIFE*, an editor had looked down at my shoes and told me that polished shoes were an affirmation of a man's lifestyle. Since then I always made sure my shoes showed a brilliant shine.

"Do I know this cowboy?" We were exuberant seeing each other. Homer hadn't changed much, but at six feet he had grown much taller than I and was quite good-looking. I looked down at his shoes; they were highly polished. He would fit right in at Time-Life. He did not limp as much now. While still restricted by his brace, using a cane, his stride was smoother. After reminiscing, our attention turned to lunch as we ordered papadums and mango chutney, a delicious helping of tandoori chicken, vegetable curry, and naan. Our appetites had not changed much, only the selection of restaurants and variety of food. I had a great job and was looking for a boat. Our friendship that first bonded in New Orleans was still close and connected.

I had another plan, the best yet, and sent Homer off to the available loft with an address and a name. Having crossed Fifth Avenue into the maze of small, winding streets, he discovered brownstones surrounded by strings of wash lines crossing over alleys and cobblestone passages. He passed a playground near Sheridan Square and saw a man strike a kid in frustration. It appeared that the young child had overturned his Red Radio Flyer, a small wagon filled with a bag of groceries, a minor accident caused when hitting a sidewalk obstacle. The parent cursed and yelled at the kid, as the boy cried and collected the contents from his overturned cart. Homer winced at the sight. He crossed the street to take issue, as the indelible, familiar pain of abuse came back in a stirring moment, but the boy and the man and the wagon had disappeared in the crowd, and all that was left was an orange rolling toward Homer.

Nearby was the White Horse Tavern, a saloon where poets and journalists, surrounded by clouds of writhing smoke, scribbled notes and discussed their writing. Homer paused, wanting to be one of them and share their tables. Then over to a small theater, the Cherry Lane, where playwrights and actors made a career struggling downtown, not far from the next uptown subway stop, Broadway.

AN UNEXPECTED SURPRISE

"Afternoon sunlight streaked through a window over a Georgian doorway. It was all very Irish."

—Homer Sincere's journal, 1960

An anteroom inside the Cherry Lane displayed playbills from the theater's past productions in black frames. A few actors waiting to read for a part in an upcoming play were milling around.

"Just put your name here," a young actor said to Homer, handing him a script.

"Homer Sincere."

"Nice name. Have a seat."

Why did he give me a script? He leafed through a familiar play by Sean O'Casey. He remembered an afternoon lecture given by Father, held outside on the lawn at La Vieille Maison, about Irish poets and playwrights.

O'Casey surrendered to a woman's voice.

"Come in, please," she called to him. Homer openly stared at a beautiful woman with strands of blonde hair. Serious full lips, a bright voice, and her Louisiana-blue eyes got his full attention. Something familiar.

Absorbing her words, he was unable to control his feelings and tried to remain steady. He had not forgotten her.

"I'm Daisy Philips," she said, all business, concentrating on the script she held in her hand, while with the other, she brushed back a wisp of hair that had fallen over her face.

"I know," he said, following her through a narrow passage that led downstage.

She held tight to the routine business at hand, paying little attention to what he had said. "Why don't you read, starting on page twenty-two?"

"Read what?"

"The part of the young man."

"Is that required?"

"If you want the part, yes."

"I'm here for the apartment," Homer replied hesitantly.

"Apartment?"

There was a frown on Daisy's face while leafing through the script to identify a page number. Then looking up with hesitant recognition and tremendous surprise, exclaimed, "Homer Sincere!"

"Do you remember me?" he asked nervously.

"Of course I do. Yes, sorry." Daisy blushed. "I'm losing it. The last time I saw you was after we danced zydeco, and I followed you on your campaign trail, a political groupie. When did you become an actor?

Recovering her composure in a moment, Daisy threw her arms around him, following with a barrage of questions. "I can't believe it! You're here, in New York! What happened to you? It was Rigby who sent you over!"

Homer was lost for words. He had come to New York to write. A momentary thought about me flashed through his mind but was interrupted when a voice off stage called, "Miss Philips, we're ready to begin."

"This is amazing. Here, take the keys. It's just up three flights, behind the dressing room and across to the left. The apartment is above the theater." She added brightly, "It's a hundred dollars a month."

"Yes . . . yes. That's okay."

"But there's a hitch. There's some noise between eight and eleven each evening, except on Monday night."

"Monday night?"

"That's when it's dark."

"Dark?"

"The theater. There are no performances on Mondays."

She waved and made her exit into the wings. "We'll catch up later! Got to go . . . can't wait to get together, and welcome to New York!"

Making it upstairs was slow and uneasy, but Homer was rewarded by finding a large, handsome room with windows facing a courtyard that reminded him of New Orleans. The eighteen-foot-high ceiling harbored a skylight with streaming sunlight falling to a seasoned oak floor. There was a window where his desk would fit perfectly. The room was enclosed by tan plastered walls with a cream trim. And a rocking chair stood in the center. A rocking chair! We southern boys know there is something calming about rocking, a habit-forming addiction on the porches of Louisiana. As Waldo would have said, "They give thinkin' a rest every once in a while."

Daisy! He imagined a sweeping musical fanfare and then a title, "My Life With Daisy Philips."

Homer settled in to look for a job. In between, with two sandwiches and a malt for a solitary banquet, he read Faulkner and Fitzgerald, Mailer and Capote, and Steinbeck. He wanted to be like Hemingway and write like Styron, and made daily entries in his journal.

"After reading Lie Down in Darkness, *William Styron indisputably becomes my literary hero. He wrote the first few pages after being fired as a junior editor from a publishing house, McGraw-Hill, in the basement of a New York brownstone off Lexington Avenue. His stream of consciousness narrative took my breath away. I unabashedly confess my admiration and that I will try to copy him in any way I can. Every phrase, every line is crafted in a way that sings and dances, a way that can change color and tempo, easily and mysteriously. He is a man of letters, a master storyteller. Surely, his novel would have been on Father's list."*

Most mornings were as empty as the yellow pads on his desk waiting to be filled with plot outlines or, at the very least, observations. The yellow pad and the Venus #2 pencil were distant opponents. He sat in the rocking chair, thinking, rocking some more, collecting his thoughts. It was always his refuge, his home for reflection, and only felt more secluded with pinging rain on the skylight overhead.

For many writers, there is a peculiar resistance ritual, and Homer fit the typical pattern. Stalling, he took a shower after his breakfast and a walk around his apartment, constantly looking for a diversion before he could get down to the business of writing. After sharpening thirty yellow pencils with clean erasers and placing a green rubber band around the bundle, he decided that he would have to put on a sweater and take inventory of the articles in his bathroom medicine cabinet:

One blue toothbrush.

A tube of Colgate toothpaste with the secret ingredient Guard-All.

Johnson & Johnson waxed dental floss.

Yardley lavender soap.

Two Band-Aids.

A half-used bottle of antibiotics.

An almost empty bottle of mouthwash.

Three razor blades.

Bayer aspirin.

Lemon & Orange aftershave lotion.

For some time he studied the labels as if they were the promotional palaver on the back of a cereal box. Then back to reading books and returning to Hemingway. He wrote Hemingway, he pretended Hemingway, he became Hemingway.

"Barcelona. It is a lovely spring day when we start for the front. Last evening coming into town, it had been foggy, gray, dirty, and sad; now it's bright and warm; pink almond blossoms color the gray hills. The window in my hotel room is open. I lie in bed and hear the firing from the front line just a few blocks away. The rifles go pow, ta-crong, ca-phong, crangg with the hisss of passing bullets. They say you never hear the one that hits you. That's true of bullets because when you hear them, they're already past you. Overhead, light bombers are protected by circling Messerschmitt pursuit planes; bombs drop all around. I will need a khaki safari jacket with "Correspondent" on the sleeve, and remember to send my morning dispatch from Madrid."

For weeks, Homer checked the classifieds in the *New York Times* and *Village Voice* for any editorial job. Rejected after a dozen interviews, he qualified as "overqualified." He heard the excuse over and over again and couldn't imagine why or how he could break through.

There were days and nights between disappointments. Write what you know, said Hemingway, find your muse, listen to your voice.

A letter from his old schoolmates, Nick and Bobbo, caught up with

Homer. The letterhead introduced the Nick and Bobbo Superior Laundry and Dry Cleaning Company.

NICK and BOBBO SUPERIOR LAUNDRY and DRY CLEANING

Dear Homer,

Remember us? We've followed your speaking career with the Governor and see one of Rigby's photo credits every so often. Anyhow, we remember the good times at La Vieille Maison, the good old days. After school, we opened a laundry and now have ten stores, still growing! I'm not sure if you heard that Father died. He really meant a lot to us. We may have let him down in our studies, but I think we made up for it in our entrepreneurial skills. I think he would have been proud of us all.

Hope we meet someday.

Your friends,

Nick and Bobbo

MEETING HENRY LUCE

"Henry Luce looked up at me from behind his desk with the most formidable and imposing eyebrows over the bluest eyes I had ever seen, and asked the most inquisitive questions."

—Homer Sincere's journal, 1960

A ringing telephone sent Homer into the adventure he had longed for. It was an appointment at *TIME* that I had arranged.

Waiting in the reception hall, he read the words etched on a marble wall.

"To see life, to see the world, to eyewitness great events, to watch the faces of the poor and the gestures of the proud, to see strange things, machines, armies, multitudes, shadows in the jungle and on the moon, to see man's

work, his paintings, towers, and discoveries, to see things thousands of miles away, things dangerous to come to, the women that men love, and the many children, to take pleasure in seeing and to see and be amazed, to see and be instructed, thus to see and to be shown is now the will and the new expectancy of mankind."

The thirty-fourth floor of the Time-Life building had two corridors that led to a blue-carpeted, teak-paneled executive area. On one side hung a painting of the tall chairman, Andrew Heiskell, leaning back with arms and hands stretched behind his neck; on the opposite, a painting of Henry Robinson Luce, Editor-in-Chief, with blue pencils and papers, editing pages of copy. Nearby was a collection of engraved plates.

Homer was invited to the inner office.

Henry Luce set an unattainable schedule and then spent the rest of the day trying to catch up with it. He was a keen, attentive presence, anxious for perfection, and unforgiving of disappointment. Surrounding a large teak desk, on all four walls, there were floor-to-ceiling exposures of Manhattan. Homer marveled at the supporting islands of jammed skyscrapers with soaring towers, reaching across to five water-edged boroughs making up neighborhoods, each with its own ethnic character. The beauty of Manhattan's skyline was one of forced compression, a panoply of buildings in which beauty was unto itself. It was the work of many architects and builders, each concerned with their own creation, each blissfully unconcerned with the whole. Every scale was exhibited from the four-story townhouses to topless towers, and it was the cramming together of so much diversity that gave New York its myth and enchantment. To some extent, Homer thought it was like a scene in a play that never ended, for it was the cultural theater of all nations, and all the languages of the world jostled together happily enough. Chinatown, Little Italy, Harlem, the Lower Eastside, to the north, Harlem, to the west a Spanish touch, and all around the town, corners of Europe at every turn.

Henry Luce wore suspenders that matched a tan gabardine suit jacket hovering over a well-traveled, black leather office chair. On each side of his balding crown were puffs of white hair. He was slim, and his mind and body were both intellectually and athletically fit. The Editor–in-Chief of all TIME Inc. magazines peered through steel-rimmed glasses, and if he was not shuffling papers in neat stacks, his focus followed his ever-present blue pencil, editing and checking a current lead story. His eyes were blue and penetrating. Swiveling around in his chair and gazing briefly at the Hudson River, he asked, "Why do you want to be a journalist, Sincere?"

"Because it's the only thing I want to do, sir."

"I took the challenge once at your age," Luce said. "Britt Hadden and I were eager to do a magazine called *Facts*. After we graduated from Yale, we wrote a prospectus and raised about $85,000. That was in 1924.

"I called a friend of mine at Doubleday who took us to see Doc Eden, head of Doubleday's Development Operations, supposedly a brilliant man. Do you know what he told us? He told us we didn't have a Chinaman's chance to launch a magazine.

"Was there room for another magazine? No one would have thought so until a professor at Yale who was an editor of the *New York Times* literary supplement told us: 'You've got to develop a style that will exactly suit your purposes, and when you do that, you will have made an appreciable contribution to journalism.' I suppose we all have the same need to do something no one else has done. A Chinaman's chance! Doc Eden didn't know I was born in China."

Luce stood up stiffly, pacing, pushing his left hand across the back of his head, and holding a cigarette in his right, its ashes dropping on the dark blue carpet. His patrician face reflected energy; his slightly nasal words tumbled out without a pause.

"Why writing, reporting? Why not art or music?"

"Writing has always been a refuge to me."

"From what?

"Real life."

"But at the magazine we deal with real life."

"I understand, sir. I should have said books are a refuge for me. Passages of time that exist on paper and nowhere else. And I read, of course, walking through pages of history, meeting characters that I never thought I'd meet or know."

"Discovering people like yourself."

It was an observation, not a question. Then Luce punctuated his thoughts with single words. "Poetry. Pastimes. Recollections. Reporting. Objectivity. Accuracy. Illuminating ideas," then added, "It is the most challenging thing you could do."

"Yes, sir, I'm sure of that." Homer blurted out.

"Bill Canfield wrote me about you. I knew him in China."

Homer didn't know my father had been in China; we had never discussed it. My father had spent his early years in Shanghai, a colonial city where he and Henry Luce had become friends.

"Our parents were both missionaries. After Shanghai, we went to Peking, and he came to live with us after his parents were killed."

"Killed?" Homer was confused. He had never known.

"Canfield told me," Luce continued, "about your inspiring act of courage down in New Orleans."

Homer was bewildered by what Luce was talking about. Was it the subject of his article rejected by the *Picayune*?

Then Luce's remarks came sharply. It was the first time Homer had heard anyone answer his own questions as quickly as he asked them. It was an indication of his editor's instinct, an insatiable curiosity about facts and ideas. "How many men fought in Verdun?" he asked. "Five hundred thousand," he answered. "How many Americans died in the Second World War?" he asked. "One hundred and sixteen thousand," he answered. "How many lives lost in the war?" he asked. "Nine million," he answered. "The recent World War was a pivotal event in the history of mankind, a struggle of enormous importance. We are doing a series on that Great War.

"The magazine was founded to keep people well-informed. We're creating a new column in the front of the magazine: 'The Editor's Note.' I'd like you to write about the men and women who contribute to our pages each week in their search to extend and uplift. Let the words and phrases congratulate themselves."

Homer went to work in an exhilarating setting where editors and correspondents lived in a crucible of crises and deadlines, searching, deciphering, filing, assembling, and reporting on the sheer drama of world events.

DATELINE

"If you ever have an important story, put it on the service. Nothing can compare with the thrill of a good story, yours alone, slowly developing and leaving its mark on history. Nothing."

—Homer Sincere's journal, 1960

Luce introduced Homer to Dick Clurman, the knowledgeable reporter and veteran correspondent who was head of the News Service. Clurman was a sandy blond man with horn-rimmed frames, in his mid-forties, who had earlier hired me. He walked Homer to the twenty-seventh floor, introducing him to several people along the way, but Homer was too preoccupied to remember their names. Passing the library, offices, archives, and then a series of rooms called Dateline, his attention was drawn to a large glass enclosure with four brass clocks timing cities around the world. Teletype machines clattered in different rhythms, spewing out reams of paper with messages from United Press, Reuters, Associated Press, and the Time-Life News Service.

"This is the heart of our magazines, Sincere," Clurman explained. "We have thirty-five bureaus around the world: London, Paris, Cairo, Buenos Aires, and Delhi among them, with several hundred correspondents and stringers filing stories twenty-four hours a day. When we need information on anything, anytime, anywhere, the editors send out queries to the bureaus and within hours we have answers. Of course, if it's a fast-breaking story, it will be filed over the ticker so that we receive the information immediately. If you ever have an important story, put it on the service," he said. "Nothing can compare with the thrill of a good story, yours alone, slowly developing and leaving its mark on history. Nothing."

Clurman told him that each machine had a code, a number fed over telephone lines throughout the building. "Except for exclusive stories, newspapers all over the world subscribe to different services for a monthly fee. The Associated Press was born in the 1920s, when newspapers decided to pool their resources and form an agency to search out information and feed stories to other newspapers. We do the same with our Dateline service. Clacking away in irregular sequences and uncertain rhythms, it is a lifeline to the world, a journalistic epicenter for late-breaking news. From the Dateline, events and news travel all over the world."

Every reporter, every correspondent for *TIME* was a Soldier of the Word.

Homer had been enlisted into a global army.

DATELINE HAVANA.

I am speeding along the Malecón, past colonial buildings facing the harbor. The time when Cuba was alive with cruise ships and luxury hotels, gambling casinos and brothels, rum and Coca-Cola is now only a memory. It is the twenty-sixth of July. Outside the presidential palace people chant, "Fidel, Fidel."

DATELINE ASIA.

Somewhere in the bamboo jungle of this beleaguered country, an American army captain sits in a thatch-roofed hut in the intense humidity of the tropical night, bent over a map. Shorts, sneakers, but no shirt. At the first crackle of rifle fire, the captain knows: the Silver Guards are catching hell again.

THE SOVIET UNION HITS THE MOON. KHRUSHCHEV VISITS THE UNITED
STATES. THE DALAI LAMA FLEES TIBET.

MEETING IN A VILLAGE COFFEE HOUSE

*"On a black and white negative, Rigby and I would have looked alike in
many ways, but once into a print, there were differences. I had dark hair
and my eyes were deeply brown. His were transparent blue. Rigby now
wore khakis most of the time, and I had taken to wearing flannels and
tweeds. The contrasts were startling. I have never known for certain
Rigby's liking for me. Perhaps he needed approval for his ambition, company for companionship to conspire with every plan. But I think he held out
some admiration for me. Rich in imagination, Rigby was extremely well
read—a secret reader—and had an encyclopedic Rolodex for facts, at least
to my knowledge. He could speak about medical diagnoses as easily as the
techniques and brushstrokes of great artists, and what he didn't know he
could manufacture in a moment just as a magician produces the mystery
card out of a deck, rabbits and doves out of a hat, or a bouquet of flowers
from thin air. And I wondered if it were more than coincidence that he sent
me over to meet Daisy again, another one of his inventive plans."*

—Homer Sincere's journal, 1960

After Homer's meeting with Luce, he was very happy, and I was
anxious to know how the interview went. We met at a place downtown for a snack, and he had gotten a job!

I then turned to the matter of my latest assignment. "Homer, meet
Melissa. She's going down to Cape Canaveral with me."

Melissa Framboise. I loved the sound of her name, half French,
half English, an international intern whose delicious revenue included
her deliciously full breasts. I had taken her under my wing. Her misty
gray eyes were inherited from skies of Normandy, contributing to her

curiosity, which I was glad to satisfy. As she left, she glanced back with a smile that I was sure to follow.

My plan was another research project. I sent Melissa on her way: "Make sure you pick up twelve rolls of Ektachrome 100, and don't forget, I'll meet you at your apartment at five a.m."

With utmost sincerity and best intentions, I whispered to Homer, "I can't do anything without her. She's my inspiration."

I was ambivalent toward Daisy and had decided to move on to another challenge. Conquest was a familiar hunting pattern for me. Whatever my stupid reasoning was at the moment, I had no intention of hurting anyone. Homer might need an old friend from New Orleans more than I did.

Homer was curious and asked how I had arranged his interview with Luce.

"Remember Waldo and Daddy Grace?"

"Of course."

"Well, I thought I would just visualize my father writing his old pal Harry Luce a letter of introduction for his good friend Homer Sincere.

"You did that?"

"I did."

My daring had impressed Homer, though having grown up together we were in familiar territory.

"How is your dad?" Homer asked.

I started to shirk the question but answered, "I just don't think he gets it, what I am doing and all. He thinks I'm wasting my life and should be doing something more serious than running around taking pictures and playing Rhett Butler with the ladies. But the only thing I'd rather do is see the world."

I changed the conversation to an easier subject.

"Well, Homer, you have a job and an apartment. All you need now is a lady in your life, and you've reconnected with Daisy.

"Rigby, it was really a surprise. We had lost touch over the past years."

"You should ask her out. She's your type."

Homer was curiously silent. "Do you know her?"

"Just a little, she's a friend." I was convinced it was better to be vague about my relationship with Daisy.

"Doesn't she have a boyfriend?"

"I think she was seeing some actor, Jeffrey McNeil or O'Neil, something like that. I don't think it was serious."

"How do you know?"

"I know. Trust me. You two should get together. Homer Sincere, writer, and Daisy Philips, actress. Two creative souls, Chagalling.

"Chagalling?"

"You know, Marc Chagall's paintings: Lovers are always floating. I've got an idea. I have a packet of photographs of children to give to Daisy." I took a large envelope from my camera case and handed it to him. "I promised her a set of these, and I'd like you to bring them to her. You need a friend. Check it out!"

HIDDEN EXPOSURE

"There was a panel in my room, hiding something. It had been plastered over, but I could see the outline, with something behind it."

—Homer Sincere's journal, 1960

Homer's first assignment was to write about a reflective photo essay on the battle of Verdun in World War I, with photographs taken there by Alfred Eisenstaedt. Homer didn't have a credit or a byline, but it was a good opportunity for an apprentice to write about TIME's distinguished writers and photographers.

In his room over the Cherry Lane Theater, Homer researched the Great War for the new series that Luce had introduced, reading the material he had received from the publication's archives. Homer's first "Editor's Note" appeared in the front of the next issue of *TIME*.

A Call to Colors

Turning back the clock to the ghosts of the great siege, to heroes and half-forgotten songs, to the colors that are vividly and romantically far away, to the years before 1917, to a time of innocence, to a period painted in a watercolor world, the photographer Alfred Eisenstaedt and LIFE magazine have done so. They first met in 1937. This week the magazine returns to his photographs of the torments of Verdun's millions of men of whom five hundred thousand died. Back to an era when the trumpets summoned the young men of many nations, a call to colors echoing the death of the old order and signaling the birth of a new one. Eisenstaedt captures the legacy of a tortured landscape that guarded the grim battlefields and the remnants of great armies.

Clurman told Homer he was pleased that he had adopted the magazine's style and had followed his mandate to write quickly about the best photographers and writers in the country.

Sometimes Homer thought about Daisy, reflecting on her in his journal, but when it came to reality, he was still unsure of himself. She had become a beautiful, sophisticated woman. Homer felt left behind, locked in his own feelings. He wanted to muster the courage to ask her out but anxiety overwhelmed him. He still had my packet of pictures.

A muffled sound came to his apartment from somewhere. Music seemed to find him wherever he lived. First the thumping, clumping zydeco above his room at La Vieille Maison, now below his room at the Cherry Lane.

Scanning the apartment, he noticed that part of a wall had been plastered over a recessed square. He observed something odd: a panel with the outline of a small window that could be hiding an opening. He inspected it closely, then opened the panel with a knife. He heard muffled sounds from down below and looked down; a performance was in progress on the stage! He guessed that this part of the room might have been a lighting booth for the theater before its remodeling.

As seen from above the theater, Sean O'Casey came to life. With an unobstructed view from his "gallery," he watched both acts, an amenity not mentioned in his lease.

After the applause, the curtain came down and the audience left. He continued his work.

He read the diaries of George Jean Nathan, a *New York Times* drama critic and member of the Algonquin Round Table, with Benchley, Parker, Ross, and Mencken. Nathan had written: "There are two times in a man's life when he particularly needs the ear of a good friend. The first is when he's just lost his old girl, the second is when he's found his new one."

Homer reasoned inaccurately that he felt more for Daisy than she could ever feel for him. His insecurity dominated his feelings. Eventually, with my encouragement, he decided to speak with her. Practicing in front of a mirror while shaving, he manufactured some reassurance. "Hello, Daisy! Why, imagine seeing you again! Coffee?" Having gathered his courage and having splashed himself with cologne, he took the packet of my pictures and went down to the courtyard.

He was more conscious of his gait than ever before. Throughout his life, he had learned to walk steadily, but walking with the hope of knowing Daisy again, he lost his balance.

Daisy appeared unexpectedly in the courtyard. He quickly turned without losing his footing and re-entered the building. His confidence crippled, falling into anxiety, he found it hard to express more intimate feelings. Homer had never seriously dated anyone. His emotions were painfully locked inside, unable to follow their natural directions. Romantically, he was lost.

Summoning all his courage, heart racing, he walked into the courtyard, right past Daisy, toward the street. She called after him, saving him from defeat. The invisible pane that had imprisoned his feelings since childhood lifted a bit, letting in a wisp of fresh air.

"Hi, Homer. It's really nice to see you. I've been thinking about when we can get together. When do you have time?"

"Hi, there," he said blankly. It was all he could muster at that moment. He had expressed poetry in his journal, but now reality had trumped his fantasy. If he only had confidence, Homer thought, an easy way with ladies. It was easier to keep Daisy in his journal than to lose all hope. *Maybe if I wrote about my feelings, I might achieve a measure of confidence. Father's "Greats" should have included passages about intimate encounters.*

EDITOR'S NOTES

"Dateline was familiar, like the Western Union office I remembered long ago . . . words coming from telegraph keys flying through the air."
—Homer Sincere's journal, 1960

On Thursdays and Fridays, the magazine closed. Homer took to spending weekends in the empty offices of *TIME*, reading stories from editors and photographers' captions. Down the hall, teletypes clicked and clacked their reports, and assignments waited to be received and to become news. The Dateline room was compatible and comfortable, almost like the Western Union office where he had worked for a while as a kid. He longed for his own byline and assignments. And he longed for Daisy.

He went back to work.

THE EDITOR'S NOTE
JUNE 24, 1960
THE MAN IN THE GRAY TATTERED SWEATER

Staff writer Philip Yardley is a friendly man who wears a tattered gray sweater as he writes on one of the oldest machines in the building. For years, he has withstood all efforts to replace the typewriter and has worn his sweater as comfortably as he writes. The excellence of Philip's stories is the result of painstaking craftsmanship and vast experience. There is a Yardley Law: always grab the reader with the first few words and never let him go.

THE EDITOR'S NOTE
AUGUST 20, 1960
FOREVER ONLY IN MY MIND

When he was ten, Paul Schutzer found a broken camera in a neighborhood wastepaper basket. He taped it together and began shooting pictures of his native Brooklyn. Years later, after studying to be a painter, he realized that what he really wanted to do he had been practicing all along: photography. This week on assignment at the ruined barracks of the concentration camp at Auschwitz, Poland, Schutzer was so moved that it was difficult for him to take a picture. "The room was dark, and on the wall were simple paintings of flowers. When I saw them, I tried to visualize the child who had painted them. This photograph, which exists forever only in my mind, had more to say about the soaring human spirit in the face of adversity than anything I'd ever seen." You'll find his story on page 64.

Most editors and writers are not friendly to a new recruit until he or she had logged a significant contribution. Offering some of the best news writing in the world, the group at *TIME* guarded against intrusion by newcomers. As he progressed, Homer began to be included in their circle.

Self-effacing Philip Yardley had never worn a sweater and had not been particularly friendly, but after having been mentioned in the Editor's Note, he greeted Homer warmly. And now he always wore a gray sweater.

Paul Schutzer sent a message over the wire service from Europe: "Thanks for the notice, Homer. How did you know that painting was forever on my mind?"

Homer wanted to be out in the field, to measure up. He diligently polished the few paragraphs he wrote each week for the managing editors.

They told him "not yet"; the time wasn't right.

During the sixties, all at the magazine were influenced by the "New Frontier." Each crusade, slogan, poster, or button carried a sense of special commitment. In ways that no one had imagined, a new generation began to show passionately and vocally that they did give a damn.

Times were a-changin' with free speech, free love, and freedom rides. This feeling of commitment would change as the decade wore on, from optimism to doubt to disenchantment, a loss of innocence, in ways no one from an earlier generation could have imagined. In the nostalgic, drug-hazed swinging sixties, bordered with tangerine trees and under marmalade skies, one writer wrote, "A few folks won't remember too much about the decade because they weren't really there." But a lot of our caring classmates and colleagues joined the Peace Corps. Others listened to songs from a place called Motown.

I invited Homer to come and hear a folk singer in the Village. We met in a crowded coffeehouse called "The Bitter End," and as soon as Bob Dylan began to sing, Homer began looking for an answer "Blowing in the Wind."

I asked whether he had seen Daisy or gotten together with her, but he dodged the subject. I casually mentioned the great job she was doing at a special school near Columbia College. He was reluctant to talk to me about the feelings that I guessed were stirring within him. I couldn't sense what his thoughts were about Daisy and was certain he had not found out about our brief affair. It would serve no good purpose for him to know. I was glad when he asked for her school's address. Encouraging!

TEN CENTS AND A SUBWAY TOKEN UPTOWN

"A big, blowsy cleaning lady gave me directions to a room that could accommodate a palace. It could have been best described in a book of fairytales."
                                        —Homer Sincere's journal, 1960

Homer took a token, a chance, and a subway uptown to Daisy's school where he ran into someone who pointed to a room down a narrow hall, opening to an elegant grand ballroom. A crystal chandelier hung above a polished wooden parquet floor. A carousel of windows formed a circle. In its middle, the primary resident—Daisy Philips— sat at a piano, placing on the keys the hands of a young girl who sat next to her, to produce chords. Behind them, a group of children sat attentively. Entering quietly, Homer bumped into the doorframe. Daisy looked up briefly. He didn't want to interrupt the lesson, much less intrude. As he passed through a tall mahogany door, he saw a note pinned to it, glaring at him:

I regret to announce that all classes are suspended until further notice. The Board of Education has discontinued the Special Program for Performing Arts. Please know that I'm doing all I can to appeal their decision.

I'm so sorry.
Daisy Philips, Director

He left quietly. On his way back to the Village, he stopped at a music store where he bought an assortment of classical records. He thought Daisy might like Chopin's polonaises and mazurkas. Arriving at the Cherry Lane, he started to drop them off for her at the box office, but after a moment, decided to wait. There was more to be done. Just before dawn the following morning he went to nearby Chelsea. It was still quiet, with only the footfalls of a few people finding their way home. This morning, more than ever, he wanted to improve his walk, and managed quite well without his cane.

The city was empty except for a rushing yellow cab hissing over the freshly watered streets; a trucking brigade paraded off the West Side Highway for several blocks along West Twentieth Street, invading the New York wholesale market, then depositing their cargo—thousands of flowers arranged in rows of tin garden cans for waiting wholesale florists. Homer was there with them.

He selected a dozen peonies. Expanding his preparations, he stopped at a bakery and fruit stand, bought hot, buttery croissants and fresh California orange juice from Valencia oranges. Finally, loaded with packages and the new records, he audaciously knocked at Daisy's door. As we say in New Orleans, he came a-callin'.

A large door opened to a sleepy Daisy, silhouetted against a colorful Gainsborough portrait. Homer announced cheerfully, "Good morning. I just happened to be in the neighborhood."

"Homer, you live across the way. You're up awfully early."

"I hope I didn't wake you."

She glanced over her shoulder at the clock on the mantle. Eight. They looked at each other for a moment. Homer, breaking the awkward silence, began to hand over the morning's collection.

"The flowers are for you."

"They're lovely!"

"Some croissants from the bakery."

"Thank you."

"Some marmalade and fresh fruit. Raspberries are in season, and clotted cream." His words tumbled over each other.

"Homer!" she exclaimed.

"Fresh tea from Ceylon."

"Homer . . ."

"Here are some records. I know you like records."

"I didn't know it was Christmas!"

"The morning paper. I think that's all."

"Come in!" Daisy beckoned, but his courage had run out of steam.

"Just dropping by."

THE BEAUTIFUL PEOPLE

"I was afraid of losing Daisy before I found her and didn't know the first thing about boy-girl relationships. Separation and anxiety were familiar companions. I would rather write about her and play the game from moments of chance. But then something happened on a day that could have been dramatized by a great playwright.

—Homer Sincere's journal, 1960

Returning from work one late afternoon, as he was opening the door to his apartment, he was ambushed by Daisy.

"Don't you dare even think about opening that door, Mr. Sincere."

He knew who it was, and turning, he put up his arms in mock surrender.

"What did I do?"

"Nothing."

"Then what?"

"Are you going to come along quietly, or do I have to call for back-up?"

"Back-up? Who?"

Daisy sighed. "Look, just go along with the improv, okay? Are you going to come for a walk with me, or do I have to go find someone else who wants to share my companionship on a spring day?"

It was now or never for Homer.

"Why did you give me all those presents?"

"I guess to get your attention."

"You got my attention."

After a pause, he uttered, "I think you're a fine teacher, Daisy."

"How do you know?"

"Rigby told me."

"He's right. I am and I'm trying to save the program, but the board just won't listen with politics and all. I adore those kids. They are good musicians. When they play, it reminds me of my mom."

"Was she a musician?"

"Yes," Daisy replied with a side-glance.

Taking his hand, Daisy led him outside to a bench and pulled two scripts from a canvas bag. They were marked with yellow highlights.

"Here."

"What?"

"Follow the parts marked in yellow, my lines. I have to get them down for an audition. Now, help me. Just give me a line when I ask. Ready?"

"I'm not sure if I can."

Without missing a beat, Daisy continued, "It's a play by William Saroyan, 'The Beautiful People.' I'll read the part of Agnes."

Daisy began, "I never noticed the glass door in the library before, looking out past so many books. And I never noticed before, that if he wasn't waiting, he was still there. I . . . Line."

"I could have turned and walked away." Homer turned a page.

Daisy continued, not missing a beat, "I could have turned and walked away quietly. I had been walking quietly for years, but I couldn't move. I wanted to, I guess, but I just couldn't. He was alone, and then. And then . . ."

"I was too," Homer answered.

"And we had to be together . . ."

"Yes."

Daisy puts her arm around Homer.

"First we went to the steps of the library, but we just stood there. We got in the way of some people."

Homer replied, "Who were in a hurry . . ."

"Yes." Daisy turned, "They looked at us. Were we special? Different? Could they tell? There were other people coming and going too . . ." Daisy took a beat and waited for her cue.

"And we were in the way."

"When we moved we were, we were together."

"Yes, together, and we walked through the park and he kept bumping into me and I kept bumping into him and he kept saying . . ."

"Excuse me . . ." Homer carried on, following the script.

"And I kept saying," Daisy continued, "'OK, that's all right.' He said something about his shoes. He said they didn't fit. That's why he stumbled. He could have been barefoot and it would not have made any difference. I understood. I found something and I was beginning to see. The streetcars going by had people in them suddenly and they were waving and smiling. I hadn't noticed before how beautiful they were. We looked up at a flock of birds flying in formation. He pointed to them, and just then they turned and circled as if they were forming a ring above us, to include us. He was bewildered and shy. I've waited every day to meet one person in the world who understood and now I've found him. We're not so different from the others. I thought we were but we're not, and I can't forget him. When we walked through the park and looked at everything together, I discovered . . . I . . . I discovered . . . Line."

"It's not the same as looking at things alone."

"Yes," Daisy said. "It's not the same as looking at things alone. I loved him and I thought love would have been somewhere else but it wasn't. He was here . . ."

Then a long moment and, after a pause, Daisy took a sweeping bow before an invisible audience. Homer cleared his throat. She turned, her happy face transformed.

"You're a fine actress."

She reached over and kissed Homer. "How do you know I was acting?"

The she saw the gathering tears in his eyes.

"Why are you crying? What hurts, Homer?"

He shook his head, unsure if it was pain or joy or some collision of the two.

"Please, Homer, what is it?"

He took her hand and said nothing.

That night, he wrote in his journal:

"How can I tell Daisy that the first time someone said they loved me since my mother, it was William Saroyan. There we were pretending, and the

words were not meant for me at all. There is just no way to admit that to her, and I hid behind my silence, waiting for the warm afternoon to dry the evidence of my feelings."

AN IMMODEST PROPOSAL

In the early sixties, most of the eleven million black Americans in the South were still deprived of their constitutional right to vote through poll taxes and trumped-up literacy tests. In both North and South, black children were still segregated into schools that usually prepared them only for the lowest paying jobs on the economic ladder. The issue of civil rights was moot. For Homer, these concerns were familiar territory. They resonated with him, not only as a cause, but also as his mission.

Homer asked to see Clurman with a proposal he felt was essential for the magazine. "Richard," he began (they were on a first name basis by then), "I suggest that *TIME* should have a film department. Nothing new has been done here with motion pictures since the old *March of Time*. Film is a natural extension of the printed page. We have access to all the important people and great stories in the world. Why not let our photographers become cameramen as well?"

"Homer, we are print medium," Clurman replied. "While *The March of Time* was a great promotional vehicle, it never made any money. These days, we're losing about ten percent a year in advertising revenue to television, and it's the pages that pay the bills. Henry will never go for it."

Homer tried to argue that it wouldn't take much investment and we could find an outlet on television, it would be something we could call our own, like Time-Life Films. "It's the future, and with small crews, it wouldn't take much investment." Clurman resisted, as did the managing editors. Television was the corporate enemy. "We're print, that's what we do, and that's what we know well, not moving pictures. We have no experience."

"But Rigby Canfield does. We have some experience; we used to make films together."

"You and Canfield? Rigby Canfield?"

"Yes, sir. I think you saw some clips he filmed back home."

"Oh, those? Were you part of that?"

"In a way I was, and I tell you, he's got a knack to make films. And it's something I can help him with, something we both really like to do."

"Forward-looking thinking, Sincere, but we don't need knack; better stay with what we do for the time being." He was a counselor with rock-like protocol with little give to his penultimate decision.

"Could Rigby take a Filmo with him on his next assignment?"

"Filmo, who is Filmo, what's a Filmo?"

"It's a handy camera, and it could give you some idea."

"I won't authorize it, Homer, but if he wants to take a Filmo, and it doesn't take his eye off the assigned story, I'm not against it."

WE SHALL OVERCOME

Clurman had no intention of pursuing the "motion notion," as he called it. Homer had to stay in New York for "The Editor's Note," but it was a great break for me. I loved the idea, but it still didn't get Homer into the field.

In the southern states, even though some progress had been made and a controversial effort had been advanced by Governor Long of Louisiana, African Americans served notice to the nation that they would no longer endure their insufferable and hard lives. The dramatic emergence of a powerful movement, a crusade of non-violence, was orchestrated by an Alabama preacher who led southern blacks in a series of sit-ins and marches, not unlike Daddy Grace's prophetic walk to the Louisiana legislature. Despite deeply imbedded racial prejudice since the days of black slavery, and unwillingness to grant justice to black citizens in courts of law, Martin Luther King's effort had an enormous influence. Due to his courageous leadership of the movement, he was roughed up, jailed, and eventually assassinated by a white ex-convict. He had never abandoned his course of non-violent protest for civil rights.

"Someday we shall overcome," was the anthem of the moment.

The March on Washington was my next assignment for *LIFE*. I looked forward to meeting and documenting Dr. King. I wanted to show stark passion, faces of hope. I wanted to hear calls for freedom without violence. I took my Filmo to record some additional footage documenting what I might experience.

THE EDITOR'S NOTE:
LET FREEDOM RING

This week, LIFE magazine brings the idea of the Promised Land to our readers in a superb photo essay by Rigby Canfield. With a single photograph, Canfield can show a politician posture or canonize a hero. With a folio of pictures, he can open our eyes to things we never before saw or understood. Rigby Canfield was born in New Orleans. With his first camera, this enthusiastic photographer could portray the essence of the subjects he saw through the lens. As a young boy, he began clicking everything in sight, including the first light of progress in Louisiana; and now, years later, his eloquent style adds another dimension to the magazine. Whether it's a broad panorama or a candid portrait, no assignment has ever been too hard, too big, or too small for this tireless, inquisitive photographer. He has the "eye," as we say around LIFE, and his achievements are impressive. He sees the essential idea of a story and translates words into pictures that witness the significant actions of Martin Luther King, Jr. His photographs, starting on page 44, bring home the unfulfilled promise of America.

When I returned from Washington, I deposited thirty rolls of film at the photo lab, then dropped by to see Homer, who was reviewing the makeup of the magazine.

I had some of the motion footage that I had developed, and when the rushes came back from the lab, we looked at them together. I wished Homer had been in Washington with me—his passion for the subject would have lightened my load. The film turned out well—touching emotion, as moving pictures should. We showed some footage to Clurman at a special screening but still couldn't build a case for Time-Life Films. The stills were considered powerful and dramatic. When I read the latest "Note" about me, I recognized Homer's unflappable faith, his optimism, and sense of fairness. While I was still stuck in a deeply embedded traditional Southern viewpoint, not caring or courageous enough to change, my camera was objective, utterly free of prejudices. I hadn't changed much politically or emotionally, but after my experience of the March, I began to reconsider my own bias. I realized that Homer was my only true friend with a noble conscience.

Daisy called. I hadn't seen her for some time. I realized Homer's feelings for her were more complicated than I had anticipated. To me, ladies were a pastime, a conquest instead of a commitment—pretty shallow when I think about it. Why? Was it my razzle-dazzle career as photojournalist, taking me all over the world? There was no need for a constant in my life, I had too much to do, too much to see, and I pushed any need for reflection aside.

Daisy and I hadn't spoken, and her work at the Special School of Performing Arts, now closing in a few weeks, as well as preoccupation with our own interests, kept us at a distance. She told me that budget cuts across the board affected programs for special education. Music was as important to Daisy as it was to those kids I had photographed, but I could not help her. I was off on another assignment.

THE SONG OF IT ALL

"I considered the idea that if I was meant to be a Soldier of the Word, it was time to apply word to action. That was certainly the intention of

Father Rivage, and if Billy Sunshine spoke only one word, it would be courage."   —Homer Sincere's journal, 1960

After the magazine had been put to bed, Homer went to the Dateline room surrounded by teletypes. The pale gray machines stood in rows blending into penumbral silence, but like sentries guarding the news, spinning out stories from remote parts of the world about weather, an outbreak of disease, a statement from a leader, or a school closing. During the week, the room bustled with activity; copyboys tore long ribbons of text from the machines, dispatching them to the proper one of the magazine's thirty-three departments.

Homer couldn't clear Daisy from his mind; the thought of her school closing haunted him. Nothing took precedence or was more important for the kids and for Daisy, but what could he do?

He thought, Didn't Billy always try to right a wrong? Then he recalled Clurman's admonition, "If you have a good story, put it on the ticker. That's what makes us journalists in the first place."

Father Rivage would advance a noble cause in mission and message. Billy Sunshine would champion a good deed. And with their virtual support, the Soldier of the Word gathered his courage. He dialed the line to the Associated Press and filed the first "special" dispatch from *TIME*.

DATELINE NEW YORK: BY OUR SPECIAL CORRESPONDENT
THE SONG OF IT ALL

Something happened to a group of kids at a special school in New York City. They lost a teacher and what they love most: the sound of music. If budget for the Special School of the Performing Arts is not restored, there will be no more songs. Take eight-year-old Sooki Kim, who came from Korea when her family was killed. A band of GIs adopted her and brought her home to the United States. She may have lost her sight, but not her memory, and the school has been a sanctuary for her, a happier place for a better life. Somewhere between where we are coming from and where we are going, we can do more if we listen to the song of it all. It's up to our readers. If you want to help, please write to The Editors, Time-Life, Rockefeller Center, New York.

The teletype machine from the AP clacked. "Dateline: Associated Press: Received." Dimming the lights, Homer waited for the explosion to begin.

Several thousand letters filled with donations were mailed to the editors, appealing for the restoration of the program. From on high, journalism's great moderator Henry Luce sent down a query. "Who is the Special Correspondent on Dateline? Please acknowledge." There was a scuttle around the building but no reply was forthcoming.

Newspapers around the country picked up the story. Readers in New York took notice. The editors were curious and stymied. They couldn't figure out who had filed the story.

MISTAKEN IDENTITY

"Can you believe it, Homer? The program has a chance," Daisy cried, excited at hearing the news.

In celebration, Homer had brought Daisy a bouquet of nodding flowers.

"Yes, good news! It's really great!"

Daisy exclaimed, "That Rigby! What a remarkable friend!"

"Rigby?"

"I am sure that he had something to do with this!"

Homer was lost. The chivalrous Soldier of the Word had become a casualty.

He went back to working weekends, with time off during the week. Most of his free time was spent in a movie theater where he always felt good, absorbed, and not so alone.

Unspooling weekly features, a retrospective series about the

American Experience played at the Village Cinema on Eighth Street off Fifth Avenue. History, legend, and most notably, the western. Billy Sunshine's great adventures were his favorites. Judge Hardy dispensing wisdom to Andy Hardy was another. Atticus Finch pleading compassion in *To Kill a Mockingbird* topped his list of film favorites.

"Through film," as Waldo would say, "we are seein' the world."

Homer asked me to come with him to see *The Grapes of Wrath*, a story filmed in stark black-and-white emotion about migrant workers with a cause. I accepted, inviting Candice, my newest and attractive researcher.

"Honey, don't forget. I'll need twenty-four rolls of Kodachrome 200," I requested, my usual opening volley.

Turning to Homer, I confidentially added, "Huge story! I'm covering the Democratic National Convention, and Candice is going with me. I can't live without her . . ."

"Your inspiration!"

I'm sure that Homer was disgusted as Candice and I mooned over each other more than over the film. I'm embarrassed to write about such dalliances now. I hadn't lost my primary interest in films, but Candice's charm brought my raging hormones to a boil. Homer and I were at opposite ends of the relationship scale. We had different measures. Homer was in search of confidence, both as a writer and as a man. I was a still a boy playing in a Bohemian world.

THOMAS WOLFE AND JOHN STEINBECK JOIN THE TEAM

There was a blizzard raging outside on the snowy streets of New York, and Homer was warmly insulated in the Dateline room. His attendance at the recent movie marathon aroused a good dose of patriotic nostalgia—about the West, about the land, about triumph. If the editors waved the flag too often, they risked venturing into sentimental slosh, but there were some issues Homer felt deeply about, especially after seeing *The Grapes of Wrath*. The next issue of *TIME* would have no story that could rise to the standard of an Editor's Note. Homer had to fill a page, but the problem of what to write that would sustain the trusted "Note" was compounded by writer's block. Homer had to draw upon pure inspiration for the four hundred words he needed to contribute. As he moved into a stronger *TIME* identity, matching that of a Special Correspondent, he kept company with John Steinbeck and Thomas Wolfe, his favorite authors—especially Wolfe, who proved he could go home again. Homer kept returning to Wolfe's books, over and over. The magazine, he dared to think, could use some fresh thinking from old hands. He recognized that good writing needed to be cherished and that there were such writers who still had much to say to refresh the promise of the country. Father Rivage had first introduced him to many of their works with a lecture about the West. It was time for Homer to engage Tom and John in conversation; he needed them to help fill the column.

DATELINE NEW YORK: BY OUR SPECIAL CORRESPONDENT
PIONEERS AND FRONTIERS

Thomas Wolfe and John Steinbeck are on assignment. Wolfe writes: Go seeker if you will throughout the land, and you'll find us burning in the night. There, where the hackles of the Rocky Mountains blaze in the blank and naked radiance of the moon, go make your resting place on the highest peak. Can you not see us? Turn now seeker, and look another thousand miles across the moon-blazing world of the Painted Desert, beyond the Sierra's edge, to the magic congeries of lights there in the West. The continental wall juts sheer and flat, its huge black shadows on the plain, and behold, flung like stardust on the field of night, past that spreading constellation to the north, just before the jeweled crescent of a hundred towns and cities is the land.

Steinbeck replies: I can see you now, Tom, on your resting stool atop the Rocky Mountains. I see you along with the men and women who made the great crossing, carrying with them the lyric of the land that reaches us with affecting form. They allow us to live on a heroic scale and strike us with full power.

It is the promise of the plains. The land transforms us, it provides for us, it is us. Their courage made it to the high coast mountains and to the valleys where gray clouds marched in from the ocean. They made it through the rains that began with gusty showers and paused before growing into a downpour that gradually settled into a single tempo. And when the rain stopped, tiny points of grass came through the earth, and in a few days the hills were green with the beginning year.

That's how it started, Tom. And the vision men had seen. The glow in their faces will always belong to them. They made it; they made it. They made it through the rock formations that stand as churches, supported by towering redwood columns. They carried life out here and set it down. The Westering was as big as God, with slow steps until the continent was crossed.

From your resting stool, can you see me now, Tom?

I can see you now, John. I can see you now.

As soon as Steinbeck and Wolfe finished their assignment, the teletype resumed its familiar clacking. "Dateline: Associated Press"—Received. Stories about the land, the country, and making a difference were being dispatched from Dateline.

"Who's the Special Correspondent?" Luce demanded. "Thomas Wolfe can't be writing from the grave."

Clurman didn't know. He just wasn't sure. The writing seemed to have the style of Paul O'Neill and Loudon Wainwright, two wordsmith masters who didn't mind being credited. They appreciated Steinbeck and Wolfe's unmistakably authentic words, but the issue remained unsolved.

Editor-in-Chief Luce was determined to identify the real author. When no one came forward, he sent a memo. "If we have some mysterious writer in our ranks, I don't mind, but we must acknowledge authorship and a byline. I was surprised by and appreciate these good words crossing the nation. As the son of a missionary, I know the

Almighty works in strange ways but I need to know the source of this literary chicanery."

As an unintended but productive consequence, Margaret Bourke-White was assigned a photo essay on the West, which ran in a subsequent issue. Stories expanded into areas outside the usual news, inaugurating a series called "Civilization" and another, "The Ages of Man." Stories about movers and shakers, promise and purpose from different perspectives. The magazine's engine was driven toward the nation's interest. And for Homer, there was other news in play.

A MAGICAL, AFFECTIONATE CIRCLE

"When the curtain came down, it just seemed terribly sad. I was in a comfort zone of make-believe and wanted to stay."

—Homer Sincere's journal, 1961

Daisy invited the undetected correspondent to a performance of "Anything Goes!" This time Homer watched from backstage, not from the privacy of his overhead "lighting booth." He enjoyed seeing the stage manager command a large board with switches and lights from his small elevated platform, sending light and sound cues from his headset to black-dressed stagehands. In backstage corners, dancers stretched, actors rehearsed their lines, and the show was on. It was another world, another place, alive, vibrant, and magical. Flats, sets, ropes, cables, scrims, backdrops, muslin, and paint, all part of a mechanical stage apparatus that underpinned the performance.

Overhead rows and rows of lights were suspended from black pipes, projecting circles of blue and violet, pink and amber. The overture began, the curtain rose, and from his special place, Homer watched Daisy Philips. There was nothing like backstage during a performance; it was private, intimate, exciting.

It was over too quickly. When the curtain dropped in a swash of ripples, Homer awakened from the land of make-believe. Walking home with Daisy, he was giddy with delight. He thought about her talent and the difference between the performing Daisy and the real Daisy at his side.

"You're easy on the eyes, Daisy."

"An actress is only as attractive on stage as you imagine her to be off stage."

Homer pondered the notion. Daisy was attractive on and off the stage, but Homer wanted to know what she felt when she was on stage. Before he could ask, Daisy gave him the answer: "It's hard to describe. Something overcomes you. How do you write? Something happens. When the audience reacts to you, is really with you, it becomes a very seductive experience. I really love to be alone and yet an intimate part of something—the play, the words, the music. Am I making any sense? When a spotlight throws a beam of light and finds me, I step into a magical, affectionate circle."

"You have a lot of promise!" No, that wasn't quite right. Homer tried to find something more substantial to say. Daisy was more than a bright promise. But before he found his phrase, Daisy cut in, "The only thing that cuts a little ice is the possibility or the promise of affection, and that's something for you to consider."

"E.M. Forster," Homer shot back.

"Possibility or promise?" Daisy responded mischievously.

Homer needed time to think about it.

Daisy carried a large bag, and Homer politely asked, "What's that? Can I help you?"

"You'll see."

OVER A CARDBOARD SEA

"It's Billy Sunshine. That poster went with me everywhere. And much to my surprise and delight, Daisy knew all about Billy! Daisy had a million questions. I had a million answers and was ready to give a few."

—Homer Sincere's journal, 1961

Inside his apartment, Daisy saw the poster above Homer's desk and shrieked, "Homer, that's Billy Sunshine!"

He was taken by surprise.

"You won't believe this, Homer, but I've loved Billy Sunshine ever since I was little. As a matter of fact, I have a photograph of me in a cowboy hat, toting a holster—do you think that's unusual for a girl?"

"You are what you are," they repeated, smiling in agreement.

They sang together, "It's only a paper moon, sailing over a cardboard sea."

That was followed by another question: "Do you think we see something of ourselves in each other?" Daisy asked. "I think we do."

Among his belongings, Homer had an old cowboy hat. He put it on.

"You like it?"

"You really are a cowboy."

For dinner, Daisy made terrific fettuccini. At the last minute, she added some melted butter, crisp bacon, just enough garlic and parsley, topping the dish with Parmesan and Romano cheeses. "Sour cream, that's the secret ingredient," Daisy confided, mixing it into the sauce. Removing all the papers from his desk, Homer prepared its long polished surface for their meal.

"What was it like for you, growing up in New Orleans—before you met the governor and all? I've always pictured the Quarter as a mysterious place. What was your mother like?"

"She was a writer; she wrote children's stories. She died when I was ten."

"I'm sorry. I'm really sorry." Daisy paused and then asked about his father.

It was a sensitive subject, one he had long ignored. "He was a musician who played the best trumpet in Louisiana. I loved to hear him play. But someone who meant more to me was Waldo, a remarkable philosopher in the Quarter who helped me though the hard times . . . I couldn't understand why my mother went away. Waldo taught me to hope . . . but hope was not enough to save her."

Homer moved to a brighter subject.

"I have a surprise," he said, opening the recessed panel looking down on the darkened theater with just a work light on stage. "I've watched your show so many times that I've memorized all the lines, know all the songs, and could go on as your understudy." Daisy closed her eyes and didn't speak.

"Is something the matter? Did I say something wrong?"

"It's just that I might be falling in love with you," Daisy whispered. "I knew something was going to happen the very first moment I saw you again: trouble."

Homer had absorbed every word, amazed at her revelation.

"Trouble? Me?"

Daisy nodded. "I want more than anything in the world to be an actress, Homer. Not just any kind of actress, but a great one."

"What does that have to do with how you feel about me?"

"My God, Homer, I look at you and see a home, not a career."

"But you are an actress . . . I don't . . ."

"It's not about me, damn it," she turned to him. "It's about you. When I see you, I feel the same love that my parents had for each other."

Homer had no frame of reference.

Daisy spoke about her early years—her home in Le Place, her mother who was devoted to her family, and her father who owned a bookstore called the Book Nook where she spent most of her time alone, reading, pretending, longing to be an actress.

A SHORT DISTANCE IN BETWEEN

"Daisy kissed me tenderly. I had wondered what making love would be like, in my youthful fantasies. I was tentative and unsure what to do; would I please, would my lovemaking be adequate? Soon our kisses were deep and long, embracing that passionate moment when nothing else could matter.

I adored her ample breasts, slender waist, and rounded hips, all converging in perfection. We lay in comfortable silence, our thoughts aloft in different directions, like clouds floating in the sky until they vanished into memory. If I had been a composer, I would have written a song. Or an artist, painted a watercolor. But I aimed to be a writer, and I look for words. Nobody needed Monet's studies before he painted them, or Mozart's concertos before he wrote them, but I could not imagine the world without Daisy, lyrically lovely and occupying a quiet place in a spinning world. She was the stuff of sonnets and songs. Her radiance was born to shine on others and not herself, a beauty made by generosity and goodness. She expanded my vision and refreshed my spirit. Close to her, my curiosity and imagination met up with my fantasy. It was a symphony composed by creating notes into notational melody, in just the right combination. Was it music? Maybe more, maybe an artist who begins with only a vision, on a blank canvas until brushstrokes paint passion and beauty, longed for and felt, creating a still-life with texture and movement, touching the heart, something long remembered. Making a painting, making love, making music, all meeting the same equation. Something happened from the deepest feelings under a carpet of winking stars."

—Homer Sincere's journal, 1961

"Books, Homer, they always took me far away."

"I've read a lot, too, Daisy."

"I know that. Tell me, Homer, fantasy or reality, what is more important?"

Homer couldn't answer. How far was it between the two?

"The reality is fantasy brought to life," Daisy continued.

In a moment, she kissed him, and the tenderness of her kiss lifted him to the stars. She accepted Homer as he was, she never seemed to care about his brace, and that was a good feeling.

Dressed in only a petticoat, she lay in his bed on his pillow. Every action involved all of her; when she walked, the world was in step, when she leaned toward Homer and whispered, he was conscripted into her world, and longed for more kisses.

When she left the following morning, he lay in bed thinking about what it would be like to have her always in his life. How sad it would be if she were not around. Reality, fantasy, was there a difference?

YOU'RE THE TOPS

He had Daisy's attention. I was a lover, as least numerically fashioned, while Homer had a quiet but singular integrity. And his inventiveness to win her went airborne. The rooftop above his apartment had a cupola, a balcony, where he often took a break from his assignments, a place to think, a place to give his rocking chair a rest. He looked over the garden and courtyard that brought a bit of the Quarter to New York and observed Daisy strolling there. From this point of view, it was not likely that Daisy would come into a camera frame but she did. For a moment, he lost her behind a trellis. She reappeared, in time for Homer to scribble a lyric from "Anything Goes" on a piece of white paper, fold it into a glider, and set it flying. The note caught a breeze, turning, twisting, and fell close to Daisy. The flight of "You're the tops" landed safely in her hands.

Daisy looked up, squinting toward the sun. "That's not fair!"

"Were you expecting special delivery?"

"No, hand-delivered, and signed for."

"You didn't tell me that."

"And how do I answer letters postmarked from rooftops?"

"With suitable sentiment."

"Do you have a stamp?" she cried up to him.

"I suppose I do."

"Then mail yourself down, now."

He tripped down the steps until he was in her arms, then swept her to the fluffy down pillows on her living room sofa. "O Mio Bambino Caro," Puccini's lovely aria, made perfect background music. The azaleas blooming outside made a magic garden. All was in soft focus, like a scene from the movies.

* * *

They both loved books and fell into acting out plots and characters; Daisy had an enthusiasm for "bookacting," a pastime she invented, and Homer followed into her new game, just to see if he could compete.

He was good at malaproping with "The Rivals," playing Captain Absolute, "deeply enameled" of his niece Lydia Languish, a young lady "'with a very specious place in my inflection."

After reading "Hay Fever," and with a little help from Noel Coward, Daisy transformed her apartment for a drawing room comedy, with Miss Sorel Bliss making an attempt at normalcy. However, the subtext and her artistic temperament got the best of her.

In this new role, Homer spent the night at Daisy's apartment. She had a piano, and without missing a beat, he took to the four progression chords Daisy had taught him when she visited Pea Patch. She had not forgotten her improvised melody, and sitting side by side, they played together.

He had never before slept in someone else's bed, and the experience was a deeply personal one. The walls of the room were washed in light yellow and white tones. In the center, there was a large double, four-poster, canopied bed, framed by a wrought iron headboard with brass finials. A feather down comforter amply covered lavender-scented cotton sheets.

"Comfortable?"

"Very!"

"You like the bed?" Daisy asked.

"Even Oblomov would never leave!"

Daisy caught her breath. "You like the mattress?"

"What? Daisy, of course I like the mattress."

Homer slid under the covers close to Daisy. Feeling her warmth completed him.

"It's from England. The Savoy Hotel. They make all of their own mattresses."

"Are we going to talk about mattresses at a time like this?"

"I just thought you should know." Daisy kissed him, her hands stroking his neck and head.

"How did you get the mattress from the Savoy Hotel?" Homer asked.

"It was a prop in a play. You've heard of method acting. The director, Kurt Owens, wanted everything authentic, so the producers let him have his eccentric way. After all, he was Kurt Owens. So they sent to the Savoy for the mattress. Call it method scenery."

"What was the play?"

"Noël Coward's Design for Living."

"I think we should live together."

"You're serious," Daisy murmured. "And I'm afraid to deal with that. Separate apartments is better."

Homer didn't think so.

He held Daisy, his hands lightly touching her body, brushing her hair off her face, gently kissing her cheeks. This must be what Waldo meant when he said the most important things are what you cannot see. It's what you feel.

AFTERTHOUGHTS

In the morning, there was a lingering goodbye kiss when Homer left her front door. Daisy got back into bed, scrunching up under the covers in a place left warm by him. With her head propped on one pillow, she took the pillow that had been under Homer's head and placed it on top of hers. She thought about him, keenly aware of his lemon citrus scent, suggesting to her what it would be like to live with him. It was fresh and invigorating, not the smoky musk she had known on other men. She fell back asleep realizing how thoroughly she had fallen in love. When she awoke, she reached over to touch him, but he was gone. Her heart was in conflict with her thoughts, with her reason. She wasn't ready to be that involved, still not sure of what she really wanted. She panicked. In order to deflect her feelings, she had to ease her mind and put the relationship into proper perspective.

THE THREE OF US

I invited Homer and Daisy to a small party given by John Steinbeck. When I had asked Steinbeck if I could bring my team, he didn't mind at all. I had recently photographed him for *TIME* and thought Homer would like to meet this author, especially due to his deep admiration for *The Grapes of Wrath* and John's success as a Hollywood screenwriter. *East of Eden* had been a favorite film of Homer's as well. Homer was delighted.

Arriving at a Village brownstone, they were introduced to several guests. Homer had moored himself in a sunny alcove when Steinbeck said to him, "Imagine teaming me up with Tom Wolfe—that was one hell of a piece of prose. Who wrote it?"

Homer paused for a minute, proud of the essay he had penned, then answered, "One of the special correspondents."

"I really enjoyed it. I'll drop a note to Harry Luce. Really clever."

Homer looked down. I did not know at the time about his secret involvement and his journalistic forays. I was enjoying the company's search for the elusive correspondent. Usually change and shake-ups occur from the top down, not from the bottom up.

Steinbeck quickly and easily engaged Homer, discussing books they both liked. With a deep, resonant voice, white hair, a strong physique, and just enough of a beard, Steinbeck had a presence to be reckoned with. He had taken a journey across America while writing his *Travels With Charley* and used words that Homer understood: "A journey is a person in itself; no two are alike. I find that after years of struggle, I did not take the trip; the trip took me."

There were artists, poets, and producers. When a few made a fuss over Daisy, she enjoyed the attention. "That's Igor Kaganovich, the Russian dancer," Daisy pointed out to Homer. Two men played mah-jongg in a corner, clicking ivory, and chirping in Chinese. Homer was fascinated. He noticed a framed painting of blue and white, yellow and pink squares in a mosaic pattern. Looking closer, he realized that it was a montage of rejection slips, all varnished and framed. At the head of each small panel was the bold name of a publishing house. Scribner, Harper & Row, Lippincott, Holt, Reinhart and Winston, Simon & Schuster, Random House, and Doubleday were all represented.

"I am sorry," Homer said quietly to Steinbeck.

"Oh, no," the art dealer Harriet Janus interrupted. "It's art. I framed them all together for John, using a divided pattern of intersecting lines for a theater of color. A visual display of emotional wounds. I call it 'Rejection,' but John calls it 'Inspiration.'

Homer was sure Father Rivage would have enjoyed the afternoon. A literary agent talked to a publisher about poetry's declining marketplace; a young lady from the Crazy Horse in Paris described stripping and streaking; Luke Higgins, a baseball player from Philadelphia, wound up with an imaginary pitch demonstrating to Daisy how his curve ball followed a principle of Newtonian physics. Ramon Córdova, the bullfighter from Spain, and George Serban, the existentialist psychologist from Romania, had an intermittent conversation.

"A las cinco de las tardes," said García Lorca of life and death, always at five o'clock.

"Both are connected in time," replied George.

Harry Janus, Harriet's husband, suggested a refreshing philosophic art walk to Washington Square.

They filed out of the carriage house into the rambling streets of the Village, encountering a similar group from uptown that had come to visit the Washington Square Art Show. Harry led the way, with his coat draped over his shoulders. He seemed to know everyone—shopkeepers, fruit vendors, passers-by, and the street artists, who greeted him with friendly smiles. The late afternoon air turned colder, but still the sun shone on the walking gallery.

"Do you see that arch?" Steinbeck asked, pointing to the beaux-arts Washington Square triumphal arch across the park. "A man once took refuge inside that monument. Monument and man, tribute and tribulation. The two are connected in some ways, I guess."

The experience had frustrated Homer. More that ever, he yearned for real journalistic experiences and assignments to record them.

A squadron of pigeons burst into flight, their fluttering shadows moving across the square.

A DAY IN THE LIFE OF DAISY PHILIPS

With his creative momentum, Homer suggested that we shoot a new film together, like we did years ago in New Orleans.

I was always up for filming. "Sure . . . what about?"

"About Daisy."

"Daisy Philips?"

"She has a birthday coming up. It will make a perfect surprise, and I have a shooting script." Homer plopped it into my hands.

The idea was a hoot, but the thought of not telling Homer that Daisy and I had been intimate troubled me. The less said the better, I rationalized. It is not a subject a gentleman brings up. It was up to Daisy. Our relationship could add a spicy adjective to our filmmaking. I really liked her as a friend, she was enchanting to me, but Homer was the one who lived in that world.

I had a lot of growing up to do to reach Homer's level of honesty and commitment. He was more mature in his affection than happy-go-lucky me. But I'm running on about confession. Eventually, Homer made me a much better man than I was then.

Making a film with Homer about Daisy? What could be more fun than shooting a film on a subject he loved? We rented a van with a sun-roof and an open back, like what some television crews use on location.

It was essential to be so undistinguished in order not to be seen. As we secretly followed Daisy from location to location, we used rooftops and balconies, seeking unusual angles. Homer presented me an outline for our shooting script. We had a new feature player and a star!

INT. HOMER'S APARTMENT-DAY

Shooting: *A Day in the Life of Daisy Philips.*

We shoot Daisy's rehearsal from the opening in my apartment, using a handheld 35 mm Arriflex and long lens.

(We take turns looking through the camera. There's enough light on stage.)

EXT. NEW YORK STREETS-DAY

We stake out a place near Daisy's mews house and wait for her to appear.

From our truck, we film with our concealed camera.

(CAMERA zooms in.)

PICK-UPS and CUT-AWAYS

(Lots of long shots and close-ups, morning to night)

Daisy in her garden.

Daisy at the Cherry Lane Theater. Daisy rehearsing. Daisy performing.

Daisy having coffee. Daisy taking a bus uptown.

Daisy at the Special School for Performing Arts.

Daisy in a park, studying lines.

Daisy at audition.

MONTAGE.

Daisy eating a doughnut, picking up dry-cleaning, playing the piano, teaching kids, shopping, walking, greeting, talking, smiling. Shots of the performance from the back of the house.

EXT. DAISY'S COURTYARD-DAY

Cake delivered to a surprised Daisy.

(Cut and print).

We edited our film on a Moviola at Hearst Movietone News where I had a film editor friend. Using the stock library down the hall, we were able to intercut footage of Daisy with crowds cheering, parades marching, bands playing, fans waving, as well as applause by audiences in the Metropolitan Opera House and Yankee Stadium. The production team added a tuneful song from a Fellini film soundtrack (forgive us, Federico!). Italian soundtracks always had it all for me.

As a finishing touch, I used footage from long ago, shot at Louise's Snack and Chat. It was in black and white and fortunately hadn't faded—a risk with film nitrate, the composition of film at the time. I thought it made a classic opening before our film shifted to color. Homer was delighted when I showed it to him.

Our film was edited, scored, and mixed. We had shot cinema verité at its incomparable best. We secured time for our premiere at a small art house in the Village off Fifth Avenue, a refurbished theater that had space to rent before its formal opening a week later. Our timing was just right.

"This is great," said Homer. He left a note inviting Daisy to see a movie with us. "Would she like to come along?"

I was excited too. We had captured some unguarded moments, and the film had freshness all over it. On the date the movie was set to screen, Clurman detained Homer at the office on a fast-breaking story: an invasion of Cuba. There had been confidential reports that the United States had trained several thousand Cubans to liberate their homeland, and our Washington bureau had heard from intelligence sources that we had given between five and seven thousand Cuban and some Guatemalan volunteers intensive infantry training in infiltration, guerrilla tactics, demolition techniques, and hand-to-hand combat. Training camps had been established. The movement was known as the *Frente*.

"Go ahead without me, Rig," Homer said. I felt his disappointment. "I've got an invasion to attend to."

"Homer, you gotta come, you gotta be there. It was your idea, and it's your film!"

He was deeply frustrated, but Dateline had priority. I explained Homer's last-minute work demand to Daisy, with regret.

Daisy knew something was up; the movie marquee tipped the surprise: *A Day in the Life of Daisy Philips.*

After we were seated in the theater, the film began with a stirring fanfare over the titles. Daisy dissolved into giggles with each scene. She clapped her hands in pure joy.

"You boys are incorrigible, you're just outrageous. You've got it all over Candid Camera."

Afterward, we went to a nearby restaurant called Peter's Backyard. It was a soft, warm evening, and a string of lights wrapped in trees overhead added romance.

"Why did you go to all that trouble? I mean, Rigby, that must have taken a lot of time, and God—how original!" I was the beneficiary of her enthusiasm.

"Homer wanted something special for your birthday, so we sleuthed around for a few days shooting scenes from rooftops, from the back of a truck, all kinds of angles. There was one particular 28 to 300-Angenieux zoom lens . . ." I was getting technical and caught myself.

"I was afraid you would see us. Are you near-sighted?"

"I wish Homer had come. You guys are just irresistible."

I explained again, "Clurman needed Homer on an irresistible deadline. He really wanted to be here; it was his idea."

"Where did you get the footage of Homer and me dancing the zydeco? It is just incredible."

"I shot it from outside the shack, just before we went up to Baton Rouge long ago."

"And you kept it all these years!"

I needed to say something to Daisy that was a long time coming. I'm not sure even to this day what happened, but making the film and seeing her again had swept me away. I couldn't resist the temptation of taking full advantage of being close, though I knew Homer was "over the paper moon" for her.

"I want to apologize."

"Yeah, you were a bit of a cad."

"I feel I let you down. I'm sorry. Sounds hollow, but you are very seductive."

"Rigby, get real. You had every intention of seducing me, and you know it. And I enjoyed every moment. Sure, for awhile you took part of my heart with you. Now I've got it back, and I'm glad we are friends.

"Me too."

"You're forgiven."

But there was more. As I looked at her, everything I saw and felt about her drew me nearer. I invited her back to my apartment, a floor-through in an East 60s townhouse with a balcony, a mansard roof, reminiscent of the French houses on the Quarter, with wide polished doors and floors, and tall European windows looking out to an awning of treetops. I knew Daisy would like it. In the living room were some of the artifacts of my work, photographs documenting my career—statesmen, celebrities, and sailboats. In a corner where I kept my cameras, I had stenciled on a wall in Times Roman, a point size reaching twelve inches with bullets between each word, a phase summing up my mantra for photography: "The Eyes See What The Mind Does Not Yet Know."

I never invited any of my colleagues over, not much on entertaining, except for an occasional lady, and now, Daisy. I enjoyed and appreciated a bond closer than being just friends. It was more than seeing her on film. She was here, fresh and appealing, up close and personal. In a wave of desire, I kissed her. She didn't respond at first but slowly gave in.

"Rigby, I knew you cared when you helped me by writing that lovely piece, 'The Song of It All.' That meant a lot to me, and the kids. That was very sensitive and kind, and I should have thanked you right away."

I'm embarrassed to say that I did not correct Daisy about the story

Homer had filed, and took advantage of the situation. Soon we melted into a deeper embrace. It was rich and tempting, passionate and forbidden. We made love.

The next morning, Daisy pulled away and looked into my eyes. "Rigby . . . I . . . Homer."

I immediately realized and became ashamed that my elevated testosterone had run rampant and had overtaken us. Daisy meant more to Homer than she did to me. It was not just the champagne. Neither of us had said no.

Before I could say a word, Daisy continued: "Rigby, the truth of the matter is I love you both. We had a wonderful weekend—you swept me off my feet when I was vulnerable and lonely. And you did that again last night. But now there are not just two of us to consider.

"Rigby, I think I love you for all the wrong reasons, and I love Homer for all the right ones."

Her words had a sobering sting. I felt guilty, but even more, I came to realize that I had betrayed my best friend. When I had kissed her, it was not due to any competition with Homer, it was just Rigby being Rigby.

"Do you think we could keep what happened between us?" I asked Daisy.

"It was deeply between us," she responded. "We got caught up in each other, and you know something, Rigby, it's hard for me to leave." Daisy was more sober about our attraction than I was.

"I don't want to hurt Homer," I said. "He needs friends, and he's a great guy, a bit of a loner."

"You are a bit of a loner yourself," Daisy said, turning to me and caressing a pillow on my couch. She looked at me tenderly, her thoughts evidently going back and forth, yet sure of herself, not embarrassed but maybe with some regrets.

"I like company," I said, just to say something.

"In skirts." Daisy had cut right through my alibi.

"That's not fair."

"You have this incredible ability of falling in and out of love with every passing girl, out of curiosity. As soon as you finish an assignment, it becomes the snapshot of the moment. You know that I'm more than an eight-by-ten glossy! But I didn't and had to prove that to myself. I was hinged to my insecurity. You think you are not involved with me, but you are."

"I am?"

"With your camera!"

She was right. I wondered later if I could ever change. Then came the cold realization: What would I say to Homer, if anything at all?

CHECK AND BALANCE

"A 4% per annum interest rate seemed very good. Was it more than just a fantasy that I wanted to build a future with Daisy?"

—Homer Sincere's journal, 1963

Like a calendar in a movie flipping pages with the passing years, Homer's hopes and dreams were no different from mine—just different priorities, destinations, and a different approach to relationships. He opened a savings account at the Bank of New York, depositing his weekly hundred-fifty dollar paycheck to the care of its manager, Mr. Holliday. It was an unpretentious branch in the West Fifties situated in a small brownstone that was always ceremoniously quiet. It was dwarfed by the financial monoliths of Chase and Manufacturer's Hanover Trust that dominated the Avenue of the Americas. Nelson Holliday was a round, jovial man, never quite neat and always perspiring. He wore rigorously starched shirts and brown oxfords incongruous with his banker's blue suit. He explained how Preferred Savings, at four percent per annum compounded, would soon be enough to start a family.

While making his weekly deposit one morning, Homer heard a stunning announcement: The president had been shot! He stopped at a small telephone booth just inside the bank to call the office.

Chapter 10
NEW YORK 1963

There was great sadness and mourning in the country. The editors were in a flurry of activity to assemble a special issue with recollections from President Kennedy's colleagues. Theodore White and Mark Shaw's photographs provided the magazine's eloquent history of the president. After putting the story to bed, emotionally exhausted staffers went home, leaving the offices empty.

The last few dispatches had been written, edited, and put on the teletypes that were spitting and punctuating stories all over the country. In their temperature-controlled room, much colder than the November afternoon outside, the machines tapped furiously, dispatching fast-breaking news. They chattered with accounts of the fallen president. Homer wondered what he would have written if he had been at the White House. The president and Homer had something in common, significant for different reasons; they both had rocking chairs in their lives.

DATELINE NEW YORK: BY OUR SPECIAL CORRESPONDENT
THE PRESIDENT'S EMPTY CHAIR

He sits in a rocking chair while you sit on the sofa looking at him from the side. He is dressed carefully but rather informally. His trousers are sharply pressed, and he wears well-worn, well-shined shoes. His face has an everlasting tan, and he looks at you with his head slightly bent back, gray eyes glinting with an expression of interest, amusement, and mischief. After a moment, he looks through the French doors to his Rose Garden, of which he is very proud. The roses are in bloom, odd for this time of year. Kennedy loved his garden just as much as he loved to sail at sea. And there, he loved to win a race.

All of us are terribly sad that he is dead. He was a fine president. On this Saturday afternoon, the autumn skies outside the East Room of the White House make the light inside gray. The tiny golden bulbs of the great chandeliers are dimmed to faintest candlepower. It wasn't long ago, back in November 1960, that John Kennedy got up from his chair, extended his hand, pointed a long forefinger, and said, "I run for the presidency of the United States because it's the center of action and, in a free society, the chief responsibility of the president is to set forth to the American people the unfinished business of our country."

Now the rocking chair is empty.

I passed by the wire room and saw Homer composing at the teletype. I knocked on the glass window; it took several taps before he acknowledged me.

"You still working?"

"Just some unfinished stuff."

The teletype machine stopped, confirming his file had been sent, and Homer handed me a copy of "The President's Empty Chair." I read it.

"It's a thoughtful piece."

"I wrote it, dispatched it on Dateline . . ."

"You what?"

"What do you think?"

"Homer, are you nuts? Look at me."

"Yes, why?"

"Homer, you can't do that."

"Just a few words, no harm. I really had to write something."

"Homer, the wire service is sacred!"

"I know. But I felt I had to, wanted to, it was my assignment."

"Your assignment? Who gave you the assignment?"

"Me."

"How many times have you done this?"

"Only when there was something of value."

"You are the Special Correspondent!"

"Not necessarily special, but secret."

"You can't do this, Homer. Listen to me, it's well-meaning and all, but if you're caught . . ."

"I don't mean any harm. This is a sacred place, Rigby. There's no place like this room, and there was no one like the president."

We had done some crazy things in our lives but not like this. Maybe it was just "outrageous fortune," but I secretly admired Homer's daring.

We continued our assignments. Clurman had remembered the footage of the King March that Homer and I had showed him and that he had liked it. I asked if Homer could come with me on my next assignment. He knew how to use a Filmo, and I could focus on stills for the magazine.

"Let me be very clear, Rigby," Clurman said. "Your essential assignment is for the magazine. I expect great coverage and powerful photographs. If you can manage some moving footage, fine, but I want something I can run."

Months passed, and still no field assignment. Homer bought a khaki correspondent's jacket so he would be ready to participate in fast-breaking events. Rigby reminded him how important it was to read everything in the newsroom and observe keenly. The editors confirmed he couldn't go on assignment, not just yet—the time was not right. In the meantime, he wanted to measure up with the few paragraphs he wrote each week for the managing editors. He was like a Soldier of the Word, but it was not enough—he had to prove himself in the field.

He read stories filed by stringers and correspondents around the country and had a good idea what was going on in America, including its small towns. Often, a letter to the editor landed on his desk after being shuffled around the building, the last stop before the trash basket. Letters came from Batesville, Texas; Putnam County, Kansas; from Aiken, South Carolina, and Greencastle, Indiana. Some were opinions on stories, others appealed for action. One letter from Iowa particularly affected him:

Dear Sir,

I'm just a simple man with a home and a horse in Peachville. I've lost my farm. A long time ago, my people had a hard time making it from Pennsylvania. Walked most of the way. We have been told by the court to move but we don't know where to go. I've had my place for many years. Just a small piece of land that I lease and call my own. My father and his father lived here too. We take care of our land. But now it is being taken away to make room for a dump! Can you believe it?

I understand the government wants to bury some kind of chemical waste that has polluted our stream nearby. I see it coming because of that new plant up the road. Nobody paid any attention when many dogs got sick, and one of my mine died from lapping up some water there. I used to go swimming in that cool stream on summer days. We need that water to grow things, especially when the rain is a long time coming. Now nothing's worth a damn. Imagine that! I cultivated my land for over forty-five years and grew some of the best corn and lettuce, and even a few peaches. I hear a lot like that is going on around the country. We're losing something of value. I read your magazine, and I was hoping one of you might let folks know what is going on here. Sure would be appreciated and help us a lot.

And if you come out this way, come on by for some of Momma's supper and sample her fine peach pie.

Sincerely,
J.W. Grand

The editors were not really interested in answering letters, though they could be used to gauge what people were thinking. If someone took the time to write, Homer thought he should respond. How would Steinbeck and Wolfe feel about pollution, about their beautiful land and waters? It was about the land and righting a wrong, a major value belonging to Billy. And Father Rivage's verbal essay about the beauty of land and resources. These simple thoughts, from a simple man, inspired Homer and again he took to Dateline.

DATELINE: NEW YORK: BY OUR SPECIAL CORRESPONDENT
A TOWN CALLED PEACHVILLE

Some sixty miles west of Burlington, Iowa, on Route 70, there is a town called Peachville, population 30,000. On the outskirts, a turnoff called 8th Street leads past a few shack buildings, a beer hall, and an old brick warehouse. Nothing much has been happening in Peachville, except for a chemical plant polluting the river. Further down the road are small white houses with front lawns and backyards. People live the kind of life that takes them to the office in five minutes or hunting in the country in ten.

Peachville, Iowa, is far away and far removed from the politicians and power brokers in Washington and New York, but people have feelings and opinions in this heartland. They shop at Sears, Roebuck for a stove and J.C. Penney's for the kids' new clothes. They go to church on Sunday and the Rotary Club on Wednesday. Life has not changed much for these folks except for something called pollution poisoning their river. Farmers are losing their farms. They're losing their crops but they are keeping their personal values. The good people, the folks of Peachville, with their fine fruit pies, deserve to be heard.

Simple letters flooded in to Letters to the Editor. This time the building reverberated due to the Special Correspondent, the secret correspondent. The staff was amused, but Corporate wasn't.

"For Christ's sake," Luce dispatched, "Can't anyone own up to this editorial chicanery so we can all sit down and enjoy a slice of peach pie?"

AN IRISH INTERLUDE

While things were heating up in the building, Daisy's exciting invitation was a convenient opportunity for the Special Correspondent to take a break. Daisy still felt guilty about me and the events of our evening together two years ago—complicated, confused, and impulsive. What could she do? Bookacting could go on location!

"Let's take a trip," she suggested to Homer. "How about if we go to Dublin? I want to introduce you to my Irish heritage."

"I didn't know you were Irish."

"I'm not."

Homer could hardly contain himself. He grabbed Daisy and held her. He couldn't stop smiling. "Why not?"

They looked like a couple of refugees from *The Great Gatsby*. Daisy had taken to wearing long beaded gowns in keeping with the character of her latest part at the Cherry Lane, and Homer adapted to a set of tweeds. He looked every bit the part of a young, brash man in his mid-twenties. They escaped from the Cherry Lane, flew overnight to Heathrow. From Victoria Station they took a train to Wales that would connect with the morning ferry to Dublin.

Warm in their compartment on British Rail, they bounced easily from side to side, cozy with hot tea, crumpets, cucumber sandwiches, and English cheddar cheese with Branston relish. Only the sound of a hooting whistle interrupted their conversation. Two lovers traveling on a train, known only to each other. Could this be a film like *Brief Encounter*?

Homer felt completely comfortable with Daisy, soothed by the gentle rocking of the carriage going *rickady rackady* over the tracks. They snuggled under crisp linen sheets on the lower birth. When her hair fell across his face, he closed his eyes and smelled the scent of lime and sugar lemon, a familiar citrus scent; Daisy had taken to wearing his cologne.

They stood on the deck of the ferry the next morning. A sweeping fog broke occasionally to give them a peek of Wales as it receded. The breeze felt wonderful and somehow made a mug with hot tea taste even better. There was a ripple of sunlight, a crisp wind, and the Irish Sea sprayed their warm faces.

They were on their way to Ireland, the land of poets.

Daisy broke into an Irish brogue, and Homer knew what was coming.

She had brought along some books, and they continued book-acting. Now he rescued Rose from Brighton Rock with the help of Graham Greene and followed the free-floating narrative that James Joyce had bestowed upon Leopold and Molly Bloom.

No plot was too complicated or muddled. When it started to rain, Homer knew he was going to play the game again. Especially when Daisy produced a book of Irish plays by Sean O'Casey and John Synge. He took refuge in their stateroom, but Daisy couldn't wait.

"God save all here."

"God save you kindly!"

"Ah, it's glad enough I am to be out of the rain, out of God's leaking firmament, into the tidy room of a decent woman, I say."

"Can I be of assistance?"

"To the 'Playboy of the Western World'?"

"Yes, indeed, I've had no food since Father Reilly's bell announced the long and quiet dawn, and my stomach is aching, so it is. I'll be troubling you for a piece of the pride of Mayo."

"The pride of Mayo, is it now?"

"Oh yes, cut bravely in a muddling hunk thick at one end and sloping to a thin edge at the other, a slice of butter gold shining like a sunset over Crossmolina with a bloom in it that would make even the Royal Pope appetize and his Holy Cardinals smile."

"I'm sorry, my dear, but you have been at this place in New York these last months, and you have lost your lilt, but would you be doing for a Kraft grilled cheese sandwich and a hot bowl of fine Campbell's tomato, invited to our table, to warm the fine morning chill and replenish my man?"

"A fine woman you are, the blessed angels shall be called down to witness."

They amused themselves in this utterly ridiculous fashion. Homer was sure he had taken a measure of retreat from the Soldier of the Word canon. Daisy was so well read that he could not resist the temptation of playing into her script.

"Imagine," Daisy said, "Two Americans at sea, pretending to be Irish."

The conversation turned to his job at *TIME*.

Her eyes reflected Homer's concern.

"You still want to get out into the field?"

"I do, and I think I will. But you know, Daisy, it's not working out. I'm thinking about what I really want to do. I hate to change time and place, but they follow along. Truth is that I've always loved cowboys, and maybe that's what I should be writing about. You know, Rigby and I wanted always to go to Hollywood. That was the plan."

"You wouldn't be thinking about riding off into the sunset now?"

"Not a chance."

"Billy Sunshine is still part of you. I think you want to ride with the cowboys."

"I always have wanted it. Hard for me to run away from them. I think about Billy Sunshine a lot, sometimes I even dream about Billy calling me.

'You gotta go to Hollywood. I think that's your future.'

'Go West.'

'California, son. It's the dream. That's what is important. It's where we come from and where we're going. I'm going to need a script. Saddle up, boy! 'We've got a lot to do.'

"We'll have to play out one of Billy's scripts, Homer. That's what we'll do!"

For a moment he felt conflict inside him. He had the same child-hood dream as Daisy. He wanted to be recognized as a writer as much as Daisy needed to be an actress. Or did he want to be a cowboy? For a while he wasn't sure, but Daisy restored his confidence. "You'll make it to Hollywood yet!"

Homer asked, "Where do we go from here?"

Daisy wasn't sure. "Paris, Singapore? Hollywood? I need a line. You're the writer!"

"I need a plot!"

Back on deck, a rush of wind took Homer's long, thick brown hair and blew it across his forehead.

A fine day was breaking through a white, wet mist when they reached the Irish coast. Approaching from the sea, with pale blue flashing lights from beacons that were twin blurs in the distance, Dublin kept them guessing until the last moment. They passed a light-house with a long shadow leading to a promising mirage, the green-gray hills of County Wicklow.

Along the streets of Dublin, green double-decker busses churned up O'Donnell Street. Daisy and Homer were stirred by the sight of great eighteenth-century buildings. The miles of modest houses were warmed by the intimacy of their multi-colored doors, each decorated with an arched fan of translucent colored glass, separated by slim white pieces of wood embracing ribbons of sunlight. Their shifting reflections in changing seasons, reflecting a blue sky and wandering clouds, may have inspired Yeats when he visited the city from the West Country.

Half a mile downstream of the river Liffey, they visited bars flow-ing with Guinness ale. Garrets nearby reflected the tradition of writers and storytellers, Joyce and Shaw, Swift and Wilde, who in voluntary exile wrote unforgettable portraits of their native town that would always be ready to welcome literary trespassers. Homer remembered Father's lectures on the great Irish writers.

Further down, Ireland's great government buildings, called the

Four Courts, with rambling courtyards with architectural symmetry, had been recently sandblasted, leaving dramatic sweeps of white columns, leading the eye to the long facade of Trinity College marked by its round blue clock chiming over an abundance of assets.

On Grafton Street, Georgian houses surrounded St. Stephen's Green bearing the imprint of past generations of Dubliners. At its center, on a silver pond, two swans dressed in pristine white feathers navigated their course while a flotilla of gray ducks sliced through the calm water, leaving a small rippling wake. In this welcome quiet moment, Homer found himself staring at Daisy. She would catch him looking. How could he make life better for her? He knew their time in Dublin would be too short. It was long on remembered kisses.

Finally, Homer gained courage. "I want to marry you someday."

Daisy spluttered. "I know, Homer. It's just not the time. I don't know what to say, I just don't know. We both need to be further along in our careers, don't you think? But you are as important to me as any words I could ever say."

"Will you think about it?"

"I will. I promise."

He wondered if they would ever be together or end like cowboy movies, just riding off into the sunset. He knew he loved Daisy and she was still finding her way. He had relied on her steadfast glow of love and longing, perhaps unconsciously enough as one among an assortment of painted scenery, props, and costumes, which supported his thinkable notion that life was rich, purposeful, and filled with reward, and a fact emerged that her adoring glance was reward enough. Then a single tear spilled down his cheek followed by a summer shower lasting just minutes, leaving the garden wet and drooping.

For the next few years, Homer was stuck with the Editor's Note. Daisy took small parts, sometimes in road companies. The distance between them was not easy to bridge. They were not only apart but Daisy was somewhere else. When she returned, Homer was overjoyed. Daisy took a part in Sandy Wilson's "The Boy Friend," which premiered at the Cherry Lane. He took the opportunity to watch from his apartment—she was amazing. She hoped for a good notice, and Homer was going to do something about it.

A review of Daisy's performance in the chorus of another off-Broadway show appeared mysteriously, not only on the news service, but also in *TIME*. I suspect our drama critic picked it up from Dateline. With twenty million readers each week, a brief note in the news magazine made a difference.

"'The only thing that cuts a little ice,' E.M. Forster wrote, 'is affection or the possibility of affection.' The current production of 'The Boyfriend' at New York's Cherry Lane Theater has non-stop affection, and Daisy Philips is a bright star of the New York stage. She won't be forgotten, hitting home to the heart long after the curtain rings down."

RIGBY CANFIELD'S AMAZING ACHIEVEMENT

"In the pre-dawn air strikes across the Arab world, Israeli jets all but eliminated Arab air power."

—Homer Sincere's journal, 1967

Careers were taking direction and adventure. I was getting more assignments, offers were coming in for Daisy, and Homer never stopped pitching film, to Clurman's utter exasperation. Big stories continued to break.

Then came an extraordinary turn of events: as fate would have it, Clurman eased up.

"I'm really sending you out to the field this time, Canfield!"

"I asked if Homer could come with me."

"He might be ready, but let me be very clear, Rigby. Your essential assignment is for the magazine. I expect some great coverage, powerful photographs. If you can manage some moving footage, fine, but I want something I can run."

* * *

In 1967, war had broken out between Israel and its Arab neighbors who intended to destroy the Jewish state. We were off together on the assignment to cover it. Homer knew how to use the Filmo, and I would concentrate on stills for the magazine. I aimed to get out into the field before the secret correspondent problem caught up with Homer.

After touching down at Tel Aviv's airport, we dove into a Mercedes taxi. Along the Mediterranean, waves pounded rocky promontories. In the crowded streets, we heard sounds of Hebrew, animated conversations of hot-tempered people in sidewalk cafes, and loud shouts of peddlers selling utensils from two-wheeled carts. The sound of an orchestra rehearsing Beethoven's Fifth came from the windows of an auditorium, mixing with the robust voices of young soldiers in military trucks, singing pioneer songs. They were on the way to the front to defend their homeland. The chance of dying didn't seem to be a reality to them.

Homer and I were registering at a small hotel outside the city when a high-decibel screech cut through the air. No warning could have prepared us for the experience of an actual air raid. Most people in Tel Aviv assumed it was a drill. A few ambled dutifully to shelters. Others scanned the cloudless skies and shrugged. It was indeed only a drill. Homer and I were more afraid of winding up on an operating table than we were of battle, but that was all part of the assignment.

Homer wanted to get into the action. But we had to wait until the following day for our Time-Life credentials to get the needed permission from the Office of War Information.

In surprise pre-dawn air strikes on the threatening Arab air forces, Israeli jets had all but eliminated Arab air power before it could attack. With only a few planes still able to provide air cover for them, the enemy's tanks and infantry had little protection under the clear desert skies. In their pre-emptive strike before morning light, Israel's fighter-bombers had destroyed the Egyptian air bases in the Sinai Peninsula, a major site of the missile buildup against Israel.

A massive Egyptian column was reported to be rolling out of its base at al-Arish, headed toward the Israeli border. An Egyptian radio announcer delivered the full reality of war. Our people have been waiting twenty years for this battle, roared Cairo. Now we will teach Israel the lesson of death. All the Arab armies have a rendezvous in Israel.

At the Office of War Information, there was a map room where officers with earphones monitored the activity of the war at a square table that displayed the region's geography in scale. As enemy movements in the desert were reported, orders were given and strategy devised to meet the constantly shifting situation in the field. As one would expect in a movie, the officers of the Israel Defense Forces were played by men and women dressed in starched, well-pressed khaki uniforms with epaulets signifying a blue Star of David—a lean and efficient cast organized with functional mobility, a flexible military command with files of gun-metal cabinets, and a large wall-to-wall map flagging field movements and outposts. But this was no set design; this was real.

Correspondents' credentials were not easy to come by. Each journalist's qualifications were evaluated and assessed before anyone could cover the battle. I asked to be assigned to an assault unit. The staffs, both civilian and military, were reluctant to give anyone permission to cover the war from the front lines.

We argued with the authorities, asking to see the person in charge. The top man appeared, wearing a nameplate that read General MacPherson. I wondered if he was Jewish. He announced that permission to accompany the troops would not be issued.

"General MacPherson," Homer spoke up with Talmudic reasoning, invoking what he remembered of the Old Testament, "Have you forgotten that, according to Mosaic Law, there must be two witnesses for every battle?"

"Three," someone shouted. "Four!" the other UPI photographers chimed in.

The general looked surprised. "You've got me. All right, you can join our boys. We move out in an hour."

"How long do you think the war will last, sir?" I asked.

"I predict six days," the general responded.

We were given a Jeep and told to meet at a certain area of the city. Homer turned on the radio. It carried folk tunes, rousing Israeli pioneer songs, and stirring military marches. Then Defense Minister Moshe Dayan spoke, "Soldiers of the Israeli Defense Forces, on this day our hopes and security are with you."

All of Israel's reserves had been mobilized. The radio called out the code names of the units: Love of Zion, Close Shave, Men of Work, Alternating Current, Open Window, Good Friends. Throughout the tiny nation, young men scrambled into the streets, half in uniform, half in mufti, bundles and knapsacks thrown over their shoulders as each headed to a prearranged secret rendezvous.

Busses delivered reservists to their units in the field. They also rode in laundry trucks, taxis, and private cars that had been drafted along with Israel's men and women. They were all elements of a superbly organized and functioning system that Major General Dayan had created when he was the Israel's Chief-of-Staff. Tanks, each manned by a single regular of Israel's fifty-thousand-man standing army, waited in convenient tank parks for the two or three reservists required to complete each crew.

Our Jeeps accompanied the tanks as they moved out in the direction of their assigned battle sectors and rendezvous points. They were part of a battalion of mechanized infantry with the mission to spearhead an armored strike across the Negev Desert against the approaching Egyptian army.

It was going to be an important story. "Faster," I urged the driver of my Jeep. The heavy vehicle raced along the dusty, barren ground, careening over potholes through clouds of dust until we collided with a rumbling tank at an intersection. I still don't know how the accident took place. As the metal-on-metal screech ended, it became clear that the collision had folded the army green Jeep with its hood camouflaged around the bumper in a crumpled embrace. Underneath the vehicle trickled oil and water, as incompatible as the Israelis and Arabs.

My arm and leg were badly hurt.

"Rigby?" Homer cried. "Are you OK?"

"My arm's hurt." I tried to get out, but my leg was broken.

An officer's head popped through the opening of the tank, yelled something in Hebrew, backed off, and proceeded across the intersection.

An army ambulance drove up, and a field medic put me on a stretcher.

"You go on without me, Homer."

"I can't leave you now, Rig."

"You've got to. We've got to cover the story."

"Give me your cameras then."

"They're brand new," I said while handing over my three Nikons and film. "If you need any filters, they're in the case with the lenses." I pointed to an aluminum box in the back of the Jeep. "And here's the Filmo!"

There wasn't much time. Homer jumped into a passing taxi, on his way, a battle-ready Soldier of the Word!

TRADING PLACES

"Everything came together in one sweeping moment out of the Old Testament. I knew the Filmo, but didn't know how to use Rigby's Nikon. I was scared, but there was no time for fear. Father Rivage had called me a Soldier of the Word. And I was. Shells were exploding all around us as my driver maneuvered his vehicle through clouds of Negev sand that blinded some troops on the road."

—Homer Sincere's journal, 1967

Homer joined the Israelites, charging into the land of *Ben Hur* and *The Greatest Story Ever Told*. He entered a page of the Old Testament, as past, present, and future dissolved into each other. He was unnerved but had no time to think as he followed half-tracks and tanks on the road.

Shells were exploding nearby as his driver maneuvered the vehicle like a dodge 'em car at a carnival. Clouds of Negev dust choked and blinded the Uzi-carrying troops advancing along the road.

The cab arrived near an Israeli firing position, and Homer shouted, "Keep the meter running. I'll be back."

In the distance, Herod's city Tiberias rumbled with Israeli Sherman tanks, tracking past walls leading to the Sea of Galilee where Peter had fished near the Syrian bluffs. A low haze of artillery smoke and high, black-waving plumes from air strikes hid the battle.

Heavy machine gun and small-arms fire impacted the area. Mortar rounds exploded, raising showers of rocks and earth. To protect himself from bursting shells, Homer took cover behind a truck. To his left, tanks were blazing with fierce, crackling fires and black smoke soaring skyward; planes screamed overhead.

Homer was frozen in fear. Except for the movies, he had never experienced war. Films ran through his mind: *Sands of Iwo Jima*, *Bataan*, *Watch on the Rhine*, and *Sergeant York*. But this was no movie; grenades, lost limbs, bloodshed, men wounded and killed in battle. He could see no glory in war.

"I'm over here, my name is Dov," a voice shouted toward him. "You all right?"

"Are you from the Office of War Information?" Homer asked, disregarding the man's question and inching his way under the fire coming toward them. His brace slowed his progress as he crept along the ground.

"Dov Levy. I'm a photographer."

They reached and shook hands.

"Been here long?"

"Never shot so much film in my life."

Homer wound the Filmo and shot until it needed rewinding. He tried to load film into my 35 mm camera. It was difficult, but he accomplished it. Trying to change to a wider-angle lens, he found it impossible to attach it to the mounting. There was a release to press, and he fumbled for it. The camera suddenly sprang open, and film unwound, exposing it. Closing the case, he mashed his finger.

Dov looked over. "Say, need some help?"

Some understatement. "Yeah, I'm having a little trouble."

Dirt poured down on them, set into motion by an exploding mortar as Homer tried to protect the camera, more than his life, under his correspondent's jacket. He could easily operate the Filmo but didn't know much about the mechanics of still cameras. His assignment was to come back with great action photographs. He also knew that Rigby would be quite upset if he came back empty-handed, with a dirty or, worse, damaged lens.

"Can I have a look?" Dov asked.

"Sure."

"Say, isn't that the new Nikon F with aperture priority?"

"I think so, but I'm not a photographer. My buddy is one, but he got hurt."

"I really like this camera," Dov said. "It's got a nice feel to it . . . a single reflex. Mind if I try it?"

"Sure. Go ahead."

"Fast lens!"

The Israeli photographer stood up and had clicked several shots when a bullet zinged past him. Crouching back down quickly, he said, "Real nice camera. Want to sell it?"

"Well, maybe," Homer replied. "How long have you been here?"

"Four days."

"You got lots of film?"

"I've got this war up the kazoo. Want to trade?" Dov asked.

"Trade?"

"Yes, coverage for the camera," he said. "Seems like a good deal."

"Good idea. How about six rolls for the camera?"

"Black-and-white or color?"

"Three of each."

"Okay. You have any accessories?"

Several other Israeli photographers crawled over from a trench and looked at the new model Nikon F with aperture priority.

"I have a couple of camera bodies, filters, and lenses—all kinds of lenses."

Dov yelled, "I'll take the 125 lens for an extra roll of film."

"Deal."

Another photographer offered six rolls for the three-hundred millimeter lens.

Homer whispered to Dov, "Is he good? I don't want to get stuck with any overexposed film."

"One of the best."

Homer negotiated with the others, ending up with nineteen rolls of film, then crawled under the continuing firing back to the cab. The whole action had taken less than an hour, following a tradition and heritage of great traders along the Mediterranean for centuries.

He was shaken by his first experience in war and deeply impressed by men who could stay calm while in the line of enemy fire. His first venture into photojournalism and trading under fire gave him a lot to think about: the futility of war, the agony and heroism of battle, and the efficiency of trade.

My leg was in traction and my arm in a cast when Homer arrived at the tent hospital.

"We've got something in common," I announced. "We're a pair of limping Bobbsey Twins."

"You okay?" Homer tossed me the nineteen rolls of film. I thought it was incredible.

"I think we got coverage." Homer was earnest. "Didn't get any motion picture film, but a lot of stills. It was some experience, Rig!" I was amazed.

When the rolls were developed, the pictures were crisp and sharp. Ingenious angles and points of view, in color and black-and-white. I marveled at Homer's eye for photography. Even the shots with my telephoto lens were impressive; he had been at the right place at the right time! Homer was too busy shooting stills with no time to use the Filmo. We had a lot of coverage that impressed even Clurman. Maybe there would be a place for documentaries and Time-Life Films after all.

When the story ran in *LIFE* with photographs of the battle, the caption read, "Witness to Our Time, photographed by Rigby Canfield." The story later won the Overseas Press Club Award for war photography, an undeserved honor I should have felt guilty accepting, but I did. Homer always made me better than I really was.

ANYTHING GOES

"Your usual table, Mr. Canfield?"

I always liked courtesy. The Café France was dimly lit and crowded. When it rained, as it did this evening, conversation seemed better. Like listening to an English accent or reading subtitles in a foreign film, it always seemed more interesting than it actually was.

A waiter, dressed in a well-pressed black tuxedo with a high-winged collar, brought a bottle of vintage champagne, marked by a diagonal stripe crossing the elegant gold and white label, and placed it into an ice bucket. On the table, set with polished silver on a white linen tablecloth, sat a bowl of spring flowers. Homer and I had returned from our assignment in Israel. Daisy had called me about a part she had been offered in London's West End. We were all celebrating an evening all together. I left my newest assistant at home.

Along a back wall of the café, photographs of performers and posters of Broadway shows were displayed. A pianist near our table played Gershwin tunes, adding a bit of nostalgia to the occasion.

"This is a wonderful party," Daisy was delighted. "And congratulations, Rigby! Photographer of the Year!"

"Daisy . . ." I started.

"No one is more deserving," Homer said, saving me from having to explain.

Daisy added, "You're our hero!"

Now it was my turn to be at a loss for words. Some hero! I thought. Homer was the hero, but I didn't say so.

We enjoyed the evening immensely. At one point, when the piano player took a break, I took over the keys and imitated Perry Como.

"I thought I'd serenade you guys, a little background music."

They seemed surprised that I played much better than I could sing.

Rippling the keys, Daisy joined me at the piano and started to play. "It's my turn, gentlemen!" She sang a personalized lyric from "Anything Goes":

"In olden days, a glimpse of stocking
Was looked on as something shocking
But now, God knows,
Anything goes.

Good editors too, who once knew better days
Now only use Homer's phrase
Writing prose,
Anything goes."

We all had a good laugh, and Homer exclaimed, "I didn't know dinner came with a show!"

I asked Daisy to dance, and we did a few turns around the checkerboard floor.

"Rigby, you are as smooth on a dance floor as you are in expressing yourself."

Daisy loved to dance, and with all those dancing lessons in the Quarter, I was just as nimble on the dance floor as I was behind a camera. I showed off some nifty steps I had learned from Madame du Bois, then noticed with a passing glance that Homer looked uneasy. Only then did I realize how awkward Homer must have felt. With his brace, he could never keep perfect tempo. I saw him glancing away, seemingly rewinding the past. It was not just the dance, but he had caught something else in a look between Daisy and me.

I had become increasingly uncomfortable, considering my indiscretions with Daisy. I announced that I had an early flight the next morning and needed to pick up some equipment, apologizing for breaking up the party.

"I'll leave you two in the company of Cole Porter!" I said as I left.

"Homer, would you like to dance with me? I'd like that," Daisy asked later.

Homer refused.

"Is something wrong?"

Just then, the piano player returned. His playing swept Homer away with its melody. He felt it was magic how music, just a congregation of notes, could strike such a personal and responsive chord in him.

"You're a dreamer, Homer," Daisy said gently.

"I know."

Daisy reached over and kissed him softly on the lips. "I'm going to miss you…"

Homer wondered if trouble was brewing again.

"It was great that Rigby organized this get-together."

Then Homer just came out with it. "What's going on between you two? I saw how close you danced."

Daisy took a long pause. "I never told you, but Rigby and I went out a few times before you came to New York. I adore you both."

Homer looked down to cover his concern.

"It was just a twist of fate, but then you came along and everything changed."

It could have been a movie. Homer, Daisy, and me, like *Jules and Jim*, François Truffaut's movie about love and life and relationships, and three friends.

"I'm not going to see him anymore. Surely you know that."

Homer wasn't sure what Daisy meant. "It's okay, Daisy. I just didn't know you had been seeing Rigby."

"The last time was after the film you made for my birthday. It was wonderful and thoughtful, Homer, a delicious present, and I love you for making it. I'm sorry you couldn't come that evening. I realize that something came up at your office."

"I hated to miss your birthday, but I called when I finished work, I remember. You weren't home."

"I was with Rigby, Homer. I shouldn't have been, but I was, and I don't want to lie. But it was years ago. Ages."

It wasn't so much about truth as it was about the confusion Homer felt. He wanted to ask more, but her words stabbed him, cut him open, hurting deeply, something he never expected. Had they been intimate? Not Rigby and Daisy. They would never cross that romantic line knowing how he felt. He pushed the thought from his mind. It couldn't be real; his stupid lack of confidence was at play. Daisy added the other bit of reality. News was coming faster than he could accept or absorb.

"It's a big break for me."

She held his face in her hands, feeling sad, conflicted. For Homer, it wasn't just the change that he needed to face, but the accelerating realization about Daisy and me that took his breath away.

"I better stick with my writing."

"I need to know something. Did you have anything to do with that notice in *TIME*?" Daisy asked curiously.

"'The only thing that cuts a little ice is affection or the possibility of affection'." Homer's mood brightened.

"That's my line!" Daisy exclaimed. "Did you write that review?"

"Why would I do that?"

"Because you love me," Daisy replied.

And he did.

MIXED FEELINGS

"It is painfully difficult for me, and the mixed emotions give way to mixed feelings over Daisy's good fortune. I am going to miss her. Maybe if I make more entries and outline ideas for movies I can avoid the hard question. Was I betrayed more by Rigby than Daisy? It is hard for me to reconcile when I love them both. I can't write about familiar empty feelings, but I can gloss over them by recalling a Cole Porter lyric—"It was just one of those crazy things."   —Homer Sincere's journal, 1967

It was ironic that Homer had written about Daisy, introducing her to the world. He wanted everyone to see Daisy as he did, her lovely talent and warmth as an actress, and by doing so he diminished his chances of a deeper relationship with her. Her offer was pretty heady stuff for anyone in show business: stepping from off-Broadway to a starring role in a London production! I was not sure what to do, or what the consequences would be. I did feel that he would be at a loss.

Chapter 11

THE SECRET CORRESPONDENT EXPOSED

They found Homer out. The offense was clear: *TIME* reported the news, and Homer had disobeyed its rules. As a Soldier of the Word, he had failed in his duty. His name was expeditiously excised from the masthead. Not due to any restructuring or reshuffling of the corporate troops, but fired. When Clurman confronted him, he admitted to being the "special correspondent."

I attended a staff meeting called by Henry Grunwald on whom Luce had bestowed his editorial legacy. Henry was a fine but inflexible managing editor. "The stories Homer filed were at least authentic," he said. "He is a good essayist and did a fine job with the Editor's Note. I'll admit that he has the qualities that make us journalists in the first place: taking a stand, righting a wrong. We should have recognized Homer's frustration, but frustration is no excuse. He knew the rules. He was innovative in pushing for a film department, and in the long run, he may be right. Take the Six-Day War, Rigby. We gave him a chance to report on that 'conflict's credible cause,'" Grunwald alliterated in Timespeak, "but Sincere didn't, not one word, no reporting, no file except a few captions for your extraordinary coverage, Rigby. When Homer was assigned to weekend duties, he read the stories filed Saturday afternoons just as the magazine was put to bed. And sometimes, with self-appointed responsibility, he would write a review or send out a dispatch from the 'special correspondent.' He knew that the Dateline desk is a rotating responsibility of the editors on the News Service."

I came to Homer's defense. "All he was trying to do was to prove himself; he wanted to do what we do out in the field. You can't blame him for that. So he created a few assignments for himself. You guys never gave him a real break."

I was surprised at my daring, but what I said was true. I should have spoken up about what happened on the way to the front lines—Homer had saved the day, and my ass—but I didn't.

"Here at *TIME*," Grunwald said, wrapping up the meeting, "We have a journalistic duty to keep our readers accurately informed. We all know that. Accuracy is essential to any weekly news magazine. I am afraid that we'll never know how many dispatches Homer sent out over Dateline. Hundreds of stories break every week. For all I know, he could have launched a few more astronauts into space. Accuracy is *TIME*'s charter and mandate."

HOLLYWOOD CALLING

"We see what we want to see in others and ourselves, by need and necessity. Looking back to the idle summertime afternoons at the Rialto, I wrote repeatedly in my diary, 'A really neat movie.' My comments were always the same. But these really neat movies shaped and defined my life. I confess to my thoughts without apology, the enormous influence they had on me, my life, my way of seeing things, and my dreams."
—Homer Sincere's journal, 1969

Grunwald observed life as he saw it; Homer described it as he wanted it to be. Homer had done what many staff writers dreamed of. His stories were true and based on facts; they were engaging and did no harm, and they made news. But in the last analysis, copy has to be fact-checked and vetted so that it conforms to the company's editorial policy. I felt for Homer but there was no way to protect him from his violation of *TIME*'s rules.

While losing his job at *TIME* had depressed him, over the next few years, Homer would also lose his enthusiasm for New York. Despondency arrived like a slipcover over a tattered chair. Writing in his journal helped him keep the fantasy and lose the reality. When he wasn't writing, he was lost, deeply lost, with inescapable sadness.

Spending days and nights without sleep, he committed his story to paper, recording his life, pouring out details and descriptions. It surprised him how much he was able to recall and how much meaning it had for him. When he was not recollecting personal history, he wrote down story ideas and treatments for films, refreshing the magical movie dream that had begun in New Orleans.

Sometimes in a turn of events, a visitor returns, arriving just in time to offer some support, some direction. Surely enough, according to Homer's journal, Billy Sunshine rode right into his apartment.

"Hi, Partner, it's been a long time." The cowboy was back.

Homer, in total amazement, took a moment. *"I'm surprised."*

"Well, I happened to be in the neighborhood."

"Now, Billy, you just being in New York, it's a stretch."

"That's what imagination is for. Take what you want, believe what you will."

"Where have you been?"

"I've never left, son. Surely you have been growin' up, working, seem to be doing okay."

"Got fired!"

"I heard. Mind if a sit a bit, have a drink of cold water? Been ridin' hard."

"Lost my girl."

"Not sure about that. Daisy's just finding her way."

"And Rigby. A bit of a betrayal, don't you think?"

"I'm thinking, but I'm not judging. Human nature. Oh, Rigby is just tripping himself up, foolin' around."

"Lost my job."

"So you said. What you aiming to do? They could use you out at Century."
"That's your old studio."
"Hope they haven't given up on old Billy. Need the words. You up for it?"
"About cowboys?"
"That's all I know."
"I'm up for it, you bet!"
"Courage, loyalty, legend...the spirit of the land."
"I've missed you, Billy! Like old times."
"Old and good times."
"Yeah, Billy, old times."
Billy turned, leaving behind his engaging smile. *"I'll be expecting ya."*

Over the following weeks, Homer mailed story treatments to Billy's studio, mostly *TIME* articles adapted for film, refreshing his magical movie dream that began in New Orleans.

When a phone call came, he was astonished. Century Studio liked his ideas!

Jordan St. Clair, Head of Production, one of Hollywood's senior executives, was on the phone. "I've been reading your stuff. I always read the magazine. There may be a movie in 'The Six Day War'—nice piece of work. I'm going to be in New York next week. Let's have lunch." *TIME* had been the credential that had opened the door.

From the first, St. Clair was soft-spoken and warm. Homer heard the suntan in his voice.

"Kid, that story was engaging . . . dynamite. Colossal! Fantastic." St. Clair talked like a front page ad in *Variety*. He told Homer about his new unit. "I want seasoned writers who can craft a story, an original." Then, speaking as if in confidence, "Homer, would you like to join us? The General has authorized me to build the finest team of producers and writers in the world. It's going to be like the old Hollywood when movies had pizzazz, a certain something. They entertained! You know? You know what I mean?" St. Clair started to yell. "We want to make one hundred percent quality. And the only way I know how to do that is to come to New York and look for writers, not Hollywood flakes but real talent. I'm offering you a one-year contract. With an option, of course . . ."

A WISH AND A WORD

Refreshed by St. Clair's enthusiasm, Homer nearly shouted, "Yes, yes, of course!" He could now fulfill his early wish to write not only about war, but about cowboys . . . yes, putting down the gun, yes, about legends of the brave, the lonely, the West! . . . yes, about heroes who fought and forged ideals . . . these were operative words. Yes, he could write a film starring Billy Sunshine. He was at last going out to see Billy! It seemed to be providential, but was Jordan St. Clair a Soldier of the Word?

While Homer embarked in a new direction, I found my boat, the one I had dreamed about since steering the pirogue on the bayou. My fifty-four-foot sloop built in Sweden was called the *Starlight*. I had first seen her in an illustrated story in *Yachting* magazine when she was under lease for the winter months by Nicholson Yacht Brokers in St. Martin. The boat had been returned to the Johansen shipyard in Malmo, Sweden, to be refitted. The owner, a Swiss watch manufacturer, had decided to buy a motor yacht in the Mediterranean and put the *Starlight* up for sale. My life's dream went into her. After winning the Photographer of the Year award, I had received a generous contract from *LIFE* to initiate a new series, and I would start by photographing my adventures at sea. A Portuguese seaman named Manuel Ortega, who had distinguished himself by breaking a transatlantic record, would captain the boat.

Our first leg would be to sail from Malmo across the North Sea to London, then on to Spain and through the Strait of Gibraltar to the Cinque Terre coast on the Italian Riviera. From there we would sail along the coast of North Africa, then cross the Atlantic to the Grenadines and finally to the Bahamas. My trusted Leica would be my companion, and I wanted Homer, my best buddy, to sail with me, bringing a Filmo. I had thought that Time-Life films would be our next step toward Hollywood, but when I asked Homer, I learned he was making his own plans. We had been apart before, but as best friends we should be able to pick up where we had left off, recollecting experiences to talk, share, and laugh about. I worried how Homer would do without the immediate promise of Daisy in his life. I hadn't been of much help.

SAILING ON

"Rigby was giving new meaning to words. Betrayal, the word was almost foreign sounding to me. I was not the first person to experience broken trust and hurt. I knew something about words. You can't see them but can read them and surely feel meaning before expressing language. Some words I did not want in my emotional dictionary."

—Homer Sincere's journal, 1969

Our last night together in New York was spent at Homer's apartment over the Cherry Lane. We talked into the evening. As he packed his things, he seemed remarkably calm, considering that he had recently been fired. But he look exhausted and very tired, with much on his mind.

"Let's get something to eat," I suggested. "The Blue Mill is just around the corner." But Homer had little appetite.

I was excited about the prospect of our sailing the world, but Homer's mind was on going West! But there was something more.

"It's time to move on," he said, his voice trailing off.

"Everyone loved your work, but the editors just didn't know what was real."

"It was all real, Rigby. All the reports, the dispatches; there was nothing made up or phony."

"Jesus, Home, you changed the magazine around. You got people thinking."

"Thanks, Rigby," he replied, forcing a smile.

His expression clouded. "Yes, it's all real."

And then I told him, "I've found my boat."

"You've finally done it!"

"I want you to come with me," I said, adding glibly, "The eyes see what the mind does yet not know."

Homer turned squarely, looking at me with crashing reality. "Maybe the mind sees something else, Rigby." I then knew what Homer had suspected for sometime. "I can't, Rig, I don't want to."

"What about Daisy?"

"You mean about you and Daisy, don't you?"

Finally, it had come up. "She told you, I guess."

"Before she left—as much as I could hear, Rig, and just enough that I could bear. I don't know what more to say, and if I did, I'm sure I wouldn't want to say it. I've always admired and looked up to you as my only and best friend. But now your dishonesty is without thought—it's become a kind of style. What happened to you, Rigby? You were always better than this. I never imagined you would hurt me, especially knowing how much Daisy meant to me. She's in London. You've found your dreamboat, and I'm going to write film scripts as I've always wanted to. Sorry we won't be together; we all have things to do. We're getting older. I have to move on. It's not difficult to understand."

Disappointment, sabotage, expectation. It is toxic and unsettling. I shot from a lens long out of focus, out of balance, dissonant, disturbing—where was the perspective? Emotions are harder to find when hope loses its way, and the deepest feelings are diminished by an unutterable act. How could Homer forgive what was given, forget what was gotten, preserve in an instant what was gone?

There was a photograph of the two of us on his desk, and he took it and looked at it a long time. With a symbolic act, he let the frame he was holding just drop to the floor. No anger, no slamming it down, just a dropping memory. The picture and the reflection from the broken glass were broken and uneven.

Homer had stepped up to the plate, hit a home run—a stunning connecting hit—knocking me out of the ballpark. I had no defense. How could I say sleeping with Daisy had meant nothing to me? I had tried to be a friend and companion when she was new to New York. Then the birthday night, when Homer was detained, swept me away, ending in confusion and guilt. It was the wrong thing to do.

"Homer, it was a while ago."

"Oh, time just marches on."

"Homer, I'm at a loss for what to say."

"I'm not and I don't mean to give you a laundry list, but you are as phony a friend as you are Photographer of the Year...considering the chance I took for you." Homer was hitting hard.

"What are you going to do?"

"Going to give Hollywood a shot. Got an offer from Century Studios."

"You going to see Billy?"

"First thing I'll do!"

"Isn't he getting kinda old?"

"He's got the stuff called loyalty."

"Hollywood! That's great, Home! Makes a lot of sense. Christ, we made enough movies back home to last a lifetime. Hollywood!"

"See you around, Rigby."

In a swift, vagrant lack of sorrow, with some forbearance Homer insulated his feelings. No more reflection of loss, resentment, and remembered pain. My shame did not harmonize with Homer's resentment, my action had not engendered a lasting friendship; we went our different ways. As I left, I noticed Homer pull out an object that carried meaning, one that Father Rivage had given him a long time ago. It was a cane with a silver handle and a means of support. Though I had really wanted Homer to come along, I was glad for him. For one who had dreamed most of his life, going west was a vision come true. The studios and the weather were ideal, conditions favorable for a perfect flight into the world of make-believe.

When I walked away that night, a massive weight pulled at the center of my being. I had betrayed our friendship and wondered if it could ever be repaired. We were connected through our past. Homer was a part of me, and Tennyson's line was never more true: "You are a part of all those whom you have met." Maybe I was the one who really had been alone all of my life, even more so than Homer. I was damn close to self-pity. I was at a rally with empty banners and bunting, at a party where no one came.

I hoped that Daisy would come back into his life, and mine too, with the same forgiveness that Father Rivage had spoken of long ago. When I got to London, I'd make sure Daisy was okay. I was envious that she and Homer had enjoyed a real relationship, at least for a while, something that I had never found. I was somehow reminded that my foundation was built by a mother who ironically cared more how things *looked* instead of how they were.

Part Three

HOLLYWOOD, CALIFORNIA
1970

Chapter 12
CALIFORNIA 1970

━━━━━━━━━━━━━━
━━━━━━━━━━━━━━

It was a California dream to be sure, but this journey would be different for Homer; this time he was going home. The sun was brighter, the palm trees sharper against a postcard sky. Maybe this is what people saw before there was Hollywood. They came when there were oil fields, when Fairfax and Wilshire was a flying field, when Sennett and Griffith set up their cameras on mud flats.

He had arrived with a desk and a dream, like the seekers and searchers, the explorers and the dream merchants who had preceded him. They still came when anyone who could say three words had a good chance to be in talkies. It was the time when Aimee Sample McPherson shook her tambourine, when dirigibles raced each other through the skies and Earl Carroll lined up the girls. The best gathering place then was the Garden of Allah where W. C. Fields, Gene Fowler, John Barrymore, Gene Autry, and Billy Sunshine hung out at the bar. They came with ambitions to succeed and visions of ready-made fortunes. And they bargained for land, discovered oil, made movies, and played in a balmy climate of clean ocean air. Every dawn promised a lucky break, the setting of a new record. For many hours each day, there were late afternoon shadows, a consequence of tall eucalyptus and palm trees that loomed over the City of Angels.

The movie people fulfilled hopes, created myths, and reached new heights in building castles of dreams. Why not? The country was built on expectations; every street's sunny side beckoned. And if their audiences wanted not only oil derricks and palm trees but also glittering movie star-dom and rococo facades, the moviemakers could shift real to reel. Sam Goldwyn, glove maker; Louis B. Mayer, dressmaker; Jack Warner, pushcart peddler, all "men of the cloth" whose visions and daring projected larger-than-life images all over the world. Men like Selznick, Lasky, Sennett, Griffith, de Mille, Roach, and Mayer, became pioneers of fantasy, creators of a dream machine. Everyone believed the sun shone on easy money and an easy life in an easy climate. It promised the fulfillment of the American Dream, with speed and mobility, the chance to choose what you wanted to be. It was the era of Grauman's Chinese and the Brown Derby, producing a Mediterranean melody of fabulous facades to glorify the new era of film.

"Let's go to the movies!" was the cry that led to the coming attrac-tions and popcorn memories created by Century Studios, the dream machine producing more stars than there were in the heavens. It was a magic projector of fast guns, falling horses, anxiety-ridden marshals, and far-ranging forays where the boys took a shot of red-eye then rode into the sunset with no regrets while a radio singer crooned.

The movies had conveyed vast audiences to a land called Oz and to find the *Treasure in the Sierra Madre*, to a mysterious port called *Casablanca*, and to dangerous places at *High Noon*. There was no place like Hollywood, where the players danced a minuet, a few steps for-ward, a few steps back.

The make-believers lived in small pockets among the orange groves, scattered from the foothills of the Sepulveda Pass to the ocean. It was a special part of the earth, unlike any other. Just as Greenwich, England, told the world's time, Hollywood commanded the entertain-ment hours; as Mount Everest's thin air turned men dizzy in bursts of achievement, the dizziness of Hollywood became legendary.

HOMER SINCERE GOES TO THE MOVIES

"Since childhood, intimate acquaintances were more distant than I might have wished, except for Billy Sunshine. Now I was up close, in

awe, with an almost sense of dazzle and allure by the surrounding stars who colored my imagination. My movie compass directed me to a large home behind a great gate with a brass plate on the outside that announced, SUNSHINE."

—Homer Sincere's journal, 1970

Holding true to his vision, behind the wheel of his new red Ford truck, Homer Sincere drove into Hollywood with his collection of books and notebooks packed in his desk, carefully protected by a canvas cover.

His road map led him into the Bel Air hills, to the huge iron gate where a tarnished brass plate announced SUNSHINE.

The house was a sprawling, shuttered brick hacienda, situated on twenty acres, with stables and riding rings where jump bars had been set up. Spacious lawns were bordered by gardens glowing with bougainvillea, daylilies, and camellias, framed by towering magnolias. Billy's place!

Homer drove to the front entrance. When no one answered the bell, he rang again. Still no one. On his way out, he spoke to a gardener, "Hi, I'm Homer Sincere. Is Billy around?"

The gardener was Asian and spoke little English. "Billy away, he be back."

"Please tell him Homer dropped by to see him. I'm his friend."

"Sure, I will."

"Thanks!"

Homer's contract said he could stay at the Beverly Hills Hotel for up to three weeks until he found a place to live. As a guest of the famed hotel, he had a veritable United Nations at his call: Kevin, the Irish doorman; Ernest, the Swiss desk clerk; Sven, the Swedish pool attendant; Dino, the Italian maitre d'; Jacques, the French chef. His cottage was near the pool. The cabanas around the pool were reserved for starlets and dealmakers, all in vivid Technicolor, and there were frequent calls to the cabana bunch from a loudspeaker from publicists or studios.

"Call for Mr. Lancaster. Call for Mr. Douglas. Call for Mr. Robertson. Call for Mr. Wasserman. Call for Mr. Sincere!"

For his residence, he eventually leased a guesthouse on the former Will Rogers estate, just past Brentwood. It was an artist's studio with a large atrium, high ceilings. The doors opened to a private, secluded garden. Off the main house was a small pool no one used. The fireplace in his living room was five feet high and, shades of La Vieille Maison, had Italianate fruit baskets carved into its marble mantel. It became his favorite habit to warm himself before a roaring evening fire.

TIMING!

"There was a marble block on Jordan St. Clair's desk, a highly polished square with TIMING indelibly carved."

—Homer Sincere's journal, 1970

"Good morning, Mr. Sincere, you're in Bungalow 24." The guard at the studio gate welcomed him. "It belonged to Cary Grant."

"Cary Grant."

"Two parking places in front of your bungalow are assigned to you."

HOMER SINCERE was painted on a wooden sign topping his space.

"Welcome to the studio," said Jenny, the amiable middle-aged secretary assigned to him. She had striking red hair. "Mr. St. Clair would like to see you in the executive office building as soon as you get in."

In his new office, a bay window overlooked a small garden with bougainvillea and hibiscus vines. An ideal place to work! His desk had already been placed near a window bathed in afternoon light; vases around the room held fresh flowers.

Jenny was as efficient as she was friendly and organized his cards and the details of his complicated life with military precision. She had worked at the studio for years. A photograph of her daughter in a simple silver frame stood on her well-organized desk.

"Jenny, can you find Billy Sunshine for me? I want to say hello. It's very important.

"Billy hasn't been around the studio for a while, but I'll locate him for you. Now you better get over to see Jordan."

"Fine. I can't wait to see him!"

Jordan St. Clair shared the first floor with three other executives in the producers' building. He was a man with emotional latitudes. He could have been an actor, with a style of emotions ranging from charm to coercion. He was as good looking as he was smooth, smartly disguised in well-fashioned suits, a suntan from the sunny side of Hollywood, and he offered a perfectly engaging smile.

Ed Riker, known as "the General," was head of the studio. Homer noticed that the decorations in every office were the same: military campaign desks and brass lamps. On the walls were sepia photographs of English colonial officers fighting in India—all very *Gunga Din*, very Kipling, very proper and formal, very Soldier of the Word.

An object on Jordan St. Clair's desk drew his attention: a marble block with the word TIMING deeply incised, facing the visitor.

"Like the offices, Homer? They are decorated in an eighteenth-century British regiment theme," St. Clair confirmed. "Riker had the art department copy the originals in his warehouse."

St. Clair read a press release about his new unit written by *Variety* columnist Army Archard. It included a mention of Homer.

"Jordan St. Clair greenlighted the launch of his new writers' unit today, adding luster to the writing scroll at Century. He has signed noted journalist Homer Sincere, top correspondent from TIME, who tops his list of acquisitions. 'We're delighted to welcome writers like Sincere to the Studio; he will be a great asset to our expansion program,' St. Clair announced."

It occurred to Homer that he had been assigned to a new regiment. He had joined Century's fighting forces and would soon be given orders and rations.

Jordan looked Homer squarely in the eye, announcing, "I want exciting projects for the studio," and then added quietly, "Do you like the bungalow, kid?"

"I do," Homer replied, struck by Jordan's strange style. The corporate culture was very different from what he had experienced at *TIME*.

"You've met Jenny, then?"

"Jenny is very nice."

"She has skills," he confided. "One hundred percent remarkable skills. You'll be surprised—not your average secretary from the pool, but exceptional, and reserved for our most promising writers. Like a mother."

Like a mother. One of our most promising writers. He accepted the sentiments with modest politeness.

"Sincere," said St. Clair, "we're a team. Let's hit the canteen!"

A CUSTOMARY LUNCH

"The menu was divided into 'Main Features' for entrees, 'Short Subjects' for side orders, and 'Coming Attractions' for dessert. True haute cuisine."
—Homer Sincere's journal, 1970

In the commissary, people were seated according to rank and film gross. A platoon of executive vice-presidents and stars were accommodated in front. Following the custom, when a film earned back its gross under the studio's unique accounting system, its producer joined the front-line troops as an honorary privilege. If the film didn't net out its return, that same producer was relegated to the back of the line, a fortification called "the Trenches," where a formation of production personnel and contract players sat. They had the lowest status in the studio hierarchy. St. Clair always sat in front.

Sixteen waitresses in starched white mini-aprons, hair in sprayed bouffants, each in charge of her own territory, were commanded by a maitre d' who strongly resembled Gilbert Roland, the star of silent movies. With polished black hair and a thin mustache, moody and temperamental, he danced among booths and tables, pulling out chairs with practiced aplomb. His mannered arms arched over his head as if he were fencing with Errol Flynn, sidestepping, dodging, and smiling. On the walls hung imitation Hirschfelds. Bob Hope's nose, Loretta

Young's eyes, and Cary Grant's dimpled chin were prominent.

As they made their way to the front, the faces of the producers and executives seated in booths turned to follow them. "This is Homer Sincere," St. Clair announced. "We captured him from TIME/LIFE."

The maitre d' made a delicious fuss over St. Clair.

"Will it be your usual today, sir?"

"Yes."

"Ah, the Cobb salad." The maitre d' scribbled and dispatched a piece of paper to his assistant; he knew St. Clair's stomach by heart.

For Homer, the maitre d' suggested the Clint Eastwood Spaghetti Western Special—fast-action carbohydrates—and for dessert the Doris Day Apple Sponge Cake, homemade and bouncy.

St. Clair took great care to point out that Homer was at the Number One table.

"Where does the General sit?"

"Oh, he never comes here; he has his own dining room in his suite at Headquarters."

Homer wondered if it was a field tent or a fort. But to have your own dining room impressed Homer.

St. Clair spotted a colleague nearby. "See that son of a bitch over there?"

"Which one?" Homer asked.

"The one with the gray hair and the dark suit."

They all wore the same smiles and the same dark suits; it was Riker's designated uniform that went with the furniture. Homer was the only person wearing tweeds.

"That's William Ornstein, two booths over. You'd better watch him." St. Clair leaned over and asked Homer confidentially, "What's your sign?"

"Sign?"

"Yeah, like Libra, or what?"

"I'm a Gemini."

"Oh, one of those," he said. "Two people, huh? The twins, huh? Well, that son of a bitch over there is a Scorpio, one hundred percent

Scorpio, and he'll sting you, he'll sting you real good."

Ornstein was a barracuda in the studio aquarium. The General had them all swimming under maximum stress to see who would kill the other.

Hope I'm not about to be tossed into the tank with them, Homer thought.

Jordan St. Clair waved Ornstein over. Standing with counterfeit enthusiasm, they hugged each other.

"Hey, old buddy, how's your project?"

"Looks like a go, but that asshole director, Biff Lockhart, got his head up his ass. To make him surrender his ground, I'm going to need reinforcements."

"This is Homer Sincere." Homer was introduced. He wondered if he should wave a white flag.

"Hello. I've read the notices in *Variety* and *The Reporter*. Welcome to the studio." He confidentially turned to Jordan. "You're building some staff," he said sweetly.

"I am. It all starts with the script, our marching orders."

"Pretty soon the whole studio will be under St. Clair occupation."

"Now I wouldn't mind that," Jordan confirmed.

"Well, I can say I knew you when." Ornstein laughed. "Lunch next week?"

Homer noticed a studio custom. When anyone said "lunch," they shook hands, their left hand turned out as if it were their right, with a squeeze—evidently a secret code in a fraternal society.

When Ornstein was out of hearing distance, St. Clair turned to him, "I hope Lockhart ruins that son of a bitch."

Homer realized it was a war zone.

"You have to watch your flank, can't be too careful." St. Clair's eyes flicked around the room and finally rested on Homer.

It was time to get down to business. "Jordan," Homer said, "I believe Hollywood has made more westerns than any other kind of film, and Century's made more films than any other studio. I think there's an opportunity today for heroes and what they mean to us."

"Tell me more, kid."

"I'm developing an idea. About cowboys."

Jordan looked at him, squinting his eyes. "Is this the big idea?"

"I'm working on it. It's called *The Last Cowboy*."

Jordan studied him, and nodded slowly in a thinking sort of way. "Let me have a look."

THE GREAT STUDIO

Century was known as the great studio, the one that created everything from Gable's smile to Grable's million-dollar legs. Its writers had introduced a whole new vocabulary: Colossal, Stupendous, Fabulous, Extravaganza, Spectacular, Suspenseful. "Here's looking at you, kid," "Sweetheart," "Play it again, Sam," and "Frankly, my dear, I don't give a damn."

In the early years, Billy Sunshine movies were made at his ranch and grossed more money than most studio films. Century's old guard wanted him badly. After he came to Century, the studio was soon acknowledged by the movers and shakers in the trade as "The studio Billy built." Towering over its soundstage was a bigger than life poster of Billy Sunshine. At night, a searchlight illuminated the legend, the first star to command a million dollars a picture with a percentage of the gross. And when Billy wasn't collecting profits, he was playing poker; when he wasn't playing poker, he distributed currencies holding value and fun to kids who loved him.

For Homer, the most important movies were those that reinforced his imagination. There was nothing like them in the world.

He watched all kinds of films—Billy's westerns, classics like *The Treasure of Sierra Madre*, *Thunder and Dust*, *High Noon*, and *Duel in the Sun*. Spending several hours a day in screening rooms, he made notes on three-by-five cards, outlining characters and themes, long shots and close-ups.

Sometimes, at the end of the day, he walked in the Ventura hills where California Oaks fell over one another. And in walking, as most of us sometimes do, he had an essential dialogue within himself. In his solitude, he heard music—Daisy, singing "On Top of the Wind," as Fitzgerald once wrote. He wished for her now. Drifting on the tide of his thoughts, he accommodated his loneliness, and when he returned home, he played a hi-fi recording of Pachelbel's Cannon, which accented distant recollections of the people and joys in his life.

A POSTCARD FROM HOLLYWOOD

Los Angeles has been called a place where people come to reinvent their lives. It's a city full of contradiction. Built over a major seismic fault, on the edge of one of the world's most inhospitable deserts, the city developed like the extension of a Hollywood movie set, a sprawling urban fantasy. Los Angeles was a suburb in search of a city, a ramble of gullible bricks and wayward plaster that got misdirected. Extraordinarily, there was not a single work of art that was a recognizable icon of the place—no Statue of Liberty, no Taj Mahal, no Big Ben, no Empire State Building, no Pyramids, no Golden Gate Bridge. It was the only major city in the world that didn't really have a postcard image, except for a few palm trees and a billboard on a hill reading "HOLLYWOOD."

I had heard from one of our correspondents that next to the movies and real estate, shopping was the recreational pastime and the largest industry in Los Angeles, but not for Homer—he wasn't one of the serious shoppers down on Rodeo Drive. Homer caught sight of his first celebrity almost shyly stepping through the shadows, poised for recognition. Audrey Hepburn was unmistakably thin in a smartly tailored Chanel suit, her auburn hair swept back in a characteristic chignon, wearing a strand of pearls and discreet *Roman Holiday* big black sunglasses, subverting attention. In her engagement-ring hand she was clasping a small light blue Tiffany box tied with a white silk ribbon, of course, but before he knew it, around the corner there was another Audrey Hepburn, identical, down to the blue box, and then another and another. It seems that the original had been printed for a special edition. Homer could hardly believe his luck having spotted the annual migratory patterns of Audreys that had taken wing. Could there have been a flock of Gregory Pecks far behind?

I was sailing on top of waves somewhere in the North Atlantic. I received a letter when I arrived in port.

Dear Rigby,

I'm sorry our last night together ended as it did. I've pinpointed you on my map and think you must be in Stockholm.

My work at Century is coming along pretty well, and I've spotted carbon copy celebrities. I have a screening room where I watch movies, and my assistant Jenny keeps me on course. Whatever I need, she is here to help with research, office supplies, even my expense report. She has the knack of ordering in mountainous sandwiches from at place called Art's. They are so big I can't finish them. She's a guide through the studio system and if I were still at Time-Life, I'd write an Editor's Note about "Jenny the Invincible."

I know you love your boat and hope that you are enjoying every minute playing Captain Cook!

Homer

RIGBY CANFIELD VISITS LONDON

The *Starlight* had a mahogany hull and crisp white sails. "With the wind at my back and a star to sail her by," I was on the first leg of my voyage, enjoying an entrancing calm at sea. I thought about Homer a lot. All our lives, we had dreamed of making movies together, but my thoughtless behavior on a fateful night had upset our friendship and plans.

I was caught up in a navigational agenda of charts and currents. After leaving Stockholm, I found the winds of crystal-pure air filling my unfurled sails as I navigated the North Sea. I would write Homer from London. He seemed to be doing fine.

Entering into the Thames and docking in London, I checked the papers for items about the theater. One review described Daisy as "dancing on daffodils" and I knew why the Brits thought that.

I took a room at the Queen's favorite hotel, Claridge's, near Hyde Park. Soaking in a steaming hot bath in an old-fashioned English tub with English soap and plenty of water, I enjoyed a luxury I greatly missed at sea.

As usual, Time-Life connections came in handy. Terry Spencer, a photographer who insisted on accommodating me, secured a pair of theater tickets for the press. He was amused by my grungy appearance in my sailing gear. A classic photographer, he was as talented as he was elegant, wearing the quiet confidence of having produced more *LIFE* covers than any other staff international photographer. With a shock of brown hair, just graying slightly at the temples, his eyes had sparkling spring-like appreciation that brought alive English landscapes and pastimes. Terry was just as natty and meticulous as his smart camera case. He carried his Leica and Nikon cameras in a specially designed, steel re-enforced tan leather box he had crafted by a saddle-maker in Argentina, housing small green felt compartments inside to hold his lenses.

"It's not quite proper," Terry suggested politely while valuating my wardrobe. "In London, one dresses for the theater."

I took a giant step into fashion when he introduced me to his favorite "bespoke" on Savile Row who could be counted on to provide a smart, well-fitting blue blazer.

We talked shop, as photojournalists do, about recent assignments. I told him I was no longer shooting stills but making documentaries. He was keen to hear whether Time-Life had any interest in filmmaking. Walking through London's narrow streets, we shared the appreciation for the scene. Our thoughts were motivated by the subconscious skill of seeing the world through a personal lens, calculating, for instance, how long the English summer light would last, probably well into late evening. There were avenues of diplomacy and money, where traffic moved at a reasonable pace and where the sounds of car horns would be an intrusion. When I photographed the gray and white Georgian terraces, I waited for the last bit of twilight to soften with a hint of rose to paint their doors and matching shutters. Weather had always been the rightful obsession for the British, and a drizzle, spitting with intermittent moisture, paused in the light air from Marble Arch to Eaton Square. In the summer, when the days are crystalline clear, a description would simply be *glorious*, and allowed me to believe that London and its countryside, on late evenings like these, were the most beautiful on earth.

When Terry and I arrived at the bottom of St. James, I marveled at this place and its deep green lawns. Muted sounds came from pubs with echoes of laughter and conversation lilting from every public room: The Swan, The Anchor, and The Cheshire Cheese. With time before curtain, we walked past Pall Mall into the Strand, where we took a light supper at the Savoy Grill: I favored a Welsh rarebit, a traditional dish made with cheddar cheese. We started with cucumber sandwiches and enjoyed some glasses of ale. The tastes of Worcestershire sauce and English mustard added a spicy touch to the meal, a great improvement over the ship's grub I had been accustomed to. Terry introduced me to Merrydown apple cider, which proved not to be as good as La Vieille Maison's. Father Rivage came to mind for a moment; he would have enjoyed our walking tour leading to the river's edge. We were on the ground where Samuel Johnson and Charles Dickens had walked, where many shops were emblazoned with the crest "By Appointment to the Queen."

At the theater, we sat in the Dress Circle, one level above the Stalls—a term from Shakespeare's days when the Globe Theatre's patrons stood on the ground floor. During the first act, Daisy's performance touched me; by the third, I knew she was irresistible. I managed to sneak several photographs for Homer.

I met Daisy backstage after the performance, and we walked together over cobbled lanes to the Mirabelle, a smart London restaurant in Mayfair. She had matured over the years, with success building her confidence. The coolness of the wet English air seemed only to radiate her fair peach complexion, complimenting her style, wearing a large rimmed hat that hid a mysterious summer smile underneath. Her pleated tailored skirts had just enough swish to turn the most conservative head to embrace and admire, because wherever she went, she left a sweeping presence.

Taking a seat at a preferred table, Daisy beamed and said, "You are full of surprises. Really nice to see you, Rigby. I'm so happy you came."

I was too. She was wearing her success comfortably. Offers for roles were streaming in.

"I wish Homer were here," said Daisy, "I really do. He would love it. Have you heard from him? How does he sound?"

"Pretty good. The young man has gone West! We had a bit of a tiff, as they might say over here."

"Over what?"

"Over you."

"I understand," Daisy said quietly. "That's why I haven't heard from him."

Then she opened up to me. She had deliberately been keeping Homer out of her thoughts in her dressing room, but after a performance, when she felt alone with her emotions, her defenses crumbled. "I never know what to think. He's like a puzzle; no matter how hard I try, I can't put all the pieces together. Maybe I see something in him that is much deeper, maybe I see something in him that is inside me, in a very real way."

"Maybe it's not so complicated."

"I wish I could commit to a relationship, but I can't just now."

It was a notion I understood. "Maybe you should tell him, Daisy." What more could I say?

Our conversation moved to small talk: London, theater, my trip, and the weather.

"Can I write to you? I want to stay in touch," Daisy asked, when I dropped her at her flat.

"I'll be at sea. But you can always reach me on the marine radio, the call letters are STARLIGHT."

When I filed my first report and dispatched twenty rolls of film taken at sea by courier from Time-Life's London bureau on New Bond Street, I ran into an old British actor in a nearby pub called the Garrick, a favorite gathering place for journalists and actors. We had met in New York long ago.

Ronald Fielding had been a star in Hollywood movies in the forties but was swept back to Europe after he was blacklisted in the McCarthy era. He was a classic actor whose handmade shoes were made at Lobb on St. James and tailored suits on Savile Row. I asked if he knew anything about Century Studios. Fielding had nothing good to say, particularly about Jordan St. Clair, the number two man at Century. The parent company was the TransCorporation of America, known as TCA. It was owned by General Ed Riker, a man with no abiding character, an oilman who discovered that show business was more fun than drilling. Riker was known on Wall Street as a genius. He bought businesses that were in trouble, made them profitable, and sold them at an enormous profit. He knew how to translate liabilities into assets. However, Century was not only losing money but also its creative spirit. TCA bought the old Goldwyn and Century studios, making it possible for Riker to build "Movieland" for star-seeking tourists who wanted to visit behind the scenes and glimpse a star or two. The studio had created a tour that combined movie memories and how movies were made.

See where Hitchcock filmed *North by Northwest*.

See where they shot *Casablanca*.

See the stuntmen. See the cameras. See the makeup department.

See the flats and the sets and the magic of Hollywood.

See the two-story billboard of Billy Sunshine.

Soon, the tour business was making more money than the movie business. Fielding guessed that the General was making a few films each year to give the illusion that Century was a real working studio. And to sweeten the package for a future buyer, he built a film library.

He didn't have to make a lot of films, just a few that Century would declare "in development," with no intention of actually producing them. Just before they were ready to be made, he would lay screenplays off to the vaults or packages to another studio. He also built a sprawling compound with bungalows. The one called Century Headquarters housed executives who fought for power, and in the wars of film fighters, Jordan St. Clair always won. But the General's true agenda was not making films at all; he had found Hollywood's real financial jackpot: real estate.

"Real estate?" I was surprised.

The old actor grinned his famous grin, tilted his head, and raised his eyebrow.

"You really don't understand the movie business at all, do you, Canfield?"

I shook my head.

"You see, my dear fellow, all the big ones, Crosby, Hope, Sinatra, they all owned, and I mean literally owned the town. Their fortunes were not made from films and residuals, but from their investment in land. Take Bob Hope—he was smart, insisting that Paramount buy a few hundred acres for him. It made the studio an exceptionally desirable place to work.

"So, you see, to provide a tax advantage, the studio gave them land along with their salaries."

He smiled again, a glossy display of teeth. "Besides, I own some Century stock. As far as I am concerned, they can give the land back to Mexico as long as I get my dividend checks. Films, dear man? You are dealing with Riker, a master manipulator and puppeteer."

At Portofino, I tried to reach Homer by telephone, but got Jenny on the line instead. Homer had apparently convinced her that I was the world's greatest photographer. Though we had never met, she told me how much she liked my work. And working for Homer was a job she truly enjoyed. He was learning how to get things done at Century. When I asked if he was having any fun, Jenny said Homer sometimes went to The Brown Derby, near Hollywood and Vine, where the studio crowd dined, later mimicking their startling behavior for Jenny.

Restaurants in Beverly Hills had fleets of Bentleys and Mercedes parked outside, Jenny told me, prominently arranged in pecking order, according to their owners' star or executive status. We laughed as she described Homer dropping his red Ford truck right in front, letting the puzzled attendants guess where to park it. After work, he sometimes invited her to restaurants that were as good anything in New York, Musso & Frank on Hollywood Boulevard and Chasen's in Beverly Hills.

Of course, he couldn't get anywhere without driving, and the open road is where he wanted to take the wheel and go his own way with his navigational sights set on the classic route Highway One— the old coast road between Los Angeles and San Francisco that passed through the fishing village of Monterey, Big Sur's spectacular bends and craggy turns, and the wind-blown, scented cypress trees in Carmel. On a literary note, he discovered authors who had left their landmarks—Fitzgerald, West, Chandler, Kerouac, and Steinbeck, who produced the greatest Californian story of all, *The Grapes of Wrath*. It was easy for him to imagine Okies in Model T Fords when they finally reached journey's end.

But what Ronald Fielding had told me about Century troubled me. Was the studio really not serious about film? Had Homer found his place in the sun or was he in a dream factory, sleepwalking with its actors and producers and directors? I wanted to believe that he, like others before him, was part of a generation of writers and directors that reflect an appealing national culture, not one focused on trends and keeping books for tax-deductible expenses. The newer films had an independent perspective while the focus studios had become indifferent. The business was changing. Backlots were subject to frontal assaults; studios were subservient to agents who controlled the total package. It seemed the studio system and its art of moviemaking had disappeared and would never return.

SOUND EFFECTS

"I heard an odd booming sound, followed by a short whistling and a long rumble. Shhhhh. Balooooom!"
—Homer Sincere's journal, 1970

The small block with the inscription TIMING was still displayed on Jordan St. Clair's desk; Homer had been at the studio for two months and was now at work on the second draft of *The Last Cowboy*.

"Production is going to be postponed for a while," Jordan informed him. "We go with the trend."

"The trend?"

"Kid, the trend is important to us. Did you see *Love Story*? Looks like contemporary drama is in this year."

"The trend—who starts trends, Jordan?"

St. Clair looked blankly at him and laughed, his voice and thoughts opening from a well-oiled hinge. "Well, I guess sometimes we start 'em, sometimes we end them. In the meantime, don't forget . . ." St. Clair pointed to TIMING.

As Homer read scripts and offbeat films that the other majors and independent studios were producing, like *Five Easy Pieces, Annie Hall,* and *M*A*S*H*, their connection with the trends ran through his mind. He heard explosions in the distance, an odd booming sound: a short whistle followed a long rumble. Shhhhh. Chrummmm. It was an ominous noise. "Special effects . . . ?" he called Jenny.

"They're dynamiting Lot Number Two," Jenny said. "It's being torn down to develop real estate."

Dynamiting! He went over to what was left of the European Square, finding a mass of rubble that reminded him of a battle scene. Workmen and tractors everywhere were in a demolition derby. Part of the trend? Timing?

"Hate to see it go," a workman said. "Especially where Gene Kelly sang 'Singing in the Rain.' On that street, over there."

Down an empty cobblestone alley was Backlot Number Three, a small American town with an old railway station, corrals, gangster alleys, and period settings where the studio had made *Gone with the Wind* and *Meet Me In St. Louis* long ago. It was a movie itself. A poster of Billy Sunshine that towered above western streets and storefronts was coming down. His eyes panned a long balustrade that led to an image of Hollywood he had seen every Saturday as a kid. It starred Fred and Ginger, Hopalong Cassidy and Errol Flynn, Gary Cooper and Billy.

In his notes, he wrote as if about a dream: *"About thirty cowboys in dark silhouettes, riding hard and fast over boundless land toward the mountains. They have large leather mailbags, and I ask what's in the bags. They don't tell me. They ride together, thundering into the distance until I can't see them anymore."*

HOME ON THE RANGE

"You had a call from Billy Sunshine's office," Jenny told Homer when he arrived at his bungalow.

"Finally. When can we meet?"

"After I told his assistant about the project, she said that she would be glad to set up an appointment, and as soon as you are further along, he'd be delighted to meet."

"Great news!" Homer exclaimed. He wondered if Billy knew they were tearing down the backlot?

Then St. Clair called from Headquarters.

"Hey, kid, we're going to see Riker. We'll just be there a few minutes, a formality."

Homer followed a colony of small red-tiled, honey-colored bungalows housing producers and writers on the lot along the path to the steel fortified tower, passing starlets smiling at him. He paused just long enough to accept words of encouragement, punctuated with flirting glances for a new writer. There were enough pretty and promising actresses around the lot to insure that any contract should include a double indemnity clause before playing humpty-dumpty.

Outside headquarters was the timely choreography surrounding the few active soundstages being prepared for the day's production schedule; make-up artists carrying their kits into trailers, costume grips hustling down alleys, trucks unloading scenery, directors in electric-powered golf carts scooting along and dodging crowds of passing extras. All seemed to be a normal and usual day.

Getting out of the elevator at Riker's office, Homer noticed the same furniture, but the outer reception presented two secretaries guarding their respective posts at campaign desks with TIMING engraved on larger marble blocks.

The General was heavyset, with white hair, smoking a slim cigar. He postured in a way he thought General Patton might have commanded his army. Jordan St. Clair actually saluted him!

"Homer Sincere." The General glanced at Homer for a moment. "At ease, Sincere."

"Thank you, sir," Homer replied. "It's a fine place to be, Century. Makes great movies."

The General's hospitality was direct in his opening salvo. His granite blue eyes shone with currency in their construction. "Mr. Sincere," he barked. "You have something in mind for us?"

"Yes, sir," Homer said quietly, still standing near the door as dense cigar smoke dimmed his vision. "I have a project called *The Last Cowboy*."

Through the haze, the General looked toward Jordan. "The timing has changed."

"I understand, sir, that it's all in the timing," Homer said and took a deep breath. "But we can make this movie on the Western lot, which will save a great deal of front end money."

The General offered a patronizing smile. "This new wunderkind of yours doesn't understand the accounting system yet, does he, Jordan?"

Jordan returned a wan grin. "We cover most of our operating expenses studio-wide by not saving money on the front end," Jordan said in a quiet, understated tone.

"As for filming on the backlot," the General continued, "Century is building a model city there, Mr. Sincere."

"You are really tearing it down?"

"It's going to be very profitable," Riker offered with some authority.

"One hundred percent," St. Clair confirmed.

The General spoke confidently out of the side of his mouth in muffled tones while puffing on his cigar, as if the conversation needed that for emphasis. When the smoke cleared, Homer was shown the model of the building that was to replace the backlot.

St. Clair began, "Homer, it's important. The tax people are making unreasonable demands, so we've got to diversify. It's a multi-million dollar project; it's dynamite, Homer. Do you see the big idea?"

"What idea?"

"The idea whose time has come, for the studio, for California. It's a vision for the new tomorrow!"

"Yes," he said, sighing. "It looks very good." What were they doing? he wondered. His disappointment was only matched by his astonishment.

"We've designed a solar-powered community for the twenty-first century, with our own set designers creating an environmentally correct living space for the future. There is a plan for single-family houses, cluster housing, parklands, a driving range, recreation centers, and even a few movie theaters."

Sliding walls, built-in atriums, doors with push-button combinations without locks, self-cleaning bathrooms; all were part of TCA's concept for living. Standing over the new project, General Riker's eyes rolled wildly with delirious happiness. Dotted all through the miniature model city were miniature movie posters and parts of movie sets called landmarks.

"Isn't it great? Home, home on the range, where the deer and the buffalo play," the General sang.

He had it wrong; they were antelopes, not buffalo.

"Join me, Jordan," the General requested, swinging his left arm to add patriotic rhythm. "Home, home on the range."

What is happening to the movies? Homer thought. What is happening to me?

Then the big "idea" occurred to him.

"You're building a village on the backlot, so why don't you call it Sunshine Village, Jordan? It's a tie-in for the movie I'm writing for Billy Sunshine."

"I like your thinking, kid. It's one hundred percent. I like your commitment," the General said after a pause, dropping his tune. "Sunshine Village would be perfect, and it'll be like the old days, having Billy back on the lot. It will make an attractive package. Tradition!"

"Billy Sunshine will be fantastic in the film," Jordan added. "It's one hundred percent." Homer was getting the lingo.

The General interrupted, "See if we can get John Wayne to make a cameo appearance."

"We can?" Homer felt better.

"Yes, he loves Billy. Don't be surprised if Douglas and Lancaster show up. They're friends, and it will be Billy's first film in years.

"How will they fit into the script, Jordan?"

"Now, Homer, that's your department."

A new Billy Sunshine film! His first in ten years.

THE SHOOTING SCRIPT

EXTERIOR: WYOMING: DAY

"To the gentle rolling plains of Wyoming, almost bewildering in its beauty, where the countryside rolls on endlessly to the horizon. The West, where men retain a sense of struggle and achievement. A cowboy rides into town greeting a kid waiting for him."

At first the writing came easily, the pages turning and flowing quickly, but now there were no words on the page. Where were they? Somewhere, but where was somewhere? Something was happening, but he wasn't sure what . . . Maybe if he spent more time in the projection room . . . that was the answer . . . The words would come on arrows to the target. Watch the films, listen to the dialogue, the words would surely arrive, but his words fell into a slow dissolve and into the same dream: dark silhouetted cowboys riding hard and fast over boundless land toward the mountains with saddlebags. What's in the bags? He didn't know. Horses' hooves thundered, fading into the distance, and again they were gone.

A troubling uncertainty haunted Homer. He jotted down in his notebook about his meetings with Riker and St. Clair, meetings that were oddly calm and devoid of feeling, driving toward emotional congestion. At the same time, there was something in Homer, keeping him on track, a feeling of dignity harmonizing with the nature of his writing, trying bravely to accept the reality of Century, but he couldn't. Homer was blessed with the myopic vision to see the best in humankind.

OUT-TAKES

"Meetings and hearing something I could not hear. Who were these people, who had different notions about film, and the movies I wished for?"
—Homer Sincere's journal, 1970

"A cowboy rides into town, the street is deserted, but the jangling sound of a rickety piano comes from a local saloon. The rider dismounts in front of the watering place, dances through the swinging doors. He is young, affable looking, with a smile as he enters and sees the lady. She's beautiful. She's not alone. Inside the doors he stops, the smile freezes on his face. The music continues tinkling from the player piano. The cowboy is here for a reason."

Jordan St. Clair called Homer back to Headquarters for meetings and to discuss the screenplay.

"I need some more time, Jordan."

"I've read several drafts of your story, kid, and I don't think it's gonna work just now."

"What do you mean, Jordan?"

"Don't you read the trades? Billy is at Cedars. He's been ill."

Homer didn't know. Jenny had just spoken to his office. Had something happened?

"Listen, kid, I like you. I really do and hear me please, if you want to work at Century and be part of the team."

"What about *The Last Cowboy* . . . Billy Sunshine?

"He's history, son."

History? He couldn't accept what St. Clair was saying. And before they discussed another draft, St. Claire announced, "What I want to talk to you about is another year's option we have on your contract—we really like you, but there are a lot of changes going on at TCA, and I want to share them with you."

"What changes, Jordan?"

"You know what I mean. We may have to cut overhead a bit, nothing personal, but we want to put the film on hold. It's timing, and that's the way it has always been. We just can't go with it now, but the General thought it would be helpful if you wrote a few promotional brochures, because we are going to need some good press . . . maybe something in *TIME*, to promote Century Village."

"Century Village? You mean Sunshine Village. I don't think . . ."

"No," Jordan interrupted. "The marketing people at headquarters think Century Village is better—the name has a certain panache, and we are moving on. The General has ordered the demolition of Backlot Number Four to make room. I don't think we need the western street. We're looking toward the future, not the past."

"Marketing people?" Homer stated his case. "Jordan, is that where you and the General live, in some marketplace? You hold the charter to the greatest studio ever built, one that gave rise to a national culture. Century created a screen tradition—an afterglow resonates for audiences everywhere. It is so special that there is no place better where the lore and legends of our country, the manner, the speech, the myths, the chase, the romance, can be imagined."

"Are you finished?" Jordan asked.

"Yes, I guess I am. But what about Billy Sunshine?"

He placed a restraining hand around his shoulder and adroitly addressed the subject. "Not now," Jordan said. "It's timing. And anyway, no one cares about cowboys anymore."

BACK AT THE RANCH

"Cowboy courage and loyalty mean a lot to me. Why hadn't I found Billy before now? I was waiting to finish the script. It will be a great comeback and a film that he will want to make."

—Homer Sincere's journal, 1971

A vision swarmed through his mind, but as suddenly and irretrievably as smoke, it seemed to vanish. It was not for lack of oxygen, but for sheer character that Homer returned to find Billy. He checked Cedars, finding Billy had been admitted, and he had to see him. When Homer arrived, he noticed a man across from him in a waiting room, sitting primly in a wooden chair, a kind-looking man of indeterminate age, with puffs of gray hair on each side of his balding head, neatly dressed in a three-button dark gray suit with a Billy Sunshine tie clip. His eye winked behind his steel-rimmed glasses when he discovered Homer looking at him.

"You here for Billy?"

"I am, a fan, and you?"

Another wink. "Friend. Partner. All sorts of ties to Billy." He patted the seat next to him. "I'm from South Dakota."

"Have you come all the way to visit Billy?"

"Oh, I just live over the hill, out in the Simi Valley, and you?"

"I'm from New Orleans."

"Care to talk?"

Homer walked over, reaching out his hand. "I'm Homer Sincere."

The man guided him to the chair beside him. "My name is Harry Gabriel. I noticed you limping a bit there. Fall off a horse?"

"Yes, I fell off."

Homer tried to remember where and when he first heard the familiar name, and then, in a flash, it came to him.

"Harry Gabriel, the screenwriter?"

Gabriel tilted his head. "One and the same."

Suddenly, Homer retreated to old patterns . . . he couldn't speak and waited for the words to catch up with him. Homer had seen every movie Billy made, and he was sitting next to the man who wrote them.

"How's your script coming?"

Homer stared at him—how did he know? Did he have ink stains on his fingers?

"This is Hollywood, where everyone's either an actor or a screenwriter. You don't strike me as an actor."

Homer stuttered an answer, "I'm nearly done with the outline, and a few scenes."

"What's it about?"

"It's called *The Last Cowboy*."

"Well, you look like a cowboy to me. Tall, lanky, tan, winning smile, and a wink in your eye." Gabriel paused. "Interesting title." Gabriel contemplated. "Don't worry, son. I have it on authority that Billy is going to get better."

Homer felt better with Gabriel's reassurance.

"Now tell me, what's really going on with you?"

"Well . . . I was fired from Century."

"I see. Nothing new at Century—another casualty hits the dust." Harry Gabriel fell into his own thoughts, then suddenly grinned. "Is it a good script?"

"I think so, but maybe not the right time," he shrugged. "I'm having problems."

"Maybe I can help. How long do you need to finish?"

"A month, maybe. No more than that."

"Why don't you come out and work at the ranch?"

"The ranch?"

"Maybe we can help each other. I'm having a few problems too, but if you're interested, I'd like to invite you over."

Gabriel chuckled, tearing a piece of paper off an envelope, and wrote down directions.

"You come on out when you're ready; we'll get you fixed up. Won't be fancy accommodations like the studio hands out, but the atmosphere is good."

"Are you sure?"

He leaned back, crossed one leg over a knee, and puffed his pipe. "I'm sure. After all, that's where I wrote most of Billy's films."

That night, a letter Homer had not been expecting interrupted his excitement:

Dear Homer,

You are the best man I have ever known. I wish I could live up to your expectations, but I don't know how. I said you were "trouble." I take that back. The trouble is me. My career is very important, especially now. Being an actress is something that I have always wanted and being onstage makes me happy. This sounds selfish and shallow, I know. Please try to understand. I feel this will come as a disappointment to you. I am not so stupid as not to know your thoughts. I know who you are and how you feel. And I am torn, I really am. Part of me knows I would be happy with you. There is something else inside me that is afraid, and I'm fighting to balance my deep feelings for you. And please know, what happened between me and Rigby was just a passing interlude that holds no meaning. You hold all that is good, and I'm afraid I've hurt you. You'll write great screenplays, and I expect to be there opening night next to you!

Love, Daisy

The words were just flickers on his screen. The projector needed a new lens. He did not want to think about it and tried to push Daisy out of his movie. It was not the first hurt in his life, just another emotional punch. He reasoned he would have to work harder to be somebody and his "something is wrong with me" scenario resurfaced in full force. He needed a home, someone, and something, a map to follow. There was no Waldo or Father Rivage, no Rigby to invent a plan. He had entered Century in triumph and was stumbling out in failure. A cry for help came from some deeper place inside him and was answered by a man called Harry Gabriel.

MAKE YOURSELF AT HOME

*"It was perhaps the most beautiful place I had ever seen. Billy's Ranch!
Driving under the arch, I gave a casual wave, well, more than a casual
wave, rather a snappy salute left over from 'Headquarters.' This amazing place was out of time and out of fashion, and in a way, out of sorts,
but for me, a new home. I loved every square foot that stirred my dusty
memory."*   —Homer Sincere's journal, 1971

Driving north out of Los Angeles toward the hills to see the man
from South Dakota, Homer found the ranch to be a group of tired
buildings overpowered by weather, weeds, and bushes. A broken
down fence surrounded the property and attempted to divide the
spaces between the barns. At the entrance, a rusty iron structure
announced "Sunshine Studios." It looked very good to Homer.

Miss Faye, a lady of indeterminate age, wearing a flowered rayon
dress, met him on the porch then showed him to his room. Mr. Gabriel
was waiting nearby.

"Welcome to the ranch, Homer Sincere. Please make yourself at
home!"

"Thank you, Mr. Gabriel, it is really very special for me to be
where Billy made films. Wow!"

"Well, all the early ones before the big blockbusters, and please
call me Harry. We used to have quite a spread, but over the years
we've sold off parcels of land, and with the price of California real
estate, we've managed to pay the taxes with a little left over."

It was the two hundred acre ranch that Billy built before he went
to Century, where he had made sixty-three movies, all two-reelers,
with wardrobe, props, sets, cameras, and stages, all museum-like. A
backdrop of the great western plains of the San Fernando Valley was
deposited just outside his back door.

"I have copies of the films, and we'll be getting a few more back at the end of the week. Some TV stations want to run a few in the late night movie slot, and I must say, those residuals sure come in handy."

Outside he met the three caballeros, Angelo, Raphael, and Francisco, easygoing Mexican ranch hands who sat on the porch of a mock saloon on a run down back lot. Francisco strummed a guitar and grinned.

A dusty stray circled him for a few minutes, studying the new arrival, reminding him of Walter, and rubbed against his leg as if to say, "Hello, Homer. Glad you're here." The dog followed him everywhere and with an affectionate pat, he welcomed a new friend.

Mr. Gabriel pointed to an opera house facade that adjoined a plywood bank. "Lily Langtry sang there," he gestured, his arm showing the way, "and that's where Billy caught Jesse. And over there is the jail where Billy provided accommodations."

It was an amazing place—out of time, out of fashion, out of sorts, but a familiar post for Homer and a new home that matched his dusty memory.

"We filmed exactly the way I saw them ,and writing for Billy kept me busy," Mr. Gabriel said, then added, "Billy had one simple rule: be true. That was the code."

Miss Faye played a 78 RCA Victor phonograph record, producing the tinny muffled sounds of an old Western song, which filtered outside to Homer and Harry Gabriel.

"No one could sing like Roy. Just listen, Homer." Mr. Gabriel was lost in reverie as he mouthed the words ". . . Happy trails . . . happy trails . . . until we meet again."

"You go ahead and wander a bit, and then come up to the office for some tea. Miss Faye will have it ready," Mr. Gabriel suggested. "And take your time."

A truck backfired. When Homer looked up, his flatbed red truck carrying his desk and books came to a stop. The ranch hands unloaded them, taking his gear into his room, and helped him unpack. Among his things was *Canto General*.

"Spanish?" asked Raphael.

"Won the Nobel Prize for Literature."

"Prize? Like the lottery?"

"Yes. Pablo Neruda from Chile." He pushed the book into Raphael's appreciative hand.

Later, Miss Faye brought a large silver tea service and biscuits to the office where posters of Billy in his films—*Cheyenne Pass*, *Sunset in the West*, *Trail of Sorrow*, and *Prairie Lands*—lined the walls.

Miss Faye whispered to him, "At first, I didn't know just who you were, Homer Sincere. I thought you were from the bank in Nevada."

"The bank?"

"They have been putting pressure on Mr. Gabriel lately, and he's doing everything he can to get us back into production. I am very glad you are here—he needs a partner."

A partner? Homer was curious to know more and, looking around the room, noticed a tarnished brass horn behind the large oak desk—maybe a call to colors? But with no activity on the lot, he realized that he might be the production arm of the ranch and wondered if Mr. Gabriel had told the bankers that Sunshine Studios would soon be making a film. Homer pondered this possibility; perhaps the Sunshine Ranch had seen something Century had missed. But there was one thing for sure, Harry Gabriel was serious about them helping each other. The studio was in need of some fixin' up, and Homer enlisted the Spanish-speaking trio to pitch in.

Then came the big idea: real estate!

If Century Studios had a tour, and Universal, why not Sunshine Studios? It was THE original ranch where westerns were made, and it was just down the road from Knott's Berry Farm, which did a sprightly business.

Over the next few weeks, Raphael, Francisco, Angelo, and foreman Homer Sincere dressed in white coveralls and painted buildings and fences in patches of sunlight. Landscaping followed, and the work took his mind off Daisy.

The buildings were given new life and like an old piece of tarnished silver restored after a good polish, the ranch shined! In no time at all a group of thirty people gathered in front of the main office where a "Tour" sign was posted overhead, coming to see the Ranch, Billy's place, paying visitors and tourists! Wearing laced tan boots and breeches, looking more and more like Cecil B. de Mille, Harry Gabriel led groups down the western street.

Costumes reclaimed from a wardrobe closet were restored and dry-cleaned, cowhands played new roles as cowboys, Angelo, dressed as a marshal, guarded the jail, and the singing troubadour Francisco, fitted up in a black mariachi costume dotted with silver rosettes, roamed the lot, appreciating the sound of his rolling *R*s and tenor voice. On cue, Raphael galloped furiously down Main Street creating plumes of yellow dust just before the customers entered Miss Faye's Sunshine Souvenir Shop to buy sarsaparilla, red-eye, Billy's Bar-B-Q Sandwiches, photographs and posters, cards and key chains, and Billy's red handkerchiefs to wipe off the dust that had accumulated on their apparel.

Each morning Harry Gabriel stopped by Homer's office—during the "authentic" feature of the tour—to introduce Homer Sincere, a real screenwriter at work. Almost larger than the office hung a Billy Sunshine poster. The tour got bigger day by day.

A STAR TO SAIL HER BY

I had received a cable from Jenny. She was worried about Homer. Things were no better when I reached her. She told me that Homer had been fired from Century, but that they'd still kept in touch. But he hadn't returned her calls in weeks, and she was unsure of what to do.

"Should I come over? Homer always spends a lot of time by himself."

"Perhaps I'm just overreacting," she replied, easing my concern.

If I sailed back, it would take weeks. Even if I flew, my time frame for the transatlantic crossing would not allow me to hold to my schedule and meet the assignment's deadline. With delay, I would be sailing against tides and currents.

I called Homer, but there was no reply.

It took twenty-eight days to cross the Atlantic, and as I was sailing from Martinique to Barbados to the lower Grenadines, a stunning opportunity was stirring. A gale force five hurricane was predicted and, by all reckoning, if I sailed due south I'd be in the eye. I imagined filming the storm's tremendous winds and turbulent waves; beauty was at its core, and I wanted to capture the stillness in its panoramic center. Not surprisingly, my crew refused to sail on with me and disembarked in Grenada, but promised to catch up with me in Aruba. I sailed on alone, and in the days before the storm, I had a star to sail her by. Then with assurance, I positioned the wheel toward the center using radar and my charts. No photographer I knew had ever attempted the challenge before, and I would ride toward the eye until the storm broke and subsided into unimaginable calm.

FINAL DRAFT

"The dream was different this time; the cowboys were waiting for me in the distance somewhere along the California coast near Santa Barbara, inviting me to ride with them. They were all on horseback with a vivid orange sky behind them, their horses shuffled easily, waiting for the moment when the reins were released to gallop away. "We're riding to the other side," they called to me, waiting, impatient, and restless for just a moment in time. Then the horses bolted out into the open countryside, wide and free, into gray-green plains along the blue-capped Pacific. They galloped hard, carrying large leather pouches, saddlebags filled with words. Turning into the hills, they reached the high point that almost touched the heavens and emptied their bags, spilling the contents into windy sweeping updrafts. Up, up, up, until they fell, floating over prairies and plains, to the continental wall, the great divide, falling like stars."

—Homer Sincere's journal, 1971

In his room, everything was sunny and clean. He wrote in a corner surrounded with western blankets and saddles, under rugged expose beams framing the heavy plaster walls, revising pages, over and over again, for *The Last Cowboy*, but once again came face to face with a colossal case of writer's block. The pressure of writing and measuring up to Harry Gabriel's expectations overwhelmed him. Then, without introduction, at a crucial moment, someone called to him.

"Homer!"

Harry Gabriel rose like an apparition in the doorway, offering a tin cup of black coffee. "That's a really beautiful desk. Antique?"

"Belonged to my mother. It's followed me all my life."

"Keeping it in the family. That's a nice thing to do."

"Part of me, I guess."

"I'm glad to help you in any way, research, stories, anything at all."

"I have the concept, and I want to have a full script for Billy, a perfect first draft, one we can all be proud of, but the writing is not easy on this."

"Don't worry about the script."

"Easy for you to say, Harry. How's Billy doing? Doing better, recovering . . . ?"

"Up in Santa Barbara . . . doing okay."

"That's good, Harry!"

"Sometimes the words have a way to go, got to dust them off, but I find they're usually traveling not far behind, just a little late leaving the station."

"I'll be expecting them, Harry."

"They should arrive soon, and I'm sure they will." They was almost a slight tone of urgency in his voice. "You are a good writer, son, and your words, your script, are going to mean a lot to Billy. He is THE Cowboy. It really feels good to be thought of, not forgotten, and Billy needs a good screenplay."

Harry Gabriel turned to go. "Homer, I guess you find this place is all a little different, but I'd like to say it's been here waiting for you, and I want to thank you for all the help you've given the ranch. I hope I can make it up to you in some way."

The statement of appreciation prompted Homer to ask, "Have you lived here a long time, Harry? I imagine you are a lot like Billy."

"I guess so, since I wrote most of the words. Before I came, I used to play in a band. Yep, been here most of my life. Now when you finish, you ride on up and see Billy."

"Ride?"

"Ride . . . drive, just a figure of speech."

Homer closed his eyes and imagined sitting with Billy on a porch under a red tile roof, talking about life and friendship, the big, the small, the special things that matter.

Finding a book by Willa Cather, he read her elegy about the land, uplifted by the wide western spirit inherited by those who had pioneered the "road-making West." Willa reminded him of the "precious, incommunicable past," a phase remembered from Father Rivage.

He drowsed somewhere between writing, sleeping and waking. Night came quickly. The descent of darkness arrived with a winter calling, and he rose quickly, silently, and turned on a lamp. A wind from a partly opened window shook the sheer curtains; they trembled slightly, as if being touched by an unseen hand. Bonding his connection with Billy and Willa, words and ideas clamored for attention in his mind. Outside the window, oak leaves rustled as if they were words making thin dry scrapings against the screen. Then they entered, slowly at first, and then faster and faster, and Homer could hardly keep up. Everything Homer ever knew, all the prose and poetry, everything he wanted to say about loyalty and courage and cowboys found their way into the scenes of a 104-page screenplay.

"Wait for me, Billy, we're going to ride together."

Homer finished *The Last Cowboy*.

On his veranda, before the sun paused in the sky, holding on to a pink minute before sunset, he decided that he was going to "ride" up and see Billy the next day—the drive was less than a hundred miles along the Pacific.

The following morning, he looked for Harry Gabriel, and Miss Faye told Homer that he and Raphael had gone to the post office and had not returned.

Homer felt happily enriched, walking past a leaking fountain with slow trickling notes.

He was dressed in khakis with a colorful plaid shirt. Miss Faye commented on his polished boots and gave him a cowboy hat to wear. He hadn't worn one in years. The hat was made of tightly woven felt and slid onto his head, bringing a comfortable recollection.

"You want to look real good for Billy," she said.

With an address and a manuscript, he was ready to leave and Miss Faye complimented him as she gave him a box lunch. "You look fresh and handsome. Give Billy our best."

Angelo had washed the truck until it gleamed, reflecting the blurry green-gray countryside swishing past him. He drove around a series of concourse curves, then the road ahead became straight and clear. Homer was taken with the endless blue coastline, giving his eyes a rest from the towering California oaks that had stood quietly for years, sweeping over a rolling land that expanded into forever. For a moment, he thought he saw cowboys riding along.

A few hours later, passing the leafy lanes along the San Ysidro Road in Montecito, he approached the entrance to a home for actors.

BILLY SUNSHINE!

"I could imagine Billy reading the screenplay. Looking over the pages, Billy's fingers tapping on the cover, and he will smile. 'You remembered old Billy?'"   —Homer Sincere's journal, 1971

When he asked to see Billy Sunshine, a nurse told him that Billy Sunshine wasn't there. Had he returned to Los Angeles?

"Will Billy be back? My name is Homer Sincere." Homer offered his hand.

The nurse looked at him curiously.

"You haven't heard? Billy Sunshine died last night. I guess you didn't know; it's not made the news."

"Oh no, Billy didn't die."

"I'm sorry," the nurse said. "I am very sorry. You knew him?"

"I was his friend."

"He made a lot of friends here, too."

Her words broke into a tide of sorrow. Homer felt the same sadness rolling ashore to his feelings after the loss of his mother.

The reality was chilling.

"I'm sure it can't be. Billy is fine. You must be mistaken. I have a script I've just finished and he's waiting to see me."

"Be easy, please," the nurse said soothingly. She walked him outside to a courtyard enclosed by rows of hedges.

"Just rest here for a while. Can I offer you anything?"

He openly wept, and then the sun shone, breaking and opening the clouds.

Just beyond the courtyard was Billy!

A little older since the last time he saw him, looking out to a view that gave way to miles of orange groves leading down to the ocean.

"Homer, over here!"

He entered the conversation hesitantly, unnerved, bewildered, but relieved.

"I knew you were OK. How are you feeling?"

"Not too bad, legs a little stiff."

"You're looking good, Billy."

"Oh, a little tired. Enjoy the trip?"

"I thought I saw you riding along, was that you?"

"Yeah. Out with the boys. After work, we like to ride into the sunset, you know how cowboys are."

"Like a movie."

"Not to change the subject, but take a look, son, look who's here."

Nearby was Father Rivage in his black robe with his white socks hinting underneath.

"Hey, Father!"

"Here to see Billy?"

"I am. Remember, I'm bit of a Billy Sunshine fan myself!"

In the distance something came closer. Waldo's wagon! Waldo waved, his gold tooth sparkled in the light.

"Here are some fresh oranges. I'd give you a rhyme but nothin' rhymes with orange 'cept orange."

His mother turned to him. "You wrote it all down?"

"I did, momma."

"Hey, partner," Billy interrupted, with a touch of western gravel in his voice. "I'm mighty glad you came up to see me."

Homer handed him The Last Cowboy.

He tapped on the script. "You remembered old Billy?"

Homer wondered if this was the end of the trail.

"Who's that young man outside?" Homer overheard a supervising nurse ask as she came on duty.

"A friend of Billy Sunshine."

"It's a shame no one told him."

She walked over and stood beside him as he wrote a few last words in his journal, quietly waiting a moment before interrupting:

"It's late, Mr. Sincere. I'm afraid you'll have to leave now."

"Yes, sure, it's been nice to rest here for a few minutes. Thanks."

He went back to his truck, and soon it began raining hard, pouring in torrents. In a few miles, the rain paused long enough to leave a ribbon of fog rising off the road from the humidity.

On a long piece of highway, with the rushing wind whistling over him, he saw a trail of cowboys riding hard on the plains near by. He accelerated to catch up and saw Billy and the boys riding, then faster, chasing them until he was alongside the cowboys thundering and blurring the grass green and brown countryside. The valleys in the distance were made faint by intervening oak trees. Homer drove on an endless road, waving his hat out of the window shouting. A short distance down the highway, he saw a man standing in the center, a familiar figure, looming, becoming larger, in thick enveloping mist. To the side, the cowboys were waving to him from the passing landscape, and Homer kept up alongside, running with them, into rain beading like teardrops; hard wind was now sweeping past the truck. The man ahead was closer, he looked like his father, and then he became a powerful gray shadow blending into the thick, rising fog. Homer turned his attention from the cowboys to the man, an out-of-focus image. He shouted, "Please, out of the way, please," but the shadow kept coming closer, overtaking him.

STARLIGHT

Sailing toward Barbados through treacherous white caps, the *Starlight* approached the eye of Hurricane Luis when an English Coast Guard cutter intercepted me, sounding a deep horn. I was exhilarated, wearing yellow slickers, slicing though tremendous waves. The ocean was beating havoc on the sides of my boat, but she was seaworthy and built beautifully, and I could easily handle her. There was a new groan of thunder ending in a gigantic crackle. The air seemed to be ripped apart. Water sloshed onto the deck. I was a little frightened, but not enough to take my eye off the impending opportunity.

"It's okay. I know what I'm doing," I shouted through the hard winds and sweeping rain.

The captain, holding a yellow megaphone to his mouth, shouted, "No, you don't, you're sailing into a storm in the path of Hurricane Luis."

"I know," I shouted back, furious at losing the momentum of my tack that would soon break away from the eye. "I'm a photographer, and it's now or never."

The captain interrupted me, yelling, "Mate, if you go any further, you are going to capsize. We can't be responsible for you. This storm is dangerous!"

"I know what I'm doing."

"You better keep your radio on."

The cutter pulled away. With the wind blowing harder, I didn't take their warning and headed into torrents of cutting water with a ninety-knot wind filling the sails, flying over the sea with incredible speed.

My boat thrashed over twenty-foot waves and I was at a point of exhaustion approaching the final barrier, into a wall of sweeping rain. Just beyond I knew there would be the great calm and quiet I was looking for. I could hear it—the clouds had a light blue tint, almost as if the sun were trying to burst through the dark gray; then, all of a sudden, I felt a pain in my chest, something was wrong.

For a moment, I thought I heard a teletype machine clacking, and in a quick flashing instant, I saw Homer in a premonition. My heart sank. With just enough energy to change course, I turned up the volume on the marine radio to check my navigational bearings. Instead I heard a navy radio calling the *Starlight*.

I tried to find the frequency but a voice trailed off into static and the radio crackled out.

Cold with rain, the cutter who had intercepted me hours before again found me. "Are you Rigby Canfield?" the captain shouted. "I have a message." I could hardly hear over the storm but I heard enough to know that something had happened to Homer.

I followed the cutter to a harbor in Martinique and took a plane first to Miami, then to Los Angeles, and drove to a small hospital in Ventura County. With such irresponsible ambition, had I intentionally, or perhaps unconsciously, put myself in irretrievable and inconsolable danger?

There were hours of flashbacks over the years to the adventures Homer and I had shared. One memory stood out, of a carnival long ago. My movie mind wandered back to our childhood days in New Orleans where our love of film began, our friendship cemented, and we came face-to-face with our hero.

DANCING FOR THE KING OF CHINA

"Yellow light spread like hot butter until it covered thirty shining golden cowgirls, all on white horses, each carrying an American flag, circling the cowboy in a glistening gold-glittered embrace, holding the audience's breath a little, with dazzling affection."

—Homer Sincere's journal, 1946

I closed my eyes, and heard the loopy, sweet sound of a calliope and saw the spotlights searching a windy, evening sky. Lines of red, blue, and yellow lights swung in the wind, back and forth, like great beaded necklaces. The Midway had a Ferris wheel, rocket rides, and games where men knocked down three wooden milk bottles trying to win a kewpie doll for their wives and girlfriends. The music played and a merry-go-round took riders past the brass ring. Eating pink cotton candy and ruby candied apples, we followed a sawdust walk to the end of the grounds where tents sporting large murals advertised The Fat Lady, The Man in the Iron Lung, The Siamese Twins, The Tattooed Man, Colonel Tiny Tim, and The Mermaid, all with colorful large canvas paintings behind them. Pitch men stood in front on individual platforms, a feature of traveling carnivals presenting unusual and exotic attractions.

Underneath Homer's floppy cowboy hat his eyes were transfixed, and he asked questions that I easily answered between snapshots.

"Rigby, does that man really have an iron lung?"

"Well, sort of. Maybe not a real one, though."

"How about her? Is she really a mermaid?"

"Well, she's got scaly skin and calls herself one."

"And the Siamese twins? Are they from Siam? Are they really stuck together?"

It was all a bit of a put-on. "People think these people are real and that's what counts." The truth, like the Fat Lady, sometimes got padded.

Walking over to a booth, Homer set the Wheel-of-Fortune spinning, hoping for a dime's worth of chance, but the number passed and he didn't win. Turning away from the wheel, he looked for a clock and strained to see the time. Seven o'clock and only an hour to go until Billy Sunshine's show started.

A man wearing a straw hat, red blazer, and sporting a bushy mustache was next to the tent where motorcycles zoomed around a velodrome defying gravity. But it was more than a heavy dose of gravity that lifted my happiness because nearby, right next to him, was Sweet Lorraine, dressed in layers of soft blue veils that lifted lightly in the wind.

"Here she is, folks, Sweet Lorraine!" The man in the red jacket held a megaphone up to combat the noise of the wind. "Sheeeee has danced for the Prince of India and the King of China. Sweet Lorraine! Hurry! Hurry, hurry, hurry!

"You've never seen such an astonishing act, so revealing, so dynamic, so sensational! Inside this tent, Lorraine will dance just for you. The hundred veils will come off—one at a time! Just twenty-five cents, two bits, twenty-five little pennies, one silver quarter. No one, but no one," clearing his throat and lowering his voice, "under sixteen years of age admitted."

"Hurry!

"Hurry!

"Hurry for the most exotic, most erotic dance you will ever see!"

We moved upstream against the flow of people until we arrived in front of the barker's platform, watching the men line up. Homer and I followed closely behind.

I thought Sweet Lorraine was the most beautiful woman I had ever seen. I put my camera up to my eye and took a quick picture of her, and when I lowered my camera, Sweet Lorraine was smiling right at me.

I was dumbfounded and stood open-mouthed, oblivious to the barker's aside of "No cameras allowed, gentlemen."

Sweet Lorraine disappeared behind a curtain.

"We gotta go in, Homer."

Homer looked at the man in red and then at me; it wouldn't be the first time we went somewhere we weren't supposed to be—skipping school or spending hours at the movies, taking expeditions inside the Quarter, even making trips up the bayou. And besides, the man had called us gentlemen; maybe he thought we were at least sixteen. Exactly forty seconds later, we were inside Sweet Lorraine's tent with fifty men, all smoking Camel cigarettes, milling around in front of the stage.

The lights went out. Sweet Lorraine appeared in a violet spotlight, dancing seductively to rhythmic music, her black hair falling over her curvy voluptuous body, moving her torso in a sweeping, undulating motion that slowly allowed all but one delicately transparent veil to fall to the floor.

I could barely breathe in the suddenly quiet crowd. Fascinated, she was better than anything I had seen in the movies, and when the lights came up, Sweet Lorraine stepped through a curtain behind the stage, as the once-silent men erupted into a hooting, hollering, whistling audience.

"Folks," the barker said, raising his hands, "If you wanna see, really wanna see something you've never seen before, if you wanna see what the King of China saw, gentlemen, if you wanna see that last, thin, little transparent veil of silk slide right off, it's gonna cost you twenty-five cents more. She's going to do what she's never done before in America, she's going to reveal all tonight! On this very stage! For the first time and the last time, a historic moment folks—for only twenty-five centsssssss!"

We all dug into our pockets.

"Now, if you don't wanna see this fabulous show, please exit on the left side, gentlemen."

Homer thought we should leave and started for the exit.

"Are you kidding?" My voice almost cracked. "She's beautiful, and the guy says this is historical."

Taking two quarters out of my pocket, I again broke my rule of never paying our way into any place we could sneak into.

Tossing the coins to the barker, I turned to Homer. "Now this is the real thing, not like those pictures in Dad's medical books, no sirreee!"

Soon the thumping music started, lights passed from green to amber to blue to red, the music grew louder, and then, after a moment that heightened the crowd's eager anticipation, Lorraine eased out from behind a deep red velvet curtain, dancing, and everyone became very quiet again, even quieter than before.

The last veil came off, and there she was! I couldn't believe I saw nakedness in all its splendor. Homer was embarrassed and covered his eyes, while the crowd went wild and Sweet Lorraine stood before me in white high-heeled shoes. If that weren't enough, in the midst of the whistles and applause, she wiggled and blew a kiss directly at me.

"Holy cow! Out of all the people in here, she likes me best!" Finally, in the middle of my rapture, a voice suddenly boomed, "What are you goddamned kids doing here?"

My face drained of blood at the sight of a huge policeman slapping his nightstick against his palm, and I took off like a shot for the nearest canvas wall, scrambling under it with Homer right behind me, his mismatched legs inspired despite their impediment. The sound of laughter followed us.

Homer kept up with me, stumbling, and then finally, leaning breathless against a tree, gasping and out of breath, whispered, "This is great."

While the cop was watching Lorraine, we weaseled our way in to see Billy Sunshine.

I remember hearing the loudspeaker echoing throughout the Midway: "Ladies and Gentlemen, the Billy Sunshine Show with Billy Sunshine live and in person will start in just a few minutes."

At a side entrance, the fire door was open. We snuck in and saw the show, an indelible moment in Homer's life.

Homer's applause blended with the crowd, though we had little idea of the folks being introduced before Billy appeared. Then, insulting our affection at the height of the introductions, we were simultaneously grabbed by the collars.

"Got you, you little sneaks."

Homer's eyes widened, filling with water.

"You two are coming with me."

"Wait a second," I shouted over the noise, reaching into my back pocket, pulling out two orange tickets. "We didn't sneak in."

The cops looked at the tickets, grunted, and let us go.

"Where'd you steal these?"

I shook my head. "You can ask my father, Dr. Canfield. He bought them for us."

Now it was the policeman's turn to blanch. I saw the machine falter in his brain, like some cog had jumped off its track, and if Homer hadn't been shaking like a leaf, I might have pressed the advantage.

The man mumbled something like, "Enjoy the show," and then walked toward the exit. I put my arm around Homer's shoulders and faced the stage again.

After the introductions were over, Billy sang a song before launching into a series of stories, speaking intimately to the audience and finishing the last line of his monologue with his signature—"You are what you are and sometimes a little more." The words echoed endlessly through the loudspeaker system as Billy pulled back on the reins and the Palomino reared again. Everyone cheered, coupled by stomping the floorboards in the floodlit area that thundered in appreciation.

After the show, we went to the stage entrance for an autograph. I was antsy, wishing for one last look at Sweet Lorraine, hoping to take a picture before it was too late. Arriving at the stage entrance, Homer saw Billy come out with Johnny Diamond. Maybe Billy would welcome Homer the way Lorraine had welcomed me.

I found an escape route and disappeared into the crowd until I could just see the top of a white Stetson, then I yelled back to Homer, "I'll be back in a flash!"

Finding my way through the crowd into a dark passageway that led toward my Sweet Lorraine's tent, the biggest on the midway. She was sitting alone inside, surely waiting for my arrival. Hearing voices around back, I tiptoed toward the sound and into a dim light shining from a round, porthole-like window on the side of a small, metal travel trailer.

Lorraine sat at a dingy table, lighting a cigarette with a shaky hand, blowing smoke toward the ceiling and nodding toward someone sitting out of my view. It was the policeman speaking in a low threatening voice, saying something about paying up or he would "shut down" her act. She responded with a frown, shaking her head, interrupted by a winking glance meant for me; my appreciation for Sweet Lorraine was avid with radiance and desire.

Putting my hand to my lips, I blew her a kiss, which initiated a grin —a sad kind of grin, drooping downward, as if she were going to cry. Then came the sound of the scuffle of a chair scraping across the floor.

"Is somebody out there?"

Taking off, I ran in and around tents and rides, realizing the cop had his own radar, following twenty yards behind me until I finally burst into the middle of a huge family, with about ten kids, camouflaging myself within the group, not looking up until the cop passed by, cursing. At least Lorraine was out of harm's way.

That's when I saw a tall ladder leaning against a light tower at the east edge of the fairgrounds. An inspiration called me to find a place for the perfect shot of the entire fair.

Racing over and climbing the tower, I had reached a small ledge at the top of the ladder and got on a platform when I heard a dark chuckling below and, leaning over as much as I dared, there I saw the cop, his hands on the ladder, advancing. My sinking premonition saw him climbing up and tossing me to the ground below.

"Got you, you little bastard."

The cop took the ladder and carried it away.

"I'll teach you to eavesdrop on police business," he said, his voice trailing off. As if on cue, the floodlights pouring onto the fairgrounds evaporated one by one. The bright, multi-colored midway twinkled to a glimmer. Attractions wavered and went dark. I focused on the tableau of lost energy and diminished purpose and took a picture. Only after the Ferris wheel, my final oasis of light went out, did I start to worry.

Then I heard a faint whistle fifty yards away. "Paper Moon."

Waving my arms, I called, "Homer! Over here."

The whistling stopped.

"Rig, where are you?"

"Up here."

"How—"

"That cop, he chased me up here and then took the ladder away. See if you can find it."

I was covered by the darkness again as the lights continued to pop out in clusters over all the attractions, which had drawn its power from the city and now parceled it back. Leaning back against the wooden pillar, I waited until Homer's voice returned.

"I can't find the ladder, but I have this."

Easing to the edge and looking over, I saw him standing with something around his left arm.

"When I throw this rope up to you, catch it and tie it to something sturdy."

It took three tosses before I snagged the end and could tie it clumsily to the rail, over loops and bars, fast and frantic, hoping for some structural security.

"Sure it's tied good enough?" Homer's voice sounded far away.

I wasn't sure; the knot seemed to hold well enough.

"Okay, come on down," Homer whispered. "I'm holding the other end, and I won't let you fall."

Moving with caution, I swung my left, then my right leg over the railing. The ground seemed to be a mile away, though in reality it couldn't have been more than thirty feet. The wind caught me and I lost control; I started to swing aimlessly, but Homer pulled the rope taut.

Hand over hand, my legs curled around the rope, I inched toward the ground, but at the same time, something was happening above. I could feel it, the way the lousy knot was sliding open, releasing its hold on the weary rail.

Homer was just below.

"Home?" I cried as the rope flew free.

Airborne, unsupported, Homer broke my fall.

"Jesus, Home, you just saved my life!"

Homer denied it, but when I looked into his face, I realized that in a funny sort of way, he liked to think he had helped me in some important way, and he had. I put my arm around Homer's shoulder and the two of us walked in step, brace and all, Indian fashion, careful to avoid any cracks in the pavement.

"Billy was just great," Homer said excitedly. "And he was with Johnny Diamond."

"Johnny is his pal," I said. "They play cards and stuff."

"For fun or for keeps?"

"I don't know, but I wonder if he plays marbles. I betcha I could beat him."

"I think you could too, Rigby. You can do anything except tie a knot."

We relived and laughed at every joke, savoring every nuance and every gesture of Billy's show, rubbing our palms, which ached from clapping so hard, and when we were some distance from the fair, still with happy memories, we walked on in silence.

"Billy said it was good to see me, Rigby," Homer said breaking the quiet. "Can you believe it?" Homer was lost in endless applause.

"Hey, Homer, whaddya think? If we let Sweet Lorraine know where we live, maybe she'd come over for dinner or something?"

"Oh, wow, Rigby. Don't they have a schedule? I mean, isn't she real busy dancing for the King of China, all sorts of kings and stuff?"

I was still deep in thought. If she came to dinner, this could be an opportunity to photograph her. I could use the garage as my studio, to arrange her at every angle, letting my camera document her in my scrapbook of posterity. After all, she was Sweet Lorraine, a star, and I wondered curiously, thoughtfully, if I would have the chance to see her perform ever again.

When we got to Homer's house, we found the eviction notice that had started us on our Hollywood dream.

The wheels touching down at LAX broke my reverie, and I was in a hurry to get to Homer's side.

HEY HOMER!

"He took a critical turn. I didn't think he was going to make it, but he's coming out of it," the doctor announced as we headed for the intensive care unit where I found my best friend. "He's been through a lot. It was a bad accident, his brace got caught in the brake of his truck, and it careened out of control. I think he may have swerved to avoid hitting someone. It was raining and the truck rolled off a bank, and he was trapped. He's under a bit of sedation."

The doctor pulled the white curtained sheets hanging from a curved rod around Homer's bed, giving privacy from the rest of the ward. Homer was unconscious.

"Is he all right? Christ, I hope so."

"He's had some trauma, but his vital signs are improving. He's strong, getting good care. Harry Gabriel has seen to that."

I waited outside the unit until morning, dozing off from time to time, until a nurse tugged at my sleeve.

"I think you can see your friend now."

I entered the room. "Homer."

He was bruised, weak, and wet, and his face was pale, with his hair going every which way, but then a sparkle shone from his eyes in an instant.

"Hey, Rigby."

"I'm here."

"That's really good."

I breathed a sigh of relief, "You feeling okay?"

"I'm okay."

"Hey, I think you saved my life again. I had this crazy notion about sailing into the eye of a hurricane, can you believe it?"

"Better than falling from a platform because of a loose knot and a lousy rope. Rig, you crazy or something? Try climbing Mt. Everest, it's safer."

"You're going to be fine. I called Daisy."

"How she doing? I bet she's great."

"She's going to come over."

"She shouldn't. I don't think that's a good idea. Besides, Rig, she has always had a thing for you. You're a pretty fantastic guy and I can't blame her."

"How much medication are they giving you? Homer, you are her man!"

"Don't think so, Rig. I took my best shot."

"I took a one, too, and one that I should never have taken. I was wrong, Homer, dead wrong. I hope you can manage to forgive me?"

He turned in his bed to get more comfortable.

"She loves you, and you're going to make it."

"It's good to see you, Rig."

When I put my arms around him, he looked up, his eyes watering just a bit, not from any sadness, but from a part of him deeply inside.

"Sailing into that hurricane! You are fearless. What's the name of your boat, the *Starlight*?"

"Yes, the *Starlight*."

"Nice name, *Starlight*. Sunshine, Starlight. You heard about Billy Sunshine?"

"A big loss. I heard it on the news."

"I felt pretty badly about losing him; it hurts. We all have secrets, Rig."

"Secrets?"

"Yeah, we all have one. All of us, something held deeply inside."

"You're probably right."

"The whole slam bang of it all. We've been together a long time. I feel I've been in a movie."

"Jeez, Homer."

"I got pretty hurt, I guess."

"You'll be up and about in no time."

"I will for sure and you gotta see the ranch! You'll enjoy meeting Harry Gabriel. He's quite a guy."

* * *

I called Daisy to report about Homer. Her sentences came in staccato phrases.

"How bad was the accident? Did he get my letter? I'll break my contract. I have an understudy!"

"He's doing fine. Really, Daisy. Finish your run. I'm sure that's what Homer wants."

"I adore you two, and I really love that guy."

"I've known that all along. We both do."

A stage manager knocked at her door; it was time to go on. Her audience was waiting.

CAMPFIRE TIME

When I arrived at the ranch, Mr. Harry Gabriel was ready for me. I was glad to meet him and see the place—Homer's amazing ranch!

"You're Rigby . . ."

"I'm sorry to hear about Billy Sunshine—you were his friend for such a long time."

"Yes. We were very close. Thanks for mentioning it, and thanks for coming over. Meant a lot to everybody. I'm sorry, too."

His words of consolation began to tumble in my head like a house of fallen cards.

Through the long room, past the square windows, I could see the dining room, shadowy, empty. Crystal and linen were laid out on a sideboard, very neat and ordered.

"I must tell you I knew Billy had been ailing. That's when Homer and I first met—in the hospital—and I thought it would really brighten up Billy's spirits to get a script, let him know he really counted."

"That's where you found Homer."

"We found each other. It was more than a chance introduction. I'm just sorry he and Billy never got together sooner, with appointments they were supposed to keep."

I thought for a moment about something Homer once told me,

words Father Rivage invoked about keeping appointments never made.

"Going to be a service of any kind?"

"No. Billy wouldn't go for that. When you go, you're gone, he used to say."

"Homer talks about you with real affection. I appreciate how much you look after him."

"Heck, he looked after us. He needed a place and I enjoyed the companionship. I wanted to get the ranch going again, and I had a hunch he could help. Now tell me, how's the boy doing? As soon as I finish some chores I'll get back over to see him. I know you coming was the best tonic of all, and from all indications, he is going to be fine."

"His doctor says so. I think he's past the critical stage; he'll be up and back here in no time."

"I'm sure of it."

Harry asked if he could show me around the ranch, some of his favorite nooks, asked if I'd like to join the tour.

He took me into his dusty office filled with photographs of old movie stars and posters from Billy Sunshine's movies. A wagon wheel light fixture hung from the ceiling in the foyer, yellow lights blushed alongside Remington statues of cowboys on bronco horses.

"Can you tell me anything about the accident?" I asked.

"One of the officers investigating told me several cars had stopped along the road and there was a witness. Weather was terrible, lots of fog. A bystander saw the crash and described seeing hundreds of pages floating in the air afterward, first in an updraft and then falling on the highway. She collected them all and brought them here to me, a manuscript. She said she had seen a group of cowboys close by, riding over the countryside, in the background so to speak."

"Who was she?"

"I'm not sure. She was a nice looking lady wearing a wide brimmed hat. I asked her name, went out to get some refreshments to offer her. It was really nice of her to come, but she left before we could talk, and I never did find out who she was. She just went away."

Miss Faye brought in a silver tray with hot chamomile tea and butter cookies. Mr. Gabriel gave me a large black-and-white photograph of a smiling Homer posing in front of the Sunshine Studios with his arms around the Mexican cowboys and Miss Faye.

"I took it myself," Mr. Gabriel said proudly.

It was a nice shot. "You know, Homer looks like a cowboy."

"Mr. Canfield, Homer is a cowboy."

"He's a very good man; he has some kind of courage."

"Are you better for knowing him?"

"I am."

"Me too."

"You've come a long way, better rest up a bit before getting back to your boat."

"She may have to sail without me. I could have capsized. It was pretty serious, Harry."

"What are you going to do? You're welcome to stay here, talk a bit."

"I'm not sure where I'm headed. I need to do some thinking, find some answers."

"I know about that. We cowboys often sit around and, if it's an early fire, we reminisce, greatly exaggerating stories about our past, and if it's a late fire, when the coals are simmering, we plan where we are going so we can ride the next day. That's what we cowboys do."

Harry Gabriel thought awhile, and then his clear blue eyes met mine. "You looking for answers? Well it's none of my business, but if I may say something—and take this from an old hand—you can't go looking, you got to wait for them to come to you. And when they do, you have to be ready to listen."

I chewed on that for a while.

"They come alright. I've waited for the answer, too, especially when times were bad, but then good times bring an answer."

"Many bad times, Harry?"

"Mostly good. One of the best came just when Billy was about to lose the ranch."

"How was that?"

"You ever play cards, gamble a little?"

"Can't say I have. The only gambling I've done is on the weather and hurricanes."

"Well Billy gambled, played cards in the old days, dancing with chance, just for the fun of it. At first the losses didn't amount to much, but when the studio shifted away from cowboys and we didn't have much work, Billy started gamblin' and it bothered me a lot. But we needed money. He played with Johnny Diamond, Billy's sidekick, you know, and we played cards on the set between takes, just a way to pass the time.

"Billy could always beat Johnny in the movies, but never in real life. Johnny was too good, but get this, one day, a movie arrived, a piece of film from out of nowhere, clear and sharp with Johnny playing cards, and you know what that film showed? Johnny had a tell, and his foot would slide back, like this." Harry demonstrated the slide. "Sliding back nice and easy every time he was bluffing and faking it. Well, it was a gift from heaven. Billy kept on the lookout when Johnny's foot was sliding back, and then he had 'em—raised the stakes big time, and won back every penny he ever lost to Johnny Diamond. He even bet the ranch once, but he got it back!"

"Johnny Diamond?"

"Yep. Those two were scoundrels, but Billy won fair and square, well, almost fair and square," Harry said with a consistent twinkle in his eye.

I had a flashback from the poker game we filmed long ago and left Sunshine Ranch. Harry Gabriel brought me a great deal of cheer.

A BOY NAMED SAM

Over several weeks of recovery, Homer took walks around the hospital ward, rounds similar to the one he had taken many times before at St. Exupery's Infirmary. From time to time, he'd offer a book or magazine to patients, talk to them, and one day he visited a young boy who had been admitted to the ward. He had a deformed leg, and needed an operation and a brace. The boy was bright and probably had been alone most of his life. His parents were from Mexico, hard working people who placed their hope on modern medicine. There was a new orthopedic procedure: breaking bones, re-setting and letting them heal all over again. Painful I'm sure, but a better way to gain new footing.

When the doctors weren't around, Homer dropped in to see him.

"What's your name? Mine is Homer."

The young boy, happy to have a visitor, said, "It's Sam."

"I don't know anyone named Sam, but I do now! Good name. If I ever change mine, can I use it? Sam Sincere!"

The boy laughed.

"Would you like some company?"

Sam nodded vigorously in agreement.

"How about if I tell you a story?" The boy agreed.

Homer spoke about heroes and cowboys, and his particular hero Billy Sunshine, the greatest cowboy who ever lived. Learning to walk would be nothing for Billy.

"I guess you have some trouble?"

"Yes, I have."

"After your operation, we'll walk together. I know something about that."

Over the next few weeks, Homer led the way, and before Homer left the hospital, he promised, "Sam, when you get out of here, come visit me at Billy Sunshine's ranch not far from here. We have horses and a lot of open land and we'll ride together like cowboys."

YANKEE MAMA

I went back to New York, and met with Clurman to examine the 35 mm slides of the storm I had taken on assignment. I also announced that I was finished with the around-the-world sailing stories.

"I'm selling my boat to make a down payment on a ranch out west."

"How about one last assignment? I've gotten authorization to start a documentary division, Time-Life Films. You've been angling for it for years, and we're partnering with the BBC."

The company had finally caught up! My mood brightened instantly. "That's great!" I hesitated for one instant, then said, "Sure."

"Fast-breaking news coverage, and we have to compete with technology."

Homer had known all along.

"It's an assignment you are suited for, and I promise you'll be on land. I'd hate to lose you at sea."

"Okay. I'm ready."

"We all know your amazing job covering the Six Day War, and Larry Windsor, our man in Hong Kong, asked if you would come out and join him. It's really escalating over there and he could use some help in Saigon. We'd like to launch with a film about helicopter warfare."

"You talking Vietnam?"

"I am. You up for it?"

I had mixed feeling about the war, but I would have a chance to validate my reputation, prove my mettle as a war correspondent, or at least make me an honest one. I accepted the assignment immediately. "If you don't mind, Dick, could I take someone who deserves a lot of credit and who can really be useful? We can hire him freelance."

"Who you thinking of? Not a lot of stringers want to go into a war zone."

"Homer Sincere."

"What's he doing now?"

"He's been working in the movie business and has gotten plenty of experience. I'm sure he really can add a lot."

"I remember, sure, film was his idea. Yes, why not? I liked the guy, but please keep him away from Dateline," Clurman admonished. "While you're out there, get some footage of Larry in action. It will help the marketing people."

I called Homer. "How you doing?'

"Much better. Ribs were hurting a little, but I feel good now, fully recovered."

"Let me tell you why I'm calling. I have some great news. Clurman is starting a film division, and Homer, he remembered that you brought him that concept in the first place, and we have an assignment! I want you to come. It would mean a lot me, more than I can say. This time we can finish up what we've always wanted to do. I want you to come and cover helicopter warfare with me. We'll be riding on 'em like cowboys, and I bet it's something Billy would like, defending a cause, protecting the land. It's important stuff, launching a new film division. It's what we've always dreamed of doing."

I knew that Homer would prefer handing out flowers to bullets, but when we talked about the assignment, Homer viewed it as an opportunity to make an important statement about what was really going on out there. I knew I didn't have to worry about him filing any unauthorized Datelines!

"I can get us a damn good fee, maybe to help keep the ranch going. And I'd like for us to be back together. Come on, Homer. Just think, a film division for TIME. We've done it! And by the way, there's a new Arriflex-16 with pre-loaded film magazines. I'll bring one with me. If you can make it, we'll meet Larry Windsor in Hong Kong."

We joined up with Windsor as soon as we touched down on the island crammed with colonial houses, traditional temples, and non-stop shopping. The territory was part of China before the nineteenth-century Opium Wars. Then the island, just a hop over to Indochina, was ceded to Britain.

Taking the Star Ferry over Victoria Harbor, past junks and sampans, we reached the Peninsular Hotel, the grandest of the old hotels built in the far-flung reaches of the British expatriate world.

Windsor wore thick glasses and, like Robert Capa, was known around the office as the bravest of war correspondents or the most near-sighted, claiming there was only one way to cover a war, to get out into the field with the men he photographed, accepting their dangers and fears. Taking risks was part of the package, always knowing what he was doing, pre-planning, aware of his surroundings and his own vulnerability. His trademark was carrying a battery of cameras dangling from his neck and shoulders at all times, a photographer's photographer, and I was thrilled to be in his company. Homer admired him greatly and had written an Editor's Note about him when Larry was covering the bloody conflicts in Cyprus and the Congo. In 1965, he began snapping pictures in Vietnam and soon became a fixture on the U.S. helicopter patrol circuit for *LIFE*.

Before we set off, Larry, a Brit who first learned his trade working in darkrooms as a lab technician in London, entertained us in a sensational apartment on top of "The Peak," with views reaching Kowloon on one side and Aberdeen Harbor on the other. Homer and I had always enjoyed great food and this feast was no exception. The dinner—ginger soy over bean sprouts, Peking orange duck, rice noodles drizzled in herb butter, and a fresh lemon vinegar cucumber salad—was served in the well-appointed dining room he had fitted out with red lacquered furniture.

Time-Life correspondents were always advising me, how to dress suitably for the occasion; first Terry Spencer in London, and now Larry in Hong Kong. "To get you guys ready, I'm taking you to my tailor; you need your correspondent's kit." Of course Homer was delighted to wear one, too, pleasing both his imagination and self-image.

Ascot Chang had opened his first store on Kimberly Road, and Larry, who had both style and talent, took us to this shop to have our functional, multi-pocketed poplin khaki correspondent jackets made. Ascot, who was Chinese, had adapted a suitable English forename. He was one of best shirt makers in town with a fashion-conscious celebrity clientele—and Larry's friend. As we approached his place, Ascot took a Mandarin moment, hiding behind bolts of cloths in his shop, finally peering over a polished mahogany cutting table to plead, "I don't do khaki." Larry charmed him into taking our measurements and he produced our well-fitted jackets in two days.

Flying into Vietnam, I was overwhelmed by the sublime beauty of the country's natural setting: the Red River Delta in the north, the Mekong Delta in the south, and along the entire coastal strip a patchwork of brilliant green rice paddies, with soaring mountains beyond cloaked by dense overgrown forests. It was hard to believe a war was raging below. Soon we were checked into the Caravelle Hotel, one that still retained its French character leftover from the colonial years.

The streets in Saigon bristled with energy, a flurry of bicycles peddled by women wearing the national dress, black silk pajamas and wide straw hats. Pilots wearing green combat gear were stationed just outside the city at a U.S. command post, giving advice and assistance to the Vietnamese government both fighting a war of no return. I heard a local group singing the latest Beatles' song. "I Wanna Hold Your Hand." I didn't understand Vietnamese, but the message was the same in any language. Our hotel's bar was a humming editorial newspaper room of colleagues who had set up offices with tools of a journalist's trade—desks, telephones, cameras, and bourbon—and was filled with the journalistic clatter of a dozen typewriters.

I was surprised to learn that the bartender was both the recipient and dispatcher of the daily reports about the Viet Cong. He was the local Dateline source, and his intelligence was remarkable, knowing our movements in the field at all times.

We went out to the command base. Our tour was just another day's work for the U.S. Marine Helicopter Squadron 163. In the sultry morning, after introductions were made, the crews huddled at Da Nang for our mission. We were assigned to an "Eagle Flight," a formation of Huey's, helicopters with an open cabin. We were given three-inch steel plates to sit on and an armored vest to wear, in case we took Cong fire from below. We were to accompany an airlift to deposit a battalion of Vietnamese infantry to an isolated area about twenty miles away, and Army Intelligence reports indicated that the area was a rendezvous point for the Communist Viet Cong who had come down the Ho Chi Minh trail from the north.

Among those listening to the briefing was James Harley, crew chief of the copter Yankee Mama 13. We would be riding in Harley's machine. We asked ourselves whether this mission would be a no-contact milk run or, as had been reported in recent weeks, the Viet Cong would be ready and waiting with .30-caliber machine guns.

We knew the mission was not without risk, but Larry and Homer had been in action in the front lines before; I had not. Built into this assignment was reporting and documenting in the words of "just what the hell was going on in 'Nam."

Windsor, an old hand, was much cooler under fire. Yet when we lifted off the tarmac, everyone was frightened knowing the Vietcong had dug in along the tree line and would be waiting for us to commit to the landing zone. Once airborne and well on our way, one pilot in the lead ship shouted over the intercom, "Colonel! We're being hit." Back came the reply, "If your plane is flying, press on."

We did, flying back and forth to the landing zone to add support of another load of troops. On our next approach to the landing zone, Harley spotted Yankee Mama 3, its engine still running and the rotors turning, but the ship was obviously in trouble.

"Why don't they lift off?" Harley muttered over the intercom. Then he set our ship down nearby to see what the trouble was. I was shooting the last battery-operated Filmo as fast as the film advanced. Windsor was in front, his camera fixed to his eye, and Homer was leaning out of the open door of the cabin running footage with the Arriflex. We only looked at each other occasionally, scanning the fields, saying nothing. One of the crew from YM 3 came lurching across the tall grass toward us, followed immediately by another. They were the co-pilot and the gunner. Both had been wounded and had to be helped aboard.

War makes victims and can deny its true heroic moments of sacrifice and courage. No war can be reckoned as good, and this was more than a movie with most of the blood and gore washed away for the benefit of a PG rating. It was one of unspeakable sadness.

In the cockpit of YM 3, Homer saw the pilot slumped over his controls, and Harley said to one of his crew, Charlie Vogel, "See what you can do to help that man." Before Vogel could respond, Homer had barreled out of our copter, running over to Yankee Mama 3 with Vogel following behind him. From a stone building some seventy yards away, a Viet Cong machine gun sprayed the area. I was so involved in shooting from the other side of the ship, I hadn't realized what had happened until I looked over to where Homer had been and saw his notebook and the Ari camera left alone on a bucket seat. Homer and Vogel scrambled up to the pilot in the downed chopper to drag him out, but he couldn't be budged. To get him into a more upright position so he could get greater leverage, Vogel switched off the YM's engine but the rotor blades kept turning. Bullets had ripped open the Plexiglass, and the aircrafts skin had holes all around.

Homer was kneeling alongside the ship for cover against the V.C. fire. Vogel managed to drag the pilot out, and Homer lifted the man in his arms and carried him over the field, never realizing he himself was wearing a brace, running sideways, staying out of the path of strafing bullets, breathing hard. I watched him running, slowed by his brace but moving as fast as he could, almost as if he was in slow motion. "Come on, Homer, you can make it!" As he approached the copter out of breath, the rotor revved up. Harley jumped to the ground pulling the pilot onto Yankee Mama 13. Windsor kept shooting the action.

Homer was hit and dropped to the ground. I jumped out; my first instinct was to ease his issued flight vest, but he had blood around his face and throat. I could see where a bullet had ripped through his neck. With Vogel's help, I dragged Homer into the copter. Our radio and instruments were still in commission. We climbed fast to get the hell out of there. Homer's face registered pain and his lips moved slightly. If he said anything, the words were drowned out by the noise of the copter. He was losing all color and I worried about how long he could hold on. Harley was dressing the wound, whipping the bandage across his face, then blood started from his nose, and a glazed look came into his eyes. He tried to say something to me, and he left with a grasp, a final warm squeeze to my hand before it went cold. I tried mouth-to-mouth resuscitation, but Homer was dead. No one said a word. It was as if all the air became an ocean. It was not rain, but cold, solid water that washed over me.

There was a crack of thunder. It was over as quickly as it had begun, one red spouting flash of violence. Yes, it was over. I lifted my hands to my face, a sudden, angry, almost childish gesture as if I were striking myself with a fist—then, with a single wave of my hand, I touched Homer gently and remembered, "Be not afraid. We are flowers in the field."

ON A NOTE OF TRIUMPH

With ineffable sadness I, Rigby Canfield, *LIFE* photographer, joined Homer's production company. I tried to brave my loss without showing too much sentiment when speaking about Homer, his affection for the magazine, our friendship. Yet overwhelming guilt met me at every turn. I had lost my best friend, and I had talked him into taking this assignment. He did it for me; he didn't need it. Homer was doing fine at the ranch. I would have traded my life for him right then and there, and the loss of Homer left me inconsolable.

Clurman expressed his condolences, "He was a courageous man, one of our own. We should write something alongside Windsor's Yankee Mama story, something fitting, a few words about combat, about being a soldier."

I felt that what Clurman said about being a soldier was incredibly ironic. Maybe Homer had been a Soldier of the Word all his life, spiriting humanity, but what he held sacred more than anything, what he loved most, was deeply personal and reflected who he was more than anything else. I had a better idea.

"Dick, he really held the values of a cowboy. Let's send out a dispatch for Homer. I think he'd like that!"

"A dispatch?"

The staff came together in the Dateline room. Looking over my shoulder, they made suggestions helping me with the words, restorative and clear, as I sat at the Teletype machine.

DATELINE NEW YORK: BY OUR SPECIAL CORRESPONDENT.
TO THE NATION OF KNOWLEDGE.

"Make that correspondents!" someone yelled, and I typed in,

BY OUR SPECIAL CORRESPONDENTS.

These words are for the Cowboys. Yep, for all the hard-riding, two-fisted, guitar-playing heroes we rode with every Saturday afternoon. This is for you. You grappled with the world, you held the stars, you fought for ideals so we could become more than we are. You filled our imaginations and took us to heroic landscapes of courage on western trails and Monument Valleys. And Homer Sincere, you were true to your word. You forever shape our smile.

LIFE ran an essay on cowboys with a collection of photographs: The Duke, Roy Rogers, Gene Autry, Billy Sunshine, and Clint Eastwood. The story received responses from readers around the world. Anyone who remembered their childhood with affection and imagination was as fond of cowboys as Homer.

I mentioned to the staff that an old ranch in California was in danger of foreclosure, one that could become a center for abused and handicapped kids and a cowboy legacy. I introduced my new plan, the best one I ever had.

To my surprise and delight, Dick Clurman took my proposal to Henry Luce and Luce took it to the board. The board liked the idea and approved a significant donation to The Sunshine Center, and I had an appointment to keep.

I returned to the ranch and Harry Gabriel was as sad as I was at losing Homer. I had never felt so bad. A lifelong friendship had been lost in an instant, and I could not imagine being with out him. I was in a free fall without a parachute, and I didn't know how to land.

I spent hours alone, remembering all the people who had made this good man. Waldo, Father Ravage, Daddy Grace, and his Billy Sunshine. I concluded that when Billy died, Homer's movie had probably come to an end. He lived his life in those movies, interrupted at times by stark reality. I know now that he left the ranch to come with me on assignment because I asked him to. He never complained, covering a battle that left a wall of casualties. It had been an unexpected ending, a heroic act, and I tried to move on to find a world better than he had left behind.

"Big things are done in small ways," Harry Gabriel remarked.

Raphael, Angelo, and Francisco were bigger than life to the new kids who came from all over the country, teaching them how to ride horses and play the guitar.

In the main building, near a pond bordered by weeping willow trees, was a library stacked with hundreds of books. With refurbishing and new construction, the words became a constant—building blocks if you will.

Then destiny knocked. I heard a voice behind me and before I turned around, I knew who it was.

She looked a bit funny in Levi's, a red plaid shirt, and an old floppy hat.

It was Daisy.

"I thought you might need a partner," she said. "Didn't you know that I always loved cowboys?"

Chapter 13
THE RANCH

THE LAST ROUND UP

On late afternoons around four o'clock, a wind kicks up gusts of sand and sage until it subsides. Campfire is always a special time, a friendly time, but sometimes it waits impatiently for the sunset to unwind. I remember when Angelo brought out an old chuck wagon and rustled up some chili, steaks, baked potatoes, and freshly harvested corn over a mesquite-wood fire. Miss Faye, revered for her butter cookies, had a special recipe stashed away in her kitchen inventory. She mixed three kinds of ice-cold lettuce to make a salad with finely chopped baby red tomatoes, bacon, and blue cheese, topped with a few orange slices and currants to disguise the garlic. It was a contrast, but I thought it went pretty well with the thin grilled pork chops with dill. Francisco organized a mariachi band of twenty musicians dressed in black troubadour pants studded with gleaming silver buttons. Their music swept across the valley, resonating for miles around. It was Campfire Time at the ranch.

One Indian summer evening, after building a roaring bonfire, Raphael hung a white sheet between two California oaks, a silver screen for *Montana Sky*, one of Billy's best films. The kids were wide-mouthed and breathless when Billy rode Apollo hard, leaping over a twenty-foot divide high above the Colorado River with its water racing and swirling below. Billy always performed the stunt himself.

Guitars strummed and baritones sang in Spanish. The children wrapped themselves in geometric Navajo blankets, fending off the brisk night air as they huddled around a leaping fire toasting marshmallows. Harry Gabriel had changed into his Buffalo Bill outfit and started a story. "It was a dark and quiet night, a group of cowboys sat around the campfire light." Then he turned and asked, "Rigby, tell us a story."

With the fire washing my face in shadows I continued, "It was a dark and lonely night, a group of cowboys sat around the campfire light, the thundering hoofs of a black horse came closer." I passed to Raphael, "Tell us a story."

Raphael carried on, "It was a dark and rainy night, just as the sound of the thumping hoofs approached, there was a loud eerie scream." After the scream, another cowboy picked up. "It was..."

The plot followed with twists as each pint-sized cowboy was called to add to the tale, steering in the most improbable directions including space aliens, invading bears and black cats, The Lone Ranger and Billy Sunshine!

Daisy couldn't resist performing and took to the stage.

To the accompaniment of an upright rinky-dink piano on the back of a truck, Harry Gabriel played and Daisy sang show tunes.

Afterward, taking a moment, Harry took me aside, confiding, "Rigby, I have something I've been meaning to do, to talk to you about, and I can't do it with anyone except you. I feel pretty stupid about forgetting this, but just before Homer went up to see Billy, I'd gone to the post office and a letter had arrived for him. I was keeping it to give to him, but I never got the chance. I thought I'd give it to you."

I opened it, and it was from Daisy. If it was a brush off, then best left unsaid and unread.

Dear Homer,

Not a day goes by when I don't think of you. Maybe I needed time to realize that there is something more, really, something more for you, for me, for us. Playing the same role night after night becomes very routine. I know that spending a life with you would be full of surprises and wonderful. I can't think of a more exciting role!

Please forgive me for being so dumb. But this time apart has given me time to appreciate what is important. You always knew that, and I hope you haven't given up on me. Write me into your script, cowboy. My contract is ending soon, and I'm coming home to you. And if somebody has taken my place, there is going to be drama in the high country!

I love you with remembered kisses,
Daisy

The letter had arrived too late. I folded it and put it away in my pocket.

After bedtime, I saddled up a horse and cantered into the desert over a lake of platinum glass reflected by the moon. I rode into the foothills and followed a trail, crossing a creek, taking me higher to a mountain ridge, where a sprinkle of lights flickered from ranch houses. In the distance, a smoldering fire with glowing embers shimmered. I dismounted in a clearing in the pines, on top of the world. I retrieved Daisy's letter from my pocket, examining the envelope: a light blue stamp upon which a three-masted schooner rested at anchor, commemorating something, obscured by the postmark's waving lines. I took her letter to Homer and tore her glorious words into little pieces and threw them to the wind. They sailed in an updraft, twirling and floating, over prairies and plains, to the western part of the continental divide, like swirling sparkling silver words falling for Homer. It was better that way.

Daisy loved the ranch. At times, I wondered how hard it had been for her to give up acting. But once she did, she dedicated herself to the kids, who seemed more important to her.

Her outspoken stop-and-go, spark-and-dash, her playfulness, her inventive sense of drama never changed. I thought about staying on, but I knew I couldn't replace Homer. He would always be between us, and I wanted him as a part of us, not a barrier. There would not be another like him, with his disarming core of innocence, his way of seeing life not as it was but as he wanted it to be.

Before leaving the ranch, Harry Gabriel had a call from an independent producer at a Hollywood studio who heard Harry owned a treatment called *The Last Cowboy*. He thought the timing might be right for a movie about cowboys.

"All that hard work paid off. That boy can write! It's one helluva story and I'm not selling it cheap. They are going to have to play or pay!"

"Harry, I'm going to ask you a favor. I want you to attach me to that film. I want to direct it, and I want to be part of the production. I can do it; I know how to direct films."

"Done," Harry said.

He negotiated a deal, with me as directing consultant, and my fee brought a small endowment for the place. It was something I needed to do.

Chapter 14
New York 1972

SUNSET

In September 1972, *LIFE* folded. Several hundred people had been on the staff. For most of them, working for the magazine was important, and for many, like me, who had invested our energy and youth there, it was a momentous closing. *LIFE* was created with ideas, powerful pictures, and it became bigger than life itself. The magazine taught me how to observe the world. The last issue had stories on the astronauts, the Olympics, Liz Taylor, Liza Minnelli, and Nixon eating with chopsticks in Hanchow. On the cover, tucked under the dateline, was just one word, "Goodbye."

Many of the studios in Hollywood changed too. Republic, RKO, Century, United Artists. MGM—"with more stars than in heaven"—was the last of the majors to lose its celestial jurisdiction.

I moved back to Louisiana after the magazine suspended publication, accepting a part-time appointment at Tulane teaching a course in journalism. When I least expected it, I found a beautiful brunette steel magnolia that I had known from dancing school, Jennifer Carpenter, from an old New Orleans family who collected art and, to my delight, had acquired a few original paintings attributed to an artist signed Rivage.

Jennifer was on equal footing with me. We both loved photography, and we opened The Canfield Gallery in a white Victorian house, which quickly expanded to include photographs. In the atrium were some of the finest pictures from photojournalists who had documented the world's passing parade. Across the hallway were pictures I had taken beginning in childhood. They were more than casual snapshots. The expression of events were as fresh in my mind that day as they were then, and I could easily recall with instant replay. By a large open window was Homer's desk. And there I began writing his story, which you hold in your hands.

HOME AGAIN

"Love and friendship are the only things that remind us that we are not alone in the world."
　　　　　　　　　　　　　　　　　　　　　　　—Homer Sincere

The days in New Orleans have a stillness to them, especially when the heat is passing from summer. Now and then in the early morning during the great hush, a solitary leaf shakes and tumbles through the Vieux Carré as the mist lifts in the Quarter.

It is wet air and violent heat, June sunshine and afternoons of sudden warm rain, cold shadows in alleys that echo jazz from Bourbon Street where elegant restaurants and cheap jive joints come alive again.

The foghorns sound from boats on the lazy Mississippi, a train chugging somewhere in the distant silence. There are odors of magnolia buds, and fog rises to a humid hedge.

A Creole scent hovers over black skillets. Rich chicory coffee, a salad of fragrances mix with sour weeds and wildflowers from empty lots next door.

Hot beignets turn out at the Morning Call's marble counters with silver sugar bowls.

The long, soft summer of New Orleans moves into a chilled winter sky that hangs heavy over the grillwork balconies.

Mardi Gras costumes are being sewn, ball gowns and chain mail, harlequin suits and mad court clothes that will be worn before Lent.

With carnival only a few days away, preparations take on a furious tempo, sequins and lace, velvet and feathers fly from one room to the next. And in a kitchen, off a plant-lined patio, someone makes a bowl of orange cream from fresh orange juice, sugar, sweet milk, and eggs. Cooked and frozen and finally served with a dash of brandy, it will give people the tingling energy they need to get through the last preparations before carnival begins.

For a moment in my memory, there's a marching band from Preservation Hall led by Waldo and Daddy Grace, with kids dancing and jumping and following behind. In a blink, they pass and are gone. Behind the Government House and across the square is an old Western Union office.

A few miles away is La Vieille Maison, an old building with a lot of Spanish moss growing over its stately doors, a place that is a testament to a man called Father Rivage. And when I see a beautiful sunset over the Quarter, I know he must have painted it.

By St. Exupery's Infirmary, a newsstand interrupts the Quarter's history. An old horse and wagon passes by and momentarily obstructs The Rialto's marquee that reads: *The Last Cowboy*, a film I like to think I had something to do with.

Next door a penny arcade is alive with energy and computer games where a couple of boys play; one is a ten-year-old, stringy, lithe, and sunburned from days spent in the street and on the levee. His too-long dark brown hair straggles down his neck and flops into his wide brown eyes. *Bing, bing,* the arcade games are in motion—the boy is engrossed.

"Hey, you want to go and see the movie?"

"Yeah," he says without missing a *kapow*, his hands turning in sequence on a dial.

A beginning to childhood caught near the Mississippi River, a trawler moves sleepily along in the rising wind, above it, a whirling cloud of birds. An apricot sun drops westward rolling the scene into darkness, just like in the movies.

Old heroes have faded away, helicopters and missiles have replaced summer soldiers. The cowboys are gone.